MIDNIGHT DESIRE

SHARI NICHOLS

CITY OWL
PRESS

MIDNIGHT DESIRE
Raven's Hollow Coven, Book 1

CITY OWL PRESS
www.cityowlpress.com

Cover Design by MiblArt. All stock photos licensed appropriately.

Edited by Heather McCorkle.

For information on subsidiary rights, please contact the publisher at info@cityowlpress.com.

Print Edition ISBN: 978-1-949090-32-1

Digital Edition ISBN: 978-1-949090-31-4

Printed in the United States of America

PRAISE FOR SHARI NICHOLS

"Great read and start to a new series. I'm excited to see more of as it comes out!" - *Book Junky Girls*

"An emotional, action packed, YUMMINESS ride!" - *Carrie Book Fairy*

"I can't wait for what is next in the Ravens Hollow series. I give this book 5 Fangs!" - *Maria Suarez, Paranormal Romance and Authors that Rock.*

"Action packed steamy paranormal romance with a host of intriguing characters." - *Crystal's Many Reviewers*

"Her plot was solid, her characters were complex and her writing hooks the reader right from the start and never let's go! Think of a multiple loop, fast, curving, upside down roller coaster and you have an idea of what you are in for with this book." - *Stephenee, Nerd Girl Official*

"The chemistry between the characters is awesome! You won't want this story to end. Looking forward to the next book by Shari Nichols." - *Chris Clemetson, Romance Author*

"Nichols is excellent in setting the stage. The reader is instantly transported into a believable, three-dimensional, magical world." - *S. Wilk, Romance Author*

"A gripping, sexy read you won't be able to put down. Nichols manages to infuse her characters with life and love, making them jump off the page." - *M. Kate Quinn, Award-Winning Author of Romantic Fiction*

"I was hooked from page one! A titillating, fast-paced read, this edge-of-your-seat paranormal romance kept me guessing." - *Sky Purrington, Bestselling Author of Time Travel Romance*

"Paranormal has never been my cup of tea. However, I am starting to rethink that notion." - *EJ Cohn, Romance Author*

I dedicate this book to Mike, for the unwavering love and support. You're truly the best! XOXO

CHAPTER 1

A ball of dread unfurled in Willow McCray's stomach and pricked along her skin. The sensation confirmed her earlier premonition of death.

Willow trolled through Fusion, the dimly lit heavy metal bar, while all around her a colorful mix of otherworldly beings gyrated to the thump of the seductive beat. Emotions of the crowd swam high and swirled through her head in a sea of lust and euphoria.

Tonight she came here with three objectives: find her best friend, get the bloodstone amulet, and walk out the door alive. She tried to scope out the place for her quarry, affectionately known as Maeve the Metallurgist.

She shielded her eyes from a strobe light as she pushed her way through the mass of sweaty bodies. Willow scanned the room, but she couldn't spot her elusive friend anywhere. She glanced at her watch and frowned. It was already past midnight and there was still no sign of her. As much as she appreciated Maeve's ability to work under pressure, Willow didn't have time to screw around.

Her hand shook as she pulled out her cell and dialed Maeve's number. *No service.* She moved past the dance floor toward the line of barstools, and something crunched under her boot. She glanced at the floor and noticed a broken syringe. Wincing, she swallowed hard and kept on walking.

Considering her choice of meeting spots, apparently Maeve still liked to party, hard. She claimed smack took the edge off the brutal confines of her job. Forging charmed metal in dark, sweltering conditions couldn't exactly be a picnic. But did she have to turn to drugs? They'd agreed to meet here, but from the loud buzzing in her ears, Willow sensed trouble was on its way. She'd been calling and texting Maeve all day, and she still couldn't get ahold of her.

Guilt tightened around Willow's gut like an iron fist. When this mess was over, she vowed to get Maeve clean. Even if Maeve refused, she would haul her ass back to rehab. Not that Willow was one to talk. She'd never touched a drug in her life, and yet she'd done plenty to regret. In fact, she feared the darkness she may have permanently etched on her soul. *If I can save Maeve, maybe I can save myself.*

When Willow opened her mind to the crowd around her, the hairs on the back of her neck prickled. A ball of heat circled her head and tingled down her spine as her magick responded to the crowd.

The vision of a tall, dark-haired man with a strip of gold around his wrist swam in her head. She blinked and the image disappeared. *Could he be one of the demons trying to kill me?*

She pushed the vision to the back of her mind and glanced across the bar at a group of gorgeous incubi huddled together. *Sex incarnate* was all her mind could register as her gaze locked on the tallest of the three. He flashed a sultry smile, the promise of sin written all over his chiseled face. According to legend, incubi magick, if wielded at full force, was like catnip to most women and could enslave even the strongest female with sex. He waved and she caught a glimpse of a gold string around his wrist.

Hmm. She usually gave their kind a wide berth, but in this case, she'd make an exception. She plastered a smile on her face and waved back. The male tilted his head to the side and his red, watery eyes zeroed in on her boobs. She'd raided a bag of Maeve's old clothes and managed to squish her breasts into a black leather bustier—at least two sizes too small. She sucked air in through her nose, finding it hard to breathe. She just hoped she didn't pass out before closing. Willow pushed out her chest as he sauntered over to her side of the bar. *Showtime.*

The acrid stench of sweat clung to his clothing, along with a hint of ether, which usually came from cooking meth. "What's up, beautiful? Why don't you have a drink with us?" he slurred and motioned to his spot at the bar.

She moved a little closer to him and purposely let her fingers graze the string at his wrist so she could peek inside his head. Even if he didn't recall what he'd done five minutes ago, he might have a clue about Maeve stored somewhere in his junkie brain. *Nothing.* "Thanks anyway, but I'm meeting someone."

As she turned to walk away, he caught her by the arm and pulled. His thoughts screamed, *Screw you, bitch.*

Her hands balled into fists. She drew up her other arm, ready to counter with a thrust to his chin, when a deep male voice, as smooth as single malt scotch, murmured, "I've been looking all over for you."

The incubus let go of her and she spun around. A towering figure stood next to her. The stilettos she wore added four inches to her already tall frame, and she still craned her neck to gaze up at his face.

Eyes the color of obsidian locked on hers. His lush, dark hair matched the color of his eyes and a short-cropped beard accentuated the hard planes of his face. He wasn't only classically gorgeous, but his features were undeniably unique. "You looked as if you might need some backup," he murmured close to her ear.

"Thanks, but I'm a lady who can handle herself." *Maybe a bit of an understatement.* She let her gaze trail over his wide, muscled chest. His black suit jacket hugged tightly to his broad shoulders. She pegged it for Armani.

In a sleazy place like this, he was either a dealer or a demon. Both were notorious show-offs. Either way, she wanted to check him out and not just for his looks. She hadn't come here to flirt, but she'd play her part to the hilt if it meant getting info.

The stranger slid onto a barstool and arched his eyebrow. "I don't doubt it. But from what I've heard, their kind doesn't understand the meaning of the word no."

She glanced over her shoulder at the incubus. He scowled at her before skulking back to his place at the bar. "I think he finally got the hint. They must be slumming tonight. This isn't their typical hangout."

"Nor mine. Were you just trying to get away from that guy or are you really meeting someone? In which case, I'd be seriously disappointed." Heat flared in his eyes, and she sensed the passion burning beneath the surface.

"Oh? And here I thought you were being a Good Samaritan," she said in her best seductive voice.

His big, dark eyes trailed over her like a soft caress and lingered on the swell of her breasts, crushed against the top of her bustier. "Maybe I have an ulterior motive." He leaned into her, his voice low near her ear. "I'm in Jersey for business and I don't know anyone in Raven's Hollow. Would you consider showing me around town?"

"Are you propositioning me? Maybe you're one of those guys into the whole damsel in distress thing." Antsy, she glanced at the door again and her gut tightened. There was still no sign of Maeve. Without the amulet, Willow was as good as dead. Tonight she'd been forced to use a glamour to fake out her enemy, but the magick wouldn't last long, less than twenty-four hours at best.

Her light-green eyes were now a deep chocolate-brown and her wavy, auburn hair was blue-black and flowed down her back like a waterfall. At least her black leather trench added some coverage. Not that it protected her from the frigid temperatures outside, but it matched the outfit and concealed the two-foot long, solid steel, twin *athames* sheathed in her hip belt. A metal choker completed the ensemble.

He glanced at her collar. "The only distress you look like you're into makes me think of whips and chains." His eyes were dark and edgy, full of sinful promises. "I'm Alexandros. Call me Alex."

Most demons don't have names like Alexandros. Or dark, golden tans in the dead of winter for that matter. Reddish skin and horns were pretty much the norm. Although some, rare breeds, like the Hymara, appeared to be human but were no less deadly than their full-blooded counterparts.

Under the lights, Alex's skin glowed to a warm, toasty brown and reminded her of hot buttered rum. "I'm Willow." He offered his hand to shake, and her heart spiked when she caught a glimpse of his gold Patek Phillippe watch. Could he be the man from her vision? The moment her hand slid into his, she opened herself to his emotions. Turmoil and anger swirled all around him. She suppressed a shiver and hoped her expression didn't make him suspicious.

"A pleasure." The deep, sensual way he said the word *pleasure* made her shiver

"Well, maybe if you buy me a drink I might forget who I was supposed to meet." She held onto his hand and zeroed in on his thoughts, but he kept his mind shut tighter than the zipper on Maeve's leather pants—now digging into her skin. Apparently, Alex could block a mind probe. Intrigued, she released his hand and plastered a smile on her face.

If he was sent to kill her, she didn't want to risk getting jumped the moment she tried to walk out the door. She'd stall him in the meantime and try to figure out a way to get the upper hand.

His smile revealed a flash of straight white teeth. "I wouldn't want to get accused of plying you with alcohol and piss off the guy who shows up. He might try to kick my ass."

"Why? You look like you can handle yourself." Willow licked her lips and let her gaze trail over two hundred plus pounds of muscle. "Besides, how do you know I'm meeting a guy?"

His slack-jawed response made her chuckle. Some witches loved the idea of threesomes, choosing polyamorous relationships over monogamous ones. She just wasn't one of them. The more she pushed Alex off kilter, the better. Maybe he might even let his shields down. Most males toyed with some sort of twisted lesbian fantasy. She'd have to find a way to get him to talk. Not that she'd act on the fantasy, but who knows, if he thought there was even a remote chance, it might get him to talk.

He leaned in to her and whispered close to her ear, "Since he, or she, isn't here and you are, I guess it's their loss." Willow caught a whiff of his clean, male scent and fought the urge to sigh. The man oozed sexual prowess. Funny, the only males she attracted always ended up turning into major losers. After the last one, she'd sworn off men for good.

Her gaze rested on his face. She'd imprint every gorgeous inch of him to memory and burn out the batteries in her vibrator later. Then she realized she was fantasizing about someone who might be trying to kill her. *What does that say about the state of my personal life?* She seriously needed to get laid. "About that drink—"

"What will the lady have?" He waved his hand in the air, flashing his expensive watch, and the bartender appeared. Alex turned back to face her and smiled, a sensual curve of his lips.

"Patrón margarita on the rocks." At least the good stuff didn't give her a hangover. She tossed her small black clutch on the bar and leaned her hip against the hard, cold edge.

She glanced over at the bartender, a rangy werewolf with black, beady eyes. She couldn't question him about Maeve, not with Alex by her side.

She cringed as he poured a generous amount of tequila into her glass and then added a shot on the side. She didn't plan on getting hammered during this little foray. Her telepathy worked better without the fog from booze, but what choice did she have?

"I'll have a Glenfiddich, neat," Alex said, taking a seat on a barstool. After a few minutes, the bartender placed their drinks on the bar along with the shot, a slice of lemon, and a salt shaker. Alex touched his glass to hers and smiled. "To welcome surprises."

"To welcome surprises." *If he was sent by the Agares, he was about to get one he'd never forget.* She tried checking him out more closely over the rim of her glass. But with his mass of dark, wavy hair, she couldn't make out even the slightest hint of horns. The way he mysteriously showed up here tonight and sought her out couldn't be a coincidence. Even more reason to think the Agares sent him.

When he set his drink on the bar, she contemplated slipping a potion into his glass. She kept one in the pocket of her trench, a special concoction made from licorice root and wolfsbane. The potion acted like a truth serum. A couple of drops and Alex would be forced to reveal his deepest, darkest secrets in a heartbeat. But his steady gaze never left hers.

"That's an interesting tattoo." He reached for her hand and caressed her pentagram with his thumb. Heat emanated off him like the flame of a match. She suppressed a shiver. Alex's touch contrasted with his size and dangerous looks. The man could just be a player, a master seducer lulling her into a sexual trance with his sexy voice and pillow-soft touch before he attacked.

"It's a pentagram, a sacred Wiccan symbol, and these," she said, touching each one of the five points, "represent the elements and the spirit." She shrugged, hoping to sound noncommittal. She didn't want to get into the differences between Wicca, an earth-based religion, and hereditary witchcraft. "The guy at the tattoo shop had it in his book. He rambled on about it while he inked me. I was pretty wasted at the time."

His dark eyes lingered on her mouth as she lifted the glass to her lips. She took a sip of her margarita and glanced down at his big hands, tanned and sprinkled with a smattering of hair. Funny, she never found a man's hands sexy. Suddenly her mind filled with images of Alex trailing those big, masculine hands over her body. She wondered if he fit the stereotype. Big hands, big…

"Are you considering taking me up on my offer?" The deep timbre of his voice pulled her from a host of fantasies. Willow dug her nails into her palm to get her head back in the game. She shouldn't be thinking about this man in such a raw, sexual way.

"Why not? My car's parked in the back." She probed through the nearby crowd to check if Alex came here with bodyguards. A virtual cacophony of conversations invaded her thoughts, but nothing about protection for Alex. Once she got him alone, she'd take her chances and pray she wouldn't be outnumbered.

"Then let's get out of here, unless I've got some competition." He motioned over her shoulder to the incubus whose head now lolled forward over the bar.

"I think you're flying solo." She had set her trap and let the consequences be damned. Willow rubbed her finger along the rim of the glass and licked off the salt.

She was savoring the tangy flavor of margarita mix along with the zing of tequila as it slid down her throat. *Headrush.* No surprise there. She couldn't remember the last time she'd slept or eaten in the past forty-eight hours, existing on a combination of raw nerves and pure adrenaline.

"You missed a spot." He ran his thumb along the seam of her lip. He put it to his mouth and licked. "Mmm, sweet." Her plan didn't involve foreplay...but *damn* he was hot. In another time and another place she'd be seriously into this guy. *Too bad I might have to kill him.*

"I do like my tequila, but every now and then a girl needs something a little stronger."

"Oh? What did you have in mind?"

Now she had his attention. Willow decided to play it up for the final *coup de grâce* and offered the bait. She leaned over, allowing him to get a glimpse of the rolled-up wad of hundreds, a bonus from her last job, now tucked in her cleavage and held by her black, strapless demibra. "I'll show you mine if you show me yours," she purred.

From the way his eyes widened with a mixture of shock and pure lust as they locked on her breasts, he clearly liked the view. Good. She'd be sure to use it to her advantage. "What are we waiting for?" When Alex reached into his pocket to pull out his cash, a pack of matches slipped out and fell on the floor. He shoved some bills at the bartender and waited for his change. Willow bent to pick up the matchbook, ready to hand it back, but when her fingers closed over the cover, she caught a glimpse of Maeve's face contorted in pain.

The image changed like a haze of smoke. Crouched next to Maeve's lifeless body, a shadow of a man hovered nearby. Willow's heart thudded in her chest as the shadow turned into form.

Alex?

Breath whooshed from her lips. The matches slipped from her grasp onto the floor. No wonder Maeve never showed up.

"Hey, are you okay? You look as if you've seen a ghost." Alex placed a hand on her shoulder.

Goddess, she hoped not. "F-fine," she lied.

The bartender appeared and Alex made small talk with him as he cleared their glasses off the bar. At least it gave her a minute to think. If Alex was the one following her, maybe he'd been following Maeve as well. Panic edged around her throat and made a tight fist in her stomach. What if he tried to sell Maeve a bad batch of heroin to get her to talk, then left her to OD?

She gritted her teeth and forced her fear into cold resolve. After years of practice, she'd become adept at pushing through her pain. Shaking, she picked up her drink to take a sip and calm her nerves, when she noticed her white-knuckled grip around the glass. *Don't break it. Don't break it.* A moment later, it shattered in her hands.

"Damn," she groaned as a broken piece sank into her index finger. Blood gushed from her hand and dripped onto the bar.

"Shit. You're bleeding." Alex grabbed a handful of bar napkins, wrapped them around her finger and squeezed. "Hold on. Let me try to find a real bandage." He signaled the bartender as she squeezed at her makeshift bandage until the bleeding stopped.

When Alex turned back to face her, he removed the napkin and ripped open the wrapper of a bandage with his teeth. "I would never peg such a slender lady like yourself for crushing a bar glass. Remind me not to piss you off."

Too late. "I can't believe how clumsy I am sometimes." She couldn't deny a part of her was attracted to him. But if Alex had harmed Maeve in any way, tonight he'd pay for his sins. Did he take advantage of the situation by playing on her weakness? "It's not fair, a man as attractive as you who's also funny." He lifted her hand to kiss her bandaged finger, and she forced herself not to cringe.

"Are you ready?"

"Absolutely." Through the corner of her eye, she noticed Alex glance across the bar at a hulking male nursing a beer by himself. She sucked in a breath when she caught a glimpse of the holstered side arm under his suit jacket. *Hmm, demon bodyguard?*

Alex inclined his head toward him and winked. Did he actually think he'd make a sale and get laid? *A real multitasking, drug-dealing sleaze bag.* There could be no witnesses for what she had in mind. He wrapped his arm around her waist. "I'll follow you."

"Good, because I like to take the lead." She grabbed his hand and guided him to the side entrance of the club, used for delivery only. Once they were outside, no one would notice them, not at this time of night. They passed through the crowd to the other side of the bar and exited the building.

When the heavy door closed behind them, she froze. She stared over the railing to the ten foot drop below and her stomach dipped. Goddess, she hated heights.

Her mind reeled as she peered out into the darkness in search of stairs or something to grab onto, but only found a steep ramp covered in ice and snow. Her heart pounded in her ears…in her throat.

"Willow?" Alex's voice whispered to her from somewhere far away.

The urge to throw herself flush against the building and squeeze her eyes shut became overwhelming. *Get it together.* She bit down hard on her lip instead and forced her legs down the ramp. When her boots touched the sidewalk, she breathed a sigh of relief. "S-sorry, I forgot where I parked." She waited until his footsteps crunched behind her, then spun around.

A flicker of moonlight danced across his handsome face. Cold air filled her lungs and pebbled along her skin. "First, I'd like to get a taste of what you're offering." Willow took a step closer to him. Puffs of icy breath slipped from her lips like white smoke in the frigid night air.

"Willow, wait. There's something you should know."

"Later," she murmured and grabbed him by his collar. She tilted her head to the side and opened her mouth. She cracked an eye open and waited for him to lean into her, close enough to catch a whiff of scotch and peppermint on his warm breath, then she head-butted him.

Alex howled in pain and stumbled backward. Willow didn't give him time to right himself. Instead, she thrust out her leg to the side and hit him with a roundhouse kick under the chin. His head smashed onto the pavement with a sickening thud. Pity, the big ones always did go down hard.

She glanced at his crumbled body and then pressed her boot to his neck. At least the stilettos had come in handy.

His eyes widened in shock. A gurgling sound erupted from his throat. She pulled one of her *athames* from her hip belt and pointed it straight at his groin. "Tell me, Alex," she said with a smile. "Are you fond of your dick?"

CHAPTER 2

Something warm and sticky oozed from the side of Alex Denopoulos's head and ran into his eyes. *Blood.* The instep of her boot closed around his throat like a vise. He needed to get this crazy bitch off him and fast. If he didn't, she'd crush his windpipe.

He'd been caught off guard by her sexy, bad girl act. One minute he thought she was going to kiss him, and the next, she was trying to kill him.

"What's the matter? Not used to a chick having you by the balls?" Willow's red painted lips turned into a smirk as she brushed the blade over his crotch.

Alex glanced up at her lithe body. She probably weighed a buck twenty soaking wet, but she was kicking his ass. He didn't believe her bullshit story about how she got her tattoo, especially now, after seeing her in action. Only one word came to mind—*witch*. Black spots swirled in front of his eyes.

"Okay, lover boy, let's talk." Her eyes flashed fire.

He needed to ask the questions, not the other way around, yet another complication he didn't need. He blinked and swore a blood vessel popped in his eye.

Somehow, she maintained her balance while she reached into her jacket pocket and pulled out her cell. She flashed a picture of a young woman with long, stick-straight, black hair and shoved it into his face. Shit, he recognized the girl.

"Now I want you to look at this photo and think hard before you answer. Have you seen her? I'm only going to ask you once. Her name's Maeve Donovan. Did you sell her smack? And don't even think about kicking me," she warned, anticipating his next move. "I'd hate to start calling you Alexa." She eased her boot off his neck, keeping the tip of her blade positioned an inch from his groin.

His hands circled his neck as he gasped for air. Alex swallowed and tried to find his voice. "S-smack? Hell no." He couldn't tell Willow the truth, not yet. Besides, she'd never believe him anyway.

Hell, he'd been doing a little harmless flirting. Maybe a halfhearted attempt at mixing business with pleasure in the hopes Willow would open up to him. *Bad idea.*

"Is Alex your real name? Are you working for the Agares? Did you come here to kill me?"

"Don't you have that the other way around?" he said through gritted teeth. "What makes you think I work for the Agares?" He'd been keeping an eye on the murderous band of demons for years. But what connection did they have to Willow?

"It doesn't matter," Willow hissed, bending close to his ear. "I'm looking for my friend and you're going to help me find her if you want to keep your manhood."

He'd been staking out this hellhole for weeks with one goal in mind—bust up a drug ring and nail the kingpin. He never meant for things to end this way, or for Maeve Donovan to get caught in the middle of such a dangerous game. He'd let a killer slip through his fingertips, and now because of his screw-up, an innocent life was lost forever.

And as fate would have it, Willow might be the key to solving her murder. But in the meantime, he'd be damned before he let a female wield a blade at his balls. "We can help each other." If Willow didn't castrate him, his boss would if he let her get away.

"Wrong answer. Did you take her money and leave her for dead?" Her voice took on a steely edge.

This one gave new meaning to the term armed and dangerous. Where the hell was Cayden? He left his partner sitting at the damn bar. He needed backup. *Now.* His earpiece had gone flying when he landed flat on his back on the pavement.

"No, goddamn it. I'm not who you think I am." If he could give the others a heads-up, they'd come in a heartbeat. He'd just have to live down getting his ass kicked by a girl, a hot one no less.

"Want to bet? Answer me. I'm losing patience." Willow hooked the tip of her blade into the seam of his pants, and with a flick of her wrist, exposed several inches of thigh.

"Whoa, take it easy." He let out a string of curses and tried to wriggle away from her blade, scraping his elbows against the concrete. When he got the chance, he was going to strangle her.

Her gaze narrowed as she stared at his face. "What are you anyway? A demon?"

"You've got this all wrong." Before he could convince her otherwise, she slammed her knee into his chest, expelling all the air from his lungs.

When she reached down and ruffled a hand through his hair, he swore she took a clump with it. Then her fingers probed his skull, inspecting the sides and crown of his head. "What the hell are you doing?"

"No horns. You're a human?"

"Yes, I'm human." For a split second her blade wavered. Alex used it to his advantage and jerked upright out of pure rage. With one quick jab to her wrist, the sword went flying across the pavement.

He pushed to his feet, grabbed her arms, and pulled them behind her back. His legs wobbled beneath him and, for a moment, the world began to spin. Tiny stars filled his vision, and his head began to pound. Hell, the little witch had probably given him a concussion.

"Who the hell are you?" He didn't expect her to tell him the truth, but he had to ask anyway. Alex tasted blood on his tongue, spit it onto the pavement, and then gave her a slight shake.

"None of your damn business." She struggled, trying to break free. He squeezed her wrists tighter behind her back. If she didn't calm down, he'd subdue her the hard way.

"I told you already," she breathed. "I'm trying to find my friend."

"By acting like some sort of witch vigilante?" He wiped his mouth on the shoulder of his rented monkey suit. "Listen to me, I have seen your friend, Maeve." He turned her to face him and held both of her slim wrists in one hand.

"Y-you've seen her?" Her eyes widened. "Tell me where she is."

"First, you're going to answer my questions, and then I'll answer yours. Understood?" He tried to clear his head, but the stench of garbage and rotten fumes from the sewer grate flared in his nostrils.

She trembled, probably from anger, and then nodded.

"How long have you been searching for Maeve? And why the hell didn't you just ask me inside if I knew her?"

She snorted. "Yeah, as if you would've come clean. I find guys into the whole drug scene aren't big into questions." Her eyes trailed over his expensive suit before resting on his face. "They like to cover their tracks."

"What? I'm not a dealer." The agency forced him to dress the part to blend in, and now it was easy to see how she'd gotten the wrong impression.

"If you're not working for the Agares, and you didn't come here to sell drugs, then what are you doing hanging around a place like Fusion? I think the real question is: Who the hell are you?"

"Someone who cares." Right after he said the words he wished he could take them back. She'd never believe such a sappy line of bullshit. Too bad it was true.

"Yeah, right," she muttered and rolled her eyes. "Screw you, asshole."

"And to think I almost kissed you on that dirty, little mouth." She sure was a feisty one. "Dammit, Willow, you have to listen to me. We're on the same side." He never expected things to turn into pure shit so fast. "You're right. I came here with an agenda. But it wasn't to harm you or sell drugs to your friend. I'm not the type to hurt a female. C'mon, what does your intuition tell you?"

"That you're a liar. Will you let go already? You're hurting me," she moaned in a choked voice. He loosened his grip on her wrists.

"You deserve it." Guilt stabbed at his gut like the edge of a blade. He'd never get used to going head to head with a woman, no matter how strong.

Over the years, he'd encountered a few witches like her, but none who demonstrated such a rare, preternatural speed and strength. He eased up and let out a long, strangled breath. "It appears we both thought the other was someone else. Tell me more about Maeve. Did you report her disappearance to the police?" He didn't think the RHPD was out combing the streets for her.

"I'm not answering your questions," she snapped. "I don't trust you."

"Yeah, well that makes two of us, babe, but I'm telling you the truth."

"Okay, I'm tired of fighting you." She sighed before her body went limp. "I still don't know who you are. But I believe you didn't hurt her. Now will you let go of me?"

"As long as you don't try anything." Alex figured he'd gotten through to the rational part of her brain.

"Agreed," she mumbled, sounding defeated. Shadows covered her face, which made it impossible to read her expression.

The moment he released her hands, she stomped on his foot with her spiked heel. He let out a string of curses as searing pain exploded in his toes.

"You shouldn't trust me either, babe."

Dark and sleek as a panther, Willow started to run, but Alex caught her around the waist. She shrieked in his ear like a goddamn siren and then elbowed him hard in the solar plexus. He doubled over, grunting in pain. The minute he let go of her, one leg shot out toward his face in a flurry of spiked heel and black leather. He ducked and caught her by the ankle.

Every last bit of his control slipped. Adrenaline surged through his body as his temper roared to life. "I don't care if you are a female, no more Mr. Nice Guy." Alex flipped her over onto her back and used all his body weight to force her down into the pavement. He took both her hands in one of his and pinned them above her head. Now she couldn't punch him or slap him in the face. She might be strong as hell, but he outweighed her by at least a hundred pounds.

"You like to play games? I can play too," he said. He clenched his teeth and wrapped his legs around hers to keep her from kicking.

"You'll regret this." The wind kicked up and blew her hair in every direction, and he had a sudden urge to wrap his hand around all those glossy strands.

The blow to the head had doused his earlier arousal, but feeling every curve of her luscious body squirm and buck beneath him brought it back full force. "So far I'm not," he murmured on a ragged breath.

Her face flushed. "Bastard."

"Funny, you didn't think so earlier, when you practically flashed me your tits." And Alex still couldn't get the image of black lace and all her creamy skin out of his mind.

"This isn't a game. Someone's life could be at stake. Now let me go."

The glow of the street lamps illuminated the curve of her face and the outline of full, red lips.

Even though he wanted to throttle her, he didn't have the heart to tell her the truth, at least not in her current state of mind. The exotic scent of her perfume, a mixture of vanilla and wildflowers, clouded his brain. Damn she smelled good. His erection pressed painfully against his jeans. He might be an agent, but he was still a man.

Confusion clouded her eyes. "Tell me where she is. Where the hell is Maeve? I saw you next to her. Don't try to deny it." He became hypnotized by the soft flutter of her breath and the rise and fall of her chest.

Was she talking about a dream or some kind of vision? "Who are you?" he asked for the second time tonight. Only now his voice sounded rough with lust and something dark. He gazed at her breasts, nearly spilling out of her leather top, and suppressed a groan. She reminded him of a dominatrix and fed into every one of his dirty fantasies.

For one crazy moment he thought about giving in to desire and pulling down the scrap of black leather to lick her pale flesh. But this wasn't the time or the place. His eyes roamed over her body and he noticed a second silver sword strapped at her hip. He tightened his hold on her wrists and recalled how only minutes earlier she had the other one pointed at his crotch. "Why should I tell you anything about Maeve when you tried to mess with my junk?"

"I find it gets people talking," she panted, still struggling to get free.

Another gust of frigid air blew over them and it made her nipples harden against the thin leather. He stifled a groan. "I think you've done enough talking for tonight." In fact, he could think of much better ways to quiet that sassy mouth of hers. His gaze traveled to her lips. She bit down into her lower one and he grew harder still. He wanted to rub his face along her neck, inhale her scent, and kiss all that smooth skin.

Now all he could think about was devouring her lips, kissing her until she was breathless and shaking, especially after the way she'd teased him tonight. The allure of her beauty and the sexy sway of her hips and ass called to him on a primal level. He would've followed her almost anywhere, hard as stone, heart pounding in anticipation.

When she looked up at him, the color of her eyes shifted from brown to an intense shade of green. Everything about this female was a mystery, one he wanted to solve. "Alex," she whispered, with an edge of need in her voice. Her breaths grew shallow. Her eyes glazed with passion, and then she gazed at his lips.

The witch is beckoning me to kiss her.

"Willow," he whispered. Alex was about to give in and finally taste her lips, when a loud, buzzing noise reverberated across the alley. It deflated his arousal like a bucket of ice to the groin. What the hell was he doing? He blinked as if he'd been in a trance. *A sexual one.*

Did she try and put him under a spell to get away? He wouldn't put it past her. Then why did it seem as if she was going out of her mind with desire for him as well?

She's a witch after all, and witches can never be trusted. Her kind seethed with power—and trickery. She wielded her magick like a sword. His hands clenched into fists as he reached for his cuffs from his back pocket. He pulled her up to a standing position then slammed them on her wrists.

"What the hell do you think you're doing?" She tried to back away, but she wasn't going anywhere.

"I think you can figure it out, smart girl." He walked over to where he'd dropped his earpiece, dragging her along with him, and retrieved the black dot off the ground. After he attached it to his ear, he let out a deep breath.

A male voice pounded through his mic. "Alex? Are you there?"

"Yeah, I'm here, corner of Belleville and Union Avenue. The back alley of Fusion and I'm not alone. Tell Cayden to get his ass out here. I'm at the side entrance."

Willow turned toward the landing to the scrape of footsteps. The mage who'd been sitting in the club walked up to Alex and patted him on the back. His tall, menacing frame contrasted with his three-piece, navy pin-striped suit and tie. Close up, he was almost as gorgeous as Alex, with bright blue eyes, short cropped blond hair, and black horns that ran along the side of his head. *A demon.*

"Sorry, man. I didn't think you needed me." He glanced from Willow to Alex and winked. His eyes flickered over Alex's busted lip and the bloody gash on the side of his head. "Uh, you okay? Where's the son of a bitch who did this to you? If I'd been here I would've ripped him apart. Did he flee the scene?" The demon glanced around the deserted alley before he reached into his pocket and handed Alex a crumpled-up bar napkin.

"Nope. This hellion clad in black leather, she's our perp." Alex glared at her as he dabbed at the bloody gash on his head, fury emanating from every pore. His lips twisted into a cruel smile. "This party's officially over. You're coming with us."

Undercover cops? Well, that figures. "Look, I apologize for attacking you. But you didn't exactly identify yourself or flash a badge. This is a simple case of mistaken identity. I thought you were someone else. How was I supposed to know you were a cop? Has the RHPD changed their uniform to Armani? What are you arresting me for anyway?"

He shrugged. "I'd tell you, but the list is way too long to recite."

"I know my rights. Aren't you going to read them to me?" Willow didn't want to think about what would've happened if they hadn't been interrupted. Her only excuse for having such a raw, sexual reaction to Alex could be blamed on tequila.

Alex ignored her and pulled out his cell to type a text. What if Alex used his undercover act on Maeve to bust her with drugs? It could explain her vision. She hoped she was somewhere safe, riding out a vicious bout of withdrawal.

"If you're an undercover cop, why aren't you going after the real criminals? The druggie lowlifes in there who'll sell an eight ball to any kid on the street? Why bother wasting your time talking to me?" *Flirting his ass off was more like it.* "Did you think you could bust me?"

"Trust me. We're going after the druggie lowlifes in there," Alex said, pointing to the door. "On a regular basis. And it's nothing personal, sweetheart. It's called a stakeout. You flashed me a wad of cash, which made me think you wanted to buy drugs, but it's not the only reason."

"Oh?" Their eyes locked and, for a moment, she forgot to breathe. She took in every inch of his chiseled face, and then her gaze moved lower to big, broad shoulders, a muscular chest, and a narrow waist. The man really was all kinds of fine.

"I hoped you could shed some light on an investigation." He angled his dark head toward the nightclub.

Most likely a drug ring at the club. "Really, by almost sticking your tongue down my throat? Is that standard interrogation practice?" His aura turned from gray to black, signaling anger. Chalk one up for her.

"I do what the situation warrants. I was undercover, playing a role, nothing more." His gaze rested on her choker and her skimpy bustier, before trailing down to her skin-tight leather pants. "And what's your excuse, unless of course you're deliberately trying to look like the BDSM poster child?"

She tried to give him the finger, but her hands were cuffed. "Bite me."

"Tempting offer, but I'll have to decline for now. Look," Alex said, running a hand through his hair, making it stand on end. "You have a right to know. I'll tell you everything. I promise. But it's better if we do it back at headquarters."

"I'm not going anywhere with you, and I want my other *athame* back." She spotted it across the alley next to a trash can lid. "I need to make a call to my attorney." Not that she had one, but he didn't need to know she was bluffing.

"The call comes later. Where I'm taking you, we do things differently."

Differently? Before Willow could ask him to elaborate, a set of blinding headlights flashed in her eyes. Tires screeched across Union Avenue, emitting the stench of burnt rubber. An unmarked black van careened down the alley and stopped in front of the curb.

The door slid open with a hiss and two hulking figures with reddish skin and big black horns stepped out. *Crap.* Fire demons. They weren't exactly buds.

"Looks like our ride's here." Alex pushed her toward the van.

"Who are you people?" She swallowed hard and tried to formulate a plan of escape over the buzzing in her head. Willow might have a shot at Alex and his partner, but not with the fire demons. Outnumbered and at a slight disadvantage without the use of her hands, she gathered all her strength to try to squeeze her way out of the cuffs, but they didn't budge.

"Don't bother, Willow. They're reinforced with lead."

Realization slammed into her gut with the force of a freight train. "Lead?" The metal was already working its way under her skin, weakening her powers and draining the source of her magick.

Her heart pounded in her chest. She took a step back as panic edged around her brain. Before she could make a run for it, the one called Cayden walked over and pushed her hair off her shoulder. He pulled out a syringe and shot it into her neck. "This is so you don't remember where you're going."

Bastard. Her mind became fuzzy. Tiny silver specks filled her vision. Her arms grew heavy and listless. The sensation intensified and coiled down her back like a striking snake. She tried to take a step, but her legs buckled beneath her.

"Easy there." Alex caught her before she hit the ground.

"Y-you're not cops." Her voice sounded muffled. "You're w-witch hunters." Her world spun before everything faded to black.

CHAPTER 3

"*W*here the hell am I?" Willow lifted her chin in defiance at the demon bureaucrat seated across from her at the large metal table. Even folded into a chair, he was enormous. From the way his head loomed over her, she guessed at least seven feet tall, with pale, red skin and black, curvy horns pointing straight out of his head.

"I'm Commander Smith and you've already met Special Agent Denopoulos," he said, inclining his head in Alex's direction, avoiding the question.

"Special Agent Denopoulos?" She glanced at Alex, who stood rigid in the corner of the dark room, his face partially hidden in the shadows. He no longer resembled the Armani-clad player from the night before. Now he wore a white button-down shirt open at the neck, a Kevlar vest, and a small gun hung in a holster from his belt.

Annoyed, she frowned down at her wrinkled leather pants; at least he got a chance to change. She rubbed a hand over her eyes then massaged her sore wrists. "How long have I been out?"

Her head throbbed with a slight hangover and a lingering fuzziness from the sedative. Her stomach rumbled, and she couldn't remember the last time she had eaten. She needed a toothbrush, a shower, and fresh clothes, preferably not of the leather variety.

"About four hours give or take." Alex moved into the light. A bandage now covered the gash on his head. She wondered how much flak he was getting for his injuries. She'd never meant to hurt him, but under the circumstances, what choice did she have?

"Four hours?" Willow didn't have four hours to spare. She needed to find Maeve and disappear.

"Do you have any idea why you've been brought here, Miss McCray, to the Magickal Bureau of Investigations?" asked Smith in his deep, monotone voice.

She glanced around the room, taking in the bland gray walls and sparse metal furniture. Nothing about her surroundings made her think this place could be the headquarters for a secret mage agency. But something about the energy in the room made a bone-crushing sense of foreboding swirl through her head.

"Actually, no. I'm not clear why your agents felt the need to drug me and use kidnapping as a means of getting me here. Perhaps you can enlighten me?"

Smith picked up a pen from his desk and clicked it. "Maybe this will help." Immediately, the bland gray walls spun around to reveal floor-to-ceiling computer screens. Life-size moving holograms with the words "Wanted Criminals" flashed from different angles all around the room. An array of ruthless-looking creatures moved in a blur of streaming color and loud beeping noises. She braced her hands on either side of the desk. What did she get herself into?

"Our agency instills and upholds the sacred written laws of the *Arcana* throughout mage society." Smith's face remained impassive. "In essence, our mission is to keep the mortal population safe. You're here, Miss McCray, because you've broken the law, as well as the Wiccan Rede, of Harm Ye None."

"This has all been a terrible mistake." The antiseptic smell of the room made her head throb. She swallowed hard and rubbed her temples. "The details of last night are still kind of fuzzy, but he approached me." She pointed an accusing finger at Alex. "Not the other way around."

"A mistake? Let me refresh your memory. You attacked an MBI agent without provocation, and let's not forget solicitation of an illegal substance for another, not to mention the other laundry list of misdemeanors in your file," Alex said, his tone dripping with sarcasm.

"Okay, I get it." She turned back toward Smith. "I attacked one of your agents, who, by the way, didn't exactly identify himself." Willow let out a deep breath in an attempt to diffuse the burning in her gut. "But is that a reason to drag me here?"

Alex made a sound deep in his throat. "C'mon, tough girl, you can do better than that."

"Look, I only attacked you because I thought you hurt my friend. What was I supposed to do? And for the record, the whole solicitation thing was an act," she whispered, suppressing the urge to slap him across the face.

His audacity burned her to the core. Anger swiftly turned to shame. Goddess, she'd flashed him. Her face flushed at the memory. How was she supposed to know Alex was an MBI agent? And then there was her nasty habit of swinging first and asking questions later. Her hair trigger responses always did get her into trouble, but never like this.

An image of Maeve wavered in her mind's eye, and then disappeared. "I know Maeve's here. I can sense her presence." An ice cold sense of dread slid down her spine. "Let me guess, one of your guys caught her doing smack, which I don't condone by the way, and brought her here. But how do her actions endanger the mortal population? She's only hurting herself."

"Agent Denopoulos and Agent Teague have been trying to infiltrate a drug distribution ring at Fusion for some time, with no success until very recently." Smith pursed his lips. "We have reason to believe the kingpin is someone you're acquainted with."

"Are you referring to Tristan Saint Claire?" *My former boss.*

Smith's red eyes flickered to Alex's before meeting hers again. "We've been working closely with an informant, someone on the inside, who was willing to get our agents a meeting with one of his top scumbags. Our Intel confirms that he's been trafficking heroin and meth to the mortal community. Until a sudden turn of events, the informant, Miss McCray, was Maeve Donovan."

Her heart thudded in her chest. *Maeve an informant?* Was she risking her life to stay out of prison? "Funny, she never mentioned it. Are you going to let me see her?" When Willow looked into Smith's eyes, his pupils dilated, a sign of deceit.

Demons couldn't always conceal their thoughts with shields. How had Alex managed to do it as a mortal? She spotted Smith's pen on the desk and brushed the tip with her finger. His thoughts invaded her head with the force of a bullet. *Shit, this could get ugly. Trust me, you don't want to see the Donovan woman, not in the condition she's in.*

"What did you people do to her?" Willow dropped the pen and stood up so fast her chair hit the floor. The sound of metal smashing against wood left a ringing in her ears. "Why don't you tell me what condition she's in, Commander Smith?" The lead poisoning must've worn off. At least her powers were still intact.

"Nothing." Shock flashed in Alex's dark eyes. "Now take a seat."

Smith's mouth dropped open and formed a perfect O. He glanced at Alex and frowned. "Funny, Agent Denopoulos never mentioned the preciseness of your psychic abilities."

"I didn't know. I kept my shields up the whole time I was with her." Alex shrugged and rubbed a hand over his beard.

"Lucky for you." Smith pulled out a shiny black square from the inside of his jacket pocket and began typing. "We did a background check on you while you were sedated. You're quite gifted. Too bad you're wasting your talent working for the Shadow Cabal."

"Apparently, you guys have been busy." *Great, they didn't waste any time delving into my past.* After Willow righted her chair, she sat back down and glanced across the room at Alex. He was gazing at her with an odd expression on his face.

Before she could give him the evil eye, Alex walked over to the coffee maker and filled two paper cups then covered them with lids. She salivated, ready to chew off her arm if she didn't get a caffeine fix. After he made his way over to the desk, he plopped down in the chair next to her.

"You must be starving and probably a little groggy after last night." Alex placed a steaming cup on the desk, along with some sugar packets and a couple of creamers. He reached into his pocket and pulled out a bag of trail mix. He laid it on the desk and smiled, which made his eyes crinkle at the corners. "Sorry, it's all I could find in the snack machine."

"Hopefully, this isn't my last meal." Her fingers closed over the bag and her stomach rumbled in response. She tore open the top with her teeth and poured the trail mix into her mouth. After she emptied the bag, she sighed, starting to feel a little better.

"What do you people want with me? Don't get me wrong; I'm finding the whole good cop / bad cop routine pretty entertaining, but I'm sure there are bigger badasses out there you could be questioning right now." Alex scooted his chair closer to her side of the desk and she became aware of two things—his tall, imposing frame, and the clean, masculine scent of his cologne. She tried not to stare, but the way the material of his plain white button-down clung to his wide shoulders and broad chest was downright drool worthy. His muscles visibly bulged beneath the fabric. No man should look this sexy so early in the morning.

His dark eyes danced with amusement. "Rest assured, Willow, your ass is at the top of our list. You've got some interesting friends. We'd like to ask you a few questions about them. Drink up. You'll need a clear head." Alex pointed to the coffee. "I'm not sure how you like it."

Willow smiled as she ripped open the sugar packets and emptied them into her cup. "Black with three sugars and easy on the sedative."

"Glad to see you haven't lost your sense of humor." Something told her from his solemn expression, she was going to need it. "And just so you know, we haven't done anything to Maeve. I promise to let you see her when we're done here. I give you my word."

Exhaustion mingled with relief. She took a sip of her coffee and regarded Alex over the rim of her cup. "Why should I cooperate? Have I been officially charged with a crime?"

Smith offered Willow a sidelong glance. "You'd be hard-pressed to find any Wiccan mediators willing to come down here on such short notice at this time of the morning. Why not answer our questions and get this done here and now?"

Her stomach tightened. "You've made it pretty convenient, haven't you? I'll make sure my lawyer hears about this." She needed to confirm that Maeve was okay and find a way to get the amulet; if not, she was as good as dead.

"I'll give you the opportunity to call him or her, but we'll have to keep you confined to Hellios in one of our holding cells in the meantime."

Ice cold dread formed a knot in the pit of her stomach. She'd heard the mage prison was something straight out of a nightmare, a fifty-foot stone tower on the peak of a mountain. The cells were supposedly the size of a Cracker Jack box with buckets for toilets.

Her breath caught in her throat as she imagined getting confined to a cell at the top. When she skimmed her fingers over Smith's pen again, a swirl of gray skated on the edges of her consciousness and burst to the surface with the force of a crashing wave. The image of several maddened creatures screaming and pulling their hair out in hunks flashed through her mind. "N-no, please."

"I thought you might come to your senses and see it our way." After Alex walked over to one of the wall-sized computer monitors and scrolled through the screens, a series of different images of her face in some of her more colorful glamours popped up before her eyes. Willow wrapped her arms around her body in an attempt to stave off the chill in the room.

"Should I call you Willow McCray, or how about Willa McPherson? Or maybe it's Silver Munroe? We've been watching you, giving you enough rope, figuring you'd eventually hang yourself."

Her hands began to shake, so she stuffed them in the pockets of her trench. She couldn't bullshit her way out of this one. "Working for the Shadow Cabal forced me to use different aliases and glamours to disguise myself." Willow ran her fingers through her hair and shifted in her seat when she realized a strand had turned from black back to red. Speaking of glamours, hers was starting to wear off. "My real name is Willow McCray."

"I'm guessing the fact that nothing they touch is even remotely aboveboard might have something to do with it." His steady gaze stayed fixed on hers as Alex took a sip of his coffee. "Last night you asked me if I worked for the Agares, even mistook me for one of their assassins sent to kill you. It sounds to me as if you're involved in some dangerous shit. Exactly what kind of work do you do for the Cabal?" he asked in a cold, hard voice.

"I work as a psychic consultant for the Cabal's various corporations. Typically, I sit behind a glass partition in a boardroom and read the minds of those on the other side. The Agares have a long history of business dealings with the Shadow Cabal. It's probably fair to say, I may have pissed off a demon or two along the way."

"You say you work for the Cabal's various corporations. Are you aware that they're fronts for their more lucrative endeavors, like money laundering, prostitution, and drug trafficking?" Smith said from across the table. Alex crossed his arms over his chest and peered over at her, his dark eyes intense. "Tristan Saint Claire has suppliers, the lowest scum of society, pushing to kids all over this city."

"I-I didn't know. I swear. Everything was done in secret." When Willow closed her eyes, a combination of words and pictures swirled through her head and then turned blood red as they crystalized into thoughts. Her eyes popped open. "I see something metal, like a belt buckle with the letters SG engraved in the center, maybe this person works for Saint Claire."

"We'll take it under consideration." Alex glanced from her to Smith and back again, then scribbled onto a pad. "You say you're a psychic consultant. What kind of consultant carries knives?"

One who works for a monster like Saint Claire. "A girl in my line of work can never be too careful."

"But you don't just work as a psychic, do you?" Frustration bloomed on Alex's handsome face. "If you answer truthfully, we might give you a deal."

She exhaled a pent-up breath. "I've done various jobs for him, including acting as a personal bodyguard to protect him against some of the more ruthless creatures in our world. I'm not proud of what I've done, but I did what I had to in order to stay alive." She sipped her coffee, the taste bitter on her tongue. "Saint Claire's been trying to rise through the rank and file of mage society by eliminating the lower level demonarchies. I've wanted to break free for a while now, but I never managed to until recently."

"Is that when he put a hit on you?" Alex asked, rubbing his beard.

She nodded. "Saint Claire demands loyalty. Once you're in, you're in for life. Very soon after he got word of what I was planning, he put a hit on Ronan, the Agares King, and ordered me to do the deed. When I refused to go through with it, Saint Claire purposely leaked the whole debacle to Ronan out of revenge. Now his guards are after me."

"Ah, so that's the reason Ronan put a hefty bounty on your pretty head." Alex walked back over to the desk and sat down. "Maybe Saint Claire wants to punish you. He has quite the reputation as a ladies' man. Perhaps this was all part of some lovers' quarrel? Is that why you were trying to break free?"

"How dare you try to insinuate that I was sleeping with Tristan Saint Claire. I despise the demon. No matter what you think of me, I don't kill for sport, Agent Denopoulos." Willow tried to ignore the tight knot of shame in her gut. "There's nothing personal to our association. He recruited me because I have a unique set of skills which makes me perfect for the job."

Smith's gaze darted to the bandage on Alex's head before it rested on his pen. "I think we've seen some of those skills firsthand, which brings us back to the matter at hand. What were you doing at Fusion last night? Why did you solicit Agent Denopoulos if you weren't there to buy drugs?"

Alex leaned back in his chair and tried to remain stone-faced as Willow pulled open the belt on her long, leather coat. She turned toward him and her brown eyes flashed to green. "He fit the image of a man in my vision. I only solicited him for drugs as a way of getting him outside to talk. I thought he was sent by Ronan to kill me. I don't do smack, never have." She shrugged the coat off her slender shoulders and lifted her bare arms. "See, no track marks. Satisfied?"

Satisfied? Hell no, and I still have blue balls to prove it. His mouth dropped open at the sight of her breasts pushed up to her chin in the scrap of black leather she called a top. Alex coughed to break the awkward silence. "Okay, you can put your coat back on."

His groin tightened as she leaned forward to push her arms back into her coat, flashing yet another view of her gorgeous cleavage. From the moment she strutted across the club, he couldn't take his eyes off her. She'd been funny, sassy, and sexy as all hell. *Too bad she's a criminal.*

Now, every time she glanced in his direction, it set his teeth on edge. He was thinking about Willow McCray in a raw, sexual way, for one reason and one reason only—he'd been living and breathing this damn case every waking minute. He seriously needed sex, the hot and sweaty, no-strings-attached kind. In fact, when this case was wrapped—he'd make it his number one priority.

"You say you don't do drugs. Then what the hell were you doing at a notorious hangout for pushers and burnouts?" Alex asked in an attempt to diffuse the sexual detour his thoughts had taken on.

"I was meeting a friend to say goodbye before I went on the run," she said in barely a whisper.

"Yes, we've heard," Smith said, tapping his phone. "Maeve Donovan, aka Maeve the Metallurgist. I wonder if she was forging you a weapon, maybe one to use on Ronan?"

"No, she was forging me an amulet, one used to protect, not to kill."

"How do we know what to believe?" Alex rubbed a hand over his beard. "You say you don't do drugs, and yet you must've known Maeve was hooked on smack. How do you separate the two?"

"I watched her throw away her life for years, falling deeper under the pull of addiction." She blinked and her eyes swam with tears. Finally, a chink in her leather armor. "It was like watching someone drowning in quicksand. I know you probably don't trust a word I say, but you can trust this—after this ordeal is over, I'm going to help her get her life back on track. I swear on the Goddess."

And for the first time in twenty-four hours, Alex caught a glimpse of real vulnerability underneath all the hard edges.

He admired her loyalty to her friend, even if it was misplaced. Guilt formed a tight knot in his gut. He couldn't tell her she was too late. Smith had insisted upon waiting until they were done interrogating her. No matter what she did, she deserved to know the truth. He glanced at Smith and nodded. Now it was time to put an offer on the table.

"Excuse us for a minute." Smith placed his cell inside his jacket pocket and motioned for Alex to follow him to the corner of the room.

"The way I see it, we can send her case to the Council," Smith whispered. "But they're so backed up with files, chances are they'll let her rot in Hellios before they figure out what to do with her. In the meantime, I think she can help us. She's clearly gifted. I'm willing to bet she can lead us to straight to Saint Claire. Besides, she has an emotional connection with the Donovan woman that could work in our favor."

"Hold on. Where are you going with this, Smith?"

"She's on to something. I can feel it in my gut. Besides, Saint Claire sure as hell wouldn't put someone on the payroll if she wasn't good at her job. I guarantee he wants her back. Who knows, maybe we can use her as a bargaining chip down the road. I'm guessing she has enough dirt to help bring the sonofabitch down. Have you talked to your buddy at the department?"

"I put a call into Mulroney a few days ago. The last I heard, he has a team in place trying to infiltrate the Cabal's prostitution ring, without

much luck." Alex had worked with Garret Mulroney on the RHPD for
several years before coming to work for the MBI.

"Then you agree, using the girl is worth a shot?" Smith loosened his tie
and then glanced in Willow's direction before facing Alex again.

Getting drugs off the streets of Raven's Hollow and putting scum like
Saint Claire behind bars was Alex's number one priority. In fact, it was
what kept him awake long into the night. But getting a felon like Willow
McCray to hand over her former boss on a silver platter was highly
unlikely, no matter how good the offer.

Alex sighed in exasperation. "I don't like it. She attacked me. We can't
trust her. She's a goddamn witch." His dislike of witches was well known
throughout the agency, and now Smith was asking the unthinkable, forcing
him to work alongside one.

"Regardless of your personal history, I'm willing to take the risk."

Alex cursed and attempted to shove a hand through his hair, but it
caught on the bandage wrapped around his head. He stole a glance at her
hopeless expression and he almost felt sorry for her until he spotted the
dried blood on his fingers. His anger returned full force. "Yeah, if she
comes through."

A tendril of unresolved sexual heat made the memory of their bodies
tangled together flash through his mind. He could still recall the
overwhelming urge to kiss her—to caress her. His need had shattered all
reason and nearly made him trash every code of conduct.

His jaw tightened. "She's way too unpredictable, and my guess, not
above using spells and trickery. It's too dangerous. Since when do we
recruit private citizens, felons, no less?"

"We do what we have to when we have a killer on the loose, besides,
she committed misdemeanors, not felonies. I'm sure Mulroney can attest,
the RHPD uses psychics, witches, in fact, all the time." Smith glanced at the
gash on Alex's head and smiled wide. "At least we know she can take care
of herself."

"That's splitting hair on the felon thing. Once a person is willing to
commit misdemeanors, it's only a matter of time before they commit
felonies. If this backfires, it's on your shoulders." Alex tapped his foot in
agitation.

"And yours. I'm assigning her to you. From now on, she's your responsibility." Smith smiled. "C'mon, let's make her an offer she can't refuse."

Alex followed Smith back to the desk, sat down, and tried to rein in his temper. What the hell did he just get himself into?

"You're a smart woman, Miss McCray, and my guess is a resourceful one as well." Smith cleared his throat. "It would take time to get your priors to stick for an extended period of time, especially with no witnesses. But we can enforce the current charges against you and keep you locked up in Hellios until we can get you a meeting with the Council. Frankly, that could take weeks, maybe even months, and even then, I can almost guarantee they won't vote in your favor. In the meantime, we're willing to offer you a deal to keep you out of prison."

"I'm all ears." Willow sat up straighter in her chair.

"I think we may have gone over to the dark side," Alex said, shooting a glare at Smith before facing Willow again. "But here's the deal. You'd have to agree to work for the agency as a consultant of sorts. Think of it as a chance for you to use your powers for good instead of evil."

"Is this a joke?" she snapped. "Come work for the MBI?"

"Trust me, Miss McCray, this is no joke. We're taking one hell of a risk. But it seems like a waste to let someone with your skills rot in prison. If you agree, I'll assign you to work directly with Agent Denopoulos, since you two have already become acquainted. We could use a psychic with your abilities to assist him and Agent Teague in taking down a drug ring and finding a killer, and then I'd ask you to turn over everything you know about the Shadow Cabal and Tristan Saint Claire. I'd want names of his accomplices, locations of strongholds, meeting places, and all known criminal activity."

"Are you asking me if I would become an informant? Is this how you got Maeve to do it? Did you threaten her? I've already got Ronan after me. You think I want Saint Claire on my back as well?"

"You might not have a choice." Alex crushed the cup in his hands and tossed it in the trash.

"You'd need witnesses who'd be willing to testify against me in front of the Council for those charges to stick. I'm afraid you'll have to do better." She licked her full lips and it made Alex's cock twitch.

Alex turned toward Smith, whose expression screamed, *Give her anything she wants.* Her arrogance niggled at him. "If you agree to our terms, I'll erase your file when this case is wrapped up. Think about it, you'll never hear from us again. You'll be a free woman."

Her demeanor changed from cockiness to bewilderment. "Even if I did agree, you're forgetting one minor detail." She leaned her head against the back of the chair and stared up at the ceiling. "The Agares will hunt me down until they find me."

"At least you'll have your magick to defend yourself. If you choose Hellios, I'm afraid your powers will drain the second you set foot through the door. The cells are embedded with lead, and even though the prison is protected by mystical boundaries that very few can penetrate, I put nothing past an angry demon. We can offer you no guarantees, but we promise to do everything in our power to protect you once you're in our custody." Smith tapped his long fingers on the desk.

"I guess you've thought of everything," Willow whispered, finishing the last of her coffee.

Alex glanced at his watch and stood. "I'm afraid we're out of time. What will it be?"

It took her less than a minute to speak. "Let me get this straight, door number one is a cell at Hellios? And door number two is a temporary stint with your agency? I might be considered a traitor by my kind, but I choose door number two. I guess I've switched employers. When can I see Maeve?"

Now came the hard part. He only wished the ending to this drama had played out differently, for everyone's sake. Alex expelled the breath he'd been holding. "We'll need you to fill out some paperwork and get fitted with a tracking device, but we can take care of the rest later. Is there anyone you need to call, family or friends?"

Pain flashed in her eyes before her expression went blank. "No, no one."

Sympathy twisted in his gut as he slipped on his jacket. "Okay, then, why don't you come with us?"

Willow followed the two men down a long, dark corridor. Her head swam, still trying to process the sudden turn of life-changing events. She couldn't dwell on that now. She didn't want to think about her fate. All she could think about was Maeve. The more she tried to tune into her, the more she sensed something was terribly wrong.

They passed a glass case filled with every size gun imaginable, and she wondered what kind of ammunition the MBI used, since bullets didn't work on most mages. "Hey, where are you taking me?" She shivered as a couple of ghosts floated past and faded into the walls. Alex and Smith ignored her and stopped when they came to the end of the hallway.

When both men turned toward her at the same time, their expressions were unreadable. She glanced from one to the other. "What's going on? Anxiety is emanating off both of you in waves. What are you two hiding?" She reached out to graze Smith's elbow and froze when she saw the sign for the morgue. The room began to spin.

"I'm sorry, Willow. I don't know quite how else to say this, but Maeve's gone. I'm afraid she was murdered." Alex placed a warm hand on her shoulder.

"W-what did you say?" Shaking from head to toe, she took a step back and reached out to the wall for support. "No, she can't be." Disbelief warred with sorrow as his words sank in. A gut-wrenching sadness gripped her like an iron fist. Tears stung the back of her eyes and clogged in her throat, but she refused to let them see her cry.

"I'm afraid it's true." Smith's voice echoed through the empty corridor with a brutal finality. His words left a hollow place inside her chest she didn't think would ever go away. "Please, come this way." He gestured toward the sign for the morgue. "I'll meet you inside. Come in when you're ready," he said and disappeared through the metal doors.

"Look, you don't have to do this part." Alex pulled her to the side. "There's no need to prove anything."

"I have to see her." She squeezed her eyes shut and offered a silent prayer to the Goddess for strength. When she opened them, Alex was gazing at her with a solemn expression on his face.

"I'm warning you, Willow, it's bad. This isn't like anything I've ever come across."

Her stomach twisted with nausea. "Where did you find her? Was she in her melt shop?"

"When our agents got there they found the place burned to the ground. We were able to recover a few things, her tools and a couple of swords. We're holding everything as evidence until the case is wrapped. I do have something with me I want you to look at, a necklace." Alex pulled a small metal box from the front pocket of his jacket and placed it in her hands.

"The amulet?"

"It must've been important for her to store in a fireproof box. I don't want to seem cruel, especially at a time like this, but maybe you could see if you can pick up on a clue that could help lead us to her killer."

"Fine, but I want to see her first." Willow pushed through the doors and the walls closed in all around her. The cloying, rotting stench of death and decomposing bodies caught in her throat and burned her nostrils. She swayed, ready to pass out, but Alex's strong arms wrapped around her waist. "Why are you being nice to me?"

"Don't read too much into it," he said and dropped his hands. "I'm just doing my job. You said you want to see her. Better to get this over with. She's back there in the freezer."

Shadows played across the bloodstained walls. The dampness in the cavernous room made her shiver. They walked toward a table filled with envelopes tagged as evidence and she caught a glimpse of a demon wearing a long, white coat covered in blood. He hovered over a table filled with dead bodies. When the demon looked up, his fingers were wrapped around the handle of a tool that resembled a saw. He held onto it like a kid with a new toy.

"We need to get you out of here unless you want to see brain matter up close." Alex steered her past the tables of bodies. When Willow spotted an empty bucket in the corner of the room, she wondered if someone had put it there for her benefit. Luckily, she'd only eaten the trail mix.

"How are you holding up?" Alex whispered close to her ear.

"I'm f-fine," she lied. She took several deep breaths to ease the queasiness in her stomach and the hole in her heart. Now with Maeve gone, she was all alone.

Alex handed her a mask off one of the empty tables. "Trust me. You're going to want to put this on." She slipped it over her face and walked into an ice -cold chamber where Smith waited beside what looked like an enormous filing cabinet.

"We detected black magick on the body. Perhaps you can trace it back to the practitioner?" Smith asked, pursing his lips. "I'm sorry. This won't be easy for you. We retrieved Miss Donovan's body from the bottom of the Hudson two days ago. Although the ME believes she was in the water a lot longer. I don't know quite how to say this, but I'm afraid the flesh is missing from her limbs and her chest. Prepare yourself."

"Whoever did this wanted to make a statement," Alex interjected. "These are not nice people Maeve was involved with. I'm afraid she knew the risks."

"Do you have any clues how to find her killer?" Her voice sounded shaky and weak. The cold pricked along her skin like icy needles.

"There's a gaping hole about three inches in diameter in what's left of her neck." Smith slipped on a pair of latex gloves before turning to face her again. "We have our theories as to what kind of weapon could do this kind of damage, but nothing concrete so far. We found traces of skin and an unknown substance that's definitely not human under her nails. The ME's still conducting the autopsy. We'll know more after he fills out his report."

He unzipped the bag and Willow sucked in her breath as she stared at Maeve's body. Her skin was flayed, red and raw. The flesh was gone in certain places like a deer carcass left on the side of the road. She couldn't bear to look at her neck. All that remained of her chest was painted black with the word "Whore" carved into her skin. Bile rose from the back of Willow's throat and she thought she might hurl.

A mixture of anger, horror, and guilt made her gasp. "Y-you said you found her at the bottom of the Hudson. How?"

"We keep sonar and special surveillance equipment down there and in most of the major waterways. It allows us to monitor the activities of all the sea creatures in our world. We are the law over numerous selkie and mermaid colonies living below us. One of our monitors detected black magick and sent a signal to the area. Our divers went down to check out the source and pulled up Maeve's body." Alex rubbed his chin, giving her a moment to process. But a moment wasn't enough. Hell, a lifetime wouldn't be enough. He went on. "Look, Willow, she may have been mixed up with the wrong crowd, but in the end, she was trying to make things right. As much as we all wish we could bring her back, we can't. All any of us can do for her now is to try to find her killer. We need to stop him before he does this to someone else," Alex said, shaking his head, staring blankly at the body bag.

"I swear I'll find this maniac and make him pay for what he did." Willow blinked and tears slid down her cheeks.

Smith cleared his throat and took a step back, clearly uncomfortable.

"We're counting on it, but leave the justice to us. We'll give you a minute to be alone with her."

When they stepped out of the room, Willow offered a silent prayer to the Goddess to take Maeve's soul on to Summerland. *"All you can do for her now is to try to find her killer."* Alex's words reverberated through her head.

Maybe she could at least pick up a clue—or some sort of vibration. She opened the box and slipped the glittering silver chain around her neck. The moment the amulet touched her skin, she slumped forward as if she'd been punched in the gut.

Maeve stood in her melt shop with her back to the door. She was gathering up her things, rushing to get out of there, when the door creaked open.

"Going somewhere?" A deep male voice reverberated through the small space and made the hairs on Willow's neck stand on end. "You startled me. No. I-I was cleaning up."

The male stepped closer, his face hidden in the shadows. "What's the matter? Am I keeping you from something or perhaps someone? Are you going to meet one of the special agents I've seen you talking with?"

"W-what? No.

"You always were a terrible liar." He caressed her cheek, making her wince. "I'm afraid I can't let you leave. Not now. Not ever."

"Please." Maeve began to sob.

Smoke filled the room as he whispered a series of words. The sound of Maeve's gut-wrenching screams and cries rang in Willow's ears. Pain exploded over every inch of her body. Red-hot bursts of fire lashed across her skin. Flesh, muscle, and tendons ripped away from bone. Blood rushed hot and heavy. Her body sank to the ground in agony. "Goddess, forgive me."

Willow became faintly aware of Alex picking her up off the freezer floor. He carried her back to one of the empty tables and set her on a chair. "Willow, you're as pale as death. You were screaming." He rubbed his hands up and down her arms to get her blood flowing.

Shaking, she blew into her frozen hands. "S-so...cold."

"What the hell happened?" Alex threw a clean lab coat over her shoulders.

"I had a vision. I felt every awful second of Maeve's murder. The killer mutilated her while she was still alive. She was dead long before she hit the water." She was rambling now, but she couldn't stop herself.

All the air left her lungs and before she knew what was happening,

Alex handed her the bucket and she spilled the contents of her stomach into it. He placed his hand on her shoulders and held her hair off her neck as her stomach continued to convulse with dry heaves.

When she lifted her head Alex handed her a towel and she wiped her mouth. "Who did this to her?" she choked and scooted the bucket away.

For a split second, his macho veneer cracked. "We were hoping you could tell us."

CHAPTER 4

*A*lex parked the conversion van in front of the glowing neon sign for the Raven's Hollow Inn. The sun was starting to bloom on the horizon, a burst of orange fire in a bright blue sky. He cut the engine and turned toward his sleeping passenger. She'd given this address right before she conked out, and now the little witch was still out cold. Even in sleep, Willow's breathing remained chaotic and her expression tense.

No doubt the emotional strain of seeing her friend murdered was taking its toll. He reached across the seat to remove the blindfold he'd put on her before they left HQ, and she didn't even stir. In some crazy way, a part of him felt protective of her. No one deserved to find someone they cared about murdered in such a heinous way. He knew what that was like, only too well. But in his case, he had two brothers, parents, and a slew of friends to lean on. He didn't know where he'd be right now if not for them. He couldn't imagine going through something so horrible alone.

Stop feeling sorry for her. She tried to kill you.

Now Willow McCray was his headache, property of the MBI. He'd been ordered not to let her out of his sight until they figured out what to do with the foul-mouthed little witch. Whether or not she could actually help them find the killer was still anybody's guess.

"No, you can't have her," she pleaded and then began to mutter in her sleep. Her head thrashed from side to side against the headrest. Sweat beaded on her forehead. Willow screamed and slipped her hands around her neck, choking and gasping for air. A sound of terror gurgled up from her throat.

Alex shook her awake. "Hey, you're safe. You were having a nightmare."

Her eyes flew open and darted around the interior of the van. She blinked. "Where am I?" Panting, she let go of her neck and began to shake. Her face was pure ashen.

"We're in front of your hotel." He handed her a bottle of water from the cup holder. Alex wanted to ask her why she didn't stay with family or friends, since she had grown up here. But from the haunted look in her eyes, he guessed it was a bad idea. "What were you dreaming about? Was it the past or the future?"

Her hands shook as she brought the water to her lips. She set down the bottle, a look of pure terror flaring in her eyes. "I'm not sure, but I think I may have witnessed another murder."

Willow struggled to catch her breath and process the details of her dream. She only hoped it wasn't a prophetic, one, because, that meant another witch was dead. "I felt everything as though it were happening to me." She couldn't stop gulping air and became lightheaded. She pushed her head between her knees. "I think I'm hyperventilating."

"I stopped at a drive-through. I thought you might be hungry." Alex handed her a greasy paper bag that reeked of fast food. "Try and take long, deep breaths into this. Are you okay?"

Her face flushed hot. Talk about seeing someone at their worst. "Spectacular. You've already seen me puke. Now you get to see me losing it. What's next?" Willow took another long, deep breath into the bag. When her breathing became normal again, she pushed her hair off her face and sat up.

"You were telling the truth." He glanced at the amulet now swinging from her neck.

"You're surprised?" Willow flashed him a look of nonchalance and shoved the chain of the amulet back under her bustier.

"I'm relieved, actually. It's good to know you're not a liar, just a criminal. Let's hope it protects you. Tell me more about this dream. Do yours usually come true?"

What a dick. She turned toward him, gazing at his strong profile and the curve of his sensual lips. Too bad he was a gorgeous dick. "There's typically a seed of truth or symbolism in them, yes, but I've never experienced anything like this before."

The amulet had connected her to Maeve in life and apparently now in death. If the killer had inadvertently touched it before he'd killed Maeve, maybe it had opened some sort of psychic link with him. A chill ran down her spine at the thought.

"It might be your imagination at work after everything you witnessed. Either way, I'm not taking any chances. I want you to describe this dream to me in detail while I record you. My recorder's linked with my computer so it'll replicate everything you say in the form of pictures, like a built-in sketch artist." He pulled out a small microphone and set it on the dashboard. "Try to tell me anything you remember. Even the smallest detail may be significant in some way."

"Okay, I'll try." She closed her eyes and allowed the dream to form a picture in her mind. "I see a woman. She's tall with dark hair. She's chatting with a guy and they're doing the usual stuff, laughing and flirting. She doesn't sense he's a mage because he's using a shield to block. But I can feel his powers, they're strong…deadly."

"Where are they? Is it Fusion?"

"No. They're in a house. His, I think." Her head started to throb.

"Can you describe what it looks like or where it is?"

"The space is dark and creepy. There are pentacles hung all over the place. I see skull and devil shaped statues. Gargoyle heads are hung all over the walls, like the leader of a Satanic cult lives here."

"What's happening in the room?" The steady sound of Alex's breath and the deep timbre of his voice kept some of the darkness at bay.

"The woman isn't showing her powers yet, but I can detect she's a witch. She knows this guy and has had a thing for him for a while now. I can make out the gold color of her aura; it signals excitement and attraction. He hands her a beer and grabs one for himself."

"Okay, good. What else? What's he saying to her, Willow?"

"Freaky shit. Small talk at first, and then the conversation abruptly shifts to how all witches are whores and they deserve to die. He's muttering about blood and sacrifices."

"Can you see him?"

"He's tall, with brown hair and dark eyes. I can't make out any more details. He's lighting a candle. I see a tattoo on his forearm, a snake."

"A snake? Okay, now we've got something. What about the girl? What's she doing?"

"She's trying to get the hell out of there, but I think he slipped something into her beer. Her head starts to pound. She feels bone-crushing fear as her magick slips from her body. It's like she can sense that he's going to hurt her in some way. She spots a kitchen knife on the counter and tries to fling at him with her mind, but it only manages to clang to the floor. She starts to scream and begs him to let her go, but the bastard only laughs like he's playing with her, enjoying the hell out of the whole thing. When she tries to kick him, he slaps her and starts pulling out knives with funky swirling blades. He forces her down on a chair with his magick and ties her wrists and ankles while she begs for mercy. It only gets him off. He uses one of the knives to slice off her clothes."

"Can you see any of his facial features, any distinguishing marks or scars? What's he wearing?"

"I still can't see his face. It's still only a blur. But I see he's wearing torn jeans with a belt buckle, and it keeps scraping against her skin. There are letters engraved into it, the same ones as before, SG."

"Anything else?"

"I know this sound crazy, but I smell something funky like dog shit or manure. Maybe he has an animal. That's all I got." She opened her eyes and blinked against the light. Alex shut off his recorder and nodded as though trying to digest it all. "Any thoughts on the significance of the letters SG?"

"I'm not sure." Willow ran a hand through her tangled hair.

"I'll follow up on this. Maybe you can be useful to us after all." Alex pulled the speaker off the dash and shoved it in his glove box.

"Don't look so surprised. This is what Saint Claire paid me the big bucks for."

"I'll bet. But here, we try to save innocents, not corrupt them. I'm sending everything to Smith. It's a long shot, but who knows, maybe something will pan out," he said, sounding skeptical.

Her face flushed at the jab. "As much as I love sitting inside your freezing cold car while you insult me, I need to shower and change." Her head was splitting.

"I didn't mean—hell. I think we're done here." Alex adjusted the MBI issue laser gun in his holster and then reached behind the seat for his briefcase. She swallowed hard at the sight of his gun. The sheer power from the beam could turn most mages—witches included—into a pile of ash. After he shoved the bag of fast food into the front pocket, he swung the strap of his briefcase over his shoulder.

He got out of the car while she stretched her stiff limbs. By the time she opened the door, he was already standing at her side. "Here's how this is going down, you get a shower, pack up your stuff, and we get on the move, ASAP. Are we clear? I need your key card. Where's your room?"

"Are you always so bossy?" Willow fished it out of her purse and handed it to him. She slammed the door and put up her hand. "On second thought, don't answer that. It's through the courtyard, second door on the left."

He glanced over at her through thick, dark lashes. Even if he was a royal pain in the ass, the man was hot. "No, just efficient. One of us has to be."

I hate him. "Yeah, keep telling yourself that." She took a step forward and swayed. Dizziness hit her like a twenty-pound weight to the skull. Black spots filled her vision. She leaned up against the door for support. Cold steel seeped through her coat and made her shiver.

He put a hand out to steady her. "What's wrong?"

"No biggie. I got dizzy all of a sudden." She needed to purge the dark magick from her system. If there was a twisted link connecting her with the killer, it had managed to zap all her energy. "Give me a minute."

"Trouble is, I don't have a minute," he muttered and before she could protest, he scooped her up into his arms and carried her down the long, winding path toward her room. "I suggest you wrap your arms around my neck. I wouldn't want to drop you on your leather clad ass," he said without a hint of humor as they passed the office and the flashing motel sign.

"Wouldn't you?"

"After the stint back in the alley, could you blame me?"

And he wasn't going to let her forget it anytime soon. "Guess I bruised more than your head." Willow wrapped her arms around his neck and her fingers brushed at the thick strands of his hair. It was as soft and silky as she imagined. She wanted to sigh but moved her hands to rest on his collar instead.

When she glanced over her shoulder at a couple with satisfied smiles exiting a room, she bit down on her lip and turned back to face him. "You know how this must look."

The twinkle in his dark eyes was pure sin. "Like we're both about to get lucky? Don't people usually frequent these places to have sex, Willow?" The way he rolled her name off his tongue shot heat straight to her core. "I suggest you go with it because right now you don't have the strength to fight me."

His arms tightened around her body and she shivered. He made her feel safe, protected. So this is what she'd been missing out on for the past few years, a strong, sexy man for the taking. *Yeah, don't get used to it,* her inner voice warned.

"Are you cold?" Alex pressed her closer to his chest and she caught the scent of his woodsy aftershave. Why did he have to smell so good?

No, I'm burning up. "Maybe a little."

He tucked her under his coat and without thinking; she snuggled against the hard wall of his chest. They walked in silence the rest of the way. She'd almost forgotten what it felt like to be held by a man.

After her last boyfriend betrayed her, she'd vowed to stay away from men for good. But that didn't mean she didn't think about sex, *constantly*. *This is why I have cobwebs growing over my privates.* Well, it could be the reason why her body was having such a strong reaction to Alex.

She followed his gaze as it zeroed in on the '73 baby blue Mustang convertible parked outside her door. "Nice ride."

"How did you know it was mine?"

He flashed a smile. "Easy. It has trouble written all over it. Too bad you won't be driving it for a while."

"Define a while?"

"You're going to have to get used to taking orders and playing by the rules."

"Lucky me. It's bad enough I have to work for you. Now I'll be forced to ride in that monstrosity to boot?" Willow motioned over her shoulder toward the van. "What about my car? I can't leave it here."

"One of our guys can clear up your bill and drive it back to the agency." Alex set her down and kept his hand at the small of her back. The protective gesture warmed her from the inside out. He slid in her keycard and the door opened with a hiss. "Home sweet home. Do you need help getting inside?"

"I can manage." She pressed her hand against the door for support, ready to pass out. It wouldn't do her any good to get used to having a man as attractive and virile as Alex hanging around. Once this case was wrapped up, she'd probably never see him again. And good riddance. Hot as he was, he was also extremely high-handed, and according to his conversation with Smith, which she was able to pick up on thanks to her amulet, he apparently hated her kind.

"I need to chill out for a minute." Her bed called to her. She dragged her tired body into the room and plopped down on the edge of the lumpy mattress. She let out a long, slow breath, relieved to be back among her things. "Feel free to make yourself comfortable," she muttered and pointed to a desk chair.

His gaze narrowed in her direction. "You okay?"

Her head continued to throb from the dark sludge inside her body. She scooted up the bed and grabbed a potion bottle off the night table. She gulped the green concoction and frowned at the bitter taste. "I should start to feel better soon."

"What are you drinking?" Alex walked to the other side of the room and took off his coat. He hung it across the back of the chair and took a seat.

"It's a tincture of herbs and vitamins that replenishes my energy and diffuses any black magick which may have seeped into my system."

"I didn't realize such a thing could happen." Concern flashed in his eyes so briefly she thought she imagined it. "I'm not used to working with a witch," Alex said with more than a trace of disdain.

Anger pulsed through her veins at the implication. "Then we're even, because I'm not used to working with a mortal. What's your beef with witches anyway? Did one of us steal your lunch money when you were a kid?"

"Look, it's nothing personal. I don't like witches or anything they stand for, and trust me, I never will."

"I see. You're not even trying to hide your disdain. I guess it's probably better to lay it all out in the open so I have no illusions of civility where you're concerned. Thank you, Agent Denopoulous, for telling me exactly what you think," she said with a lift of her chin, trying not to show how much his words stung. When she crossed her legs over the side of the bed, a zing of energy pulsed through her veins. The greens were already starting to do their job by cleaning the sludge from her body. Willow pulled a white candle from the nightstand drawer, whispered an incantation, and then flicked her wrist. She needed to zap any remaining dark energy.

"No one said I wouldn't be civil. I'm a professional and will act as one at all times. I just want to make it clear, I wasn't the one in favor of letting you work on this case in the first place, mainly because of the danger involved."

"Oh? Were you more in favor of sending me to Hellios?"

"What I think is irrelevant at this point." He looked as if he wanted to say more but pulled out a tiny piece of plastic that looked like a guitar pic instead. "You're here. Let's try and make the best of a bad situation. Now there's a matter we need to take care of first."

"Does it have something to do with that thingy in your hand?"

"Good guess." He walked toward her and knelt on one knee at the edge of the bed. Her eyes tangled with his and then moved lower. He was big, and impossibly broad, a wall of solid muscle. Somehow the room seemed smaller with Alex sharing the space. He leaned forward and tingles broke out along her skin.

His closeness unnerved her, especially when she caught another whiff of his musky scent. His searching gaze rested on her lips and his eyes turned molten, flaring with sexual awareness. He sucked in a breath and a rush of heat swept over her skin. What it would be like to kiss him?

"This thingy is a tracking device." His voice pulled her from her sexual haze. He held up the small, triangular shaped piece of plastic. "Once I insert it, there's no getting away. My advice, don't try anything stupid, because I'll find you."

"I agreed to help. I didn't realize I'd be your prisoner. What's next, are you planning on cuffing me to the bed while you take a pee?" The second the words flew from her lips, she wished she could take them back. Images of Alex binding her wrists to the back of the headboard and pleasuring her until she screamed flashed through her mind. Her cheeks heated.

Alex must've guessed the train of her thoughts because fire smoldered in his eyes. His gaze trailed up and down her body and lingered on her bustier. Her nipples hardened in response. He pushed her hair off her shoulder, and his fingers lingered for a moment. This time his eyes were weary as they met hers. Clearly, Alex was attracted to her but didn't want to be. "Stay still." He pressed the tracking device into the side of her neck. It burned and pinched as it dissolved into her skin. "Done." He got to his feet and pointed toward the bathroom. "Now would be a good time to shower and change while I send this new intel about your vision to Smith."

"I bet the tracking device was your idea. You thought I was going to run rather than face what's ahead of me, didn't you?" This whole situation, not to mention his overbearing ways, made her want to scream. Before her anger got the best of her, she got up from the bed and walked to her suitcase. She never did get a chance to unpack and guessed by the sudden turn of events, she wouldn't be staying long. Her heart sank at the reality of never seeing Maeve again.

After rummaging around through her stuff, she reached for her robe and toiletry bag. She counted to ten, grabbed them both, and then turned to face him again, hoping to avoid a confrontation.

He walked toward her, closing the distance between them. He placed a finger under her chin. "Yes, but now it's up to you to prove me wrong." The challenge in his words belied the gentleness in his touch.

Willow tried to ignore the trail of heat licking across her skin. He'd barely touched her and yet she couldn't deny the effect on her body. What could Alex do if he really put his mind to it? A host of sultry possibilities, one more erotic than the next, flashed through her head.

"Why are you looking at me like that?" His voice sounded dark, melting her insides like warm chocolate.

Busted. "It must be your overactive imagination," she lied, taking a step back.

"I don't think so."

She glanced away, desperate for a little privacy and distance from the sexy agent Denopoulos. It was time to clear her head and put a rein on her sexual fantasies. Hmm, maybe she could masturbate? A good orgasm or two might be what the doctor ordered. It could take away her stress. Goddess knew she could do a better job at pleasuring herself than he ever could. Someone so arrogant couldn't possibly be a good lover. Could he?

"Willow?"

Whether she liked it or not, her fate rested in his hands. He had enough power over her; she refused to give him anymore. "Look, there's a Starbucks about a mile up the road. I'll need about an hour to get myself together."

"Sorry, I'm staying put." He walked back over to the chair on the other side of the room and kicked up his shoes on the small table as if he owned the place. "I've been ordered to guard you at all times."

Anger warred with shame. "You put a tracking device on me. Where could I go? How about when I need to use the bathroom? Are you supposed to stand outside the door?"

A mischievous glint flashed in his eyes. "Pretty much. You're lucky I don't go in there with you." Alex glanced at his watch and pulled out his cell. "You have ten minutes starting now."

His arrogance rubbed her raw. "I refuse to shower with you in this tiny room. That's got to be considered some form of police brutality."

"I'm not the police, sweetheart. Unfortunately for you, none of that applies. You're wasting time. You just used up thirty-five seconds. Chop, chop."

She muttered a curse and slammed the bathroom door in his face. Hellios was sounding better all the time.

CHAPTER 5

*A*lex stifled a groan, imagining rivulets of water sluicing over Willow's creamy skin. He needed to control his overwhelming lust toward his new charge. Curious to find out more about her past, he pressed a button on his cell and pulled up her file once again. His suspicions confirmed she wasn't lying about being a loner. She was never married and there was no record of a live-in boyfriend.

The only child of an alcoholic mother and a deadbeat father, her home life couldn't have been ideal. She'd lived like a gypsy until she landed at the coven. Coincidentally, it was the same one Maeve Donovan had resided in at the time of her murder. Why had Willow kept that particular nugget about her past a secret?

Apparently, she left the coven at the age of sixteen. The question was why? From that point on, everything in her life had gone downhill. He rubbed his beard and read on. Funny, her file had been pristine right up until she went to work for the Cabal. Not so much as a misdemeanor crime had tarnished her youth. How did her life take such a downward turn? He pressed a button on his cell and the screen went blank.

Now he had more questions than answers. His earlier training as a cop had shown him the worst side of humanity. He'd arrested his fair share of bad parents over the years. The kids were always the ones who suffered.

Eventually, when left to their own devices, most turned to a life of crime and became runaways, forced into prostitution and drugs.

Did Willow's parents abandon her? Was that the reason she went to work for a dirt bag like Tristan Saint Claire? He was still pondering the question when his cell beeped.

Smith: *Stay put for now.*

Great. He didn't trust himself to be alone with her, not with the bed only inches away. Frustrated, Alex slammed the phone on the table. Despite her shitty home life, what could possibly drive an innocent girl like Willow McCray into organized crime? She was a mystery, one he would probably never solve.

No matter how curious he was about her, he'd have to tread lightly. He was in a position of power, which meant his attraction was way out of line. He couldn't afford to get distracted, yet another complication he didn't need. What could he be thinking, allowing himself to become attracted to a felon, a witch no less? No matter what she might bring to the table, he could never trust her kind. He'd been burned before. He refused to make a mistake that could put both their lives in danger.

Freezing, he rubbed his cold hands together and glanced around at the sparsely furnished room. He walked to the thermostat and turned up the heat. The ancient-looking radiator groaned and hissed before blowing warm air into the tiny room.

He looked around at the stained curtains and frayed bedspread. To say the place was a dump wouldn't be a stretch. If Willow was making the "big bucks" working for the Cabal, then why couldn't she afford a nicer room? The woman was an enigma in every sense of the word, from her unwavering loyalty to her friend to her knack for breaking the law and bending the rules.

When he heard the shower cut off, he reached for the bag of chicken nuggets and fries from his briefcase. He popped them in the microwave and pressed the button. It wouldn't do either of them any good to have her passing out from hunger. He was waiting for the ping to go off when the bathroom door flew open.

"I hope you managed to keep yourself entertained." she said, sounding suspicious. In a puff of steam, the woman in question stood in the doorway clad in a fluffy, white, terry cloth robe. The scent of vanilla and strawberries wafted through the air.

His gaze trailed over her freshly washed face, down her body, to her bare feet. Her toenails were painted a soft pink. Would her nipples be the same color? He ached to know and chastised himself for it. He'd be sure to suppress any and all lust-fueled thoughts moving forward. They'd only lead to trouble. To his surprise, everything about her appearance was a complete and utter contrast from the leather-clad siren from the night before.

"You're lucky we were ordered to stay put." He glanced at his watch and shook his head. "You went over time by five minutes. What if we needed to be at a crime scene?"

"I'm sorry, but it's been forty-eight hours since I had a shower and I still have the grime of the morgue on me. Jeez, are you always such a ball buster?"

"Hell yes, especially when I'm on the job. Well, now that you've used all of the hotel's hot water, do you at least feel better?" he asked and pulled the food out of the microwave. He set it on the table.

"You have no idea." She wrapped her arms around her body and sighed. "But no matter how hard I scrubbed, I couldn't seem to get the stench of death off me."

His gut tightened at her words. A part of her was probably still in shock. They hadn't given her the chance to digest the impact of Maeve's murder. In his experience, reality would set in soon and no matter how tough she appeared, she'd probably crash and burn when it did.

"I don't think it's something you ever get used to."

"I suppose not." Her voice sounded so lost and sad, he couldn't help but soften toward her. Willow sniffed the air and placed a hand on her stomach. "What do I smell?" But at least she was asking about the food.

"I thought you might be hungry." He swallowed hard as she strode into the room. He thought she was hot as a brunette, but he'd been wrong— dead wrong. She was even more stunning as a redhead. Her damp, red hair curled around her shoulders in soft waves. The robe hung on her small frame as if she were playing dress-up in someone else's clothes. "When was the last time you ate?"

Without her stilettos, he towered over her by a good six inches. She appeared more fragile and innocent somehow. *But you know better*, his inner voice warned.

"Sitting down to a meal sort of slipped my mind." She picked up the food from the table and gobbled it down like a starving prisoner. "I've been on the run from a band of bloodthirsty demons," she said in between mouthfuls. She swiped a packet of honey mustard sauce off the table, dipped her chicken, and took another healthy bite.

He glanced out the window and folded his arms across his chest. "No demons breaking down the door at the moment." He turned back to face her, and their gazes locked and held.

"Well, I appreciate the gesture. Thank you." When she was done, she threw her trash in the garbage and grabbed a napkin off the table to wipe her mouth. "What? Why are you looking at me like that?" she asked and dabbed the corner of her mouth again.

With her face scrubbed free of makeup, he couldn't get over her natural beauty. She carried herself with a quiet confidence and a down-to-earth manner that surprised the hell out of him. "Your appearance, it's different. I like you much better like this, without the glamour." Alex let his gaze trail over her face.

"Not many people see my real appearance anymore." She brushed the crumbs off her fingers and appeared self-conscious as she regarded him with a cynical smile. "I almost forget what I look like."

"Seems like a waste if you ask me. You're a beautiful woman, Willow, in or out of a disguise."

She remained silent, apparently at a loss for words.

Maybe she wasn't used to compliments. Was there anyone in her life who told her she was much more than Saint Claire's personal lackey? He needed to break the awkward silence, so he pulled out an extra cell from his briefcase and set it on the table. "You'll need to answer this phone at all times. It's untraceable."

"Lucky me. I guess the MBI will be paying my phone bill from now on." She reached for the cell and walked to the end table to drop it in her purse. "What's your angle in all this? I'm still trying to figure you out." She cut across the room and rubbed her hands over the noisy radiator. "Cranking up the heat, feeding me, is that part of your job description? It's almost as if—"

"As if what?"

"You care what happens to me," she said softly.

"Believe it or not, I do care." *More than I should.* He gritted his teeth to keep from crossing the room and showing her how much. "You're working for me now."

Her face fell, but she quickly tried to hide it by crossing her arms across her chest, which pushed up her breasts. He stifled a groan and glanced away.

"There must be an ulterior motive."

"Believe me, there's no ulterior motive. I heated up the food because I figured you'll need all your strength for what comes next." From what he'd gleaned about her past, she probably wasn't used to anyone doing something nice for her, not without a quid pro quo.

"Why don't you tell what comes next, Agent Denopoulos, or should I call you Alex?" She stalked over to her suitcase and pulled out a scrap of black lace. His breath hitched. Now he knew for sure there was absolutely nothing beneath her robe.

"Call me Alex." She must've caught him staring because her cheeks flushed a lovely shade of pink that made the front of his pants tight. She shoved the underwear in the pocket of her robe.

He inclined his head to the side and pretended not to notice. "We wait for orders on how to proceed. We've got a team at the coven going through Maeve's room looking for any evidence. A diary, a business card, that sort of thing."

"I feel helpless standing here doing nothing." Willow began to pace. "He's out there, possibly killing another innocent as we speak. Isn't there anything your agency can do to find this maniac?"

"I understand how anxious you must be to solve this case and find the animal responsible for Maeve's death. This is personal for you, but things don't happen at the snap of a finger. Be patient."

She stopped and turned toward him. Her eyes widened, practically shooting daggers at him. "You're damn right it's personal. Maeve was my best friend, my family. Maybe that doesn't count for anything because of what I did or who I worked for, but it doesn't take away the pain." Her bottom lip trembled.

"No, it doesn't. If I didn't say it earlier, I want you to know I'm truly sorry for your loss." This was the part he wasn't prepared to deal with— her falling apart on him.

"Thank you," she said with a sigh.

He decided to redirect the conversation. "I think we need to get a few ground rules established. You'll follow my orders at all times, no questions asked, and when I tell you to disengage from a situation and retreat, you will."

"Do you always talk like such a robot?"

His temper flared. "Do you agree?"

She lifted her hands in the air. "Fine, whatever you say."

"And one more thing, you will agree to never, under any circumstances, use magick on me."

"I guess a personality spell is out of the question then?" The corner of her lip lifted in a smile and it made his chest tight. Damn, she really was beautiful.

"You think everything's a joke? This is a murder investigation. Do I need to remind you what's at stake?"

"Of course not." Willow rolled her eyes. "Fine. I vow to the Goddess to never use magick on you. Will that help you sleep better at night?"

"I'll sleep better when this psycho's behind bars." Alex placed his cell on the table. "We might as well do something constructive while we wait. The more I know about your powers and how they work, the more it'll help us when we're out in the field. How did you light the candle without a match? Did you teach yourself how to do magick?"

"I'm what you call a hereditary born witch." She sat down on the bed and let out a breath. His questions seemed to mollify her. "My mother and my grandmother were both witches. It's in my blood. I've read tons of books on the craft over the years and studied with a mentor and took tons of classes. Eventually, I learned how to channel energy with my mind. It didn't happen overnight. My abilities grew over time. There are other witches who can learn the craft through study and practice, but those that are blood-born are more powerful. Their abilities can be vast, from physical and mental strength, to spells and potion making." She stretched and waited for him to respond.

"Interesting. Please go on." He'd be lying through his teeth if he tried to pretend he wasn't riveted to her every word.

"The clairvoyance and the mind reading developed when I was a child and became more fine-tuned through meditation and listening to my intuition. Most psychics are also empaths, which means we can sense others' emotions."

"Sounds like one hell of a responsibility." A responsibility she apparently had no choice in taking on.

"It can be sort of a mixed bag. You take the good with the bad." She frowned and toyed with the belt on her robe. "When I have a premonition, I see a picture in my mind. I never know beforehand if it'll be from the past or the future. Certain smells, sounds, even textures and colors, can trigger the images and make them more vivid. I can pick up on thoughts by the residual energy left behind on an object or through touch. Did I answer your questions?"

He nodded, impressed by the depth and breadth of her powers. He'd never be a fan of witchcraft, but at least her brand of magick didn't sound like the dark kind. "Thanks for filling in the gaps."

"Can I ask you a question?"

He nodded. "It only seems fair. Shoot."

"What's your deal with witches? Do you hate all of us or just a select few?"

His jaw clenched. "I don't hate anyone. Let me make that perfectly clear. Next question," he snapped, immediately regretting his tone, but he refused to go there, especially with her.

"I'm afraid I'm at a serious disadvantage here. You know so much about me and I know almost nothing about you. I imagine this kind of work leaves little room for a personal life. Do you have a girlfriend? Or a disgruntled ex-wife or a dozen kids somewhere?"

"No on all counts."

For a minute, she almost looked relieved. "What made you want to work for the MBI?"

He shrugged, not sure how to answer. "I worked for RHPD for seven years. My goal was simple, really. I wanted to get drugs off the streets and put away the scum responsible for selling smack to kids. In the end, I felt I could do more working for the MBI than the police department."

Willow shook her head as realization flickered in her eyes. "Did you know someone who suffered from addiction?"

Her perceptiveness caught him off guard. "My younger brother Gus was a junkie." The words spilled from his lips before he could take them back. "He fell in with the wrong crowd as a teen. He started selling drugs and then eventually doing them. By the time my folks had realized the extent of his addiction, he was in over his head." His heart thudded in his chest at the memory. Maybe that was why he was feeling such a strange connection to her, a kinship born out of addiction. Watching someone you care about self-destruct could do strange things to your head.

"What happened to him? Is he okay?" she asked in a tone laced with compassion.

"He's sober now, thanks to a six-month stint in rehab and a twelve-step program. He has a sponsor and counsels other kids to prevent them from falling into the same traps. Funny, it has been years since I've talked about this with anyone."

He was surprised at how easily he revealed such a deep, dark secret to a stranger. The fact that she'd been through a similar ordeal with Maeve may have had something to do with it. But he hadn't expected to feel so comfortable talking to her about the subject.

"I guess we have something in common. Now I understand why you want to go after Saint Claire. It seems we both have a personal stake in bringing him down. You still think Maeve was murdered by the front man in his operation?"

"Unfortunately, we never got a meeting with him. Maeve was killed before we got the chance. But everything certainly points in that direction. As long as we're doing question and answer time, I was wondering how you and Maeve met. You two seem like an unlikely pair."

The background check on Maeve revealed she'd accumulated a record a mile long, mostly all drug-related. "Not really. We met when we were kids at the same coven and found we had a lot in common." Willow walked to the closet and pulled a pair of jeans and a big, wool sweater off a hanger. She walked back to the bed and sat on the edge.

"How come you never mentioned that you lived at the same coven with Maeve before now?"

"Sorry, I didn't think it was important." The way her whole body tensed confirmed she was hiding something. "We both had challenging childhoods, parents who could barely take care of themselves, let alone a child. Living at the coven gave Maeve some stability, but she was always troubled. She couldn't get over her mother abandoning her, and she never met her dad. She got hooked on meth by the time she was old enough to climb out of her bedroom window. She'd promised to quit. I was going to help her too, as soon as I got on my feet." She sniffled a bit.

"People sometimes use unhealthy outlets as coping mechanisms for their pain." He was finally starting to get insight into the scars hidden beneath the surface. Maeve had turned to drugs and Willow had turned to a life of crime.

Embarrassment flashed in her eyes. "Thanks for the psychoanalysis. Hey, I thought you were a special agent. I didn't realize you were also a shrink."

He must've hit a sore spot. After all she'd been through, she probably had major trust issues. He understood why she wanted to keep her secrets close to the vest. He picked up a napkin off the table and waved it in surrender. "I'm sorry. I was only trying to help."

"No, it's okay." She cracked a smile. "I'm not used to talking about my past or Maeve's. I'm not myself right now. I'm grieving and angry, still severely sleep-deprived."

"Grief can eat you alive, Willow. In the end, Maeve was trying to do the right thing by giving us the dirt on her supplier." Alex was starting to see a softer side beneath the hard shell. He fought the urge to cross the room, pull her into his arms, and take away her pain. Witch or not, they were on the same side now, in a manner of speaking anyway, and he hated to see her in pain. He leaned forward instead and rested his hands on his knees. "She would've succeeded too, if he hadn't killed her before we could nail him. I want you to know I never meant for this to happen. I feel somehow responsible for her murder."

Her expression of sorrow made it clear that the impact of his words and the loss of her friend had finally started to sink in. Maeve was dead and gone. Now there was no going back to save her from a killer or from herself for that matter.

"When this mess is over I'll have to make a funeral. I knew she was trying to change. I promised to help her, if only—" Her voice broke off with a sob.

"Hey, it's going to be okay. I promise." Alex opened his briefcase and pulled out the worn, jet-black stuffed kitten he'd been holding onto for days. He walked to the bed and knelt at Willow's feet. "I was planning to give this to you at some point." When he lifted her chin and gazed into her watery green eyes, his chest tightened. He placed the small stuffed toy in the palm of her hand.

Tears spilled from her eyes and ran down her cheeks. The sight made his gut twist. He never could stand to see a woman cry, especially a beautiful one. "Shh, don't cry." He reached out and wiped away her tears with his thumbs.

She glanced at the torn piece of fluff and sniffled. "How in the world do you have him? I gave him to Maeve on her seventh birthday. I used to beg my mom for a kitten before I went to live at the coven, but she always said I wouldn't be able to take care of one. Funny, I've been out on my own for ten years now and I still haven't gotten a damn cat."

"You can start fresh, Willow. Turn over a new leaf, maybe even get a kitten. Maeve said this little guy was her good luck charm. She gave him to me to use as a protective charm the night I was supposed to meet with Saint Claire's front man. This was her last selfless act."

"Why her?" When she drew her hands over her face, on instinct, Alex pulled Willow to her feet and folded her into his arms. He couldn't have stopped the impulse if he'd tried, and right now, he didn't want to. She cried against his chest, gut-wrenching sobs from the soul.

"Let it all out." Alex rubbed her back and ran his fingers through her damp hair as her whole body shook with grief and exhaustion. She felt so good, soft curves flush against his chest. He wished he could hold her all night long. And then the realization of what he was doing sank in. What am I thinking, comforting her like this? Somehow she managed to blow through his defenses without the use of magick.

When her sobs began to subside, he pulled her away from his body. Tears glistened on the ends of her long lashes and once again he was struck by her natural beauty and her sudden vulnerability. Her wild scent flared in his nostrils and fired his blood. She parted her full lips and he wondered what other parts of her lush body were the same ruby red color?

A part of him wanted to make her scream his name and claw at his back while he sucked and flicked his tongue over her nipples. He'd spread her legs and lick every last inch of her until she begged him to stop.

Another part of him wanted to punish her, especially after all she'd put him through in the last twenty-four hours. But he couldn't deny he wanted her with a base male hunger that made his cock throb painfully against his jeans.

Her eyes widened in surprise as she looked up at him. Willow was psychic and empathic, which meant she could probably sense the lust he was barely containing, brimming just beneath the surface, and fuck if it didn't ratchet up his desire even more. The images in his head, never fully explored, forced him to grind his teeth with restraint. She was a witch, and his pseudo-partner to boot. Jesus, it wasn't right, but hell, this attraction was raw and unrefined—one they both needed to explore. Could that be the reason why he found himself removing his gun holster and placing it on the table?

"Willow." He walked back over to her, his heart pounding with every step. He lowered his head to hers and caught her mouth in a languid kiss. Her lips were soft and pliant as they molded to his. He licked her bottom lip and when she moaned low in her throat, his sense of power surged.

He tangled his fingers into the wet, silky strands of her hair. For most of his adult life he'd scorned witches, and now he was savoring the drugging taste of one. He tilted her head up to deepen the kiss, and like a flower in bloom, she opened for him. She tasted hot and sweet, like warm sugar.

Her tongue melted against his and made him rock hard. She dug her fingers into his shoulders, silently urging him on. The kiss became greedy and wild as he dragged her up against his chest. He was playing with fire, but at the moment he didn't care.

His hands gripped tight to her waist. He couldn't get enough of the slick, wet heat of her mouth. She whimpered as the kiss raged on in a scalding, erotic dance. He cracked an eye open and his gaze darted to the bed. Three long strides, maybe four, and he could have her soft, wet heat beneath him.

He wanted to untie the knot of her robe with his teeth and run his hands over every luscious curve. All he could think about was gliding his fingers over her damp skin and making her squirm. He'd bury himself deep inside her, until they were both writhing and shaking. He'd make sure to drive all thoughts of death and guilt, and broken promises from both their minds.

Her kiss became bolder, her tongue fighting for dominance with his until he thought he might drag her to the bed. He was in over his head. Shit, they both were. He squeezed her ass and pressed her hips into his rapidly growing erection. She moaned, and the sound made him growl.

Maybe, if I have her just once I can get her out of my mind.

There'd be no sweet words exchanged—no spooning after this interlude. No. This would be a case of pure lust and raw need. With that thought in mind, he loosened the tie at her waist, and tugged the robe off her shoulders.

The scent of her hair and her skin flared in his nostrils. His lips moved from her mouth to the shell of her ear and she shivered. He trailed kisses down her neck and sucked on her collarbone. The strawberry flavor of her skin melted in his mouth like cotton candy. "You taste incredible. I can't get enough of you."

Could she be putting a spell on me?

The thought whispered through his mind. He ignored it and let his eyes trail over her instead. Tendrils of her red hair were starting to dry and curl around her face. Her pupils were large and glazed with arousal. His cock grew harder still, about to rip through his jeans. "You're gorgeous."

A soft, breathy sound rushed from her lips. "Please, Alex." She was so responsive, and so damn hot.

He wanted, and damn he was going to take, to hell with the consequences. *This is unprofessional as hell and can only lead to trouble,* his inner voice warned. She was vulnerable and confused, but dammit he was throbbing for her.

There were shadows under her eyes. The sight made him still, reminding him of what she'd been through tonight. His heart sank. Here he was in a position of power, acting like a thoughtless jackass. What was he thinking?

Guilt stabbed at his gut like the turn of a knife and his conscience flickered. He couldn't take advantage of her in this state. He slowly pulled away from her and ran a hand through his hair. He let out a string of curses under his breath. He wondered why he couldn't keep his hands to himself.

"Alex? What's going on?" Her beautiful features shifted from lightness and joy to complete bewilderment. His gut clenched with guilt when he noticed her lips were swollen from his kisses. The skin around her jaw was red and abraded from the rub of his beard. There were even little bite marks on her neck.

"I'm sorry. I shouldn't have kissed you." He exhaled and wished he could think of the right thing to say without hurting her feelings. "It was a mistake." *Smooth. Shit, way to go.*

Her cheeks flushed, and then his words registered on her face as if she'd been struck. "Right. This was a mistake, big time." Willow refused to meet his eyes as she fumbled with the tie on her robe. After she tied it around her slender waist, she lifted her hand to smooth her mussed hair.

He was about to say some bullshit about maintaining his professional conduct at all times when his cell vibrated on the table. He walked over and picked it up. His heart pounded in his chest as he read over the text. *Sonofabitch.*

In an instant Willow was at his side, gazing at him with an expectant look on her face. "Any news? What is it?"

"It turns out there was something to that dream of yours. Our guys found a body in the river. You were right. There's been another murder."

CHAPTER 6

A frigid breeze blew off the Hudson and lashed at Willow's face, chilling her straight to the bone. Fumes from the nearby oil refineries and the barges caught in her nose and her throat, making her want to gag. She stood on the dock of Port Jersey and shivered, her gaze fixed on the fog rolling off the water in a big gray cloud. She tried to block the wind by burying her face in her big, wool scarf.

Alex, Cayden, and Smith stood on either side of her, pulling on latex gloves, paper booties and face masks from cardboard kits marked *Biohazard*. Brodie, a barrel-chested demon who made Cayden and even Smith look small, was cordoning off the area with purple crime scene tape.

"You're going to want to put these on." Alex handed her a kit. "Get ready for chaos. This place is about to turn into a three-ring circus." The roar of helicopters circled overhead, descending on the scene like a swarm of bees crashing a picnic.

She covered her ears with her hands. "I don't think I'm prepared for all this," she shouted over the noise. She glanced at the furious swells of water rushing back and forth, breaking violently at the edge of the dock. Her stomach clenched. *Someone was still down there.*

RHPD boats, along with several sleek black ones—which she guessed were MBI—zoomed around the murky water. When she thought about Maeve floating around in the black, icy depths, something in her broke apart, and now another innocent, no doubt the witch from her vision, had met the same fate.

A tall, striking vampire with jet black hair walked up to Alex and shook his hand. He wore a navy, RHPD jacket with the name Mulroney emblazoned across the front. The guy looked like he should be on the cover of *GQ* rather than working for the police department.

After a few minutes, he disappeared in the crowd and Alex turned to face her. "Stay out of everyone's way and let the agents and the police do their jobs. I'll ask you to do your psychic thing when I think it's warranted and when we've collected all the evidence." She couldn't deny the indignation that his cold, all-business tone fired up inside her. Why did she have to go and kiss him back? How could she think for one minute that there was more to him than a prick with a badge?

"Anything you say." She tried to school her features into an expression of nonchalance and slipped on the mask, grateful for any excuse to hide her face from Alex. She didn't want him to see the effect he had on her. "You're the boss."

He'd gone totally arctic after they'd practically ravaged each other. The lower half of her body still thrummed at the memory. The man had a sinful mouth, which only made the fact that he'd completely ignored her on the drive over even more awkward. Now, every time he glanced at her, anger flickered in his eyes.

Her gaze darted to his lips. A fresh wave of desire crashed over her at the thought of his sultry kisses and the press of his body against hers. Her nipples hardened into tight points. When she got a minute alone, she'd make quick use of her Pocket Rocket. She was currently on the verge of sexual combustion. This was simply a case of lust, nothing more.

She tried to push the image from her mind, but the sense of regret still lingered. She should've never let herself get caught up in the heat of the moment. Before she indulged in more of her mental rant, the scrape of footsteps forced her to look over her shoulder. A throng of demons, vampires, and mortals trudged up the long, narrow dock carrying video equipment, cameras, and small devices that resembled vacuums.

"It looks as if we've got company." Instinctively, Willow took a step back to get out of their way and Alex pulled her further off to the side by her elbow. He pointed to a twenty-foot patch of dock. "This is our 'safe area.' It's where we collect evidence and try to determine the time and cause of death. As long as you have your gloves on you can touch anything you need to. Whatever you do, don't give any comments to the press if they happen to show up."

Still holding the kit, she pulled on the booties and the gloves. "Don't worry. Having my picture plastered all over the news wouldn't exactly be a good idea right about now."

A throbbing pain welled up in her temples and traveled down her spine. The MBI was counting on her to give them clues that might lead to the killer. She realized her presence here was a matter of life and death. She'd never been given that kind of responsibility until now.

What if I fail?

Before she could contemplate the morbid thought any further, two heads bobbed up from the surface of the rough water clutching what looked like a human sized, black garbage bag from the icy depths of the river.

"They've got something, and it looks a hell of a lot like a body," Alex yelled, signaling to the collective group to give them space. Her heart leaped into her throat as Brodie, along with a team of divers and a group of other agents waiting along the perimeter, helped him pull the bag from the water. Together, they slid it onto the dock.

Now dripping wet and leaving a sizeable puddle beneath his massive frame, Brodie opened the bag with a pocket knife and revealed what was left of a body. This one was naked, and her head dangled from her neck. The flesh was missing from her limbs and her chest. A *female*. And like Maeve, the word "Whore" was cut deeply into what remained of her chest. Willow thought she might hurl, and put a hand over her mouth.

"Dear gods, have mercy on her soul," Brodie murmured and bent his horned head. The sulfur stench of black magick permeated the air. Willow instantly recognized the same foul scent that had lingered on Maeve's body.

"Whoever did this sure must have a hard-on for the dramatic. Has anyone called the coroner yet?" Cayden shouted and walked over with a camera. He frowned as he began snapping shots of the body, and then peeked inside the bag. "It looks like he used rocks to weigh her down. I thought the last one was bad. Between the gaping hole in her neck and the missing flesh, there won't be much left by the time he gets his ass here."

"He's on his way." Alex shoved his cell back in his pocket and pulled out a penlight. He pointed it into the bag and it looked as if he was suppressing the urge to heave. "Easy, Cayden, try to keep the gory play-by-play to a minimum. We have a newbie in our midst." He slid a sympathetic glance in Willow's direction.

"No, it's fine," Willow said, taken back that Alex would speak up on her behalf. "I'll have to get used to it at some point." She waited until Cayden was finished and then took a step closer to get a better look at the macabre scene.

The wind whipped at her heels and rustled the soaking wet plastic bag alongside the body. She surveyed the dead female and her stomach roiled again. Somehow, she thought it would be easier to see a stranger stuffed inside a bloody trash bag. At least now she was detached from the person emotionally, she reasoned. But, if anything, it was worse.

The blatant display of evil and disregard for human life made her tremble.

"How are you holding up?" A deep male voice whispered in her ear. She turned and bumped into a solid wall of muscle that threatened to knock her on her ass. Immediately, Alex's hands flew to her waist. She heard his sharp intake of breath. She swallowed her gasp and took a step back.

"I'm okay." *Yeah right.* She didn't want to look like an amateur by losing her cookies in front of all these people. But no matter how hard she tried, she couldn't seem to desensitize herself from the fact that this was someone's daughter or sister lying dead from a senseless act of violence.

He began pulling plastic containers from a black canvas bag marked "trace evidence" and setting them up next to the body. "You're looking a little green. You can let loose over the side." He angled his head toward the water. "Nobody will be the wiser. Don't always have to be a tough girl." He reached out and squeezed her gloved hand. Warmth radiated from his skin even through the latex.

Why was he suddenly being nice to her? His moods were as mercurial as the wind rolling off the water. "I'm not exactly sure how to act. This is my first murder scene."

"Yeah and let's hope it's your last."

The sinking feeling in the pit of her stomach told her something different. "Do you have any idea who she is?"

"Only the coroner can make a positive ID. But I'll give you my best guess, a witch by the name of Kimber Woods, the last person to see Maeve Donovan alive. She was reported missing from her coven a little over twenty-four hours ago. Ironically, it's the same one that you and Maeve lived in. It's too much of a coincidence if you ask me."

She didn't recognize the name, but then again she'd left the coven over a decade ago. "I don't believe in coincidences." She swallowed hard, letting his words sink in. "I thought you suspected the killer murdered Maeve out of revenge because she was about to hand him over to you. Do you think the killer's targeting the coven now?"

He shook his head, his expression grim. "Sure starting to look that way."

There might not be any love lost between her and the high priestess of her former coven, but she'd never forgive herself if she didn't do everything in her power to stop this madman. Regardless of their tumultuous past, Willow refused to let him hurt another innocent, especially if it might be another one of the women she had considered to be both a friend and family. If he was targeting the coven, then this changed everything. "Why would he do such a thing?"

Alex turned his head in Willow's direction and watched her with growing concern. She didn't act like she knew this victim, but he suspected that didn't make it any easier. "Any number of reasons, revenge against Maeve and anyone she associated with. Maybe a twisted obsession with witches, or maybe he's just a sicko." Alex was turning into a human powder keg, ready to explode at any moment. If he'd been in any other state of mind, he would've never acted on his attraction toward Willow.

Damn, he could still taste her on his lips, and now he could recall, in vivid detail, what it felt like to have every curve of her lush body pressed against his. At first, he would've sworn she'd put him under a spell, but not now, not anymore. This was more than just chemistry. It was fucking primal and combustible. He tried to mentally shake thoughts of her as a woman from his mind.

"Hey, Earth to Alex." She waved a hand in front of his face, and he prayed she hadn't figured out what he'd been thinking. Even if he had to remind himself a hundred times a day, this was one woman who was off limits. He still owed her an apology for handling the situation with zero finesse. Once they were alone, he'd have to smooth things over.

"Can you at least tell me what you're doing?" Willow tilted her head to the side, her green eyes wide and assessing. "Who knows, it could trigger another premonition."

"Frankly, I'm not used to divulging the p's and q's of a murder investigation to a witch, but if you think it might help." Anger and frustration formed a tight knot in the pit of his stomach. It was his screw-up that had caused Maeve Donovan's murder, and now he had her blood on his hands. He hadn't slept right for days, running on raw adrenaline. Alex pulled out a notebook and a pen from one of the large canvas bags. He pressed a button and the notebook hovered next to him in midair.

"Try me." She placed her hands on her hips, offering him a silent challenge.

Don't tempt me. "Fine. Every detail is significant in this kind of investigation—the weather, the time of day, any specimens from the area," he said, jotting down notes onto the smart board. "I'll look for any traces of fibers from clothing she may have been wearing before he stripped her naked, and I'll have to take a semen swab. I'm sorry, Willow. It must be hard as hell to let your mind go there. My guess is he's raping the women and then marking them with the word 'Whore' for everyone to see his handiwork. He's a sociopath."

From all appearances, this maniac was cutting into their flesh. To think he might have been raping his victims either before he killed them or post mortem made Alex want to crush something, or in this case, someone.

All the color drained from her face and once again his gut twisted with sympathy for her. Hell, it was bad enough she had to experience the murders in her dreams. Now she was forced to see all the bloody details in real time and relive the nightmare in front of an audience.

He turned his attention toward the group around the body. "As for the rest of you, anybody want to venture a guess as to why the killer would want to shoot her in the back of the neck and throw her in the river?"

"I say we have a serial killer on our hands." Cayden used a pair of tweezers to collect a few microscopic hairs from inside the bag and then placed them in one of the plastic containers. "He clearly has zero remorse about how he's disposing of the bodies."

The screech of tires forced Alex to glance toward the road. "What now?

Great," he murmured as a news van pulled up to the lot. He turned back to face Cayden and felt his mood darken even more. "By some miracle, we've managed to keep the Donovan murder under the radar and out of the press up to this point, but I'm not sure we'll be so lucky the second time around."

"Whoever she was, we have to assume she must've been acquainted with the Donovan chick," Brodie chimed in. "After all, they lived at the same coven together. They probably talked. What if Maeve Donovan confided in her and let it slip about a bust going down at Fusion, or that she was our main informant? If the killer found out, then he had a motive to get her out of the way to keep her from talking."

"You think he killed her in the same heinous way as the other victim to make it look like a serial killing?" Alex scratched his forehead with his gloved hand and let Brodie's words mull over in his brain.

"It's just a theory," Brodie pointed out.

His buddy Garret Mulroney, a detective from the RHPD, walked up holding a vacuum in his hand, his expression bleak. "I did a sweep of the perimeter. Whoever he is, he didn't leave any footprints."

"There wouldn't be if he dropped her from the sky," mumbled a familiar, male voice. Willow took a tentative step back as the towering shadow came closer. Joe Tate carried a worn, tan case in each of his enormous hands. He set them on the frozen ground and approached the body.

From his rumpled clothing to the heavy bags and dark shadows under his eyes, it was clear he'd been working overtime. His skin was even paler than usual, which was saying something. He crouched next to the body, opened one of his cases, and pulled out a pair of gloves and a mask. "Keep up people."

Alex's brows shot up. "Did you find any evidence?"

"I found a piece of a feather under the nails of the Donovan girl. It's a wing."

"Great, we're screwed six ways 'til Sunday and we still don't have a murder weapon." Alex scribbled a few notes on the board, and then looked up. "Joe Tate, meet Willow McCray. She's our psychic consultant on this case. Willow, this is the coroner." He briefly described her vision, focusing only on the finer details.

"Alex, what did you mean about being screwed?" Willow whispered close to his ear, before burying her face in her scarf. The wind picked up and blew her red waves in every direction.

"Joe found feather-like particles and bone fragments that match the DNA of a large winged creature who possesses magickal properties, which could mean the killer is a fae, a breed nearly impossible to kill. You don't shoot or stab them. You literally have to banish their souls. The ones we have managed to arrest over the years were always accused of really twisted shit like rape and murder. They're now rotting in Hellios for the rest of their miserable lives. I have a feeling we won't be so lucky this time around."

"What do we have here?" Tate interjected, forcing Alex to focus on the body and not the potential disaster they now faced.

"Could be Kimber Woods, twenty-five years of age, a witch reported missing by her coven. Looks like the same type of trauma over most of the lower extremities from a blunt force, like the Donovan murder. He's using a sharp, pointed weapon that leaves a hole in the back of the neck." Alex knelt next to the body. "It looks like the same size hole, around three inches in diameter."

Tate pulled out a small tape measure from his bag and angled it over the wound in her neck. "Yeah, three inches to be exact. What the hell kind of murder weapon could do that kind of damage?" he asked, rubbing his chin. "I've never seen anything like this."

Alex leaned closer. "My dad took me hunting when I was a kid. We went with the neighbor and he used a crossbow to kill his prey. I can still recall the way he screwed this long thin piece of metal called a broadhead into the end of a bolt, which is basically an arrow." He stole a glance over at Willow, who seemed to be digesting every word. "The broadhead opens on impact and leaves a pretty sizeable hole, depending on the width of it. I saw it cut through the bone of a white-tailed deer."

"Okay, let's say the killer used a bolt from a crossbow to shoot her in the back of the neck, but he didn't use it to carve into the skin." Joe glanced at the body before facing him again. "It looks as if he's using a ritual knife with a fine point."

"Like an *athame*?" Willow asked, taking a tentative step closer to the body.

"An *athame*?"

"It's mostly used to cast a circle or direct energy. Although, I, uh, use mine for other purposes," she said, staring at the ground.

"Well, whoever he is, he did another butcher job." The vampire glanced from Willow to Alex and back again. He pulled out a small knife and glass slides from one of the cases. "Hell's bells. I've seen freshly gutted deer picked over by the vultures in better condition."

Willow took a step closer to Alex and he stood. She pushed a stray hair off her face and whispered, "How does he handle blood and not want to, well, you know?"

"Have a snack? I think he's gotten used to it after all these years, and it's lucky for us, because he's got supernatural intelligence and doesn't require much sleep."

Smith walked up to the group, glanced at the body and scratched his horns. "I was talking to the divers and the RHPD. Any leads at this point?"

"No finger or footprints to match anything in our database," Brodie muttered, typing frantically on the keyboard of his iPad before turning toward his boss. "But I'm still looking for a match with a snake tat on the forearm."

Frustrated, Alex cursed under his breath. "Something sure as hell better turn up and quick, before this maniac kills again. Tate, I want you to check for traces of a potion in the vic's blood. Willow has a hunch he used one to dull her powers so she couldn't fight back or get away." His gaze snapped to Willow, and their eyes locked and held. He was too aware of her every move. Annoyed with himself, he looked away.

"For someone who professes to hate witches, you can't seem to keep your eyes off her," Smith muttered under his breath. The demon scratched at the scruff on his chin and surveyed Alex with a curious expression on his face. *Does he suspect my interest in Willow isn't purely professional?*

Alex tried to ignore Smith's scrutinizing gaze, focusing his attention on Willow instead. "What kind of potion would have the effect you described?"

"I'm by no means an expert, but certainly a tincture made from belladonna or mandrake root could slow you down. Only a spell using a lock of her hair or a piece of her clothing could strip a witch's powers completely," Willow added.

Smith motioned for Alex to step off to the side. "We still don't have

Maeve Donovan's autopsy report, but we'll make sure to check her blood as well. Whoever did this wanted to send a message, loud and clear."

"Yeah, well, I don't know about you, but I'm still trying to figure out what the hell the message is at this point." Alex shot back.

"It's usually about one of two things: revenge or a need to be famous. We've got to find this psycho and take him down. None of the witches in and around Raven's Hollow will be safe until we do." He glanced over at Willow and frowned. "As of right now, we have a serial killer on the loose. I suggest we strongly urge these women not to go out alone."

The sound of footsteps forced them both to turn around. An attractive female tried to shove a microphone in their faces. A press badge hung from her neck. "Would either of you like to make a statement now that you're officially classifying this as a murder case? Do you know the name of the victim? Do you have any suspects?"

Smith muttered a curse. "I'm not sure how you managed to slip past us. We don't have a positive ID yet, nor the name of any suspects. We'll make the information readily available when we do." He raised his hand. "That's all for now. Thank you."

Alex stole a glance at Tate, who still hovered over the body and was now up to his elbows in blood and gore. His stomach clenched thinking about the visit to the family. It would be the second one this week. This part of his job never got any easier.

They waited until the reporter walked away and then crossed onto the other side of the tape. "I wasn't planning on getting interviewed. How bad was it?"

"Well, it was interesting. If our killer's indeed a fae, then you may have drawn him out, let him know we're onto him." Alex pointed out. "On the other hand, it could backfire on us, and he could take it out on another unsuspecting victim."

Tate glanced at them over his shoulder and smirked. "How much worse can things get?"

Willow walked over to Alex and whispered, "Has anyone thought about how we kill him?"

Before he could respond, Tate called out his name. He was holding a miniscule scrap of brown fabric with a pair of tweezers. "You need to come see this, gents, and bring your psychic."

"What is it?" Alex stood next to Tate as Smith hovered nearby. Willow walked over to his other side.

"There's a ton of debris and garbage down there, but this was stuck inside the bag," Tate inclined his head to the murky black water. "I'll take the sample back to the lab and do some tests. I'm not sure if it came from the vic or the killer, but it might be a piece of clothing."

"Willow, why don't you give it a try? See if you can pick up something." Alex gently nudged her closer to Tate. Up until recently, if someone other than Smith had asked him to rely on a witch's premonition to solve a murder case, he would've deemed them insane. But now he had to take note of every detail of her vision and consult her on her theories. Despite his misgivings, so far she'd been damn accurate.

After she wrapped her gloved fingers around the scrap of material, she doubled over as if she'd been punched in the gut. "This belongs to him."

"Willow? Jesus, what's wrong? Are you okay?" Alex placed his hand on her shoulder, and then quickly removed it when all heads turned in his direction.

She nodded. "I picked up on his twisted essence immediately. I sense you've made him angry. He saw the news and is taking your statement as a personal challenge. He wants to make you run around in circles like a sick cat and mouse game."

His hands clenched into fists. "Can you pick up on where he is?"

"I might if you can get me a map. I'll try scrying his location."

"Try this." Cayden walked up with his iPad, displaying a layout of the city and held it in front of her. Willow pulled off the amulet dangling from around her slender neck and swung the chain over the map. After a few minutes, it continued to move around in a circle, but didn't land anywhere.

"He must be using shields or a charm to conceal his whereabouts. I can't break through them." Willow slipped the necklace back on.

"Tate, what do you have for us?" Alex asked, anxious to wrap up and get the hell out of there.

"The DNA matches to a Kimber Woods. You were spot on, Denopoulos. I found traces of heroin and booze in her blood. There's also an unknown substance I haven't yet identified."

"Let's get the body into the van and back to the lab. I'm positioning as many agents as I can spare to protect the coven around the clock. Every woman living in that house is now a target," Smith said as he helped them pack up their stuff. "Denopoulos, I want you to get your team over there pronto and check the place out. I'll text you the address from the road. Talk to the witches and find out all you can about Maeve Donovan and Kimber Woods."

Exhaustion pressed down on Alex and yet there was no time for sleep. He threw his soiled gloves, booties, and mask in a garbage bag. "They might accept our protection in the interim. But do you really think they'll talk freely to a witch hunter?"

"Don't worry," Smith said with the trace of a smile on his lips as he glanced over at Willow. "You're not going alone."

CHAPTER 7

"Two down, how many more to go?" Willow asked Alex as she continued to pace across the polished hardwood floors of the coven library. All the while, she kept repeating details of the crime scene and her vision, over and over again.

"Way to think positively," Alex shot back and plopped down in a desk chair, resisting the urge to glance over his shoulder, bracing himself for whatever could jump out at him. The last place he ever expected to work undercover was at a coven full of witches.

He refocused the train of his thoughts and let his gaze trail over her, taking in her white knuckled grip around her to-go cup. Apparently, he wasn't the only one on edge. He wished he could figure out what was going on in her head. It was the first time she'd spoken since they'd arrived at the coven, after spending several hours at the morgue. She'd been quiet and downright withdrawn when he'd informed her where they were going. He didn't think he'd earned the right to ask her if her sour mood could be attributed to grief, or perhaps there was something more going on. *Stop thinking about her as a woman.*

Willow stopped pacing and turned toward him. "Do you still think this is the killer's sick way of sending a message to the coven?" she asked, sounding weary.

His stomach knotted with guilt. They had been working her pretty hard, the least he could do was feed her. "There's no doubt in my mind, the killer's been watching the place. Maybe he managed to get easy access in and out of here somehow." He made a mental note to ask the high priestess for a blueprint of the house. He'd need to familiarize himself with all the exits, figure out how the killer could be getting in and out, or in the event he needed to make a hasty escape.

If he was acting out his revenge on Maeve, then why go after the other witches of this coven? He pondered the question, and then pushed it to the back of his mind. He glanced at his watch. They'd been there for almost a half hour and were still waiting for the high priestess to grace them with her presence.

He'd give her some leeway, considering the circumstances. According to her assistant, who'd showed them in, the lady in question was trying to track down Kimber's family upon hearing the news that another one of her charges was dead, murdered by a madman. He supposed it wasn't every day a special agent banged on your door to inform you of yet another murder, but in this case, it was the second time in a span of three days. Brodie had been assigned to deliver the gruesome news the last time around.

"No doubt he believes Maeve turned against him. In terms of motive, he could feel the need to punish anyone she came in contact with. It's his way of saying he's in charge, holding all the cards." Alex scrolled though the notes on his phone, hoping to make sense of it all. He feared something darker was in play.

"I've never been able to follow the game of football, but how do we get on the offensive and turn the tables on him, so to speak?" She took a swig from her cup then blew a stray red hair off her face. His fingers curled to push it behind her ear.

He smiled at her analogy. "We have a team of agents camped outside combing the place for clues. But if we plan on truly outsmarting the bastard, then we sure as hell better come up with a legitimate cover. I say we get our people positioned on the inside." Funny, he'd spent most of his adult life avoiding witches, and now he was about to be surrounded by a house full of them.

"Whoa, you want me to go undercover, here? I don't think so," she said sarcastically.

"You come back in as yourself. The killer doesn't know who you are."

"But everyone else does," she said, and visibly tensed. She placed a hand on her hip and his gaze was riveted to her long legs, encased in denim. He imagined those legs wrapped around his neck while he pleasured with his fingers and his tongue. His cock strained against his jeans. For so many reasons, he couldn't go there. His brain seemed to be getting the memo, but his body...not so much.

"Help me understand why that's a bad thing?" Alex could still almost hear the sexy little sounds of pleasure she made when he kissed her. He wanted to see her eyes glazed with passion, not misery. He shook his head to redirect his wayward thoughts.

When her breath hitched and her eyes became focused on his lips, he realized she must've picked up on what he'd been thinking. He wanted to explore her lush mouth again and lose himself in her moist heat. He reminded himself where they were and what they were about to do, and pinned her with his gaze, waiting for her response. "Well? Are you going to answer the question?"

"It's a long story. I can't get into it now. Besides, don't you think it's a little odd considering I've been out of here for over a decade? But now, all of a sudden, after the murders, I've had an epiphany and suddenly want to sing "Kumbaya" around a full moon with all my witch friends?"

It became clear she wasn't used to talking about her past with anyone. After the way he'd left things, he certainly couldn't expect her to confide in him. He'd have to tread lightly. "Do you have a better idea?"

"You're forgetting one minor detail. Even if I could pull this off, the high priestess would never agree. You don't know her like I do. Trust me on this one."

"She might not have a choice, and at this point, neither do you." He tried to soften his tone at the exasperated look in her eyes. "Believe me, I'm getting the message loud and clear. You'd rather be anywhere but here." The question was why. "But you're going to have to make an exception. If not for me, then do it for Maeve."

"That was a cheap shot, Denopoulos."

When she moved into the light, grief, exhaustion and a glimmer of fear tinged her features. The urge to take her in his arms and chase away her demons caught him off guard. What was it about this woman that pushed his distrust of witches to the back of his mind? It didn't matter. This wasn't the time and definitely not the place.

"There's one major detail you're not taking into account in all this. I didn't leave by choice. I was kicked out."

Before he could ask her to elaborate, a shadow of a cat appeared in the room, and then disappeared. Willow glanced at the door and froze. "That's her familiar, which means she's on her way." Willow picked at an invisible piece of lint on her sweater and tried to smooth down her tangle of red hair. Shaking, she slumped in a chair next to an antique-looking desk cluttered with fairy statues, different colored candles, incense, and even a black cauldron.

Instinctively, he reached for the lead badge, tucked in the front pocket of his jeans. All agents carried one. It worked against black magick in most situations, but then again, nothing was full proof against a powerful mage.

She glanced over at his badge and tilted her head to the side. "May I ask what that thing is that you're clutching onto for dear life?"

"It's a device that protects against dark magick." He shoved the shield back in his pocket, not sure why he felt the need to give her an explanation.

"Uh, huh, your so-called device is actually a talisman. Similar to my amulet." She pulled the reddish stone out from the chain under her sweater. "Not all magick is dark, Alex."

Christ, so she did have a point, not that he'd ever admit it. Hoping to change the subject, he turned his gaze to the desk, "Is this stuff for show or do witches actually use all this crap?" Alex rubbed his beard as he glanced at the bottles of oils, and differently shaped crystals.

"Only to turn unsuspecting males into toads." An unfamiliar female voice replied from the doorway. Alex turned to stare at a petite woman dressed in jeans and a hoodie. Her hair was short and spiky, fire engine red. Various piercings adorned her ears. Flame tats shot up over the collar of her sweatshirt.

"I guess I had that one coming." Alex flashed a sheepish grin.

"I'd expect nothing less from a mortal. They tend to think the worst about our kind." She flicked her wrist and the door slammed shut.

His whole body tensed. Spells and magick made his palms itch. "Look, I meant no offense, and I get that you've been through a tragedy, but let's not start trading insults."

The high priestess blinked, and he noticed her eyes were red rimmed and swollen as if she'd been crying. Despite her sorrow, he got the distinct impression she was a force to be reckoned with. She waved her hand at him dismissively. "Well, I know why you're here. I'm Ellen Oresky, the high priestess." Her gaze trailed over him with open, unabashed longing as she crossed in the room and took a seat at her desk. Alex wondered the last time she'd seen a flesh-and-blood male. He didn't like being ogled, especially by the likes of her.

Alex stood and offered his hand. "I know this can't be easy for you, Ellen." She was at least a decade older than he was but kept herself trim and youthful. The woman was a real cougar in the making. He'd even go so far to say she was probably stunning in her youth. "I'm sorry for your loss. I'm Special Agent Denopoulos, and you already know Willow—"

"What the hell is she doing here?" Shock flashed in her eyes as her gaze zeroed in on Willow like a laser beam.

Willow's face flamed. "Good to see you too, Ellen. I wish it wasn't under such horrific circumstances."

"Don't try to tell me she works with you," Ellen said in an accusing tone, angling her head in his direction before her eyes rested on Willow again.

"Indeed I do. I'm the psychic consultant on this case," Willow said with a lift of her chin.

"A consultant, huh?" she huffed. "Is that what you're calling yourself these days? I thought you were in deep with some demon, getting into all kinds of trouble, just as I predicted."

"You always did assume the worst about me." Hurt flashed in Willow's eyes. "Well, you should be pleased to learn you were right all along."

There were a ton of questions he wanted to ask, but they'd have to wait. Alex took a deep breath, hoping to channel the last of his patience, and took a seat across from Ellen. *I need to take back control of the situation.* "Look, ladies, we don't have time to take a stroll down memory lane. There's a killer still out there targeting the women of this coven."

"What do you plan on doing to stop him?" Ellen's voice shook with a combination of anger and grief. "I still don't get what she has to do with all this."

"Commander Smith made it clear that we'd have your full cooperation. I'll need to position a few agents on the inside to draw out the killer and protect the other witches. I'll need to bring Willow in as well."

"I don't see why that's necessary." She pulled out a tissue and dabbed at her eyes.

"As for the how, Willow can move in with the sole intention of helping to protect the women of this coven. No one, and I mean no one, will know she works for us or we risk losing more than one life in the process. Do I make myself clear?"

"Crystal," Ellen said with a scowl.

"And as for the why, Willow's intimately familiar with this case, not to mention a highly skilled psychic. We've established the parameters. Now we need to execute the plan before anyone else gets wind of it."

"Well, I might not like what you're doing, but I can see you're a man of action. You'll at least get the job done. How can I help?"

"I'm glad we understand each other." Alex smiled, grateful for the change in demeanor. "I'll need a list of every person who comes in and out of here for any reason."

"I keep a log of everyone who enters and exits the building and make them sign in and out." Her voice broke with a sob. "I enforced it for the safety of my girls, not that it did Maeve and Kimber any good." She composed herself long enough to pull open a drawer and take out a clipboard. She shoved it toward him and flicked her hand, and the pages flipped to the beginning. "Happy hunting."

He flinched away but recovered quickly enough. "I appreciate your help." Overcoming his aversion to her use of magick, he began to flip through the pages of delivery people, construction workers, wand salesmen, and repairmen. "At this rate it'll take hours to load all their names into the MBI database. It looks as if I have my work cut out for me."

"Do you want me to see if I can pick up anything?" Willow scooted her chair closer and peeked over his shoulder. Her sexy vanilla scent flared in his nostrils, and a surge of pure lust coursed through his veins.

"Go ahead, give it a try." He tried to rein in his libido and counted silently to twenty and then flipped through pages. The name of a local contractor that appeared several times in the last few weeks drew his attention. "Donato and Sons? Who are they?"

"They're contractors. We're in the middle of a construction project, of all things, to expand the ritual room. We want to accommodate our new coven members. They've been working night and day, crashing in the guest rooms. But at this rate, we'll be lucky to keep the members we have when they find out about Kimber's murder. I'll have to sell the place." Ellen rubbed a hand over her eyes. "I'll be ruined."

If they didn't catch this maniac, Ellen would lose everything—her reputation, her members, and quite possibly her home. He never thought he'd be in a position to feel sorry for a witch. And yet, here he was. He supposed he could thank Willow for the shift. "I'll do everything in my power to make sure that doesn't happen."

He read through the list of different names who'd signed in and out under Donato and Sons. "From the looks of it, they have quite a few people working for them."

"Where are you going with this, Agent Denopoulos?" Ellen glanced at him disbelief. "Do you actually think one of the guys framing the addition on my new ritual room is the killer?"

"Whoever he is, my guess is he's probably trying to hide in plain sight. I've seen it a hundred times before."

Alex glanced over at Willow, and a surge of protectiveness came over him against the ever-present glare of the high priestess. *Since when do you rely on witchcraft to solve a murder case?* "What's the verdict?"

"Sadly, nothing so far." Willow ran her slender fingers over the page where the contractor's names appeared, and then closed her eyes in concentration. After a minute, she opened them. "I'm picking up on sheet rock and moldings, but nothing dark or deranged per se."

Her words brought him back to the days when he'd worked for his uncle's construction company to put himself through college. He ran a hand over his beard as an idea struck him. "I'll need your contractor's number," he said, angling his head in Ellen's direction. "I think I may have figured out a way to blend into the woodwork without raising suspicion."

"You can stay in the rooms the contractors have been using. But give me about thirty minutes for someone to change the linens." Ellen produced a card, along with two keys from her desk, and handed them to Alex without a second glance in Willow's direction. "They're all I have available at the moment." She stood and headed for the door, dismissing them. "You'll have to excuse me. I'm afraid I have a million things to do. If you need anything, don't hesitate to ask."

He nodded. Relief coursed through him when the woman left the room. Feeling sorry for her and trusting her were two entirely different things. Besides, he wasn't about to rely on anyone who looked at Willow through such a tainted lens. No matter what she did, at least she was trying to change. He supposed everyone deserved a second chance.

"Let's get out of here." Alex placed his hand at Willow's elbow and led her into the hallway. He glanced at the numbers on the keys and hissed out a breath. "We're on the second floor. Your room's right next door to mine." It seemed someone up there wanted to throw him another curveball and test his control. He took an oath, and that meant duty trumped desire. The question was which would win out in the end. Either way, he was screwed.

CHAPTER 8

"It looks as if we'll be taking the stairs," Alex said, sounding exhausted as they passed the *Out of Order* sign for the elevator. Every few seconds he'd glance over his shoulder to make sure no one was around.

"Some things never change. I spent more time climbing up and down the stairs than doing anything else. The elevator never worked around here." Maybe it was a blessing in disguise. Willow didn't exactly relish bumping into anyone right now, especially in such a small, cramped space. She needed a clear head when she faced the others. It was weird enough coming back here without having to explain the reasons to a coven of gossipy witches.

"Well, considering this is a house full of witches, you'd think one of you would be able to use a little hocus-pocus to get something as simple as an electrical problem fixed." His gaze trailed over dark beamed ceilings and the pale pink walls as they walked. *Hocus pocus?*

"Witchcraft and magick should be used for a higher purpose, a greater good, not be trifled with for the sole purposes of convenience." Willow sounded like a damn hypocrite, but she couldn't resist the urge to defend her kind whenever Alex made a potshot about witches. Not sure what his problem was, she decided to change the subject rather than trade barbs with him.

He held up his hand. "I'm sorry. I'm too tired for an argument. Forget I said anything."

"Already forgotten. I'd love to know how you plan on pulling off this ruse of yours?" she asked, lugging her enormous tote bag over one arm and gripping the handle of her suitcase in the other. Alex had fished out her trusty old Samsonite from the trunk of the van while she looked around the place.

"Cayden and Brodie are already on it." Alex followed alongside her, lugging a black duffle bag. "They're headed to the construction site as we speak to get a truck, supplies, and company tee shirts so we look the part."

His phone beeped. "Sorry," he muttered and pulled it out of his pocket. Relief crossed his face as he glanced at a text. "My friend Detective Mulroney sent a couple of his men in blue over to investigate the murder. They arrived while we were talking to Ellen. They're questioning all the women right now in the kitchen. According to Smith, the news report about Kimber's murder has spread all over the city like a goddamn wildfire. The good news is, at least it'll give me a chance to slip in without anyone noticing, so I don't blow my cover."

"That's the first good news I've heard all day." Maybe she could avoid seeing everyone until the morning. The ten years since she'd been gone seemed to melt away in the blink of an eye. A familiar twang of nostalgia mixed with a sensation of pure dread lingered in the pit of her stomach.

How the hell am I going to do this?

"I put a quick call into Donato and Sons and the old man was more than willing to cooperate. When I put his company name in the MBI database, I found a file open on one of his employees. Funny, he practically jumped at the chance to work alongside of us. This way no one will get suspicious when a whole new construction crew shows up here tomorrow."

"No offense, Alex, but do you really think you and your posse of demons will be able to pull this off?" Willow took extra-long steps to keep up with his strides.

"We have to. Besides, I worked in construction before I was a cop. I know enough to fake it, at least in the short term."

A sexy image of Alex clad in torn jeans and a hard hat flashed through her mind. Her eyes trailed over his powerful shoulders and the wide expanse of his chest. The man had a rockin' hard body. Any female would have to be dead not to notice. "I'm sure you got your share of catcalls."

"Are you flirting with me?" He waggled his brows at her.

She rolled her eyes. "You wish. I'm simply making an observation." She tried to redirect the train of her wayward thoughts by scoping out the place. The three-story Victorian was exactly as she remembered, with its stained glass windows and decorative red wood trim.

They passed through a foyer and stopped at a large seating area with chintz sofas and oversize chairs. An altar was set up in the center. Oriental rugs and large potted plants added a burst of color and gave the room a homey feel. Beyond the foyer, there was a room covered under tarp.

The familiar scents of frankincense and lavender wafted through the air. "I guess that must be the addition to the ritual room, and where you'll be spending most of your time." Willow pointed to the area under the tarp.

He turned and glanced around. "I'll check it out tomorrow. I don't want to go sneaking around before I have on my construction shirt. It might blow my cover, which reminds me, we shouldn't be seen together."

"Yeah, it's probably not smart." Why did those few words fill her with disappointment and not relief? Alex was occupying way too many of her thoughts as it was. The temptation of being under the same roof as him, in the room next door, made her heart beat wildly in her chest. She tried to ignore the uncomfortable sensation and followed Alex as he crossed into the great room.

"We have some time to kill before our rooms are ready. Mind if I have a look around?" he asked and set his bag on the floor.

"Suit yourself. After all, this will be your new home for a stretch." She glanced at the pictures lining the walls, generations of witches who came before her, and it made her chest tight. She'd forgotten how much she'd missed this place until she stepped inside. It was as if time had stood still.

"Yeah, thanks for reminding me." Willow followed Alex's curious gaze as it swept over a collection of wands, scrying bowls, and crystal balls spread out over the fireplace and along the glass coffee table. Boxes stacked one on top of the other filled an entire corner of the enormous room.

Not sure what his beef was, she pressed on. "They must be using this room for storage until the addition's ready. Is this your first time inside a coven?"

A shadow passed over his face. "I've been outside a few before, but never inside of one." His stance was hard and rigid as he continued to glance around as though preparing himself for an attack at any moment.

"Don't worry. Our initiation ritual is only mildly painful." She laughed at his horrified expression. "I'm sorry. I couldn't resist. You just look so uncomfortable."

"Oh, I see," he said with a nod. "You're messing with me. Remember, Willow, there's always payback." Her pulse quickened at the dark promise of sin in his eyes. It was time to put some space between them.

She pushed up the handle on her suitcase and walked to the bookcase. Not that she planned on having much time to read, but the ancient grimoires lining the shelves and stacked on the floor caught her eye.

On a whim, she sifted through the titles of the worn-out, red, leathery spines. *Drawing down the Moon, Witchcrafting*, and *Banishment Spells and Potions* got her attention. The minute her fingers skimmed over the spines, a tingling sensation spread up her arm.

Before Alex noticed what she was doing, she shoved *Banishment Spells and Potions* in her tote bag. When she had a chance, she'd check the book to see if there was anything about banishing a fae or destroying his soul.

"Ready for bed?" Alex whispered directly behind her in a deep, sultry voice. His body thrummed with heat and strength and it was all she could do not to press her back against the hard wall of chest.

More than you know. She ignored the question and brushed pushed past him. "I bet our rooms are ready." She grabbed her suitcase, and headed back out to the hall, a safe distance away.

"Hey, slow down. What I meant was I think we should probably catch a few hours of shut-eye while we can. We both have our work cut out for us around here," Alex said, jogging to catch up with her.

"Trust me, it's going to be hard enough trying to convince everyone that you're skilled with a hammer, let alone trying to pass yourself off as one of Donato's sons."

"Why?" he asked, looking mildly alarmed.

"I remember Mr. Donato and his sons. They're all about this high." Her hand went to her forehead. "And baldness runs in the family, even on the wife." She smiled, eyeing his luscious locks.

He laughed. "If anyone asks, I'll say I was adopted."

"Good luck with that one."

From what she'd seen so far, except for the addition, nothing about the coven seemed to have changed much since she'd been gone, and yet there was a suffocating dark energy lurking in the air. She sensed something more sinister at play than the deaths themselves. Could she be picking up on the killer's presence? She sniffed the air and it made her stomach clench. Something about the scent was eerily familiar. She ignored it and continued on. "What exactly do you want me to do here, besides blend in?"

"I want you to go through both Kimber and Maeve's rooms—see if you can pick up on anything after our guys are done. They took jewelry, personal items, and both women's computers. We're currently checking their email correspondence to check anything suspicious."

"I'll do whatever it takes if you think it might help." A part of her was horrified at the idea of poking around through their stuff, imagining what she might find when she did. The other part of her was curious. What if she found a clue that led them to the killer? She stifled a yawn and rubbed the back of her neck with her hand.

Exhausted as she was, she didn't think she'd be able to sleep. Every time she closed her eyes, the shadowy figure of Maeve's killer appeared in her mind, along with images of blood and crossbows.

"You look tired." A genuine look of concern flashed in his eyes. "I guess we worked you pretty hard today. You did great out there, by the way, and really held your own." His praise caught her off guard and snuck under her defenses.

Color burned her cheeks. "Be careful now. You actually sound sincere."

"One thing you'll learn about me, Willow, is I don't mince words and I don't pay false compliments. When I say something, it's the truth." The conviction in his words sent an awareness pulsing through her veins. Alex was a man of steely determination, an alpha in every possible way.

"The description you gave Ellen about what I'm actually supposed to do here seemed pretty vague."

"You do what all the other witches do. If my hunch is right and the killer is watching from the sidelines, we don't want him to suspect anything."

She took a deep breath, not sure how the other women were going to feel about her shadowing their every move. She'd have to worry about it later. "I'm dying to hear what you think of the coven so far."

"This place is different than I imagined." He turned in a circle to check out his surroundings.

"Did you think the house would be filled with a group of women covered in blood and chanting to the devil, taking turns making human sacrifices on the altar?" His harsh intake of breath forced the hairs on the back of her neck to prickle. "Why do I get the feeling that's exactly what you were thinking? Either you've seen *Carrie* and *Rosemary's Baby* one too many times, or there's something else going on. Care to fill in the blanks?"

"Not really." He swallowed hard and it made his Adam's apple bob up and down in his throat. He was hiding something.

Granted, there were a few dark practitioners who used blood and human sacrifice in their black magick rituals as an offering to Satan. Only the criminally insane did such abominable things, giving the rest of her kind a bad name. "Okay, fair enough then." She decided not to press him on the subject. "You have nothing to worry about. The worst thing you'll encounter around here is an angry pixie."

He smiled, lightening the mood. "What the hell is a pixie? I don't think I've ever encountered one of those."

"Trust me, you don't want to." Curious about his past, she figured now was as good a time as any to ask him something personal. She kept her expression casual. "If it hadn't been for your brother getting involved in drugs, do you think you still would've gone into law enforcement?"

"Why would you bring that up here?" His expression turned fierce. He glanced over his shoulder again, apparently to make sure no one was around. When he turned back to face her, his brow was knitted in anger. "What if someone heard you? I told you about Gus in a private moment, Willow."

Despite how things had started out between them, they shared a connection and it wasn't just physical. She had her own dark past to contend with and it was still a source of shame and regret on so many levels. She never imagined that Alex had been dealing with skeletons in his closet as well.

"I'm sorry. I didn't mean to make you angry." She had no business sharing secrets with Alex. Secrets between men and women led to intimacy. They were already skittering on dangerous territory. She didn't need to complicate matters any further, and yet she couldn't help herself where he was concerned. She wanted to learn more about him.

Besides, what red-blooded female could resist a man as sexy and passionate as Alex? The fact that he could kiss like a sex god was icing on the cake. She'd experienced firsthand what he could do with those luscious lips. And yet, she couldn't get past his dislike of witches. If she could only find out why...

"I would never tell a soul about your brother. You have no reason to believe me, but I give you my word. Who understands the layers of shame and secrecy with addiction better than I do? I was always covering up for Maeve, making excuses for her to try to hide her addiction. She wasn't a sister, but she was as close to a blood relative as you could get."

His gaze bored into hers with such intensity tingles exploded all over her skin. "It's obvious you cared very much about Maeve."

"She was all I had." Back in the motel, she could've sworn they'd made some headway in learning what made the other person tick. Then again, maybe she'd been reading him wrong, but he was giving her mixed signals.

One minute he was kind, flirtatious and downright charming, and the next, he was cold and detached. After all, he'd been the one to pull away from her and had even gone on to say the kiss had been a mistake. *But the man was as hard as stone and moaning your name when he did*, she reminded herself.

He ran his fingers across his close-cropped beard, as though contemplating what he was about to say next. "I overreacted. I didn't mean to."

"It's okay. We don't have to talk about this anymore."

"Yes, we do. I'm wound pretty tight right about now from stress and lack of sleep. There are only a handful of people who know about Gus. I need to protect his anonymity. I shouldn't have told you in the first place."

Secretly, she was glad he did because she got to see firsthand how deeply he cared about the people he loved. He was protective of his family, a quality she admired. The simple truth was written all over his heart-stopping face. "Does the fact that I have a criminal record and was formerly employed by the main supplier of a drug ring have anything to do with it?"

"I'd be lying if I said it didn't factor in, but I believe you when you said you weren't aware of the full extent of what Saint Claire was up to." He exhaled and continued. "The more time I spend around you, the more I realize you don't lie. In fact, you're honest to a fault."

Through the corner of her eye, she caught him gazing at her. His expression became so stark and so unbelievably sexy it made her heart skip a beat.

"You surprise me and that doesn't happen very often."

They both stopped when they reached the end of the hallway. She turned to face him and smiled. "Unfiltered is a more accurate description." She pressed a hand on his arm and he followed the movement with his eyes. "You surprise me too, by trusting me enough to tell me something so personal."

Alex dropped his bag, took a predatory step toward her, and kept coming until Willow's back hit the wall. She barely registered her suitcase tip over and smack against the wooden floor when Alex was curved over her. His thick hair framed his beautiful face and made his eyes appear even darker. His expression of anger was gone, replaced by pure, unadulterated lust.

He pressed his hands on either side of her head, caging her in with his big body. "We've already gotten personal, and frankly, as much as I have no business saying this, I can barely think about anything else but kissing you and making you come," he breathed, his lips only inches away.

Her nipples instantly hardened into tight points from his sultry words and the raw hunger in his eyes. "I'd be lying if I said I wasn't tempted. But I think it would be a bad idea. Things are becoming way too complicated."

"Trust me, there's nothing complicated about the way my body has been reacting to you, Willow." His erection pressed against her thigh to prove his point. His gaze darted to her breasts and he sucked in a breath. He ran his hand down the underside of her rib cage. "From the looks of it, you're about as turned on right now as I am."

"Okay, I might be attracted to you physically, but I can't do this again." Not after the way he treated her the last time.

"I'm sorry about before. I didn't want to take advantage of you when you were so vulnerable, but I can't stop thinking about you, Willow. I want you." His jaw visibly clenched as if he were trying to rein in his control and losing.

Shocked by his brutal honesty, his words turned her on almost as much as his sultry kisses had. "I thought maybe you were just trying to comfort me."

"It might have started out like that. Do you have any idea what you're doing to me? My only mistake was to start something I couldn't finish. I was hard through an entire crime scene."

She instantly grew wet. "Please don't say those things."

"Why not? They're true." He eased her hair from her ponytail and let it fall in a heavy wave around her shoulders. He ran his fingers through the layers until she sighed. "God, you're beautiful. I've thought so from the second I saw you strut across that bar."

"You have an unfair advantage here." No, Alex had way too much power over her. She refused to give him any more.

"Let's level the playing field. Take advantage of me all you want." He caressed her cheek and then pressed an open-mouthed kiss to her neck, making her shiver.

She put up her hand and held it against his chest, secretly loving the way his muscles jumped beneath her fingertips. Female pride surged inside her at the effect she was having on him. "I'm not stupid, Alex. You're every woman's fantasy come to life." She gasped as his tongue slid over the shell of her ear. "Ellen was practically drooling all over herself staring at you." Not that she could blame her. "Watch your back. She's a man-eater."

"Don't worry. She's not my type," he murmured and nibbled on her neck.

She bit down on her lip to keep from moaning. "Yeah, well that never stopped her before."

He pulled away from her, and his expression was full of mischief. "Maybe you haven't noticed, but there's someone else I have my eye on." He ran his thumb over the pulse beating wildly at her throat. "You seem aroused and angry, and I find it sexy as hell. I know a great way to ease the tension."

"Is sex all you think about?" she asked and smacked him lightly on the shoulder.

He caught her hand and brought her fingers to his lips, then flashed a wicked smile. "Do you really want me answer truthfully?"

CHAPTER 9

"I'm sure you're used to women falling at your feet." Willow was trying to keep her guard up and protect herself from Alex's masterful seduction tactics, and failing. "We got carried away earlier, but it won't happen again. I try to avoid one-night stands and casual hook-ups." They always ended up making her feel like crap in the end. She'd been there and done that, even got the tee shirt.

"You're judging me based on your past? Some asshole hurt you and now you're making all guys pay for his screw-up? Sorry, but I don't see how that's fair."

Wrong answer. She wasn't sure what she was expecting, but there were no soothing words about how he'd never hurt her, even if they were a load of crap. At least the effort would've been nice. "You're one to talk. It's not as if you haven't judged me for being a witch. You've made your feelings quite clear, which is why I'm saying no. I mean, what were you hoping to do? Charm the pants off me with a few sweet words?" She'd learned her lesson the last time, and her ego still hurt from the aftermath.

"I'm sorry. I must sound like a jerk." Alex ran his knuckles across her cheek and tucked a stray curl behind her ear. A part of her didn't want to let him get so intimate, but her body craved his touch. Her desire was still so raw, it was hard to fight. "I admit that I screwed up. I probably didn't handle things in the best way. I lose all control when I'm around you. This isn't easy for me either, but I don't think I can fight it anymore. I'm starting to realize all witches aren't the same."

His admission surprised her and softened the crux of her anger. "Fine, I accept your apology. Look, now we're working together. I think it would be way too awkward to get involved. It can't happen again." She said the words as much for her benefit as well as his. She'd tuck the delicious memory away and savor it over again.

"Willow." Her name came out like a plea. The truth was, she couldn't wait to ease the slow, steady ache building between her legs. She planned on using the hell out of her Pocket Rocket to accomplish the task; a sex toy was far safer than Alex any day.

"Look, I'm tired and cranky right now. I haven't slept right for weeks. I need to crash for a few." The grandfather clock chimed, making her jump.

He nodded and took a step back. "It's been a one hell of a day." He pulled a key from his pocket and handed it to her.

"I agree." Before she could pick up her suitcase, he lifted it over his head and slung his duffle bag over his other shoulder. "What the hell do you have in here anyway? Rocks? This thing weighs a ton."

"My book of shadows, wands, crystals, a small copper cauldron, and a mortar and pestle for crushing herbs. Why?"

"I didn't know you were bringing the whole bag of tricks with you."

"I carry my "bag of tricks" with me wherever I go." She wouldn't dare tell him that she spent most her time living out of her suitcases. Her tiny apartment outside of Salem Proper felt so cold and temporary, she'd been there almost four years and still couldn't unpack. Ever since the day she left Raven's Hollow, she never found a place to call home.

They came to the end of the hall and she rested her hand on the balustrade of the old wood bannister. A rush of memories flooded her like a crashing wave. How many times had she and Maeve sailed down this staircase head first? It was a miracle they'd never broken their necks, or any bones for that matter.

And now her best friend was gone forever. The thought made it hard to breathe. Moisture blurred her vision. She centered herself and placed the grief in a box inside her mind to open when the time was right. For the time being, she needed to focus on finding and stopping the killer before he went after another witch. She had no doubt he would. She felt it with a certainty deep in her soul.

The pounding of footsteps made her glance up to see Alex taking the stairs two at a time. "Where am I going?"

"It's the third door on the left." Willow followed his gorgeous ass up the stairs. She tried not to watch the way the muscles in his broad shoulders and back flexed as he moved. But it was hard not to gape at all that magnificence right in front of her. How could she look at Alex and not be tempted to touch him?

She made her way to the guest room and shoved her key in the lock. Not sure what to expect, she pushed open the lacquered door, glanced around the small room, and sighed. At least it was clean and the queen-sized bed looked inviting.

When she turned back to face him, his eyes filled with heat. Alex set her suitcase down and leaned against the doorjamb. She pushed her hair off her forehead and offered a smile. "Well then, I guess I'll see you later."

"Not so fast." Before she could stop him, Alex pushed his way into the room. "I'm checking to make sure there are no monsters under the bed."

"Alex, please. It's not necessary. I can take care of myself." She wheeled her suitcase into the room and placed it in the corner next to the closet. She turned on the tiffany lamp on the nightstand.

He ignored her and did a quick search of the room. "You're okay for now. I'll have to find a way to set up surveillance equipment. Maybe install alarms to alert us if someone tries to break in."

"I don't think he's stupid enough to show up here now, not so soon after killing Kimber. Do you?" The scent of cedar and vanilla candles filled the air, a faint reminder of her old room here at the coven. The smell wrapped around her like a warm blanket. She slipped off her coat and purse, and tried to push the memory away as she tossed them on the old wrought iron bed.

"We can't predict what he'll do next. No one's safe at this point." His voice took on a steely edge.

She did another quick sweep of the small room and pointed to the salt around the windowsill. "Someone took precautions. Salt will keep most dark forces at bay, but it's not foolproof against strong magick. I'll have to see what type of protection spells they've put around the place and maybe the other girls, and I can create additional charms around the windows and doors."

"If you say so. After all, you're the expert." He smiled and she melted.

"Are you trying to score brownie points with me?" She didn't want to correct him on the part about her being an expert on much of anything these days, except getting into trouble, although the reference did bolster her confidence.

She vowed to the Goddess to get out from her old life and change professions when this mess was over. She was living the straight life from now on. This whole ordeal was a major wake-up call, a sign from above. *Karmic debt existed for a reason.*

"No brownie points." His gaze swept over her like a soft caress. "Smith believes you can find the killer and I'm starting to believe him. We'll sit down later and figure it all out and go from there."

His confidence in her abilities caught her off guard. "Fine by me. I want to try scrying him again. If we have a full coven of seven, we might be able to break through whatever shields he has up." Her stomach clenched at the thought of sitting down in a circle with Ellen and the other witches after all these years.

"I'll take whatever help I can get at this point, magickal or otherwise." He glanced at the door but didn't move from the spot. "If you need to talk, day or night, don't hesitate to knock. I guess I should let you get some rest."

How much rest could she get with Alex lying naked in bed in the room right next door? She gritted her teeth with sexual frustration as she imagined him spread out in all his beautiful male glory. What would it be like to lick the sexy V at his hips, and kiss up his sculpted torso?

"What's the matter? Does it bother you to have me so close? Do you think you can trust yourself?" His tone was playful, but his eyes were stormy. "You might find this hard to believe, but most women actually find me charming."

"I'm not most women." She crossed her arms over her chest.

His eyes trailed over her cleavage before resting on her pentagram tattoo. "No, you're a witch."

"Thanks, Obi Wan, for pointing out the obvious, and lucky you, you're going to meet a whole bunch of us soon. If you think I'm a lot to handle, just wait. I learned from the best." There were secrets behind these walls, ones that cut deep.

"I don't mean to pry, but you know something very personal about me, it's only fair to fill me in on the real story between you and Ellen." His expression grew serious. "Why did she kick you out?"

Anger pulsed through her veins as old wounds rose to the surface. "There's no sense trying to hide it from you. You're going to find out one way or another. I guess it's better to hear it from me rather than the gossipmongers. It was a simple matter of Ellen thinking I tried to steal her boyfriend."

His eyebrows shot up. "Did you?"

"Of course not." She sat on the edge of the bed. "I was barely sixteen years old at the time, and her boyfriend was forty-five. He was always a perv with all the girls, but looking back, he took a special interest in me. The whole thing was totally creepy. He suggested a threesome and became angry when I rebuffed his advances. He had the nerve to tell Ellen I came on to him, at which point she kicked my ass to the curb."

A mixture of anger and compassion sparked in his eyes. "What a lowlife. Okay, now I'm curious. What was his name?"

"I haven't said it out loud in years. Ed Milleu. Why?"

"Yeah, well he deserves a serious ass-kicking. I'd love to do the job. How could Ellen believe him and not you? All the pieces of this puzzle are starting to fit into place. Hell hath no fury like a witch scorned." He shook his head and ran a hand through his dark hair.

"Now you know what I'm dealing with. Most of the witches living here at the time took her side and labeled me as some sort of Lolita."

"I'm sorry you had to go through something like that." He closed the distance between them and sat down beside her on the bed. He moved his hands up and down her arms, and then gently kneaded her neck and back. Her body thrummed with desire from the sensual glide of his fingers. "Is that when you went to work for the Shadow Cabal?"

Shame and regret welled up inside her chest. A sob caught in her throat. "I was broke and hungry. I was lost and all alone in the world with no formal education, and zero money."

"What about your parents? From what I read in your file, they're both alive," he pointed out.

"My parents couldn't help me. My mother was young and impetuous when she had me. She never wanted to be saddled with a kid, neither did my dad." She stood. "My mom was a drifter, a witch who'd never been formally trained, and my dad is a Roma. He can never stay in one place for too long."

"What's a Roma?"

"A gypsy. He's the parent I inherited my psychic abilities from, although he calls the gift fortunetelling. He does it on the road for a quick buck, and then moves onto the next gig. There wasn't any room in his life for a daughter. I've only seen him a handful of times in my life."

"That's bullshit, Willow. Every child deserves a dad." He got up from the bed and stood beside her. He gently rested a hand on her shoulder for support. "What about your mom?"

"She fell madly in love with my handsome, adventurous father." Her voice took on a wistful tone. "When he left us, she never quite got over his rejection. She dropped me off here at the coven to develop my powers. She said she could see my potential and wanted me to get properly trained. She left Raven's Hollow under the guise of trying to bring my dad back to us. But I knew, deep down, she'd never find him. He didn't want to be found." The old mixture of pain and anger made her sigh deeply before going on. "The last I heard she was still looking. I talk to her sometimes. I get the occasional email, usually asking for money. I'm sorry. I'm babbling. I don't know what's come over me. I don't usually spill like this. You must have a knack for bringing it out in me." Mortified, she glanced at the floor.

He tipped her chin up, forcing her gaze to his. "I'm glad you told me, Willow. The little girl who never got over her mother abandoning her wasn't Maeve. It was you."

"I always prayed every night. Maybe if I was good, she'd come back for me, but she never did. Eventually, I accepted that she couldn't take care of me. This was the only place that ever felt like a home, but now I never stay in the same place for very long. I go wherever the Cabal sends me. I've stayed in every sleaze-ball motel across the country over the past ten years. I guess I'm more like my dad than I'd like to admit."

Goddess, she sounded pathetic and utterly damaged. She wouldn't be surprised if Alex ran from the room screaming. She had to redirect this conversation before she lost it. "What about your family? I highly doubt they're as crazy as mine."

"Both my parents are Greek immigrants." He shrugged, and she could see the pride reflected in his eyes. "Once they came here to the United

States, and worked their butts off, all they wanted to do was put down roots. They've lived in the same house for forty years."

"Wow, I think we had very different childhoods. We couldn't be more opposite." Even more reason to stay away from him. "You of all people probably can't imagine making the choices I did, but at the time, I had absolutely no support or resources. Going to work for Saint Claire seemed like my only option. I never had any idea what kind of monster he was, Alex. You have to believe me."

"Shh. It's okay. I understand." The husky sound of his voice lulled her into a state of bliss. He placed a finger to her lips. "I only blame scum like him for preying on innocents. You're a survivor. Now I understand why you did what you had to."

Tears stung her eyes and slid down her cheeks. Embarrassed, she swiped them away with the back of her hand. "I'm sorry for the tears." She hadn't talked about this subject with anyone in years. Maeve was the only person alive who knew the truth about her past and now she was dead and gone.

"I'm not judging you for the choices you made as a teenager. Stop judging yourself. You can't change your past, but you can change your present and possibly your future." He wrapped his arms around her and pressed her to his body. Immediately, she felt the insistent throb of his erection hard against her thigh and she gasped. "Let me make you feel good, Willow," he murmured into her hair.

She had no doubt Alex could coax her body into new heights of pleasure, but then where would she be afterward? Her gaze drifted to his lips. It killed her to say the words. But now she was in self-preservation mode. "I can't."

"You want me to kiss you. Admit it. But I won't, until you do." He leaned into her, his mouth a breath away. Sparks of attraction flickered between them and made butterflies flutter low in her belly. The scent of pheromones filled the air.

"I'll admit no such thing." She wanted him to kiss her, breathless. Deep down inside, she sensed Alex was the only man who could give her the passion, the heat and intensity she'd always craved. If the way he'd kissed her was any indication, the man had the ability to rock her world.

"I want to tell you something, although you probably won't believe me. I know you think I want you in my bed because of some notch on my tool belt, or because of something I have to prove to myself about witches. But the truth is I want *you*, Willow. I know it would be foolish as hell on both our parts, but I find myself thinking about you, a lot. In fact, no matter how hard I try, I can't stop," he said on a ragged breath.

"Alex," she whispered. He ran a hand through his thick mop of black hair. Her fingers curled at her sides, itching to do the same.

"People around me are showing up dead. I knew going into this case, I may not come out in one piece, but wanting you, touching you, and fantasizing about you isn't something I planned. Somewhere in the middle of all this mess, I let things get personal. What I'm trying to say, and maybe screwing up royally, is life is too short to have regrets."

His words stunned her—confounded her—and aroused her beyond belief. "What exactly are you proposing?"

"Let's take away each other's pain and turn it into pleasure, even for a little while." He brushed his thumb across her bottom lip.

"As in a no-strings-attached kind of thing for the time I'm here?"

His fingers moved to her hair and he inhaled a strand as he wrapped it around his finger. "You always smell incredible. I can't stop thinking about your scent, your taste, about you," he murmured. "Don't give me an answer right now, think about it. After all, we're both consenting adults. I know it's unorthodox as hell, but we're human right?"

"At least one of us is." She still couldn't forget the way he'd treated her, or the biting pain of his earlier comment. *I don't like witches or anything they stand for.* "Let me get this straight, you don't like me for everything I stand for?" she said, throwing his words back in his face. "But you're willing to take me to your bed?"

And yet she couldn't deny the thrill of excitement pulsing through her veins at the prospect of giving in to her wildest fantasies. Nothing and no one had ever turned her on like this, and she had only kissed him. A part of her embraced the challenge of making him realize all witches weren't the same.

"You're taking my words out of context. We're both risking our lives. We don't know what can happen from one day to the next," he whispered close to her ear.

. . .

"I don't disagree." But she didn't trust men, particularly those who condemned her kind. She tried to act nonchalant, as if his sultry proposition didn't stir up a myriad of emotions that she kept hidden under lock and key. Lust and longing and her raw need to be held by a man, broke through the surface with the rush of a tidal wave, but she held herself back. "I admit I'm intrigued, and I'd be lying if I said I haven't thought about this very thing. There's just one small problem: I don't completely trust you. And before I'd even consider any sort of physical relationship, there are some things I'd like to teach you first that you're in serious need of learning."

His face hardened a fraction. "I guess I earned that. And I have your answer, for now. I'll just have to convince you otherwise." He glanced at his watch. "I'll meet you downstairs at seven p.m. sharp to go over a game plan, which should give you enough time to catch up on some sleep."

Alex walked to the door and put his hand on the knob before turning to face her again. "Despite the crap I've given you, I know you'll be able to help us. I'm glad you're here, Willow."

Rendered momentarily speechless by the look of heat and certainty in his eyes, she smiled. There was a lot more to this gorgeous man than his looks. Despite their obvious differences, he was compassionate, wicked smart, not to mention, brutally honest, and most of all, he listened when she spoke. Who knows, maybe she could teach him a thing or two after all. Before she could stop herself, the words flew from her lips, "Me too."

When the door closed, Willow kicked off her boots and plopped down on the center of the bed, sending her coat and her tote bag flying. A faint buzzing sound erupted from across the room. "Oh shit."

There was a quick knock, and before she could push her legs off the bed to answer it, Alex pushed open the door and sauntered back into the room. "Hey, I almost forgot—"

Her heart slammed into her chest. "Alex?"

Immediately his gaze rested on the contents of her tote bag strewn out on the floor, and the hot pink case of her Pocket Rocket. "What's with the buzzing noise?"

"Alex, no." She jumped off the bed and lunged for it, but he was quicker.

"Hmm, what do we have here?" He picked up the case and held it over her head. His sexy grin made her insides squirm.

"Uh, it's nothing."

"It doesn't look like nothing and it sure as hell doesn't sound like nothing. Fess up and don't *toy* with me," he murmured and smiled wide.

"Real...funny." She jumped up to tear it out of his hands, but in her stocking feet, she barely reached his shoulders. "Nothing for you to concern yourself with," she huffed, hoping the floor would open up and swallow her whole.

His dark eyes smoldered. The look alone made her melt. "Everything you do concerns me. I'd love to know what other surprises you have up your sleeve. This could get interesting."

"Give it back."

"I don't know who the guy was who hurt you, but whoever he was, he's an idiot. You're funny, and smart, not to mention sexy as all hell, especially when you're mad."

His words left her breathless. "You seem to have that effect on me." She reached for it again and failed miserably. Frustrated, she blew a stray hunk of hair off her face and placed her hands on her hips.

"Well, I'd like to have another effect on you and it has nothing at all to do with anger."

"This isn't what you think. I, um, well, it is, but I can explain." Her face flushed. What kind of woman carried a vibrator in her purse? *A woman who didn't have sex for two years and six months and twenty-six days, that's who.*

"No need to explain yourself. I was just having a little fun with you. Besides, a piece of plastic is no substitute for the real thing." He stepped closer to her, his lips only inches from hers.

"This is your last warning. I'm not responsible for what I'll do."

"Neither am I." He fisted her hair in his free hand, then angled her head up and crushed his lips down on hers in a blistering kiss. He licked her bottom lip and she moaned deep in her throat. The case clattered to the floor with a thud and he pulled her flush against his hard body.

His lips were hot and urgent against her mouth. When he delved his tongue inside, blood fired in her veins. She melted from the passion in his kiss and met him stroke for stroke. He sucked on her tongue and she nearly lost her mind. The sheer heat of his mouth was like liquid fire, burning her from her head to her toes and everywhere in between.

Even in her limited sexual experience, no one had ever kissed her like this. Would Alex ruin her for all other men? The thought whispered through her mind, but at this moment, she didn't care.

His lips moved to the shell of her ear, and then he began licking and biting her neck before he stopped to look into her eyes. His were dark with arousal. "I want you, Willow."

A combination of his words and the pure need reflected in his eyes made all her protests die in her throat. She answered him by pulling his head down for another kiss. She knotted her fingers through the thick strands of his silky hair, angling his head closer.

The kiss became deeper, hotter, and more urgent. Her breasts grew heavy, her nipples tight and aching. He trailed his fingers along her rib cage and caressed the underside of her breasts and her entire body tightened with need. Then he pressed his erection against her stomach, sending a delicious tingle down her spine. Apparently, the man was large everywhere.

He broke away. "I know you want me too. I can feel it when you kiss me." She couldn't find the words to argue. He unbuttoned the top of her sweater and pushed his warm hands over the swell of her breasts.

His breath grew harsh. He ran his fingers over her pulse racing wildly at her throat. He bent his head and licked her nipple through the lace of her bra. Before her knees buckled beneath her, his arm went around her waist.

"Alex, please," she whispered on a moan.

"Baby, you drive me insane. I'm going to see how many times I can make you come."

"Is that a promise?" She shivered, her sex instantly wet. Before she could respond to his sultry promise, he lifted her off her feet and set her on the edge of the bed. Willow was so caught up with anticipation, and the intoxicating taste of him still on her lips, she couldn't bring herself to stop. She reached out to unbutton his shirt, when she heard a knock on the door. She froze.

After a few minutes, when she didn't answer, footsteps pounded down the hall. Her heart thudded against her ribs when she realized they'd never even bothered to lock the door. What if someone had barged in?

What if one of the other witches had caught her naked in bed with Alex? It certainly wouldn't help in the "blending in" department. The gossipmongers would have a field day. Her reputation was tarnished enough as it was. Did Alex even care about the potential repercussions she could've been facing? And once again she wondered if she was just a sexual conquest, or was this a way to prove he held no animosity toward witches?

She scooted off the bed and tried to catch her breath. When she glanced over at him, his jaw was clenched, his expression murderous. "Who'd be knocking on my door? The only one who knows we're here is Ellen and I seriously doubt it would be her." She buttoned her sweater and glanced at the door. "I think you should go."

"I texted Cayden and Brodie and gave them our room numbers." Alex ran a hand through his messy hair.

"Oh." What could she have been thinking? Anger welled in her chest. A few kisses, caresses, and she'd turned into a wanton female. She blamed it all on her dry spell.

He must've realized she was dismissing him, but instead of acting pissed, he seemed amused. He caressed her cheek and bent down to whisper in her ear. "I'll text you the meeting spot. Don't be late." After he picked up the Pocket Rocket off the floor, he handed it to her, a smile playing across his full lips. "If you are, I'll know exactly what you've been doing."

CHAPTER 10

The next morning, Alex, Cayden, and Brodie, along with most of the construction crew, had gathered for a meeting in the new addition. After old man Donato had made introductions all around and Alex was fairly certain their cover was intact, he sent Brodie and a few of the other guys out for supplies.

He yawned, feeling exhausted. He'd waited until all the women had congregated outside for their crack-of-dawn circle thing, then he, Cayden, and Brodie placed SED's—security enhancement detectors—on all the doors, and most of the windows. If a bird so much as pecked at the glass, an alarm would sound. And in the event of an attack, all hell would break loose.

"How do you propose we find out who the hell the bastard is? Do we question every male who darkens the doorway? 'Excuse me, we're on the construction crew, and were wondering if you've murdered any witches in your spare time?'" Alex muttered as he unpacked rolls of insulation material from a crate.

"I don't think they'll be too responsive," Cayden shot back, helping him lay the materials on the work table. While part of the crew had gone out to buy materials, a few of the men had stayed behind to do ductwork.

Alex glanced over at the three remaining guys, and nothing about them stood out or appeared sinister in any way. From what he could tell, while a couple of them did have tats, none of them appeared to be of a snake.

All three had earbuds in and were focused on the work at hand. With their paint-splattered coveralls and scuffed-up work boots, they looked like regular working stiffs. It was hard to imagine, but one of these guys could be a serial killer.

Still hovering over the worktable, Alex glanced at the materials list Donato had given him when they'd arrived in the new ritual room. The older man had been sworn to secrecy, vowing to tell no one their real identities.

"We could narrow down our suspects by going through the high priestess's list and the one Donato gave us by cross-referencing the two with anyone who has a record," Cayden suggested.

Alex shook his head in frustration. "There's one problem. Most of the work, like the electrical, the HVAC, and the flooring are all subcontracted out, but the general contractors sign into the coven under Donato and Sons."

"Great. That makes our job fun." Cayden reached for the last of the insulation from the crate and stacked it on the subfloor. "He could be walking in and out of here right under our noses and we might not ever know it's him."

"The bastard's probably hiding in plain sight, the type no one would ever suspect. But that's where Willow comes in. She was able to sense the debris found on Kimber's body belonged to the killer. If he walks through the door, she'll know." Alex glanced at his watch. "She should be down here any minute." A heady anticipation consumed his thoughts, forcing him out of his foul mood.

They had a killer on the loose and were no closer to stopping him at this point than the day before. Not only was every woman in this house in danger, but he had brought Willow here, which meant she was just as much of a target as all the others. Like it or not, he was growing quite attached to the little witch.

Cayden laughed. "Yeah, sounds like a long shot."

After the way they'd left things yesterday, Alex wasn't sure how Willow would act toward him this morning. She'd been downright withdrawn and distant when they'd met for a briefing last night. If given the chance, he'd pick up where they'd left off and take her in every position possible, as many times as she'd let him, and not because he wanted to get her out of his system, not anymore.

He couldn't stop thinking about her and the fearless way she called him out on his shit after he'd behaved like an insufferable asshole. Hell, even her stubbornness was sexy. Despite all the shit that went down, she was so ready to sacrifice herself for a coven that had cast her aside.

While she didn't trust him, it seemed like she wanted him to try and win her over. His entire perception of her had shifted now that he understood what she'd been through. He wasn't sure if it was her unfailing determination or eagerness that had him thinking about her day and night. She somehow managed to draw out a possessive, caveman side to him that he'd never experienced with any other woman. He cursed under his breath. He had no business obsessing over her when he should be thinking about solving a murder case. She was a distraction he didn't need.

"Alex? Where the hell did you just go?" Cayden's asked, sounding suspicious.

"Sorry. I was saying, she's been brought here for a reason. We need to give her the opportunity to do her thing," Alex said, sounding annoyed. He shoved the list, along with the blueprints for the addition to the side of the table. He'd barely slept a wink, and if it were possible, he was even more tired than before. She'd kept him awake long into the night with her name on his lips and his hand down the front of his boxer briefs.

"Hold on. When did you start buying into all this witchcraft bullshit? Does the fact that you want to get in Willow's pants have anything to with it?" Cayden asked, rubbing his hands on his coveralls.

"Don't be an asshole. There's nothing going on between us." Alex came around the table to help him unload the last of the materials." He hated lying to his best friend, but telling him the truth wasn't an option. Alex didn't know what this thing was between them. Well, that wasn't entirely true. She intrigued him on every possible level.

"Who are you trying to convince? I know when you're crushing on a woman, Denopoulos, and you don't exactly have a stellar track record. Think what this one would do if you pissed her off, or she caught you messing around? She'd probably kick your ass again, or worse, curse you for all eternity and make your dick fall off," Cayden said with a chuckle.

"Has anyone ever told you you're a dick?" Funny, Alex couldn't imagine ever getting tired of sexy, beautiful, tough as nails Willow McCray, the same woman who cried over a stuffed animal. His thoughts were interrupted by his phone buzzing. He pulled it out of his pocket and glanced at the screen. *Tate.* He picked up the call. "Talk to me, man."

"Well, I found traces of bone and feather particles on the Wood girl's body as well. The imprint of magick left behind all point to a fae. The way the flesh has been eviscerated, and the butchering marks on the bones, makes me believe this sick fucker's consuming his victims."

"What?" His gut clenched with fury. "Jesus, I didn't think this case could get any more twisted. What could his motive be for doing something so sick?" Over the years, he'd come across his share of bizarre cases, especially amongst the more bloodthirsty mages in their world, but nothing came close to this kind of abject violence.

"The toxicology report confirmed what I suspected. Both vics had a considerable amount of heroin and booze in their systems. Both girls were easy prey, probably no fun for a sick bastard like him to kill. But now that he's had a taste of power, he may become more selective in whom he targets. Even choose victims based on their unique talents. Dark fae can absorb another mage's power through fluid exchange, and in some rare cases, when they consume the flesh of their victims."

Alex gritted his teeth as Tate's words sank in. Automatically, his thoughts shifted to Willow. She was preternaturally strong, fast, and the only witch he'd ever come across who could read a person's mind like most people read the newspaper. A surge of protectiveness welled up in his chest. He'd kill the bastard himself before he'd let anything happen to her.

"All he has to do is watch and observe. Most witches have huge egos. They're proud of their abilities," Tate interjected, interrupting his thoughts. "If he's a master manipulator, it wouldn't take much to convince his next vic to play a game of show and tell."

"It would be like shooting witches in a barrel around here. Even more reason for all of us to stay put and go forward with the undercover op. If he has a connection to the coven, then he's watching these women every day. Did you get anything on the shirt?"

"One of the guys in the lab said it's made of hemp. Not much to go on I'm afraid. They make those garments everywhere." There was a noise in the background and his voice began to fade in and out. "Sorry, bad reception. Look, I'm beat. I'll check in later."

"Thanks." Alex ended the call and shoved his cell back in his pocket. His head buzzed in every direction as he tried to digest this new information. He glanced over at Cayden, who was staring at him expectantly. "You probably heard most of it, but I'll fill you in on the rest."

"C'mon, let's head to the kitchen. You can do it on the way. I smell coffee and I have a feeling it's going to be a long-ass day."

The coven kitchen was an enormous state-of-the-art restaurant-sized room. Baskets of fruits and clusters of candles lined the various granite and butcher block surfaces. Bundles of fragrant dried herbs hung from wooden beams. Large copper cauldrons gleamed under the overhead lights. Alex peeked inside of one, half expecting to find a shrinking head bobbing on the surface. He exhaled a pent-up breath when he realized it was filled with oatmeal. It might be unfair of him, but some ingrained beliefs were hard to overcome. Sunlight streamed in from a wall of windows, bathing the room in soft, yellow light. He gulped. It was nothing at all like he expected.

He turned his attention to the eclectic group gathered in the corner. The room buzzed with women crying, shouting, and hugging each other. The news of Kimber's murder must've spread like a bad virus. Scantily clad in nightclothes and short, silky robes, the group of young women looked like something out of a frat boy's wet dream—minus the emotional baggage. He walked to the coffee maker, filled two mugs, and handed one to Cayden. No one seemed to notice them, too wrapped up in their grief and conversations. After a few minutes, things slowly mellowed among the group. The crying reduced to sniffles and the shouting got hugged out.

Alex took a sip from his mug, turned to Cayden, and whispered, "I think it's time we offer our sympathies and introduce ourselves. Let's see if we can find out anything."

Cayden's face broke out in a huge grin as his eyes locked on the group of pretty women. "Scratch what I said earlier about this job not being any fun. I think I might like this place after all."

"Down, boy, remember, you're on the job, not here to pick up women, witches no less." Alex whispered, glancing around the kitchen. Who was he kidding? He was talking out of both sides of his mouth. Damn, he was in trouble.

"Talk about the pot calling the cauldron black," Cayden pointed out. "When I came to your room yesterday to check in, you reeked of a woman's perfume. I know you were with Willow and don't try to deny it."

He couldn't, but he still flashed Cayden a silent "fuck off" as they approached the group around the table. He turned and extended his hand to a tall, attractive female with long, dark hair. After a few minutes, her head snapped toward the door. Curious, his gaze followed, and he swallowed hard as Willow appeared in the doorway. A completely unexpected flare of protectiveness shot through him. *This should be interesting.*

Willow took a tentative step and felt all eyes around the room lock on her. She wanted to turn tail and run, especially when her heart began to hammer painfully against her ribs. She couldn't remember the last time she'd been this nervous, but she'd be damned before she gave these women the satisfaction.

Her gaze swept over the crowd, noticing a few familiar faces, but most of the women were new since she'd lived here. She stuffed her hands in the front pockets of her hoodie so no one would notice them shaking.

From across the room, she caught sight of Alex and their eyes locked. Heat shot up from her belly and made her flush. She looked away a little too quickly, feigning indifference. "Please, don't stop talking on my account," she said, glancing at the group of women congregated around the worn, oak table. After an awkward silence, the room began to buzz again.

A pure white cat with crystal blue eyes darted across the kitchen directly in front of her path and jumped onto the counter. She tilted her head to the side, and Willow swore she was listening to their entire conversation.

"Well, well, look what the cat dragged in, literally. Willow McCray, I always knew you'd come back." A stunning witch with sandy brown hair emerged from the throng. The hair was longer, sleeker, but the face was the same, and apparently so was the attitude.

"Hey, Gillian. It has been a long time. I'm truly sorry about Kimber." Willow walked over to the coffee maker and poured herself a steaming mug. Maybe caffeine and a sugar boost would give her the guts to face the others head on. She glanced around for the sugar bowl but couldn't find anything but Agave syrup. She frowned and turned back around.

Gillian arched her perfectly shaped eyebrows. "I tried to warn her. I got a message from the other side." Her expression turned introspective. "We both know you didn't come back here to offer your sympathies. What's the real reason? I hear you plan on sticking around. I think I speak for everyone when I say that would be a mistake."

"I see you're still Ellen's loyal pet. I guess some things never change," Willow said and blew on the rim of her mug.

"You'd be surprised by how things have changed around here, and for the better," Gillian insisted, waving her hand in the air at her surroundings. "What about you? Have you changed, Willow? Or are you still throwing yourself at other people's boyfriends? Perhaps you've taken up another hobby?"

All of the women around the table laughed, except for a petite blonde with a head full of long, enviable curls. Was she the only holdout? Willow made sure to plaster a fake smile across her face as if Gillian's words didn't slice open an old wound like the edge of a blade.

Yup, she'd heard all the names before. *Man stealer, Little Lolita, backstabbing bitch, tart.* Well, Gillian and the rest of these women could think what they wanted. She wasn't about to correct them on ancient history. She had more important things to do than right the wrongs of her past.

On the other hand, Gillian had put the subject out on the table, she'd be damned if she didn't give her something juicy to remember her by. "No. My hobbies haven't changed much. In fact, my appetite has only gotten bigger." Willow suppressed a grin as she set her mug on the counter and crossed to the center of the kitchen. She placed both hands on her hips, arched her back, and stuck out her boobs. "You'd better hang on to your men, ladies, because I'm back."

A few of the women glared at her, while Gillian's face flamed red with anger. Willow turned, and her eyes locked with Alex's from across the room. He must've seen the entire catty exchange, yet his expression gave nothing away. She'd kill to find out what he was thinking right now, but she'd have to get in line. A few of the girls congregating around the table had now moved to where Alex and Cayden stood. They practically draped themselves over both males, gazing at each one with open, unabashed interest.

She couldn't blame them. Willow guessed most of the women here weren't used to seeing men around the coven. Besides, both were gorgeous, but there was something incredibly sexy and almost dangerous about Alex's dark, brooding looks. "Okay, ladies, the show's over, unless anyone has anything they'd like to add?"

Another witch stepped forward, tall and thin with raven hair down her back. She was a bitch on wheels from what Willow remembered. "Hello, Saje. I'd say it's nice to see you again after all these years, but I hate to lie. Karma and all." Once again the women laughed, but at least not at Willow's expense this time.

Saje's face turned bright red. "You might be back, but you're not welcome here, Willow."

As Willow braced for another onslaught of insults and accusations, she reminded herself the reason she was there and tried to blow it off. "Bummer," she said in a deadpan tone. "But I'm not going anywhere."

There was nothing like being thrown into a ring with a bunch of rabid Dobermans. She couldn't show any fear or they'd eat her alive. Despite her ballsy façade, hopefully, no one would notice she was still shaking from head to toe.

"Of course she's welcome. Don't be such a tight-ass, Saje." The pretty blonde stepped in front of Saje and smiled. "I'm Delilah. Things have been difficult around here, as you can imagine. We've barely recovered from hearing about Maeve's murder and now poor Kimber. This is almost too much to bear."

"It's nice to meet you, Delilah. Look, I want you to know I didn't come back here to stir the cauldron, so to speak, especially after everything." Willow held her breath, waiting for Delilah to make some off-color comment to match the others. But she smiled instead, throwing Willow completely off balance. "I'm sure you've heard my name around here. I'm guessing my reputation precedes me." Willow glanced at the other witches as a fresh wave of nerves settled in her stomach.

When Delilah didn't respond, Willow crossed her arms across her chest.

"Okay, I'll bite. How come you're not ribbing me like everyone else around here?"

"I have heard about you, Willow, and not just the nasty rumors," Delilah said with a genuine smile. They both turned to the sound of high heels click-clacking along the tile. Saje and Gillian stomped out of the kitchen. "Pay no attention to them. The word is you're quite the psychic. I'm truly sorry about Maeve's death. I didn't get to know her as much as I would've liked. Deep down, I sensed she was a good person."

There was a kindness in her ice-blue eyes, an innate goodness that shined through from her soul. Taken aback by her sincerity, Willow felt lighter than she had in months. "Thanks for the support. It was starting to feel like the first day of school around here. I came back to help find Maeve's killer and I don't plan on resting until I do. Maeve would've done the same for me." Willow exhaled. "I think Gillian said what everyone was probably already thinking."

"There's no excuse for rudeness. It took a lot of guts to come back and face everyone. I admire what you're trying to do. It'll take time for them to get used to seeing you around every day again, but they'll come around."

"I love your optimism. Let's hope it's contagious," Willow said with a bitter laugh. She glanced around the kitchen to the bundles of herbs tied in ribbons and hanging from the beams "Are you still using Rocky's for your supplies?" The shop was one of her favorite places to browse when she'd lived in the Hollow.

Delilah shook her head. "No, it closed down. The owners retired to Florida and apparently couldn't find anyone to buy the place."

"What a shame. It was a cool store. I used to dream about owning my own place someday." Willow picked up her mug off the counter and smiled, feeling a tinge of sadness. It all seemed like such a long time ago.

"Funny, me too. Now we have a guy who comes here selling his wares. He doesn't always carry what we need for our potions, and he's expensive, but at least his herbs are decent. He grows them himself. It doesn't hurt that he's hot. Every girl here has a thing for him and he knows it. He flirts like crazy with everyone, even with Ellen. It's probably the only reason he's still hanging around." Delilah laughed and reached for a handful of seeds.

"It doesn't surprise me." Ellen always did have an ego a mile long and had prided herself on being at the center of male attention. Willow pushed the thought aside and decided to change the subject. "I'm curious. How come the murders haven't forced any of the girls to leave? I mean, it must have crossed your mind. Why aren't you packing your bags and running from the house?"

"Don't you see? If we leave, then he's won. We don't want to give him that kind of power over us. We're stronger as a group. When we divine together we can pool our magick. Besides, you're here to help us, right?"

"Of course," Willow said, hoping she could do something right for a change. She glanced around at the newly remodeled kitchen. All of the appliances had also been upgraded to stainless steel. Tall oak cabinets, along with a fancy ceramic backsplash had also been added. "How are you guys keeping this place afloat? And making all of these renovations? What are you doing for work?"

Delilah shrugged. "We all do odd jobs, but over the last few months we've been working for a local antique dealer. His shop was robbed of a bunch of jewelry and pricey art. Luckily, we were able to locate a lot of his missing inventory," she pointed out. "The only downside was the cops showing up at all hours to question us. They wanted to make sure we had no connection with the robberies. Aside from that, it's been quite lucrative for us actually."

Willow's mind reeled in about ten different directions at what the witches were able to accomplish as a group. "What if we try divining together to find the killer? We might be able to break through his shields with our collective magick."

"As long as we have something that belonged to him, I don't see why not." Hope blossomed on Delilah's face.

"I think that can be arranged." Willow would make sure to ask Alex for any evidence he had from the crime scene. Hey, it was worth a try. "Is there a chance you could convince the girls to meet tonight, say around midnight when the moon's at its fullest? We have to act now before he goes after someone else."

"I promise. There's nothing more important than finding the man responsible." Delilah pulled out her phone "I'm sending a group text as we speak." After she finished typing, she shoved her cell back in her pocket.

"Thank you." Willow sighed with relief. It was a start anyway. "What's your gift, Delilah?"

"I read Tarot cards, and I make my own soaps and lotions that have healing properties." Delilah reached for a small purple soap from a basket next to the sink and handed it to Willow. "Here, try it."

"Thanks. I will. Maeve told me about you." Willow held the soap to her nose. The fragrant scents of vanilla and cherry blossoms flared in her nostrils.

"You said you came back here to find the killer. I want you to know, I'll help you any way I can." When Delilah placed her hand on Willow's arm she sensed her sincerity. It would be nice to have a friend in the group.

Embarrassed by her earlier behavior, she'd made a fool of herself by playing into both Gillian and Saje's hands when she should have taken the high road. "What you saw back there, the comment about 'holding onto your boyfriends,' I didn't mean—"

"There's no need to explain. I learned a long time ago not to believe everything you hear around this place. Besides, I'm in no position to judge anyone. This all allegedly happened a long time ago, way before I moved in." Delilah's attention was diverted to the spectacle now around the table. "The way the girls are flirting over there you'd think they've never seen flesh-and-blood males before. It must be an outlet for their grief."

A surge of jealousy made Willow's pulse jump. She sipped her coffee, but the taste was bitter on her tongue. She'd never felt particularly possessive about a man, until now. The truth was, she had no claims on Alex and planned on keeping it that way. He could talk and flirt with whomever he wanted. For a man who supposedly didn't like witches, he was getting awfully friendly with them.

"Those two are hot, especially the dark-haired one," Delilah murmured, glancing in their direction.

"Hmm, I hadn't noticed," Willow whispered, hoping the lie wouldn't make her nose grow. "I was too busy dodging bullets." Thank the Goddess she didn't take Alex up on his offer and let things go too far.

Even if she did lie awake all night fantasying about him and all the wild things he'd do to her in bed. It was clear from the way he was eating up all the attention from the other girls, the man was a player. Willow tried to not to let her disappointment show. "Who are they?"

"The other girls said they're part of the construction crew for our new expansion. Trust me, none of the guys have ever looked like these two. I shouldn't be going on at a time like this. We all saw last night's newscast. You can't trust anyone these days." Delilah angled her head toward the curvaceous dark-haired witch who was making cow eyes at Alex. "That's Arabella. I overheard her earlier. She said both girls knew their killers. Do you think it's possible?"

Before Willow could respond, Alex unraveled himself from the throng of women, and strutted over to where they stood. Her breath caught in her throat at the sight of him up close. Delilah was right. He was hot, especially in a pair of ripped jeans and a simple black tee shirt. She couldn't help but admire the way the cotton stretched over his broad shoulders and bulging arms.

"I don't think we've met. I'm Alex." He extended his hand to Delilah, and then to Willow. His expression remained blank.

The moment their fingers touched, his thoughts entered her mind like a soft caress. *You look beautiful this morning. Standing here and acting as if we're strangers is making me crazy. I want to drag you into the nearest closet and ravish the hell out of you.* His voice was a sultry whisper.

Heat shot up and down her arm. Willow tried to pull her hand away, but Alex held tight. She took a big gulp from her mug instead, hoping to hide her expression.

"I couldn't sleep last night imagining you touching yourself while you thought about me. Did you? I know I did. I came so hard thinking about burying myself in your tight, little —"

Willow choked on her coffee, going into a coughing fit. Alex patted her lightly on the back. His luscious lips twisted into a smile. "Are you okay?"

"F-fine. It went down the wrong pipe."

"I should get back to work. Nice meeting both of you." He nodded at her and Delilah and then motioned to Cayden. They both turned and left the kitchen.

Mortified, Willow wiped her mouth on her sleeve. She stood there trying to catch her breath, and before she could contemplate all the ways she was going to kill Alex, her phone buzzed. "Excuse me," she said to Delilah and pulled out her cell from her back pocket.

Meet me in room 302. Three o'clock sharp. Make sure no one sees you. Alex.

Her stomach dipped to her toes at the thought of going to Maeve's old room after her murder. She felt all the color drain from her face as she shoved her cell back in her pocket.

"Willow? Is everything okay?"

"Yeah, it's nothing. I have a headache. I haven't eaten for a while. I'm probably just hungry."

"C'mon, how about some breakfast?" Delilah pulled her over to the fridge. "We usually eat together after the morning meditation, but considering the circumstances, we skipped it today."

"Morning meditation?"

"We start at five o'clock, religiously. It really sets your intention for the rest of the day and enhances our magick. I like to think it brings about peace, love, and harmony in the group. Well, in most instances. You have to join us. I bet it will help bridge the gap between you and some of the girls. It's a great way to heal old wounds."

"Seriously?" Willow suppressed the urge to snort at the idea. If there was one thing she despised more than being forced into a house full of catty women, it was getting up at dawn to meditate about peace, love, and harmony with them. But the insistent rumble in her stomach made her protests die in her throat.

Maybe if she ate something she'd figure a way to get out of it gracefully. If Delilah only knew the real reason she was here, she'd probably demand Willow leave immediately. She wasn't exactly lying to her. She was simply omitting the more sordid details.

Delilah passed Willow the bowl of seeds she'd been munching on. "They're hemp. We get them from the guy I told you about."

"Thanks. I'll pass."

"How about a muffin?" Delilah pointed to a basket on the counter. "I baked them myself. I'm learning to use herbs in all my foods. I'm not the best. Give me your honest opinion."

"Okay." Willow reached for one and took a bite. She was surprised when she didn't taste the slightest hint of sweetness. The muffin stuck to the roof of her mouth, and she wondered if the main ingredient was sawdust. She took a big sip of coffee to wash down the gritty taste. "They have a unique flavor, like nothing I've ever tasted before."

"They're carob, zucchini, and parsley. We're all vegan here." Delilah smiled.

"Surely you're joking."

"Afraid not." Delilah shook her head and pulled out a container of what looked like lumpy oatmeal, a bag of cantaloupe, yogurt, and almond milk from the fridge. She placed everything, along with paper plates, spoons, and a bowl on the counter.

"I'm not sure what you like. I do the shopping and Belinda does the cooking." Delilah pointed to a tiny elfin-looking witch with chin length blonde hair. "We all take turns helping out, but Gillian does the bulk of the cleaning and really looks out for everybody around here."

Willow shrugged. "Okay, so maybe she's not all bad."

"Trust me, she's not. She's actually a really cool girl, but I don't condone her judgement of you, especially when she's been involved in plenty of her own drama."

Curious, Willow wanted to probe, but decided against it for now. She'd find out one way or another. There were some things that never changed. No one could ever keep a secret around here for very long, and she doubted the new girls were any different.

When Willow didn't make a move to dive into any of the food, Delilah's pointed to the blender on the counter. "If you don't like anything here, we also have smoothies and almost every kind of green drink. I can make a pretty mean wheat grass, kale, and kiwi combo. It's great for energy and makes your hair crazy shiny."

It was way too early for this. "I'm guessing the eggs, bacon, and whole milk are out of the question?" she asked, glancing over the top of Delilah's blonde head into the fridge.

Delilah laughed. "We don't have anything like that here. This place wasn't vegan when you lived here?"

"No. I wouldn't have survived. The staple foods back then were hot dogs, chips, soda, and burgers. I guess I've gotten pretty used to eating junk food and it's all I live on." Willow glanced around at the odd assortment of food, and her appetite vanished. "Thanks. I think I'll stick with the coffee for now."

"How are you settling in? Is there anything you need? I feel badly about the way you've been treated so far. Granted, this is a tough group, but I've learned more about the craft living here over the past year than I have in all the books I've ever read, and the comradery is amazing. There must be something one of us can do to help you find this killer. Don't try to take this on alone, Willow."

Willow perked up at the opening. "I do need help with a spell I found in one of the ancient grimoires. If I'm right, it could be the key to vanquishing the killer."

"I'm by no means an expert. Nadia's more seasoned in that area of witchcraft. Give me the book and I'll ask her to have a look." Delilah said with a nod. "Is there anything else?"

Willow glanced over at the three witches around the table. She did a mental head count, including Ellen, Gillian and Saje, they had a total of eight women, more than enough to cast a powerful circle. "Well, there is one more thing. What do you know about black magick?"

CHAPTER 11

*W*illow climbed the stairs to the third floor and tiptoed down the hall toward Maeve's old room. Every now and then she peeked over her shoulder to make sure no one was around. Thankfully, the floor was completely empty.

The only sound came from the pounding of her heart and the creak of the floorboards. When she finally reached Maeve's door, she held her breath as she turned the antique glass knob. The door protested on its hinges, but after a little shake, it finally opened. A ribbon of late afternoon sun streamed in from the window, casting the room in pale yellow light.

Once inside, the door slammed shut behind her. She jolted and spun around while her heart pounded in her chest. She glanced around the room, but no one was there. Maeve must've spelled the door to maintain her privacy, but it didn't make the effect any less unnerving. *Even in death her essence lived on.*

No sign of Alex yet.

To think the killer could be lurking around the coven, waiting... watching, made Willow break out in a cold sweat. After years of working for the Cabal, she'd come to terms with her own mortality, but having a bolt shot into the back of her neck wasn't how she pictured herself going.

Throughout the day, she'd run into several men hanging around the coven. Some came in to deliver packages and lingered far longer than necessary, probably to get a glimpse of a house full of young, attractive women. She supposed this place was a jackpot for the UPS guy.

But then there were others, men who wore coveralls and sported tool belts slung low on their hips and seemed to blend into the woodwork. She could feel their eyes on her every time she walked by.

There was also the occasional repairman, the mailman, and even a couple of frat brothers who knocked on the door as a dare, no doubt to get a peek into a real witches' coven. She didn't have the slightest pull toward any of them. Not sure what it all meant, she pondered the connections like pieces of a giant jigsaw puzzle as she stared out the window.

Dust motes floated through the air and formed an arc of rainbow light above the bed. She inhaled and caught the faintest trace of Maeve's flowery perfume. Grateful she got here before Alex, she wanted to have one last look around in private before the rest of her friend's stuff was boxed up and given to the MBI as evidence.

She glanced over at the piles of clothes, shoes, and jewelry strewn out across the top of Maeve's dresser. From the way the drawers were still haphazardly opened with clothes spilling out the sides, she could tell someone had been in here poking around.

Alex had mentioned that the agents were going to search the room. He said they'd taken Maeve's computer, as well as her diary, in hopes of finding a clue that might lead them to the killer.

The only thing that hadn't been taken or upended was a framed photo of her and Maeve on her sixteenth birthday. Even the thick coating of dust hadn't detracted from the open joy on both their young faces. She had fond memories of that rare, happy day. One last bit of innocence for both of them—before Willow had been kicked out of the coven—and before Maeve had turned to drugs to solve her problems.

Tears filled her eyes as she reached for the small, simple frame. When her fingers closed over the edge, an image of Maeve appeared in her mind's eye. She was bent over a large butcher-block table surrounded by potion bottles and glass paneled walls. Fear and dread practically emanated from her pores like a heady toxin.

Behind her, misters sprayed lush potted plants that were lined up on the ceramic tiled floor. Willow instantly recognized the room as the coven greenhouse. The pungent aroma of mandrake root and rosemary perfumed the air. Maeve had been in a rush, using a mortar and pestle to grind the herbs together into a fine paste. *Did she sense she was going to die?*

Willow blinked and the vision drifted away like a wave getting swallowed up by the ocean. She stretched on the bed, still holding the frame, and rested her head against the pillow, hoping to see more. A high-pitched squeal made her jump. The picture slipped from her grasp and smashed onto the floor with a thwack.

The scent of sugar cookies filled the air, followed by a puff of pink sparkle dust. Small, purple, winged creatures fluttered above her head. When she tried to sit up, they dove straight for her face. Tiny claws scraped against her cheeks and chin. And before she could reach for her athame, her wrists were forced against the bedpost. Shocked by their strength, she tried not to panic. Before she could cast a spell, sparkle dust flew into her mouth, making her gag. "What the—"

When she kicked-out with her legs, more flew out from under the bed, and tied the laces on her Converses together. "Seriously." Her heart was pounding wildly in her chest by the time her *athame* was lifted out of her hip belt, the tip now pointed between her eyes, "H-hey, guys, can we talk about this?"

The door creaked open and her head snapped to the sound. Alex appeared and rushed into the room with his gun drawn. "Willow? What the hell's going on?"

"The Q&A portion of the program comes later. What does it look like?" She angled her chin toward his laser gun. "Alex, please. Shoot!"

For a split second he froze, and his eyes filled with dread. He recovered so fast, she thought she imagined it. With a steady hand, he aimed the barrel toward the pixies at her feet and pulled the trigger. The entire room shook with the force of a mini-explosion. Purple ash floated through the air and made her cough. Pixies flew in every direction, disappearing through a crack in the wall.

"Holy shit, are you okay?" Alex holstered his gun and rushed to her side, helping her off the bed, making sure to avoid the broken glass and pixie ash.

She sat up, rubbed a tiny drop of blood from her cheek. "I'm fine. They must've found a way inside and built a nest. It happens when it gets cold." When she glanced at the cracked glass on the floor, an overwhelming sense of grief and loneliness came over her at the irony. The smashed-up frame was a metaphor for the broken pieces of their lives.

"Willow?" His eyes trailed over her face before resting on the picture. "Are you sure you're okay?"

"I told you, I'm fine." She got off the bed, looking around for something to sweep up the mess on the floor.

Alex nodded. "I'm sorry about your frame, but we can always get you a new one. What were you doing before you got attacked?"

Of course he was right, but it didn't make her feel any better. She exhaled and ran a hand through her hair. "I had a vision. I saw Maeve right before her death. She was making a vanquishing potion to use on the killer." Willow didn't realize the truth of the vision until she said the words aloud.

"A vanquishing potion?" His gaze narrowed. "Did she finish it? Where would this potion be?"

"I might've found out if I hadn't been interrupted," she said irritably and immediately regretted her tone. Taking out her frustration on Alex wasn't fair to him, but she couldn't help herself. This had been the day from hell. She had no one else to vent to and he was the closest person to unleash her wrath on at the moment.

His brows knitted together. "What are you angry about anyway?" She couldn't exactly come flat out and tell him how much she resented coming back here after all these years. At least Delilah would make the experience bearable. She had no choice but to make the best of the situation.

"Does it have something to do with what you thought you saw in the kitchen this morning?" He took a step closer and she caught a whiff of his intoxicating scent, a combination of musk and pure male. "You looked jealous, and you have absolutely no reason to be. I was trying to gather information and see if the girls could fill in the blanks."

"You don't owe me anything." She squared her shoulders. "Besides, I wasn't jealous," she lied. Annoyed that he was able to see right through her, Willow bent to clean up the mess and Alex placed a hand on her arm.

"Hey, don't try to pick up glass with your hands. You'll only cut yourself. There must be a broom around here somewhere." He glanced up over the bed to the decorative besom displayed on the wall. "I'm guessing that thing is used for something other than sweeping floors?" A smile lifted the corner of his lips.

She straightened. "Mainly in fertility spells and certain rituals. I'm sure you didn't ask me up here for the lowdown on the many uses of magickal tools."

"No. Of course not. I wanted to talk to you in private. Have you picked up on anything around the coven that could lead us to *him?*" he asked, glancing around the room. "What did you find out?"

"Unfortunately, nothing concrete. I talked Delilah into getting the others to form a circle to see if we can divine his location. We're meeting in the dining room at midnight." She slumped down on the leather bench at the end of the bed and sighed, wishing they had more to go on. "I thought I'd go over to the greenhouse in the meantime and see if I can find this potion Maeve was working on."

He nodded. "Good work, Willow." His eyes darted toward the door.

She didn't want him to leave and tried to hide her disappointment by pulling out her phone. She glanced at the screen. "Well, if there's nothing else, I'll clean up and head over there."

"Wait," he muttered. When she heard the lock click, she glanced up to find Alex walking back from the door. He took a seat next to her on the bench. He moved closer so their thighs touched and she could feel the heat from his body even through his jeans. Desire coursed through her veins and fired her blood. "I can't stop thinking about you, Willow," he rasped in a voice as jagged as broken glass. "Believe me, I wish it weren't the case. This is making my job and my life complicated as hell."

"Sorry to complicate things for you," she whispered and shoved her cell back in her pocket. The truth was she couldn't stop thinking about him either.

"I didn't mean it like that." He exhaled and ran a hand thorough his wavy, dark hair making it stand on end. "This wasn't meant to happen. Look, about earlier, I didn't mean what I said...let's just say I could have used a lot more finesse. Whatever this thing is between us I know it has zero to do with spells and magick. This is real. Tell me you've at least entertained the idea of exploring this attraction between us?"

Oh I've entertained the idea alright. She imagined their sweaty bodies tangled together, rolling around over satin sheets. Then there were the multiple orgasms she had no doubt Alex would give her. A fling would never be enough, not where he was concerned. She'd want more. "I decided it would cost one of us way too much."

"I must be going about this all wrong." Alex reached out and caressed her cheek with his thumb. His touch sent prickles of heat along her skin. Now all she could think about was his hands roaming all over her body. Her nipples instantly tightened. "I want you, Willow, any way I can get you."

She swallowed hard, his words burning away some of her fears. "It's not as if I'm expecting a marriage proposal, but I need to be emotionally invested in the person I'm sleeping with and vice versa. Otherwise, it's just about the physical release."

"Then why does this have to be only about sex?" His hand moved from her cheek to the back of her neck, rubbing lazy circles, leaving tingles along her skin.

"I'll probably never see you again after this mess is over, and that could only mean that this is about casual sex."

"Who says this has to be only about sex?"

"Why would I invest my feelings in someone who doesn't like witches or anything we stand for?"

"I thought you were helping me work on that," he said and glanced at her lips.

Not sure his intentions went beyond something purely physical, she shrugged off the pang in her chest and offered a smile instead. "Working on it, but you're not there. Considering how things started out between us, you'll probably be happy when I'm far away from here."

His dark eyes burned into hers. "Not at all. I'm not your enemy, Willow, quite the opposite." She tried not to read too much into his words. He must've felt her pull away and moved his hand to rest on his knees. "Okay then, let's change topics, tell me what's been going on around here. Anything strange or out of the ordinary?"

"A local antique dealer hired the girls to locate his stolen jewelry and art, which is how they managed to pay for the new addition. The cops thought they were involved at first, and interviewed them numerous times, but didn't find anything."

"Interesting," he said shaking his head. "I'll look into it. What did you find out about boyfriends or any strange men hanging around the coven?"

She sighed. "I'm afraid I struck out big-time. No one talked about anything personal. If you haven't noticed, none of the girls are welcoming me back into the fray with open arms. But don't worry, I'll keep trying."

"Yeah, you put on quite a show this morning." He rubbed his beard and flashed a sexy smile. "You sure got my attention."

"Believe me, it wasn't my intention, but those girls pissed me off." She let out a frustrated breath, still trying to block out the memory.

His eyes softened. "I'm here if you want to talk about it."

Maybe she was being too hard on him. He really did seem to be trying. "Thanks." She picked up Maeve's scarf, and toyed with a loose thread, too affected by the deep thrum of his voice and the closeness of his body. The last thing she wanted was to have this kind of raw, sexual reaction to him. When she finally did look up, his eyes were filled with genuine concern. "Look, I'm sorry about before. I didn't mean to bite your head off."

"Apology accepted." When he was this close she could see the whiskery grain of his beard and the tiny flecks of gold in his brown eyes. The sight of a man as gorgeous and as perfectly chiseled as Alex was awe inspiring, but it didn't change anything.

"I got the feeling those ladies were giving you a hard time earlier. Telling lies about you and spreading vicious gossip would put anyone in a shitty mood. Don't think I haven't figured out what this must take to come back here and face your demons."

"Nothing I can't handle." She pushed to her feet and began to pace, feeling awkward. She turned to glance at him over her shoulder. "How come you believe my story? Considering my past, I assumed you'd expect the worst from me."

Heat flared in his eyes as he stood. "If you're asking if I think a woman as beautiful and smart as you would go after a middle-aged dude to get attention, the answer is no. You may be many things, Willow McCray, but you're not a liar. It's like I said before, you're honest to a fault. The truth is in your favor. You should tell that to anyone giving you a hard time." His voice dropped to a near whisper. "And yeah, the way I perceive witches is changing, and all because of you."

Stunned by his belief in her, she stopped and turned around to face him, resting her hands on her hips. "You make it sound so easy, like I can put everything behind me and start fresh."

"You can. Don't sell yourself short. You don't work for the Cabal anymore. This is your chance to make things right and leave your past where it belongs." He moved closer still and inclined his head to the side.

"Besides, I'm betting the ladies around here are about to change their attitudes toward you."

"Whoa, what are you talking about? Have you started reading Ellen's crystal ball?" Her gaze narrowed, not sure where he was going with this.

"No need for a crystal ball. I've got a worldwide database at my fingertips. I've been compiling data on Ellen's ex-boyfriend, Ed Milleu. As it turns out, he really did have a thing for the young girls. He was charged with four counts of statutory rape over the last ten years, involving almost legal-aged victims and convicted of one. He was also accused of sexual misconduct on the job and was let go when the woman in question rebuffed his advances. Apparently, he has a nasty temper as well and knocked his ex around pretty good."

Willow swallowed hard, almost too stunned to speak. Finally, after all these years, she was getting validation for Ed's despicable behavior, and then as Alex's words sunk in, her stomach clenched.

He'd done the same thing to another innocent. She'd spent too many wasted nights lying awake, wondering how her life would've turned out if Ed hadn't propositioned her and thereby sealed her fate. Where would she be now? It was worthless to dwell in the past. Shaking, she tried to rein in temper. "Why would you do this for me, Alex?"

"Simple. I felt as if it were high time justice was served around here." His jaw ticked. "I went to Ellen with the news and basically told her she owed you one hell of an apology. I more than suggested she set the record straight."

Her anger flared. "How could you? I never asked you to get involved. I don't need a personal bodyguard. I've told you already, I can take care of myself. It's what I do. It's what I've always done. You had no right."

Annoyance flashed in his eyes. "I thought you'd be happy about this. I did this because you deserve to have someone in your corner. I want you to trust me and know that I have your back. Besides, did you ever think it was the right thing to do? Dammit, Willow, one of these days you're going to have to let the wall you've put up come down and let me in." A swirl of heady emotions emanated off him—frustration, desire, and tenderness.

"Your intentions were honorable, but you should've come to me first. It sounds as if I put you up to this." She crossed her arms in front of her chest to hide the fact that she was shaking.

"But you didn't. Only Ed's responsible for creating the shit storm he's made of his life." He stalked closer to her and placed his hands on her shoulders. "The man's a scumbag, plain and simple, and he's finally getting what he deserves, serving a year behind bars."

"My mind's reeling in about ten different directions right now." Deep down, she wanted to trust him. No one had ever done something like this for her before and she wasn't quite sure what to make of the whole thing. She sighed with relief and massaged her temples to soothe the pounding in her head. "Thank you for getting to the truth. How do I know you didn't do this for your own selfish reasons?"

"You don't. I'm sure this is shocking to hear after all these years. But did it ever cross your mind that I did this for you simply because it was time for the truth to come out? And for the record, I expect nothing in return."

Gratitude warred with pride. "Look, I appreciate the gesture, but it doesn't matter at this point. My stay here's only temporary. I'm not going to make peace with everyone." She shook her head, doing her best to clear it. This was too much to process all at once. "You brought me in to help you find a killer, which is what I intend to do. What about you?" she asked desperate for a change of subject. "How did you do with the construction crew?"

"I've got a few names for you to check out." He pulled a Ziploc bag from his back pocket and laid it on the bed. "I made all the contractors leave their cards and sign their names on the back. I told them I'd consider their services for other jobs in the near future if they worked their butts off today."

"This was pretty ingenious of you. I'm impressed." She opened the bag and spread the cards out on the bed. When she skimmed her hands over the pile, a swirl of mingled thoughts and raging emotions almost knocked her on her ass. Anyone who thought mindreading was easy had no clue the effort it took. It was like untangling a thousand wires with a toothpick.

She blinked and a name formed a clear picture in her mind. "Antonio Perrini. You might want to check him out. I kept seeing Arabella's face in his head. His name doesn't fit with the letters SG from my first vision, but maybe those letters stand for something else."

"You think the killer could be one of these guys?" Alex asked, gathering up the cards, and placing them back in the bag.

"I can't say for sure. I'll need a personal item that belongs to the killer. Did you find anything of his at the crime scene?"

"I'll talk to Tate. Let me see what I can do. I'll make sure to get it to you before midnight." His gaze swept over her again. "You look a little drained. Have you eaten today?"

"Only if you count the old Snickers bar in my purse. I'll take some herbs to replenish myself."

"I'm guessing you're not into the whole carrots and celery thing going on around here?"

"Are you kidding? I'm pure carnivore. I would kill for a cheeseburger, fries, and a milkshake." His expression grew solemn and already she could sense his mood getting dark. "What is it?"

"I got back the autopsy report. The flesh missing from the bodies was because the killer was consuming them."

"What? No!" Her hand went to her mouth as her stomach churned. Now she was grateful she'd skipped breakfast. "Why would anyone do such a thing?" As if killing these women wasn't bad enough, he was consuming their flesh?

"He's doing it to steal their powers" Alex was at her side in an instant. He folded her into his arms and rubbed her back.

"For what purpose?" Willow pressed her face into Alex's shirt, inhaling him, loving the press of his strong arms around her. Slowly, his words sank into her brain. Maeve, oh Goddess, no... Up until now, the only thing she had to go on when she tried to tune into the killer was a piece of hemp and that damn belt buckle.

"We're still looking into it, but the typical motives are power, greed, and revenge." He smoothed her hair down her back and kissed the top of her head. "Hey, you okay?"

"Yeah, this is a hell of a lot to take in."

"I need you to be careful. I couldn't live with myself if anything happened to you." His tone was primal, possessive, and made her heart skip a beat. "Promise me you'll be careful."

She drew back to look at him. "Of course. Hey, are you flirting with me?" she asked, mimicking his question from the day before.

His smile was pure sin. "How's this for an answer?" he murmured and sealed his lips over hers in a searing kiss. At first she stilled, but when he licked her bottom lip, her defenses melted away like warm candle wax.

The first thrust of his tongue tasted like coffee and cinnamon. She pushed her fingers into the thick strands of his lush hair and kissed him back, meeting him stroke for stroke. She pulled him closer, deepening the kiss, not able to get enough of the heat of his mouth. His tongue twined with hers in slow, wicked laps.

The kiss became wilder, and she could feel him losing his tight rein of control. He groaned and pressed her body flush against his. Her nipples tightened against the hard wall of his chest.

His erection pressed against her thigh. Panting, his arms tightened around her waist. And she became languid in his arms, letting herself get lost in his touch and the wicked taste of him.

Willow wanted this man in ways she couldn't explain. He gave her hope and confidence, despite the mess she'd made of her life. The thought sent a wave of panic through her, toppling the carefully constructed barricades she'd built around her heart.

Her breath became ragged as he thrust his hips against the crotch of her jeans. He was hard as stone, shamelessly rubbing the thick ridge of his erection against her crotch. A moan ripped from her throat. They were both still fully clothed. If she let herself, she could climax from the friction alone.

Her hands went to his gorgeous ass to press him even deeper against the place where she ached and wept for him. He continued to rub against her while he fondled her breasts and pinched both her nipples through her bra.

More than anything, she wanted to forget, and Alex was the only man who could make her. To what heights could a man as sensual as Alex take her in bed? A thrill of excitement coursed through her veins. He sucked and lapped at her tongue with bold, heated strokes. She was close to going over the edge. The crest of her orgasm was building and charging forward like a freight train about to run off the tracks.

She imagined Alex could fulfill every one of her sultry fantasies, and for the first time in her life, she wanted to explore each one with him. He broke the kiss by dragging his hot lips down her neck. "I want you to call out my name when you come, Willow."

"Alex." Her sex pulsed and tingled against the hard press of his erection. He licked and sucked on her neck while she dug her nails into his back. She was burning up, silently begging for release. His hips moved up and down against her, increasing the friction.

"I know you said you were hungry. You can think of this as an appetizer," he said hoarsely and thrust the velvet heat of his tongue into her mouth again. When he pinched her nipple, her sex clenched. "Give it to me." His scorching demand was her undoing, that and the fast rubbing of his cock against her most sensitive parts. Light flickered behind her eyes. A burst of pure bliss consumed her body and mind. She screamed his name as she came and then slumped against him, ready to collapse.

"The next time I make you come I'll be buried deep inside you." He kissed her temple, her eyelids and her cheeks. He whispered how beautiful and sexy she was and how much he wanted to please her again and again. All the while her body continued to thrum with the aftershocks of a mind-melting orgasm.

When she finally caught her breath, her face broke out into a huge smile. "Is that a promise?" There was a noise in the hallway. "Crap, we should go before someone sees us."

"I'll see you later and from now on don't even dream of using any hand-operated toys. I can think of much better ways to pleasure you." Her breath caught in her throat and before she could respond, he placed a deep kiss on her lips, and left the room.

With her heart still pounding, she glanced at the door, and touched her lips. Alex almost made her believe she could leave her past behind and imagine the possibilities of a future. *Almost.*

CHAPTER 12

"What's up? Your text said it was urgent." Alex glanced over at Garrett Mulroney; the vampire was seated next to him at the counter, perched on the edge of a silver and red barstool. Fortunately, the diner was empty, which meant the dinner rush had apparently come and gone a long time ago.

Alex ran the risk of blowing his cover if someone saw him conversing with another cop. On the other hand, they both needed to eat, and he couldn't remember the last time he had a decent meal. What were the chances of bumping into anyone from the coven out here in this hole-in-the-wall in Jersey City?

"There's something big going down with Saint Claire. Our guys have been watching him and his minions, doing surveillance around the clock," Garret whispered, over the low thrum of voices and the clink of silverware. "You need to check out his operation for yourself."

"Does this have to do with Port Jersey?" Alex bit into his steak and eggs, practically groaning. After he chewed and swallowed, he lifted his mug and regarded Garrett over the rim. "Do you think the Shadow Cabal is behind the witch murders?"

The kitchen door swung open and the smell of bacon, freshly baked bread, and apple pie lingered in the air. Garret waited for the busboy to pass. "I'd say it's a definite possibility on both counts. I'm not sure what the link is yet. It's not enough that he has a hand in a high-class prostitution ring and a drug cartel. Now he's got a new hobby. He's acquired a number of art galleries." When Garret bit into his burger, blood oozed from the side and ran onto his plate.

"Art galleries? Who knew the guy was into Picasso? I'm willing to bet it's connected to his drug business." Alex made sure to keep his gaze on the revolving dessert display and not his friend. It was best to keep up the pretense that they were strangers enjoying a meal after a hard day's work, and not sharing intel on a bust about to go down.

"He's got politicians, custom agents, and even cops in his back pocket. Our surveillance shows his demons pulling large crates off of ships docked in the port. We need to find out what's inside." Garrett dipped a fry into some ketchup and the sight of red smeared across his plate was an unwelcome reminder of how much blood had already been spilled.

His appetite gone, Alex pushed his plate away. "It sounds like he's stashing drugs in the crates, which could explain why he has so many powerful people on the payroll."

Before Garett could respond, the waitress came over and gave him a refill. He waited for her to leave and continued. "Well, it's not as if we can get our drug sniffing dogs anywhere near the area without giving ourselves away. Saint Claire has guards on standby. We need to be sure and gather enough evidence before we try to go in and seize anything. It could blow our chances of bringing his whole operation down for good." Garret finished the last of his meal and wiped his hands on a napkin.

"That is a dilemma," Alex said with a frown. "But I might be able to help. We've been using a consultant of sorts, a psychic. We could find a way to distract the guards and let her give it a try." Time wasn't on their side. This case could implode at any minute. It was like playing catch with a ticking time bomb.

"A psychic huh?" Garret smiled wide, showing the tips of his fangs. "Would that be the hot redhead I saw you talking to at the crime scene?"

"Don't go there." Alex reached for a creamer and poured the contents into his mug, avoiding his scrutinizing gaze.

A commotion at the register drew their attention to glasses shattering and plates smashing to the floor. A tall brunette was backing away from the tray she'd apparently knocked off the stand. She turned and her gaze locked with Garret's from across the restaurant. That's when Alex got a better look at her. "Jesus, what the hell is Gillian doing here?" He tried to hide his face by lifting a menu. He stole a peek at her. She was decked out like she was going clubbing, not getting ready for a ritual at the coven.

She stared back at Garret and the momentary burst of excitement that spread across her face quickly turned to anger. She handed some bills to the cashier, reached for a bag off the counter, and without a word, disappeared out the door.

"You know her?" Garret asked in a strangled voice. When Alex turned toward him, his eyes were wide, almost saucer-like. His gaze lingered a few minutes longer before the vampire cursed and turned back around.

"She's a witch from the coven where the two vics resided. I think the real question is how do you know her? Why do I get the feeling there's a story between you two?"

Garret's hands balled into fists as he placed them on the counter. "No story. Our paths crossed recently. You might say Miss Howe and the witches from her coven got mixed up with the wrong people. It put them in the crossfires of my investigation."

"Miss Howe?" Alex chuckled, not used to seeing him so flustered, especially when it came to someone of the opposite sex. Women were naturally drawn to Garret's rugged good looks and the whole vampire thing. The fact that Gillian was beautiful might've had something to do with it. "Ah, no wonder why she was shooting daggers at you."

"When I saw her at the coven the other day, she barely looked at me," Garret whispered and stared off into space. Alex knew that look. In his experience, it usually meant you were done for, and the truth was he saw it every time he looked at himself in the mirror.

"Shit. I hope that didn't blow my cover. Maybe I can tell her I did some construction work at the station a while back and we ran into each other. I think my story will involve you treating me to breakfast."

Garrett chuckled and pulled out his wallet. "Yeah, yeah, fine. This one's on me. Next one's on you, man. But not a bad story. It just might work."

The waitress appeared and placed a to-go order in front of Alex just as Garrett reached across him for the check. There was a certain witch back at the coven who'd love a cheeseburger and fries. As much as he wished it weren't so, Alex found himself thinking about Willow all the time, and he had a sneaking suspicion he wasn't going to shake his craving for her anytime soon. "Maybe when this case is wrapped I can put in a good word for you with Gillian."

Garret smirked. "Trust me, by then it won't be an issue. I'll just push her out of my head."

"Yeah, keep telling yourself that, buddy, and maybe you'll actually start to believe it."

Several hours later, Alex was still trying his best to focus on the task at hand, figuring out a way to explain to the women of this coven why he was puttering around the dining room at midnight. But his mind was too preoccupied with sultry images of Willow, naked and spread out before him, to come up with anything even remotely plausible.

His cock throbbed painfully against his jeans. He couldn't wait to slide into her moist heat. If he didn't act on this raging lust coursing between them soon, he was going to take matters into his own hands, literally. If he could get her in his bed, maybe he could stop this constant fantasizing.

And yet there was a part of him that didn't think he'd ever get enough of her. He was about to text her *again* to let her know he'd managed the unthinkable, when she strutted into the room.

She looked as gorgeous as ever, clad in white jeans and a fuzzy white turtleneck sweater. Her long, red hair was pulled back off her face in a ponytail, accentuating high cheekbones, a pert nose dotted with freckles, and full, sensual lips. A touch of pink gloss colored her lips, and he had the strongest urge to close the distance between them and lick it off.

A small backpack hung over her slender shoulders. She must've sensed what he'd been thinking because her breath stilled as she approached him. "Alex? I can sense your arousal a mile away. What if one of the girls sees you? Tell me you're standing here because you have something that belongs to the killer."

"Yes, but it's not the only reason." He pulled a plastic container off the table and handed it to her. "Sorry, it might be a little cold. I'll have to give you a rain check on the shake. I'd like to take you to dinner when this mess is over."

A breathtaking smile spread across her beautiful face. "I'd like that." It was dangerous to think of her outside the scope of this investigation. Once this case was wrapped, he'd be onto the next one and chances were she'd be long gone. If only he could get her to stay. He found himself thinking about her all the damn time.

"Mmm, smells like heaven. This was sweet of you, Alex." She didn't see her strengths, only focused on her faults. She was smart, brave—loyal. Damn, he was in over his head. She opened the box and inhaled the searing aroma of beef until her eyes fluttered close. She set the container on the sideboard, picked up the burger and took a healthy bite. "Want to share?" she asked between mouthfuls.

"No, you go ahead. I ate while I was there." He enjoyed the hell out of watching her eat. "You relish your food. It's a pleasure to watch."

He guessed by the way her face flushed a lovely shade of pink, she was thinking the same thing—about all the ways they could pleasure each other. "I meant what I said before," he whispered. "I want to make you come again, only this time when I'm buried deep inside you."

Her eyes glazed with passion. "Alex? What if someone hears you?" Willow glanced over her shoulder to make sure no one was around. "I thought over what we talked about, but I still haven't made a decision. Are you trying to tempt me with food?" she asked with a smile, taking another healthy bite. She pulled a linen dinner napkin from a drawer in the sideboard and wiped her hands and mouth.

"Is it working?"

"You're incorrigible." She laughed and smacked him on the shoulder. He caught her by the wrist and sucked on each one of her fingers until a little moan escaped from her throat.

"You taste so good." Her eyes burned with desire and it was all he could do to keep from hauling her into his arms and taking her up against the wall. But she was right, the witches were due in at any minute. Reluctantly, he let go of her hand. "I took a little trip over to the Port. Saint Claire has quite the operation going on. He's smuggling in illegal cargo. I'll need you to go over there with me and check it out. What did you find out about Anthony Perrini?"

"I asked around. Apparently, he dated Arabella and didn't take it well when she blew him off. I'll be seeing her in a few. I can ask her about it then. See if I can sense anything strange." After Willow finished the last of the burger and set the container on the table, she glanced at him with an expectant look on her face.

"Don't worry, I'm going. I'll take this with me on my way out," he said, angling his head to the empty burger container. "If one of the others smells beef around here, I'm guessing there will be hell to pay."

"No doubt. Do you have the thingy?" she whispered.

He set his briefcase on the long, wood table, and pulled out the clear plastic container marked "trace evidence" and handed it to her. "Don't open it yet. You'd better digest first."

She glanced at the dried-up black piece of wing through the plastic and made a face. "Gross. This should do the trick though." The grandfather clock chimed. "C'mon, you need to leave. We shouldn't be seen together. You said so yourself."

"Okay, I'm going, but I wanted to ask where you've been for the last few hours? I was texting you and you didn't respond." His tone sounded accusatory, and possessive, but he couldn't help himself. In a short amount of time, Willow had gotten under his skin.

"Sorry. I forgot to charge my phone. I didn't think I needed to be at your beck and call twenty-four seven. I told you earlier I was headed to the greenhouse."

"I don't expect you to be at my beck and call." He took a step closer to her and glided his hands up and down her arms, needing to touch her. "But we're partners in this. You need to keep your phone charged at all times. Did you have any luck with the potion?"

"There were hundreds of potion bottles in there. I tried to go through them, but I didn't know what I was looking for. I'll start again in the morning and ask Saje for help. She's an expert on potions."

"Saje? The petite brunette who kept giving you evil looks?"

"Yeah, one and the same." Willow reached out to stroke his arm. "I can sense your tension. How about you? Did you find out anything official about the Perrini guy?"

"I wanted to talk to you about him. I've been going through his file. His former girlfriend filed charges of stalking and domestic violence against him. The man is a danger—" Footsteps echoed down the hall.

Willow's head turned toward the sound. "You should go. We shouldn't be seen together."

"You never told me if what you're about to do is dangerous."

"C'mon, what could possibly happen?" She deliberately avoided meeting his eyes.

"I'll wait for you in the ritual room. Come get me when you're done." He shut his briefcase and slung the handle over his shoulder.

Before she could protest, he placed his hand at the nape of her neck and kissed her squarely on the lips. "Be careful, and don't forget, we have some unfinished business."

Willow tried to calm the pounding of her heart when Nadia, Delilah, Arabella, Saje, Belinda, Ellen, and a witch she'd never seen before strolled into the dining room. All of them were dressed from head to toe in white. The color enhanced their magick and was used for psychic strength and power. The only one missing was Gillian. No surprise there.

The energy around the women had indeed changed and felt lighter, less judgmental. A breath slipped from her lips and drifted in the air like a helium balloon. Willow shivered with anticipation, not sure who or what they were going to find.

Her gaze drifted to the stained glass window. The drapes were drawn back, allowing a sliver of pale blue moonlight to pour into the room. Her skin tingled from the pull and power of its force. She turned back to the women and glanced over at Ellen. The high priestess nodded at Willow but made no attempt to apologize. *Be grateful for the little things.* At least she wasn't giving her the death stare.

"If everyone's ready, we can get started," Ellen said to the group and began placing different colored candles used for spell work on every available surface.

The other witches milled about the room and chatted, eyeing Willow with suspicion. Their attitude forced her to repress a sigh. While things had lightened for sure, they were miles away from being good. She moved to the head of the long table lined with pitchers of consecrated water, cauldrons, crystals, and bushels of sage, and dumped the wing in the center, careful not to touch the evidence with her hands. "Ready when you are."

"Ew, what the hell is that thing? I sense the dark magick surrounding it." Belinda reached for a bundle of sage. She lit it with a snap of her fingers and flitted around the room, clearing away any dark energy that might try to enter the circle.

"I've been in touch with the agency investigating the murders. I went to the crime scene to see if I could pick up on a psychic link with the killer." Willow cleared her throat and tried to ignore the butterflies fluttering around in her stomach. "I'm afraid I didn't get very far. I've already tried scrying him, but my magick alone wasn't strong enough to break through his shields, which is why I had Delilah ask all of you for your help. This belongs to him," she said, pointing to the center of the table. "It's a small piece of a fae wing."

A collective shudder vibrated throughout the room. Delilah was the first to step forward. She placed her bracelet in the center of the table, and then turned toward Willow and offered a reassuring smile before facing the group. "We should put anything in the circle that belonged to Kimber or Maeve. It could help channel the killer's energy."

"Thanks for doing this, Delilah. I owe you big-time," Willow whispered and glanced tentatively at the table of other witches.

"You don't owe me anything, Willow. I want to catch whoever's responsible. We all do." Delilah pulled out the chair next to hers and motioned Willow over. "I'm sorry Gillian couldn't be here. Apparently, she had a prior commitment. But we brought Meadow in to take her place in the ritual." Delilah angled her head toward the petite, dark-skinned girl with spiky purple hair. "She's great with the Tarot."

"It's nice to meet you. Thanks for coming. I didn't think everyone would actually show," Willow murmured to Delilah.

"It's the least I can do. We all want to help anyway we can. I spend a lot of time here," Meadow said with a smile and began arranging her Tarot deck.

"Um, if anyone has anything they'd like to add, please bring it forward now." Willow was finally starting to feel as if she weren't a complete outsider in everyone's eyes. She tried not to dwell on the fact that Ellen knew the truth about Ed and remained silent, never coming to her defense, or clearing the air for that matter. A knot twisted her stomach into a pretzel. She hung her pack on the back of her chair and tried to calm her pounding heart.

One by one, the women placed a trinket or memento—a crystal, a pack of matches, even a mood ring, and a business card on the table. Energy thrummed through the room and made the table vibrate.

Ellen was the last to step forward, her lips pursed in a tight line. She placed several photos, a wand, and a gleaming silver chalice on the table. Since Ellen's magick resided in the realm of fire, she waved her hands over the candelabras of white candles and immediately they flamed to life. She turned toward the cast iron fireplace and sparks of fire shot out of the grate.

The scents of vanilla mixed with a faint trace of sage and wild berries permeated the air. Meadow sprinkled salt around the table while Arabella walked around the room, chanting protection spells. Flickers of light sizzled through the air and formed a glittering circle around the group.

After Willow unclasped the chain of her amulet and placed it on the table, she unsheathed her *athame* and held it straight out in front of her, turning clockwise in a circle. She chanted a prayer to the gods and goddesses for their collective magick to take shape and offer protection.

All eyes focused on her as she unzipped her backpack and pulled out the small stuffed kitten, along with the snapshot of her and Maeve, minus the frame. Willow laid all the items on the table and picked up the salt. She sprinkled the various objects individually to keep any dark magick from taking hold.

Once everyone took their seats, the women clasped hands. "Go ahead, Willow. The floor is yours," Ellen said from the head of the table.

Surprised Ellen had asked her to invoke the circle, Willow searched her memory as the sacred words fell from her lips. "I cast this circle as a link between worlds. We invoke all the witches who came before us and honor their magick. We ask the Goddess for psychic strength and protection." Her voice trembled. There was so much riding on the outcome, so many lives at stake.

Flames shot up from the candelabras and the clusters of candles around the table. Bright sparks of magick sizzled in the air like a lightning storm on a warm summer's night. All of the women in this circle were natural born witches. Willow could sense the strength of their powers emanating from the spark of magick snapping around the room like a ball of electricity.

They released hands and, one by one, the group of witches took out their tools and laid them around the table. She wasn't sure what would happen when they attempted to divine together. Willow pulled out a black scrying mirror and tried to focus all her energy on finding the killer through the glass.

Belinda used a big, black cauldron filled with consecrated water and let candle wax drip onto the surface. Willow watched in awe as the wax began to form symbols and images. Meadow and Delilah laid out decks of Tarot cards, frantically flipping them over, jotting down symbols onto a pad. Saje and Belinda peered into crystal balls, now changing from clear to gray as shadows took shape inside the glass. Arabella focused her trained gaze on tea leaves inside a china cup, no doubt trying to find a pattern. And Nadia swung the end of an amber pendulum over a map of the city, waiting for it to land on a spot. Willow's gaze finally landed on Ellen, who waved her hands back and forth over the candle flames as images formed from the smoke.

Willow had become used to practicing magick as a solitary witch. She'd forgotten the jolt of power one got from a full coven. Gazing around at the skill and strength of the others, she realized how much she missed practicing witchcraft in a group setting.

Now it was her turn. She swallowed hard and wiped her sweaty palms on her jeans. Okay, no more stalling. But what if she witnessed another murder? Could she get to the killer this time around? Her stomach clenched imagining another innocent suffering at the hands of a madman. "I need something to pick up the wing fragment with."

"Try this, Willow." Delilah slid over a set of kitchen tongs.

"Thanks." Willow used them to pick up the dried, curled-up piece of black yuck and placed it onto her scrying mirror. She waited a heartbeat, and then removed it. She held her breath, hoping to see the killer's image appear in the glass. At first, all she saw was shadows.

Frustrated, she focused harder this time, blocking out everything and everyone around her, except for the fae. Slowly, images began to form and take shape. Pyrotechnic lights flashed in every direction, while bodies gyrated together to the thump of a sultry hard rock beat. The music grew louder and made her ears ring. Martini glasses filled with pale liquid clinked together along a shiny brass bar. She was there, but in the killer's head this time. But where was he?

The little whore isn't here yet. I should kill her for making me wait. This time I'll do her slow, make her suffer.

A deep, male voice invaded her thoughts. Who was he going after next? He picked up a shot glass and downed the dark liquid in one gulp. Willow swallowed as the bitter taste of whiskey invaded her tongue. He slammed the shot glass on the bar, and rage pulsed beneath his fingertips.

"Willow, hey, what are you seeing?" Delilah's voice called to her from what sounded like the inside of a tunnel.

"He's angry, and hungry for another kill." Like a hunter waiting for his prey, some unsuspecting female was about to fall into his trap and become his next victim. Willow blinked as if in a fog, vaguely aware of still being in the circle. A part of her, at least psychically, was in the bar. Her eyes flew open wide and her head pounded. "He's in a bar. I can't actually see him, but I can sense his presence. He's going to kill another witch. We have to stop him. We have to—"

The room began to spin. Willow became dizzy, and nauseous. She was seriously regretting eating the burger. *Karma*, her inner voice warned. All the breath left her lungs at the same time her head began to pound. She started to fall sideways from her chair when a group of hands held her in place and kept her steady as shudders racked her body. In a matter of seconds, it felt as if someone had reached inside her chest and tried to pull out her heart. Willow screamed in agony, ready to sink to her knees, but the women around her held on.

All the while, club music thrummed in her ears and lights stung her eyes. And then she became faintly aware of Ellen, Arabella, and Belinda on one side of her, with Delilah, Nadia, Saje and Meadow on the other.

"She's as pale as death. What's happening to her? Willow? Can you hear me? You have to pull back, release the connection. Can you?" Delilah asked in a panicked voice, moving her hand to Willow's neck. "Her pulse is faint. We're losing her."

"We have to see where he is before it's too late." Willow wasn't able to save Maeve, but there was still a chance to save an innocent.

"The circle's still open, Willow. The connection isn't broken, not yet. He's sensing your presence and sucking your life force from your body. If you don't pull back, you'll die. You need to sever the connection and replenish your energy," Ellen said in a calm, authoritative voice.

"I can't. I'm trying." Willow bit down on her lip and focused on shutting her mind off from the mingled scents around the bar. The gleam of the lights faded, and then the noise disappeared until she was surrounded in darkness.

"Stay with us. You're going to be okay, Willow." Arabella's voice reverberated through the circle.

"Hey, you guys, help me put her amulet back on." Hands came around her neck and secured her necklace. Willow slowly opened her eyes and blinked as Arabella's dark head came into focus. The beautiful witch pulled a packet of greens from her pocket and ripped them open with her teeth. She reached for a bottle of water off the table and poured the greens inside. She shook it before sliding the bottle over to her. "Drink every drop."

Delilah unscrewed the cap, put the bottle to Willow's lips and tilted her head back. Instantly, she tasted mint, parsley and kale, along with a hint of rosemary. Her heart rate picked up and began to beat normally again. The pain gripping her chest faded, along with the dizziness.

When Willow was able to lift her head, she glanced at Arabella. "Thanks for saving my life, but I fear we might have sacrificed an innocent in the process."

"Willow, check it out. I'm getting something big-time over here." Nadia shouted from across the table. Her pendulum swung back and forth and circled around the map until it landed on a spot in Newark. "It looks like Route Nine and Mulberry."

"There's a nightclub called SNAP on the corner," added Delilah.

"Let's go," Willow chimed in. "There's no time to waste." The ladies clasped hands again and closed the energy circle with a quick prayer. The candle flames flickered and died out.

Arabella was helping Willow out of her chair when Alex, Cayden, Brodie, and Commander Smith came barreling into the room. All heads turned in their direction, staring at the four hulking males and the giant laser guns strapped to their hip belts.

"You aren't going anywhere. I saw what happened. I was watching on the surveillance monitor. You lied to me, Willow. He could've killed you," Alex said, coming to stand at her side, dark eyes blazing, his muscles tensed for a fight.

"Yeah, but he didn't. If you heard everything, then you know we have no time to argue."

"I told you they weren't construction workers," Belinda whispered to Saje. "Who the hell are you people?" she demanded, peering at the men.

Smith stepped forward, his imposing frame making Belinda shrink back. "Who we are isn't important. All you need to know is we're here to protect all of you." He turned his attention toward Ellen and flashed his badge. "If you could keep the rest quiet, we'd appreciate it. We don't want to jeopardize our cover, but this is a matter of life and death. We've already put a call into the RHPD. They're on their way over to the bar as we speak. They're going to guard all exits. I'll stay here with all of you and make sure you're safe just in case."

His gaze darted to Alex, Brodie and Cayden. "As for the rest of you, what the hell are you waiting for? Go!"

The women started to protest and argue all around them. Ellen quickly placated the group with promises to explain it all later.

"Wait, I'm going too." Willow took a step toward Alex and swayed, still woozy from the remnants of dark magick.

"Hell no. This is too dangerous. I can't keep track of the next vic he's trying to lure out of the bar and catch this maniac while I have one eye on you."

"You don't need to protect me. I'll keep my amulet on. I'll be prepared this time. I won't get so deep in his head. You need me. I'm the only one here who can sense him. Let me try." When Alex didn't look convinced, Willow added, "Are you really willing to risk losing another innocent? There's no time to argue."

Cayden walked up and stood by Alex's side, his broad shoulders filling the space. "I'm afraid she does have a point. If we play this thing right, we may be able to draw him out and distract him from walking out of the bar with another witch."

"What are you proposing exactly?" Alex holstered a small handgun to his boot strap to match the one peeking out of his hip belt.

"Isn't it obvious? Willow has a connection with the killer that we can use to our advantage. We set our trap and use her as the bait."

CHAPTER 13

*S*NAP was an alternative dance club in the industrial section of Newark. From what Alex could recall, the owners were demons, twin brothers who liked to party, and attracted a wide range of mage clientele into their establishment.

He couldn't quite imagine the killer hanging out at a local watering hole and tossing back a cold one, but he supposed if you wanted to pick up a witch, this was as good a place as any to score. He prayed they weren't too late. He'd lost this bastard twice. He wouldn't let it happen again.

"Holy crap. I've been here before," Willow exclaimed as she climbed out of the van. "I snuck in once with Gillian and Maeve when we were underage. I don't remember it being such a hotspot." She glanced around at the crowd spilling into the parking lot.

The news reports hadn't kept women from coming out in droves, based on the line halfway around the block. This would make his job a hell of a lot more difficult. *The bastard could be anywhere. He could be anyone.*

Alex glanced around the lot in search of Garett, or any of the men in blue, before turning back to face her. "Shit, where are the cops when you need them?" Willow was standing by his side, looking tense and pale. He wasn't exactly sure what had happened back at the coven, but he knew it had scared the hell out of him.

"I want to abort the plan we discussed on the way over. There are too many damn people here. I'll never be able to keep track of you. I'm not taking another chance with your life. You do as I say, got it? We stick together. I'm not letting you out of my sight."

Whether she liked it or not, Willow was his concern. The fact that he was screwing around with her made this personal. Too bad he was falling for her, which complicated things even further.

"I told you already, I'm fine. You're being ridiculous about this. You need to stop being so bossy. You said we could hear each other with the earbuds," Willow said, holding up the tiny wire he'd given her in the van on the way over.

"You call it bossy." Alex gripped her waist. "I call it keeping you alive."

"Stop worrying about me." She arched her brows. Her green eyes darted to the spot on his forehead where she'd head-butted him. "I can take care of myself, remember?"

"How could I forget?" Instinctively, he lifted his hand to the small scar on his left temple, a reminder of her power. Still, they were dealing with a madman of the supernatural kind. "But these circumstances are very different."

Before she could protest any further, Cayden and Brodie jogged up to them wearing long wool overcoats to hide their M15 standard issue laser guns. Even if a laser couldn't necessarily kill a fae, it sure as hell could knock him back on his winged ass a few notches. If they went in there with guns blazing, they'd risk a hostage situation. They needed to take the bastard by surprise.

Cayden stepped forward, his blue eyes ablaze, and his black horns extended into sharp points. He glanced at the entrance to the bar. "This place is packed. There's no activity on the other side, must be an employee lot, but we'll keep checking. I'm afraid we're on our own here. I got a call on my cell just now from Mulroney, he said the RHPD sent a squad car over, but there wasn't anything strange going on. They had to take off on a domestic violence call."

"At this point, let's hope our killer's still inside. We'll split up and keep an eye from out here," Brodie said, placing his earbud. "Try and remember that we can hear you, Willow, at all times."

Alex stepped forward, his stomach twisted in knots. No. This was way too dangerous. "About the plan we discussed regarding Willow—"

"Everything's in place," she said, cutting him off, smoothing her red hair off her face.

Alex gritted his teeth. He supposed it was too late to backtrack at this point. He nodded at the two demons and placed his earbud. Cayden and Brodie split up, each one headed to a different end of the parking lot to keep track of anyone coming in or going out.

After Willow placed her earbud, he reached for her hand and led her toward the door. "Let's go." The full moon lit their path to the front, sending a chill down his spine. He'd overheard Ellen saying all types of magick, including black, were strongest when the moon was full.

"Wait." Willow ducked behind a parked car. "I have an idea. Take off your coat and hold it up for me."

"What? Why? We don't have time." When she started to peel off her sweater, he chucked off his jacket and held it up. Now he was the only one who had a bird's eye view of her half-naked torso.

"This will only take a sec. We left in such a rush; I never got a chance to change out of my ritual outfit. I'm not wearing clubbing clothes and it'll make me stand out, especially in this place. If memory serves, the women run around here half-naked." His height gave him the advantage to peek at her over his coat.

She pulled her turtleneck over her head and unsheathed her *athame* from her hip belt. Standing in her black lacy bra, she began slicing the sleeves off her sweater with the edge of her blade. Then she cut a deep V down the front and slid it back over her head. "Okay ready."

He dropped his coat and his jaw practically hit the ground. Her cleavage was pushed up to her neck and the lace from her bra peeked out from the newly transformed top. His mouth went dry. "I think we're both in trouble. C'mon."

"What about my *athame*? It doesn't exactly go with the outfit." She shivered and ran her hands up and down her arms.

"Here, give it to me. Don't worry. I won't give him the opportunity to get too close to you, Willow. Trust me."

"I want to," she whispered. "I just haven't had a lot of practice." She handed over the sword along with her hip belt. "We're missing one thing," she said and shook her red mane until it looked wild and untamed. She whispered a few words and then waved her hand in front of her face. Automatically, her appearance changed.

Her hair became black as night, poker straight and waist length. Her pale skin took on an olive tone; even her eyes had become darker. "Jesus, you look like Maeve's twin." His gaze swept over her again, stunned by the sudden transformation. "This is going to seriously mess with his head."

"Isn't that the point?"

"I'm not sure about this. It wasn't part of the plan." He reached for her elbow and they cut to the front of the line. Alex slipped a wad of cash to the bouncer, ignoring the hisses echoing behind them.

They stepped through the velvet ropes, and blinding lights flashed in their eyes. Earsplitting alternative music blared from speakers situated all around the club. Scantily clad women danced seductively on top of the bar, while couples swayed their hips to the beat.

"Do you think the killer's still here? Who knows if the girl he was meeting even showed up," Willow asked, sounding anxious. When he turned to face her, everything he feared was there, reflected in her eyes, and for one crazy moment he wondered if this was the last time they'd ever see each other again.

"I won't let anything happen to you. We're not here to kill him." He tore his gaze away from Willow to keep his eyes trained on the bar. He scanned the crowd, searching for any males with snake tats across their forearms. "The goal's to take him down long enough for us to get his ass to Hellios. The guards can take care of him from there. Let's go nail this scumbag."

"Agreed. You go do your thing and I'll do mine."

"Wait, are you sure you'll be able to tell if it's him?" Alex turned to face her, but she was already gone.

Willow caught a glimpse of her reflection in the bar mirror and her heart skipped a beat. It looked as though Maeve was staring back at her. Contrary to what Alex had said, she wasn't capable of making herself look exactly like Maeve, but she'd managed to capture a pretty convincing likeness.

At first, she thought this would be a good idea. She'd do anything to save another witch from dying, but now she wasn't so sure. Why did it feel as if she were dangling a piece of raw meat in front of a tiger?

As she took a step closer to the bar, her gaze locked with a tall vampire with beefy muscles. He stood at the end sipping a beer. "Are you going up?" he asked, inclining his head to the women shaking their bodies above his head. "Or getting a drink? I'd love to help with either."

"I bet he would." Alex's deep voice filled her ears.

"For the Goddess's sake, chill out," she whispered.

"Excuse me?" The vampire stared at her with an odd expression on his face, clearly perplexed.

"Uh, sorry. I wasn't talking to you." If she was going to lure this psycho out in the open, she had no choice but to draw attention to herself, and that meant shaking her ass off on top of the bar. First, she'd have to get over her fear of heights.

Letting out a deep breath, she turned toward the vamp. She reached for the beer in his hand and downed it one gulp, then slammed the empty bottle on the bar. "Thanks for the drink. I'm going up."

He smiled, offered his hand, and helped her up to the bar. Her heels stuck to the sticky surface when she tried to take a step. The room spun and her knees wobbled, but when she thought about what was at stake, it tamped down her fear.

"Where the hell are you?" Alex hissed. "I've lost you."

"Up here, on the bar." Willow began to shake her hips to the thrum of the sexy beat as she looked through the crowd, in search of the brown-haired male from her visions. But all she could make out was a sea of faceless bodies.

Adrenaline pumped through her veins as she scanned the bar area and the dance floor again. How much time did they have left before he kidnapped his next victim? Although she'd never actually been able to see the killer's face up close, she'd always assumed she'd recognize him on the spot. Now she realized how foolish that had been.

Lights flashed in her eyes, nearly blinding her. She blinked and finally the black spots began to fade. The song changed to a slow dance and the crowd parted. Her gaze zeroed in on a couple below her on the dance floor. Half their forms were covered in shadow as they moved in time to the singer's deep, sultry voice. The guy gripped his partner's hip. When he lifted his hand to take a sip from his glass, Willow caught a glimpse of the snake tattoo emblazoned across his forearm.

Holy shit. Her breath caught in her throat. Too stunned to speak, she tried to climb down from the bar, but an arm gripped her leg and pulled hard. The last thing her mind registered as she flew headfirst into the sea of bodies was whether or not someone was going to catch her before she face-planted on the dance floor.

Willow was getting passed through the crowd like a bag of chips at a barbeque. "Alex, can you hear me?" *Dead air.* Her heart stuttered in her chest when she realized the earpiece must've fallen out in the flurry. She tried to scream, but no one could hear her through the blare of music and the roar of the crowd.

I have to get to him. I have to stop him. With a Herculean effort, she dug her nails into the skin of the hands gripping her. The next minute, her elbows smashed against the dance floor and made her teeth gnash.

She covered her head with her hands, narrowly avoiding getting stomped on. When she spotted an opening in the crowd, she got to her feet and realized she was now at the entrance to the club. She turned and fought her way back through the sea of bodies to the bar.

Once she got to the exact spot on the dance floor where she'd seen *him,* she furiously scoped out the area, but there was no sign of the guy anywhere. She felt a tap her on her shoulder and spun around. "Alex?"

"Hey, I think you owe me a drink." It was the vampire from the bar.

"Sorry, no time." Willow started to walk away, but he grabbed her by the waist and pulled her against his big, barrel chest.

"What's the rush? Let's get to know each other better," he whispered in her ear.

"I...don't...like...being...manhandled." She pulled back her fist and punched him in the center of his abdomen. He let go of her and doubled over, making a choking sound.

Willow hurried to the first exit she could find and pushed open the door. After she stepped off the curb, she ran toward another parking lot. This one was empty, and she figured she was now at the rear of the club.

Cold air filled her lungs and pebbled along her skin. Frost glistened on the pavement, and she swore the temperature had dropped at least ten degrees. She glanced around at the few cars in the lot, their windows covered in mist from the chilly air. Otherwise, this area was dark and deserted.

No streetlights. She blew into her freezing hands and pushed them together to form a ball of light. She held the light in front of her body and glanced around for any sign of movement. A rustling in the nearby trees made her jump. She turned. *Who's there?* Was her mind playing tricks on her?

From the corner of her eye, she thought she saw a shadow move across the lot. She crouched behind a car, and then zigzagged in between, moving at a relatively fast pace, until she tripped over a beer bottle. Her ankle twisted, snapping off the heel of her cheap suede boot. Her arms shot out to break her fall, her hands scraping against the pavement.

Letting out a breath, she reached for her *athame* to slice off her other heel, but realized it was gone. Alex was still holding it. Crap, she had no weapon. She let out a curse and took off both boots. Pain exploded from her ankle when she tried to stand. She gritted her teeth and forced her weight onto her other leg.

She took a step and froze at the thump of footsteps. With her hand over her mouth, she ducked behind a car and caught a glimpse of a couple walking hand in hand in the side mirror.

"I've waited all this time to meet you, Gillian. Is it a crime to want a few minutes alone with you?" Willow's blood ran cold in her veins. She'd recognize *his* creepy voice anywhere. *What was the killer doing with Gillian?*

Why was she leaving a bar with a stranger? Was she trying to get herself killed? No wonder she wasn't at the ritual. Willow edged closer to the mirror to get a better look at him. He was tall and lean, with big brown eyes. He had a full head of brown hair slicked off an angular face. He was extremely good looking in a grunge sort of way, which made him even more deadly.

"Hey, where are you taking me?" Gillian asked as they moved away from the lot. "I feel kind of weird all of a sudden, a little lightheaded."

"Come with me. I know a place where you can rest for a minute." He held her up and helped her walk.

"I thought we were going to mess around in your car," she said with a giggle. "My friends are still inside. We have to be quick. They'll miss me if I'm gone too long. Uh, where's your car?" Her words sounded slurred. Crap, he probably slipped a potion in her drink, which didn't help matters. Willow would need her to fight back.

"We're almost there," he said in a sickly sweet voice that made Willow's skin crawl.

Willow edged closer and made sure to keep her head down. They were walking toward the woods. Where the hell was he taking her?

"You mentioned your ability to talk to those who've passed over to the other side? How do you do it? Do you use black magick to enhance the outcome?"

"Whoa, I never use black magick. I'm a white witch," Gillian added. "Why do you ask?"

"No matter, a power such as yours will be useful, just like Maeve's was."

"W-what are you talking about?" Willow could hear the panic slowly edging into Gillian's voice. "Hey, let go. Get off me, you bastard."

"Now, now, it's too late to turn back." He started to drag her. "I'm afraid you die tonight, my dear. Didn't your friends warn you not to pick up strange men in bars?"

Willow limped closer and Gillian let out a blood-curdling scream. "H-help me, please, someone!" She was crying now, making hysterical sobbing sounds, and trying to dig her heels into the pavement. The bastard pulled her up by the hair.

"Take this evil from whence it came," Gillian murmured. Her magick sizzled in the air, but before she could finish the incantation, he backhanded her across the face.

"Shut your filthy mouth, witch."

"Let her go," Willow screamed, as she limped out from behind the car. Finally coming face to face with the monster who had murdered Maeve gave her a rush of adrenaline that dulled the pain in her ankle.

He stopped in his tracks and spun around. "How in the hell?" His eyes were wide with shock. "I killed you."

"I'm not Maeve. You did kill her, you piece of garbage. I'm here to avenge her death and send you straight to Hell. Now, why don't we settle this, just the two of us?" She took a step closer, hoping to distract him so Gillian could get away. Alex or one of the other agents would hopefully notice her absence and be here any minute.

"Willow?" Gillian's voice came out weak and defeated as she tried to struggle out of his grip. The potion must've weakened her powers.

"Stay the hell out of my way, *Willow*." If not for the crazed look in his eyes that gave way to his madness, she could easily see how any red-blooded female could be taken in by his looks. He was the absolute worst kind of predator: a handsome, deceptive one that made women drop their guards.

"I won't let you take another witch." Willow took a step closer until they were inches apart. Her heart pounded wildly in her chest.

Stay strong, fight back. Willow whispered the words in her mind, willing her thoughts into Gillian's head.

His eyes flashed a maniacal challenge. "Have it your way. This simply leaves me no other choice. I get two for the price of one."

He whispered a series of words that Willow remembered from her vision. The next moment smoke billowed in the air, stinging her eyes and clogging her throat. When the smoke cleared, a golden cross-bow materialized inside the crook of his arm. His smile came out as a sinister twist of his lips. "Sometimes heads need to roll."

There was nowhere to hide, nowhere to run. "This can't be good." Willow closed her eyes, bracing for the pain, when she heard him grunt. Her eyes flew open.

He pulled his hand away from Gillian and scowled. "You bitch." She must've bitten him. Good, she still had some fight left in her. Willow used the distraction in her favor by going to a knee and kicking out with her good leg to nail him in the shin. He momentarily lost his balance, giving her time to land an uppercut beneath his jaw. Her hand began to throb almost as much as her ankle.

He let out a string of curses and pointed the crossbow at her neck. "I'm going to love every minute I make you suffer."

Before he could make good on his word, the back door burst open and Cayden came running toward them, pointing a laser gun at his head. "You won't get away this time," Cayden shouted. Willow glimpsed a shadow move behind one of the cars and then disappear.

"I can usually detect the filthy stench of a demon." The fae's lip curled into a sneer. "You don't play fair, demon, and neither do I." He cocked the string on his crossbow, ready to shoot. His finger was pulsed on the trigger as he squinted into the scope. He was about to release a bolt in Cayden's direction, when Alex darted out from behind a car, and pointed his laser gun at the back of his head.

"I'm only going to ask once, drop the weapon and get down on the pavement, slowly, or the street cleaners will be sweeping you up. Do it." Alex's finger was poised on the trigger of his gun, and even though his expression remained deadly calm, she'd never seen him so angry.

The triumphant gleam in the fae's eyes disappeared and was replaced with blind fury. Several tense seconds ticked by until he finally dropped his crossbow. Willow took a step forward, ready to grab it at the first opportunity. He started to bend forward toward the pavement when a loud growling noise pierced the air.

All heads turned to gape at Brodie's hulking figure barreling across the lot at full speed like a feral animal. With his head bent forward and his horns elongated into sharp points, he reminded her of a bull charging for a red flag.

The fae reached for his crossbow at the same time Willow tried to grab it away from him. But he was faster. Before any of the agents could fire off a shot, he pulled Willow in front of his body to use her as a shield. She tried to elbow him in the solar plexus, but he kept the point of the broadhead in her back. "Don't take another step, demon," he shouted to Brodie.

The maniac forced Willow to turn in Alex's direction. "Well, well, if it isn't the shooter. Go ahead, I dare you. We're not so different, you and me. We eliminate those who get in the way of achieving our goals. Only you carry a badge."

Alex's eyes flared with hatred. "You sonofabitch."

From the corner of Willow's eye, she noticed Cayden inch closer, but he was still a good hundred yards away, too far to take a shot. "Shoot the bastard, Alex. We got him," Cayden shouted.

"I-I don't have a clear shot." Alex blinked, anguish etched on his face.

Willow's breath stilled. This might be their only hope of catching this psycho. "Shoot him."

"You're closest. Take him down. Now," Cayden repeated.

"You piece of shit. I hope you rot in Hell." Alex's hands shook and his face became covered in sweat, despite the frigid temperature outside.

"Can't do it, can you? Not after you killed that poor little boy? I found the story. It was front page news. Don't want more blood on your hands, do you, Agent Denopoulos? Yes, I know who you are. I find all humans pathetic. You're all the same, no backbone. As much as I'd love to continue this little chat, I've got to fly." The fae whispered a series of words and the air around him stirred.

Thick black wings unfurled from his back and fanned out from his body like a giant eagle's. Willow screamed. The fae turned toward Cayden, who was still pointing his gun in his direction. "Don't try anything or I'll shoot her in the back." Hearing him say those words made something in her snap. Willow closed her eyes and focused her mind on casting a spell.

"Pins and needles, needles and pins.

These words will make you pay for your sins.

This is my will, so mote it be"

The fae cursed and let go of her and the crossbow, clutching his arm. Using the distraction in her favor, Gillian darted in front of him in a blur of speed and dug her hands into his shoulders. She used the leverage to knee him in the balls.

He grunted, his face contorted in anger. "You'll pay for that, Gillian." The veins in his forehead bulged as he managed to break through Willow's spell. Then in one quick move, he scooped Gillian up, and tucked her under his arm like a ragdoll. He pumped his wings as they began to soar through the air.

"No! I won't let you take her." Willow was the only one who could stop them. She was the closest. Blood thundered in her ears as she limped over to the nearest car. Pain exploded in her ankle as she climbed on to the roof. Black spots filled her vision and made her sway. *Don't look down.*

She waited until they hovered above her head and flung out her arms to try and pull Gillian down by her legs. But she caught her from a bad angle and started to slip. Her stomach dipped to her toes. She had no choice but to hold on as they flew higher.

Her world spun as wind burned her face and whipped around her ears. She caught a brief glimpse of panic in Alex's eyes as the three agents ran toward her. A moment later, they became tiny colored specks on the ground far below.

Adrenaline coursed through her veins. "Get...me...down," she screamed, but realized no one could hear her. She couldn't hold onto Gillian for much longer. She had no choice but to try and make her body weightless. She closed her eyes and whispered a spell to become light as a feather.

When she looked down, clouds floated around her like puffs of smoke. She swallowed hard and her throat became tight with fear. She squeezed her eyes shut and reverted to being six years old again.

The window to the fire escape wouldn't budge. She pushed with all her might and finally got it open. Mommy and Daddy were yelling at each other again. Daddy sounded angry and she didn't like it when Daddy got mad. There was no place to hide from him 'cept out here.

She shivered and forgot to put her coat on over her pink nightgown, the one with the fairies and stars on the front. Someone called her name from down below, and she wanted to see who it was. She tiptoed over to the side and tried to look down, but it was slippery on the fire scape and now she was getting her slippers wet.

She jumped to avoid a puddle and her foot slipped. She fell between the bars and grabbed onto the metal ladder. She screamed, "Mommy!" But no one came. Her nightgown flew out in front of her and then she was falling—tumbling into blackness.

Willow shook the old memory from her head and tightened her grip on Gillian's ankles. *Stay, focused, need to stay alive.* She didn't want to look down. Instead, she forced herself to crack one eye open. Her heart pounded in her chest, so hard, she thought it might burst.

After expending so much magick, Willow had nothing left. They'd be toast against the fae once they finally did hit the ground. A strong scent of pine and grass filled the air. They flew past trees and shrubs, a forest. She began shivering from head to toe. She sucked in gulps of cold air, ready to accept her fate, when she spotted a swamp ahead in the distance.

If she could find a way to force this maniac to let go of Gillian, then they had a chance. *Get ready to jump,* she screamed telepathically. They'd shared a connection once. Willow only hoped and prayed it hadn't severed completely, even after all these years.

We have to jump.

N-no …I can't. I'm too scared. He's going to kill us both.

At least their connection was still intact. *Listen to me, it's our only shot. You can do this. Let go of him when I tell you.*

Willow spotted a bog in the distance. As they got closer, they flew through an area of fog and then everything happened all at once. *Now.* Gillian's ankles slipped through her fingers. And then they were falling, fast, and hard. Cold air burned her throat and her lungs.

Wind lashed around Willow's face and whirred in her ears as they plummeted into a marshland. This was it. They were both going to die. Alex's face flashed through her mind. She'd never get the chance to see him again or hear his voice. She finally understood when people said life was short…it was.

Before her entire life flashed before her eyes, the two of them smacked against what felt like a brick wall of muddy water. Panic edged around her brain with the first rush of frigid water. Everything around her was pitch black, she couldn't see up from down. Tangled in a plant, she pumped her arms and legs and rushed to the surface. She coughed and took in gulps of air, trying to catch her breath.

"This water is effing freezing." Panting, she looked up and found the fae flying away like a giant bat, disappearing into the night. But where the hell was Gillian? She whipped her head around and found her face down in the water. *Goddess no.* She splashed her way over to her, flipped her onto her back and held her head above the water as she swam to the edge.

One good tug on her arms and she had her out of the water. Willow lifted her head and blew air into her lungs. "One, two, three, breathe dammit. You can't die on me, not yet. Besides, I'm the only one who can kill you." After another giant puff of air, Gillian coughed and sat up, spitting up a mouthful of water.

Tears flooded her eyes and tightened Willow's throat. Still shivering, she sighed with relief. Gillian was alive. *Close call.* "Are you okay?"

When Gillian finally caught her breath, she nodded. "How are we alive?" Gillian sat up and coughed. She was covered in mud and she had a piece of moss caught in her hair.

"Someone must be watching over us." Willow cracked a smile as a nervous giggle escaped from her throat. She began to laugh until her sides ached.

"What's so funny? How could you laugh at a time like this? We almost died." Gillian wrapped her arms around her body.

"I know, it's crazy. It must be the stress and my fear talking, that and the swamp scum all over you. I wish I could take a picture. It would be great blackmail material." Even though Willow was freezing and every bone in her body ached, she couldn't stop laughing.

"Somehow, I'm not seeing the joke," Gillian said with a frown and picked the moss out of her hair. She threw it on the ground and wiped her muddy hands on her jeans. "I was going to ask if you were okay, but I think I already know the answer."

When the last of Willow's laughter subsided, she glanced down at herself. Blood stained her jeans and her ankle throbbed, but nothing seemed broken. "We're both incredibly lucky."

A bruise was already blooming under Gillian's eye. She was covered in mud and grime. "This is crazy karma. I mean, we hate each other. But you saved my life, Willow."

"I could've never pulled it off without your help." Willow propped herself onto her elbows and pulled a hunk of weeds off what was left of her sweater. "Oh and by the way, you really need to do something about your taste in men."

Gillian sighed. "Yeah, I thought if we lived, you might bring the subject up. I always had a knack for picking losers. What can I say, you can never quite run away from the past. It's always there lurking in the background like a ghost. I'm sure the situation with my family didn't help matters."

Although Gillian didn't live at the coven when they were growing up, she'd spent enough time there for Willow to have heard the rumors. Like most of the girls, her childhood hadn't been easy. A mixture of shame and regret flashed in her eyes. "I'm sorry, Willow, for everything."

Willow didn't know what to say, not ready to accept her apology just yet, but Gillian's words made her anger recede and seemed to put a balm on some of those old wounds.

After an awkward silence, Gillian glanced around at the surrounding bogs and fields and ran a hand through her wet hair. She pulled out a stick and threw it over her shoulder. "We must be miles from civilization. How will the agents find us all the way out here? We'll freeze to death." Her teeth began to chatter.

Willow remembered the tracking device embedded in her skin. She never thought it would actually come in handy. "Don't worry, they'll be here."

"Look, I know I haven't exactly been decent to you. But maybe, after everything we've been through, we can put it behind us. I owe you my life. How will I ever repay you?"

"I think at this point we can call it even," Willow muttered and collapsed on her back.

CHAPTER 14

*C*rack, crack, crack. Alex ruthlessly jabbed his fists into the punching bag, hoping a little sparring practice would take the edge off. *No such luck.* He supposed he should be happy. Willow was safe and back in her room. But when he thought about what could've happened, he shook with fresh rage. He punched the bag again and again until his fists ached and his lungs burned. Sweat streamed down his face and beaded on his neck and back.

He exhaled and bent to reach into his gym bag for a towel. After he finished wiping off his face, he wrapped the towel around the back of his neck. He looked around the coven's empty gym. He was grateful for the privacy and didn't relish the idea of bumping into anyone in his current state of mind. Besides, only a crazy person would be working out at this hour.

His eyes darted to the clock on the wall. He'd been at it for over an hour and he still wanted to throttle something. The image of the killer's face flashed through his mind and his vision blurred. He punched the bag again. *Hard.*

"Careful, or you might end up taking the whole damn thing down, and trust me, Ellen wouldn't be too happy about it. I'm already on her shit list for accidently breaking one of her priceless fairy statues. Don't need the whole team pissing her off." Smith's voice echoed from across the room.

"Yeah, it might be the only thing I take down tonight," Alex muttered and turned to face the demon.

Smith crossed the gym and took a seat on a bench next to a rack of weights. "Ah, you must be referring to Stephen Griffiths, aka Ven Pariah. It turns out Willow was right all along. Her vision of the letters SG panned out. I took a chance and finally came up with a match in our database. We went to his last known address, an apartment a few blocks away from Fusion. No big surprise, the place was empty."

"Did the place smell like he had a pet?" Alex asked, letting the news seep into his brain.

His brows shot up. "I don't recall. Why do you ask?"

"No reason." He'd been a fool to doubt Willow's abilities. The more Alex got to know her, the more he realized the depth of her powers. And strangely, the less he was afraid of them. "What's his story? Let me guess, he started out torturing small animals before he graduated to killing witches."

"He definitely fits the serial killer profile with a couple of unique twists. He has a few priors, a domestic violence charge for threatening an ex-girlfriend with a knife, and a laundry list of other offenses against women, but no actual murders on his record until Maeve Donovan. The act of betrayal was probably enough to finally make him snap."

"She knew the risks and yet she tried to help by turning the bastard over to us anyway. I still feel responsible for her death." Guilt tightened Alex's gut. "You believe Griffiths was working alone?"

"I went through his old arrest records, and as it turns out, our witch killer was formerly employed by the Shadow Cabal." Smith held up his hand. "I can already guess what you're thinking by that look on your face. You think Saint Claire hired him to do his dirty work. But if that were true, then why not kill Willow straight away? Which leads to the question, what was his motive for wanting the other witches dead?"

"There's got to be a connection there," Alex said, shaking his head. He guessed it had something to do with whatever was in Saint Claire's cargo hold. He needed to get Willow over there to find out what it was.

"Yeah, let me know when you figure it out." Smith stood and slapped a large hand against the bag, offering Alex a silent challenge. "Go ahead, try it now." He might as well have pasted Stephen Griffiths picture directly to the front.

Alex drew his fist back and jabbed the bag, pouring all his anger into every punch. When he could finally catch his breath, he regarded Smith as he wiped the sweat from his brow. "Something doesn't add up. Going with your theory, if Griffiths was acting out of revenge, or trying to keep Maeve Donovan quiet, then why kill Kimber Woods?"

"Apparently our boy Stevie wasn't the only one into drugs. His mom was a crack whore. My guess is there wasn't a whole lot of parental supervision going on while she tended to her johns. But here's where it gets really ugly. She was murdered right in front of him when he was just a boy, by none other than his dear ol' dad."

"Well, they sure take the cake for fucked up families." Alex sighed and drew his fist back to take another punch.

"It gets better. The dad was a fae and an out-of-work loser who liked to beat up on his wife and dabble in dark magick. But you're going to love this: the mother was a witch."

Alex's blood ran cold in his veins. "He wants to lash out at all witches because they remind him of his mom? It's practically textbook." And yet the depth of Stephen Griffith's hatred was even more disturbing. "Any ideas as to why he's doing this now?"

"I went over statements he made that coincide with the violence he perpetrates on his vics. He claims to be highly intelligent and describes himself as a pure misogynist. His favorite hobby is hunting, and his occupation is a farmer. He spent most of his youth in and out of psychiatric hospitals. He's a real charmer who started doing drugs at a young age. He's known for his violent outbursts against women and obsessive behavior, not to mention owning illegal weapons."

"Like a killer crossbow? What about stealing a witch's powers? Where does that fit into all of this?"

"I read Tate's report. From what I understand, this is just some twisted way to enhance his magick and make him even more deadly. If he's indeed working for the Shadow Cabal, then I'm guessing that this is simply another perk on his resume. The agency kept an eye on him for a while, but we didn't have enough evidence to convict him on anything." Smith shrugged and crossed his arms across his chest.

"Any DV charges on his record?" Alex untied his gloves with his teeth. He pulled them off and stuffed them in his bag.

"No, nothing. My guess is none of the women he roughed up would come forward to file any charges against him. They were probably too afraid, and we can't exactly hold someone on suspicion. This lunatic means business. My fear is he won't stop until he systematically destroys all the witches of that coven."

Alex froze. "Okay, how will all this help us find him and take him down?"

"It's not going to be easy." The demon rubbed his neck, looking exhausted. "I have a feeling he's going to be more selective in the way he lures out his next victim, especially now after the news report. He knows we're onto him."

"Thanks for the update, but I'm sure you didn't come all the way down here to the basement just to update me on all of this," Alex said, glancing at the clock on the wall. "Especially since we're supposed to meet in a half-hour,"

"I figured I'd find you down here working off some steam." Smith tilted his head. "Where's the girl?" he asked, ignoring the question.

"Which one?"

"Ellen tells me Gillian's fine, considering the ordeal she's been through. She may have a broken a bone in her hand, but Saje gave her a healing potion that should mend it. She's still pretty shaken up, which is why I'm holding off giving her shit for completely disobeying our orders."

"Yeah, she almost got herself and Willow killed." Alex sucked in a breath in an attempt to rein in his temper.

"I hope she learned her lesson, and speaking of Willow, how's our brave felon anyway? I heard she sprained her ankle. You wouldn't happen to know the extent of her other injuries, would you?"

Alex could feel his jaw clench, but there was nothing he could do to stop it. "It's a miracle she's alive, considering the circumstances. She's pretty banged up." And from what he could tell, not only physically. "But she's tough. She was the only one with enough guts to actually try to stop the bastard."

Why did he sound so defensive and protective? He didn't want to discuss her injuries or her mental state with Smith, not anymore. *Things have changed. Somewhere along the line, I started to care.*

She was no longer just a *felon* to him, she was becoming so much more. He picked up his bag and pulled the strap over his shoulder, hating the fact that he'd let her down. Hell, he'd let everyone down. If only he'd taken the goddamn shot. "Why do you care anyway? You're using her for your own selfish reasons to get to Saint Claire. You don't give a shit about her as a person."

"And I suppose you do, don't you? I see the way you look at her, Alex. This has turned personal for you. Don't try and deny it. I'm sure I don't have to advise you on the dangers of losing your perspective. You had him, but your judgement was clouded. It kept you from taking the damn shot. There's no place for this kind of sappy bullshit in a murder investigation."

An investigation he alone was screwing up. "What the hell is that supposed to mean? I thought we were supposed to be protecting the innocent."

Smith chuckled. "Willow isn't our innocent here, which may be part of the problem."

What if Smith decided to pull the plug and send her case to the Council? He couldn't live with himself if anything happened to her. He refused to let his growing feelings get in the way of her safety. He had to protect her, no matter the cost. "The girl means nothing to me. I'm playing a role to get her to trust me. Nothing has changed. I want this bastard and I'm going to get him. Besides, you think I'd ever lie down with a witch?"

Smith didn't look convinced. "This time it was close, Alex, way too close. Maybe you were right from the very beginning. We should've never gotten a civilian involved. Why the hell didn't you take down the son of a bitch? What the hell were you waiting for?"

"I could've hit the girl and we would've had another dead witch on our hands." Alex glanced at the floor, avoiding the accusatory gleam in Smith's eyes.

"You're a perfect shot. You wouldn't have missed."

Yeah, you mean the perfect shooter. Alex would forever be haunted by the nick name.

"Take a couple of days off. That's an order. Work through your shit, Alex. We need you at full capacity," Smith said and headed to the door.

"You can't do this. I'm so close," Alex shouted at his back, his hands balling into fists once more.

"You're too close to this, and to Willow McCray," Smith said over his shoulder. "Trust me; this is for your own good. There's a team of agents out there right now scouring the area near the club. Cayden's in the lead for now. Don't worry, they'll find Griffiths." Without another word, he disappeared up the stairs.

His anger flared and before Alex could stop himself, he smashed his fist into the wall. He howled in pain and cradled his throbbing hand. Footsteps descended the stairs, forcing his gaze to the slim figure that now stood in the doorway. Nadia placed her hands on her hips and frowned at the sizeable hole he'd left in the wall. "Someone's going to have to pay for that."

CHAPTER 15

The coven solarium was a lush garden filled with exotic plants and brightly colored flowers of every variety. Gurgling koi ponds and glittering rocks added to the tranquil aesthetic. The flora and fauna looked so rare and tropical, Alex got the distinct impression he was walking through a botanical garden in Hawaii and not a heat-controlled room in Jersey.

It was a place of beauty and serenity, completely different from what he would've ever expected inside of a coven. The room was hot and muggy, a welcome invitation from the biting chill outside. He rolled up his shirtsleeves as he made his way deeper into the lush thicket of trees.

A bone-melting feeling of tranquility washed over him. Whether or not it was magickally induced he wasn't sure, but either way, he was grateful for the reprieve from the impending dread in the pit of his stomach.

As he turned the corner, he caught sight of Willow sitting cross-legged on a yoga mat. She was dressed in a tank top and form fitting cotton pants, which showed off the shape of her long legs. Her hair was wet, slicked back off her face in a ponytail, and her eyes were closed.

She cracked an eye open as he approached. "Alex? What's wrong? You look like hell."

"What can I say? It has been a pretty shitty night. Nothing went as planned. You didn't follow orders and almost got yourself killed." He ran a hand over his face and the back of his neck as the image of Ven Pariah flying away with her flashed through his mind. His anxiety returned full force. He unstrapped the hip belt from around his waist and handed over her sword. "I thought you might want this back."

"Almost doesn't count. I'm alive, aren't I?" She placed the sword behind one of the many small shrubs and regarded him with a wry smile.

"Yeah, by the skin of your pretty neck." He hadn't slept in nearly twenty-four hours and now things were only getting worse. Another witch had almost gotten snatched under his watch and at this point, they were still no closer to catching the bastard than they were after Maeve Donovan had turned up in a trash bag.

"I did what I had to in the moment, and guess what? I'd do it again in a heartbeat."

For several gut-wrenching minutes, he'd thought he'd lost her for good. Alex knew damn well it was a possibility going into this. But he never expected to fall so hard for her and now the thought set his teeth on edge. No matter what Smith said, there wasn't a chance in hell he was stepping aside, even if he had to do it on his own time. "You took one hell of a risk."

"Hey, at least Gillian's alive. Isn't that the most important thing?" Willow flipped her long, red ponytail off her shoulder and leaned forward, resting her elbows on her knees.

A giant bruise darkened her arm. A riot of emotions swept over him— anger, fear, longing. He'd come close to losing her, and it made his chest ache. "Of course. But I'm more concerned with how you're doing."

"Much better. Meditating in this room helps. I can draw energy from the plants and the soil to heal. I also took one of Saje's potions to help mend my ankle."

"How about the rest of you?" Alex took a seat next to her on the floor and leaned against a large stone. He pulled out his keys from his pocket and toyed with the chain, needing something to do with his hands. He wanted to tell her how brave she'd been and that he owed her a debt of gratitude for her services to the agency. The words were on the tip of his tongue, but he gritted his teeth instead. "What you did out there, hell, it must've been terrifying."

"Holding onto Gillian's ankles while that maniac flew us higher and higher, to Goddess knows where, isn't exactly what I'd call an adrenaline rush." The raw vulnerability in her eyes let the sails out of his stress bubble like a pin bursting a balloon. "I thought we were going to die." Her voice trembled on the last part.

The image of Willow standing frozen on the ledge at Fusion flashed through his mind. "Are you afraid of heights?"

Her green eyes widened and her face flushed. "Why do you ask?"

"The more we know about each other's weaknesses, the more we can have each other's back when it counts."

"Okay. I do have a kind of phobia about high places." She shrugged. "I've had it since I was a child, but it's not something I like to talk about."

"I'm glad you told me." When he scooted closer, her wild vanilla scent flared in his nostrils. Alex wanted her naked beneath him, moaning his name while she gazed up at him with passion in her eyes, not fear.

"Any new developments?" she asked, changing the subject. He didn't want to push her. He figured she'd tell him more when she was ready.

"Yeah, Smith pulled me from the case, Willow. From now on you'll be reporting to Cayden."

Her face fell. "What? I don't understand."

"Smith thinks I need to take a step back. He's convinced that my perspective's off partly because of my feelings for you."

"Feelings? What feelings?" Her pulse throbbed at her throat and he wanted to lick the spot with his tongue.

He contemplated telling her what she'd come to mean to him and that this had become more than a casual fling, even if they weren't technically sleeping together. He craved her all the time, but he also didn't want to scare her away. Besides, she had enough to deal with right now. "I think he's picked up on our mutual attraction for each other. It's impossible to deny."

"Oh." Alex thought he caught a glimpse of disappointment flash in her eyes. Was there a possibility she felt the same way? "I guess we're giving off some pretty heavy-duty pheromones. Look, no matter what happens, you were meant to solve this case and finish what you started. Smith will come around. He has to."

"Let's hope it's sooner rather than later." Alex got to his feet. If he was going to keep his distance from her, now was a good time to start. He didn't know what he felt for her exactly—desire, admiration. Maybe he was in awe of her bravery? Whatever it was, it left an ache deep inside his chest. "You need your rest. I should go. Try to stay off your ankle." When he thought about what Ven Pariah could've done to her, his blood boiled. Maybe Smith was right. He couldn't think straight where she was concerned.

"Alex, please. Don't go." Willow pressed a hand on his arm and tugged him back down. "I don't want to be alone tonight." Before he could jump to any conclusions about what she meant, she pressed on. "Maybe we could talk for a while."

"Sure." He sat back down and stretched out his legs. He needed to lie low anyway. He'd have to make a concerted effort to keep his hands to himself. It was foolish to get involved with her from the start, but no matter how hard he tried, he couldn't stay away. Probably better to end things now, before one of them got hurt. He was about to tell her as much, but the words died on his lips. *Coward.* "What do you want to talk about?

"Tell me about yourself." Her soft voice thrummed in his ears, bleeding the last of his tension away.

He flashed a smile. "What do you want to know?"

"Well, for starters, you could tell me what that thing is on your key chain." Her gaze narrowed at the small, blue crystal bead.

"Oh, this thing? It's called a Mataki. It's used to protect against the evil eye, just an old Greek superstition." He rubbed his chin. "Everyone in my family carries one."

She reached out and grazed one slender finger over the bead. "This is another form of magick, Alex, just like your badge. It's the individual practitioner that directs the spell, not the object itself. We have free will to channel magick for good or evil."

He swallowed hard. Time to come to terms with the truth. Hell, he'd been using magick all along. "I guess I still have a lot to learn."

"Don't we all? You always seem in control and so emotionally strong, but you're human. Besides trying to ward off the evil eye, what are some of your other weaknesses?"

Maybe it was time to stop being a hypocrite and admit the truth. His record wasn't exactly pristine. Now, after all these years, Ven Pariah had opened the door to his past. He had to man up and walk through it. "You want the short list or the long one?"

Her expression filled with compassion. She pressed a warm hand on his shoulder. "Does it have something to do with what *he* said about you killing a boy?"

"Funny," Alex said with a humorless laugh. "He must've dug deep to find what he was looking for. But the bastard was actually telling the truth. It happened a long time ago, Willow. Seven years to be exact. I was working for the RHPD at the time. A neighbor called in a domestic disturbance." He exhaled, reliving the memory. "By the time my partner and I arrived on the scene, all hell had broken loose. It turned into a raid on a coven of witches on the southeast part of town. There were rumors about animal and human sacrifice in their rituals."

"I remember it well. Velvet Laresh was the high priestess of that coven. She was a sadistic bitch of the worst caliber from what I've heard. Goddess, I can't believe you were the one that busted her."

His hands clenched into fists at the mention of her name. "Yeah well that term is an understatement where she's concerned. The MBI along with the RHPD had been watching her for months, but didn't have enough evidence to bring her in. My partner at the time and I were called in because a neighbor heard screams coming from the house. When we arrived on the scene, we smelled burning flesh. The place reeked of death and decay. Guns blazing, we went in. We surrounded the place and ordered them out. We were arrogant to think brute force would work against dark magick."

He became aware of her caressing his arm, silently urging him to continue. "Finally, Laresh came out," he said, not at all surprised at how every detail was still etched in his memory as though it had happened yesterday and not seven years ago.

"She had her hands up as if she was surrendering, but she was only tricking us with her magick. All the while she was weaving a spell to get us to turn our guns on ourselves. I watched as my partner peppered himself with bullets. I heard her voice in my mind, enthralling me, and yet there was another voice, a stronger one, holding me back."

"Oh, Alex, I'm sorry. It explains how you can block a mind probe." She stroked his arm. Her touch soothed him, along with the sweet sound of her voice. Both were like ice on a burn. "You must have incredible mental strength. Is that why the MBI recruited you?"

"It certainly helped." The memory of that awful night had slowly wound its way back into the forefront of his thoughts and took hold.

"Don't you see? You were meant to survive, live your life, and save the innocent. It's your destiny."

"I was the only survivor of one of the worst massacres in Raven's Hollow history, Willow. How's that for destiny? It was one of the main reasons I left the force." Alex ran his hand over his beard, lost deep in thought.

"I'm finally starting to understand your disdain toward witches. But that was black magick, Alex. Most of us practice white magick and follow the creed of harm ye none." Willow angled her body toward him. Her green eyes burned into his.

He swallowed the lump clogging his throat, not able to look away. "I'm starting to see that. Willow, you're nothing like her. You saved a life tonight. She, on the other hand, destroyed everyone who wandered into her path." Once he said the words aloud, Alex realized how true they were.

"I still don't understand what all of this had to do with a little boy."

He put his face in his hands and shook his head. Retelling the sordid details made it all come alive again. "I'd cocked the hammer on my Glock, ready to fire, but then a boy darted out of nowhere and ran in front of Laresh. I found out later it was her son, trying to protect his mom. But it was too late. I had already fired and killed them both," he said in a choked voice. He never could get the haunted look in their eyes out of his mind.

"Alex," she whispered and squeezed his hand.

He wouldn't look at her. He couldn't. "I even earned the nickname Shooter. Funny, I thought I overcame the whole ordeal a long time ago. Last night dredged it all back up again as if it was yesterday."

She ducked down to try and get in his line of sight. "It wasn't your fault. You can't blame yourself. It was an accident. Don't give him the satisfaction of thinking he has power over you."

"I let him get away," he mumbled, his anger flaring once more.

"No, you did the right thing. What if you'd missed? You could've killed me. You're a good man, Alex. A wise man once told me that grief can eat you alive, so can guilt. Don't let it. Please, let the past go. You must," she urged and pressed a warm hand to his cheek.

He was momentarily speechless. She didn't judge him, and yet he couldn't say the same where she was concerned. Deep down, he had always assumed all witches were the same and hadn't believed the whole "black and white" magick thing. But she was nothing like Velvet Laresh, and neither were the ladies of her former coven. The magick they practiced was different. She was different, kind and brave—passionate.

Her brow furrowed. "I can feel your pain," she whispered. "It's so raw."

"I don't know how to let it go." He wanted to tell her how wrong he'd been about her, about everything. She'd more than held her own tonight. When he stared into her eyes, they filled with tears, and his chest tightened.

"Let me help you." She placed a kiss on the side of his mouth, his cheek, and trailed warm kisses down his neck. "I know in my heart you would never hurt anyone," she whispered, running her fingers through his hair. "Let it all go, Alex." Her silky voice in his ear made his breath catch in his throat. All the anger and guilt he'd been holding onto all these years seemed to float away like dandelions on the wind.

"Willow," he breathed and all his resistance snapped. He pulled her onto his lap, careful not to make contact with her ankle, and wrapped her in his arms. He held her there like a lifeline. She smelled like trees and earth, like life…hope. She was his salvation against the lingering memories of death, and right now the only thing that felt real and good in this crazy roller-coaster ride they were both on.

"I thought I'd lost you." He pressed his lips to her temple, inhaling her wild scent, and pulled her against his chest.

"You were worried about me?" Her breath became ragged when he pushed his hand under her tank top and rubbed his knuckles over her silky skin.

All he wanted to do was give in to desire and make love to her until they both couldn't think straight anymore. Even if this thing between them couldn't go anywhere, he was done worrying about the consequences. He eased her back to look into her eyes. "More than you can imagine." He bent his head and closed his lips over hers.

At first the kiss was soft and sweet, but when her hot mouth opened for him, he thrust his tongue inside. He wanted her with a bone-crushing ache and felt his cock throb incessantly against his jeans. With a moan, her feminine curves melted into him. She wrapped her arms around his neck, her tongue tangling with his, firing his blood.

He licked inside her mouth, cupping the sides of her face to deepen the kiss. He could get lost for hours tasting her lips and caressing her smooth skin, but the time for teasing and tasting was long gone.

His body was strung tight from wanting her, but first he had to make sure she wanted this too. As much as it killed him, he broke the kiss. Her eyes were heavy lidded and glazed with passion. "Tell me you want this, Willow."

Her fingers curled into his shirt to pull him closer. "I want you, Alex, more than I've ever wanted anything. I finally get it. Who knows what will happen tomorrow, or even an hour from now. One of us, or both of us, could be toast. We might not get this chance again. I'm done with regrets."

He didn't answer her with words. Instead, he kissed her again, crushing his lips to hers, spearing his tongue into her mouth. But this time the kiss wasn't soft, and definitely not sweet. Mouths open, tongues and teeth colliding, their bodies pressed together. Both moaned and breathed hard, tugging at each other's clothing.

Panting, he pulled away. "We need to go somewhere private," he growled. "Or I'm going to take you right here."

"No need." Her chest heaved as she murmured a series of words. The next moment it felt as if they were wrapped inside a bubble. "Don't worry. No one can see or hear us now." Before he could comprehend what she'd just said, she kept her weight on her good ankle and straddled him. Her fingers knotted in his hair. "Now then, where were we?" she whispered, planting kisses along the side of his neck.

"I believe I was about to make you come." He cupped her breast and rubbed her nipple with his thumb. She let out a moan and sucked on his neck. "I love how responsive you are."

"Alex, please." With one tug, he pulled off her tank top and glanced at her pink nipples peeking through the lace of her bra. Seeing her half naked against the lush, green backdrop made his throat tight.

"You're beautiful." His cock strained against his jeans to the point of pain, but he wanted to take his time and savor the moment. He cupped her face and stroked her cheek, shocked and still a little raw from telling her so much crazy shit about himself, things he thought he'd never say out loud to another person.

If he could only soak her into his skin and let all the ugliness bleed away. The realization that he not only craved her, but needed her too, freaked him the fuck out. But he'd have to get over it real quick for both their sakes. The only thing keeping him from taking her fast and hard was his growing obsession to let her set the pace, to satisfy her needs before his own.

But when she moved her hips, all those good intentions went right out the window. "I want you inside me." She unzipped his jeans, and then pushed her hand inside his boxers. He growled when her fingers gripped his cock.

He lifted his head, and his eyes locked with hers. "Willow, please. Don't stop." She rubbed back and forth, curling her warm hand around the base of his cock until the tip beaded with moisture. The only sounds came from the pounding of his heart and their mingled breath inside the bubble. He couldn't remember ever being this hard.

Before he spilled right then and there, he carefully flipped her onto her back. "You still have on way too many clothes." He unhooked the front clasp of her bra and slid the straps down her arms then threw it over his shoulder. The sight of her full breasts and rosy pink nipples made him groan.

"So do you." She arched her brows and smiled. He slid her yoga pants off, making sure to steer clear of her sprained ankle. His eyes roamed over every inch of her gorgeous body. He licked his lips, gaping open mouthed at her tiny, pink lace panties.

He caressed the supple skin of her legs and rubbed her feet. He kissed his way down her body, stopping long enough to catch her wild scent in his nostrils. "Mmm, you smell so good. I could devour you." He rubbed his finger over the lace of her panties to find them soaked. "You're wet." In the natural light of the solarium, her eyes were the same color green as the leaves. Damn, she was beautiful.

"Then what's stopping you?" No need for further encouragement, he pushed the silk aside and slid a finger under the lace. He rubbed back and forth against her silky bud and then slid a second finger inside her tight sheath. She groaned deep in her throat, arousing him even more.

"You're so tight. When was the last time you've been with someone?" he asked, pushing her panties over her hips and down her long shapely legs.

"It's been a while," she murmured, her eyes half closed, red lips parted in anticipation.

The mere thought of her with another man sent a hot stab of jealousy straight to his gut. He shook it off and lifted her panties to his nostrils. When he inhaled her musky scent, his dick throbbed. "Then I think it's time to rectify the situation."

"Don't make me wait." She ran her hand along the bulge in his jeans.

"I want to make you come so hard, you forget about everything but you, me, and this moment." It was incredibly sexy having her entirely naked while he was still fully clothed. He placed feather light kisses on her hips and the insides of her thighs, loving her pleas and moans of pleasure.

"Yes, please. Lick me, Alex." He slipped another finger inside her, rubbing along swollen tissues, and circled her G-spot with his thumb.

"With pleasure." He moved his head between her thighs and licked her cleft up one side and down the other. She tasted sweet, like ripe fruit. When she arched her body halfway off the yoga mat, he buried his face in her delicious heat.

"Alex," she whispered. Incoherent words fell from her lips. She kept her legs wrapped around his shoulders, while he sucked on her tight bud, curling his fingers inside of her. She tensed and bucked, a sign her orgasm was about to crash over her. "Your mouth and your beard are driving me insane. Don't stop."

"I don't intend to," he whispered and blew on her sensitized flesh. With one long lick against her, her hips gyrated, and she came with a shriek. Watching her come apart was by far the hottest thing he'd ever seen. He placed kisses on her stomach and the inside of her thighs.

Panting, she sat up, her eyes bright, red waves spilling out of her ponytail, looking wildly aroused. For the first time in years, he felt a sense of peace and contentment, all because of her.

He wanted to tell her how he felt, but it was too soon. He'd only scare her away, so he smiled and kissed her shoulder instead. "You okay?"

"Better than okay." Willow grabbed him by the collar and unbuttoned his shirt. "Your turn to lose the clothes." Her cheeks were flushed and her lips kiss-swollen. He couldn't help but stare at her, which only intensified his longing.

"You don't need to ask twice." He pulled off his shirt and threw it next to the discarded pile on the solarium floor.

He heard the catch of her breath. She gave him an appreciative once-over that made him glad he worked out. "You are the most beautiful man I've ever laid eyes on."

"You're the one who's beautiful, Willow, inside and out." He was just about to rid himself of the rest of his clothing when she held up her hand, which was hard to focus on considering she was completely and gloriously naked.

"Wait, before we...you know, there's something we need to discuss." Her face flushed and in that moment she looked so innocent it sent licks of fire pumping though his veins.

"Protection?" He cursed and shook his head, ready to bang it against the solarium wall. "I'm sorry I don't have a condom on me. I, uh, didn't want to be presumptuous."

"It's okay. This is awkward, but I've been tested. I'm clean." She waited a heartbeat, clearly uncomfortable. "I'm not asking for a list of the women in your past."

"Hey, you don't need to worry about me. I get tested all the time." He slipped the rest of her hair out of her ponytail and ran his fingers through her silky waves. "It's an agency requirement."

Her face broke out into a huge grin. "Then we're good to go." She pressed a lust-fueled kiss on his lips. "I take a potion that works even better than the pill."

His hips jerked in anticipation. The idea of sinking into her moist heat with nothing between them made him want to spill right then and there. "I'm starting to like your brand of magick." He couldn't look away from the fire blazing in her eyes or the swollen berry color of her lips, imagining all the things he wanted to do to her.

He stood and slipped out of his shoes and kicked off his jeans. He slid down the waistband of his boxers and kicked them to the side. Willow stared wide-eyed at his hard-on, hot and pulsing, standing at full attention. He kneeled so they faced each other.

She wrapped her hand around his cock and moved it up and down over and over again until he hissed out a breath. "I won't last long if you keep that up." Maybe he'd have more finesse the second time around, and then his heart lurched, hoping there'd be a second time.

"I want you inside of me. I can't wait any longer." She gripped the back of his neck and guided him down until he hovered above her on the yoga mat. He placed a gentle kiss on her temple and lifted her hips.

"I need to get you ready first." He rubbed his length on her, letting her moisture coat the tip. He eased himself in a bit, not moving until she was ready. He clenched his teeth and sucked in several agonizing breaths, hovered above her.

She clawed at his back, moving her hips, making him lose his mind. "Please, Alex, I want to feel you move."

"I don't want to hurt you, especially after you were injured." Her scent and moans clouded his brain. Her skin was slick and drenched with sweat. Her legs were clamped around his hips, driving him deeper inside the wet heat of her body.

A groan of raw pleasure escaped from his lips as she clenched all around him. His last bit of control shattered. He sucked on her neck and began to thrust deeply. Warmth spread through him. "Willow, being inside you feels so damn good." A connection was there, vibrating between them like a live wire.

He stared down at her in wonder. She moved with him, arching her pelvis until they found a steady rhythm. "You're wet and ready for me, baby." His voice grew husky with arousal. He reached down and grabbed her breast and pinched her nipple. "I want to feel you come again for me." He took her hands and placed them above her head, entwining their fingers, and their gazes locked. It was almost too much, and yet neither of them managed to look away.

Damn, he was in over his head. "Alex, I'm going to…ah." Maybe it was her sob or the naked desire in her eyes that forced him to look away, but damn if it didn't make his chest tight.

The hitch of her breathing and the jerking of her thighs drove him insane. He began to pump harder and faster, not able to get enough of the taste and feel of her. He groaned, relishing the friction. All the times he'd fantasized about having sex with her, nothing compared to the real thing. He lifted her hips so he could thrust inside of her from a different angle.

"I can't get enough of you." The sounds of skin slapping against skin echoed inside the bubble.

With each hard thrust, her breasts bounded up, making him lose his mind. He lifted her ass off the mat, deepening his strokes. Their breaths mingled together, their hearts beating as one.

He'd been with his fair share of women before, but nothing had ever compared to this. And then he realized as her eyes burned into his, nothing ever would. "Are you feeling this, Willow?" His voice came out ragged.

"Yes," she whimpered and dug her fingers into his skin. "Don't you dare stop." She was right there with him, keeping up with the frenzied rhythm. A thin sheen of sweat broke out all over his body. His vision blurred. A roaring filled in his ears.

He was ready to implode, his orgasm about to crash over him. She circled his hips, her hair now slick with sweat. "Willow, are you close?"

Her body bucked beneath him. "I'm coming,"

A satisfied grin tugged at his lips. Hot, blissful waves of ecstasy consumed him from the top of his head to the tip of his toes. He pumped and let his own release take over. With a roar, he spilled into her. His body shook with the aftershocks of an explosive release. He lay on top of her, trying to catch his breath.

Finally, he lifted up onto his elbows and buried his nose in her neck. His muscles ached and exhaustion pulled at him. When he was finally able to untangle himself from her, he turned her over onto her side and wrapped her in his arms. He reached for his shirt and wrapped it around her body. "Feel better?"

She nodded and snuggled closer. "Much. Alex, don't go."

"I'm not going anywhere." He kissed the back of her head and decided to figure out what to do in the morning. For now, he was going to enjoy the beautiful woman in his arms.

CHAPTER 16

*A*lex made a noise deep in his throat that sounded like torment as Willow ran her hands over the hard muscles in his shoulders and chest. "I love the feel of your skin," she murmured. It was like touching silk over steel. After their first round of love making, they ended up back at her room and slept for a few hours before going for round two.

A sultry gleam flashed in his eyes "You're wearing me out. I don't think I've ever come so hard." When he reached down to gather his clothes off the floor, she figured he was leaving.

She bit down on her lip and tried to hide her disappointment. Instead, he carefully laid his things over the side of the chair and began to pick up her yoga pants, undergarments, and tank top. He stacked them on the chair, crawled into bed, and collapsed next to her.

"I'm glad I could help." After she turned on her side, she smiled and stared at the sensual curve of his lips. She'd been wildly attracted to him from day one, even when he was being a jerk. But the things he revealed, the struggles he'd been facing all alone, made her want to ease his pain. These new insights into his past from a man who appeared so tough on the outside revealed even he could be vulnerable. Her heart gave a little pang. If she wanted him to keep confiding in her then she'd have to be both friend and lover. As for the girlfriend part, for now she'd tread lightly. They still had a lot to overcome.

Her gaze trailed down the length of his body for the millionth time tonight and she couldn't help but sigh. "Thank you for confiding in me about everything." She never would've guessed that Alex was a tortured soul with a past. He'd been through hell and back and still devoted his life to protecting the innocent. Such a trait amazed her.

"I want us to start trusting each other." He raised himself up on his elbow. "I want this, Willow, you and me. If this is ever going to work, then we can't keep secrets."

But could he ever get over the fact that she was a witch? When she was with him like this, he made her feel loved, cherished even. If she let herself, she could fall, hard. But how would he be toward her around her friends, or his peers for that matter? No, she would have to protect her heart.

"When was your last relationship?" She wondered how many women he'd been with. A man like Alex must've been in love. What woman wouldn't fall head over heels for him?

"In my line of work there's not too much time for relationships." He brushed his fingers against her cheek and along her jaw. "I'm pretty much married to my job. There was a girl in college, Anna. We dated for a couple of years, but it wasn't serious. Then there was Sara. We were close, but at a certain point, I didn't see a future, so I ended things."

"Why? What happened?"

"Simple. I wasn't in love with her. How about you?" he asked and ran lazy circles on the skin above her breasts, making her shiver.

"There was someone once, a long time ago. He was a sorcerer who worked for the Cabal. I thought he loved me, but it turned out he was sent to spy on me." Even after all these years, his betrayal still stung. "Now it's just me and my trusty Pocket Rocket."

"Not if I have anything to say about the matter." He planted a kiss on her neck before gazing into her eyes. All traces of humor were gone. "I'm sorry, Willow. You didn't deserve what he did to you, especially after everything you've been through. But it was his loss and definitely my gain."

His words were sincere and heartfelt. The wall she'd worked so hard to build around her heart began to crumble. She wanted to believe Alex genuinely cared about her, with no ulterior motive or personal agenda. But could she? "Aren't you the sweet talker?"

"Who says we have to talk?" His eyes sparkled with mischief as he cupped her breast. He ran his thumb across her nipple. "I can't get enough of you," he whispered, making her sex clench.

"Admit it, you only want me for my body." She batted her eyelashes for effect.

He laughed. "I want you for lots of reasons. Your gorgeous body's simply an added bonus. I want you for your sass and your wit, and to keep me on my toes. I want you for your unfailing loyalty and bravery. I want you for your huge heart, and most of all, I want you because I don't think I'd ever get tired of trying to figure out how your brain works. I could keep going."

His words sliced her open. She wanted to run and hide, but there was no place to go. Tears swam in her eyes. She placed her fingers over his lips. "You don't have to, Alex."

"Hey, this isn't cheap talk to get you into bed. I've had you, a few times, I might add. I'm saying this because it's the truth. I don't want this to end."

She closed her eyes, letting every word and every caress sear into her brain. She'd cherish these few stolen moments forever. The more she let herself believe in happy endings and white picket fences, the more she knew she was setting herself up for heartache. She was always waiting for the other shoe to drop, and in her experience, at some point it eventually would.

When this mess was over, she'd leave Raven's Hollow and put this all behind her. She yawned, feeling the pull of sleep. "As much as I'd love to go for round three," she said in an attempt to sway the conversation. "I don't think I have the strength. My body's still weak. I need to replenish my magick."

"You need your rest." He collapsed on his back and pulled her across his chest.

She snuggled against him, breathing in his musky scent. His arms wrapped around her and held her close. "I didn't take you for the cuddling type," she whispered and let out a sigh of contentment.

"You have that effect on me. Shh, you need sleep." He caressed her back, lulling her into a state of pure bliss. The delicious memory of pleasure was still coursing through her veins when her eyes closed.

CHAPTER 17

The killer's face flashed through Willow's mind. She began to toss and turn and clawed at the sheets. A dark, twisted energy worked its way into her head like a toxin. His deep, gruff voice filled her dream.

You're the next witch to die, Willow. A man like Saint Claire doesn't take kindly to getting double-crossed. A debt is owed, and you'll pay dearly...with blood. Nothing and no one can protect you now, certainly not a mortal. I'm going to love making him watch while I kill you and consume your flesh. Such a cruel act, I admit, and yet, it allows me to absorb your powers, just like I was able to absorb poor Maeve and Kimber's. Once I kill the rest of you, I'll be unstoppable and then I can fulfill my destiny—eradicate all witches from the face of the earth. I know you can sense me now. I'm on the roof right above your bedroom door. Sweet dreams.

Before she could get away, he swooped in through the window, wrapped his hands around her throat and squeezed. Choking and gasping for air, she tried to fight him off, but he only laughed. He scooped her up and flew away with her into the night.

"No!" She screamed. Shaking, she jerked upright. Her heart pounded in her chest and her throat felt raw. She rubbed her neck as a chill ran down her spine.

"Willow?" Alex reached out to her.

"He was here, Alex. He was trying to kill me. I wasn't able to fight back. I'm still too weak." She glanced at the window to make sure the charm above the shade was still in place, but what good would it do?

"Hey," he whispered in a soothing tone. "It's okay. It was a nightmare."

"No, it was real. I sensed his presence right outside the window. He said he was here, on the roof. I can feel him inside my head. He said he was going to kill me and make you watch." She knew she sounded hysterical, but she couldn't help herself.

"You're safe. We placed SED's on all the windows and doors. They act as black magick detectors. An alarm will sound and lights will flash if that sonofabitch tries to break in. I won't let anything happen to you, Willow, I swear," he whispered and massaged her neck.

She exhaled, allowing her body to relax with the knowledge that a device was in place. When he ran his fingers through her hair, she snuggled back against his chest, and let herself give in to the exhaustion tugging at her limbs. After a few minutes, her body became boneless. When she could no longer fight the pull of sleep, her lids began to flutter. She yawned and drifted off to the comforting sound of Alex's breath.

Alex waited until Willow's breathing was steady and even before he slipped out of her bed. He quickly tugged on his clothes and shoved his feet into his shoes. He pulled out a slip of paper and a pen from his pocket to scribble a short note. He placed it on the bed, next to her pillow.

"You're mine," he whispered and kissed her temple. With her red lips parted and her face free of makeup, she looked so young, and innocent, and so damn beautiful it took his breath away.

It was all he could do not to pull her into his arms again and hold her until the sun came up. He wanted to chase all her nightmares away. He waited for the grandfather clock in the hall to chime and creaked open the door. After he pulled out his phone with the downloaded schematic of the coven, he exhaled when all SED's flashed to green. Still, he needed back-up.

He glanced up and down the hallway to make sure no one was up and about before he left the room. Grinding his teeth, his thoughts scattered in a million different directions. And yet only one kept tugging at the center of his chest. What if Ven Pariah got to her? He refused to take a chance with her life.

Pushing a button on his cell, he tapped his foot until he heard Cayden's voice. "It's me. I need Brodie or one of the other agents on duty upstairs. Now. Someone needs to guard Willow's room and it can't be me. She had a nightmare where the bastard came in through the window. I've never seen her so shaken up."

If Smith found him standing outside her door looking like a possessive boyfriend, reeking of sex and Willow's perfume, he'd put two and two together in a heartbeat. After all, Alex had lied to him about his feelings for her, and the words still felt like acid on his tongue. Out of spite, Smith might pull him from the case for good. He couldn't take that chance. "She's on the second floor, first door on the left."

"We can't designate an agent for one person. We don't have that kind of manpower right now. Besides, Willow's supposed to be working on our side, protecting the other witches."

"She's not exactly in a position to protect anyone right now, not even herself. She's injured and she's in bed resting. Besides, this maniac knows who she is and probably has a hard-on for her now."

"Let me guess, you're in her room right now as we speak. Gods, Alex, you know better than to get involved on the job. What are you thinking? And she's a criminal to boot."

"Shut up, Cayden. She's made mistakes. She's not the only one. She's a good person. You can't deny that after all she's done for us and this case." He killed a nine-year-old boy in cold blood. He was in no position to judge. "She took down a few pieces of shit the world's now better off without. She's at least trying to redeem herself. I expected this sort of thing from Smith, but not from you."

"Can you justify what she's done? You're in over your head. Did you sleep with her?"

"Not like this is any of your business."

"I think I got my answer."

He didn't give a damn at this point. He needed to protect her and he couldn't risk doing it himself. There were some things more important than protocol. What he needed to do couldn't wait. He had to follow his hunch. All of the women of this coven depended on him to stop a killer, and he refused to let them down. He'd been blinded by his past, letting it color his judgement, seeing all witches as the same, but not anymore.

"You're off the clock, man. Don't do anything stupid," Cayden warned. "I guess it's a little late for that. Think about it, are you really willing to risk everything, your entire career, and put innocent lives at risk over a hot piece of ass?"

"Watch your mouth. You're my best friend. I know what I'm asking, but if the situation were reversed, I'd never say that to you." Alex ran a hand through his hair and cursed. "Are you going to put an agent outside her door or not?"

Cayden let out an exaggerated sigh. "Fine, I'll send Brodie up."

"Thanks, I owe you."

"I've heard that one before. This time I'm holding you to it, man."

Alex ended the call and headed for the back staircase. He had someone important to see, one of the few people he knew without a shadow of a doubt would be awake at this time of the morning. His stomach grumbled. He needed food, but he wasn't the only one. He'd make a pit stop before he got on the road.

With a backward glance at Willow's door, he headed down the stairs. What he wouldn't do to get back in bed and wrap his arms around her, keep her safe. But that would have to wait, at least for now. He had a killer to catch, and if all went according to plan, the fae would soon be fairy dust.

CHAPTER 18

*A*s Willow made her way into the kitchen, she heard the echo of voices, the scurry of heels, and loud rock music blaring from an iPhone. Even after all these years of living alone, she still missed the hustle and bustle of people.

The place could be a little noisy at times, but in a good way. She'd been on her own for so long now. She still hated the long stretches of solitude and the endless lonely nights. Being here now only made her realize how much she'd been missing out on.

She dressed casual in jeans and a sweater, her hair still wet from the shower. Too bad Alex couldn't stay to soap up her back. Immediately, her mind drifted to him and delicious memories invaded her thoughts. Goosebumps broke out across her flesh. The man was sinful in every way possible. Her face flushed and her heart gave a little flutter thinking about him.

Now that he finally opened up to her about his partner, she realized there was so much more to him. He was real—and flawed, a man who still mourned the loss of his friend. Seeing him so unguarded last night deepened her attraction to him even more and doubled her chances of getting hurt.

When she'd woken up, she was surprised to find Brodie outside her door and she wondered if Alex had sent him.

She wondered how long he'd stayed before he slipped out of her room. Maybe this was only a casual fling to him, a temporary relief from the stress and horrors of a murder case. Could he really get over his issues with witches? He was the last man on Earth she should be getting involved with. *Too late.*

Before she could contemplate the situation any further, Delilah stepped out of the elevator, ran up to her and caught her in a bone-crushing hug. "Willow, you're okay. Dear Goddess. I was worried about you. We all were."

"I don't think I heard you right. Did you say you were *all* worried about me?" She raised her eyebrows at her. "I'm okay. I'm tougher than I look."

Delilah pulled away, a look of genuine concern on her striking face. "I heard what happened. You're a hero around here. The way you jumped on the roof of a car to go after the killer. You saved Gillian. Everyone's talking about it. I can't imagine what would've happened if you weren't there."

"It was no big deal." Willow waved her hand. "You would've done the same thing."

"Stop being humble. It was a huge deal. You saved a life. That's karma times three. How's your ankle, by the way?"

I saved a life. I finally did something right for a change.

Did Willow change her karma? She let the impact of Delilah's words sink into her brain. "What?" She lifted her foot off the floor and moved her ankle from side to side, amazed there was no lingering soreness, considering the pain she'd experienced last night. "It's fine, actually, thanks to Saje's potion and Nadia's healing spell. Where's everyone?"

"They're probably in the kitchen. Come on, you look as if you could use a little breakfast."

She was starving, especially after last night's workout, but the thought of digging into tofu and veggie muffins made her gag.

As they made their way through the hall, they passed two agents she'd never seen before, standing guard. She wondered where Cayden, Smith, and Alex were. There was no sign of the trio this morning. Her heart gave a little tug. Technically, Alex was off the case, she reminded herself. She wondered when she'd see him again.

They walked into the kitchen and the scent of fresh brewed coffee, scrambled eggs, bacon, and home fries assailed her nostrils. Her stomach instantly grumbled. "What's going on?"

"Come see for yourself," Delilah said, walking toward the smell of food.

When Willow stopped in the doorway, ten heads turned from the breakfast table to stare at her. The atmosphere in the room was harmonious, peaceful, and downright welcoming. "Good morning, ladies." Self-conscious, she pushed her hair behind her ear, not used to being at the center of positive attention for a change. She'd really managed to go from a harlot to a heroine in twenty-four hours? *Interesting.*

Saje, Nadia, Arabella, and most of the other girls came over and either patted her on the shoulder or gave her a hug. A collective round of "thank you," and "way to go," was murmured all around.

Overwhelmed, she stood back from the throng and struck up a conversation with Delilah. They compared notes about the murders and Willow filled her in on her premonitions. "I think you need to share your visions with the other girls. It might help. I'm here for you."

Willow sighed. "Thank you. It's good to know I have a friend."

"You do."

The clink of silverware made Willow turn toward the breakfast bar, surprised to find the other women loading bacon and eggs onto their plates. She waited until the majority had finished eating and filed out of the kitchen before she and Delilah made their way over to the food.

"This looks incredible, thank you." After Willow filled her mug with coffee, she added a healthy dose of cream and sugar, and then loaded up her plate.

"Don't thank us." Delilah's bright blue eyes sparkled. "You can thank Agent Denopoulos. He brought all this in. Of course, he asked first. He thought it would be okay this one time, considering the circumstances. He hoped we could make an exception and thought you might need a little extra protein." She picked up a piece of bacon from the pan and took a bite. "A little cheat never hurt anyone. What's going on between you two? His whole demeanor changed at the mention of your name."

"Don't be silly." Willow felt her face flush. "We strongly dislike each other. I think he's trying to make up for the fact that he wasn't the one who jumped on the car. This must be a peace offering." It made her feel horrible, not only to lie, but to do the exact thing she feared Alex would do when it came to their relationship. But she had to prepare herself for his inevitable withdrawal. Telling the women of the coven they were together would only complicate things later.

A million thoughts raced through her mind as she walked to the table. Alex had once again gone out of his way to do something nice for her—to show he cared. Her heart twisted with longing. Willow wanted to believe he was different, that he meant what he'd said. Was a future together possible? Or was this just a peace offering for him leaving?

She pushed the thoughts from her head and took a seat in between Nadia and Saje. "The potion worked wonders. I want to thank both of you." She took a bite of her breakfast, savoring the taste of bacon. "Speaking of potions, I need to ask both of you about one I believe Maeve was working on before she died."

"Delilah showed us the grimoire," Nadia said, getting up from the table and walking to the buffet. She picked up the book, walked back, and hefted the enormous leather-bound tome onto the table. She waved her finger and the pages flipped to the vanquishing spell. "We want to catch this madman as much as anyone. Do you think you can get close enough to do this?"

"Yes. We'll need to scry him again, but I know we can find him." Willow wouldn't rest until she did. "After all the bad blood, I wasn't sure you guys would help me."

"It's the least we could do after you risked your life to save Gillian. We're forever grateful, and I want to apologize on behalf of all the women of this coven for the way we treated you when you first arrived," Saje said, sounding sincere.

"We don't need to go there right now." Willow pushed her food around her plate with her fork, letting the words sink in. "We have more important matters to discuss, like the fact that there's still a killer on the loose."

"I'll help any way I can, but before we get started, I want to clear the air once and for all," Nadia said, looking anxious as she tapped her fingers on the table.

Willow shrugged, trying not to look as tense as she felt. "Okay, what's this about?"

Nadia took a sip from her mug. "I recently found out you were telling the truth all along. Ellen knew Ed was a pig. In fact, she was the one who convinced Daisy Handler, the underage girl who pressed charges against Ed, to come forward."

Before Willow could respond, Delilah stood up from the table and frowned. "Wait a minute. Ellen knew she was innocent? But she let you all think Willow was to blame?" She threw Nadia a vicious look. "All of you perpetuated your own type of witch hunt against Willow. You accused her of something she didn't even do. Considering our shared pasts, you should know better. How could you judge her without all the facts?" Her voice rose nearly to shouting level at the last word. She took a few deep breaths. "Excuse me. I need to work off this anger. I'll be in the library," she said and left the room.

Shocked, Willow shook her head and pushed her plate away, her appetite gone. "I don't understand. How did Ellen know the girl? You said her name was Daisy?"

A guilty look flashed in Nadia's eyes. "Yes. Ellen was friendly with Daisy's mother and she came here to tell her what had happened to her daughter. Naturally, she remembered Ellen and Ed used to live together years before. When Ellen first found out, she was seething with anger."

Holy shit. Ellen knew the whole time since Willow had been back and never said a word, even let the other girls think the worst. "Then how come everyone has treated me as if I had a scarlet letter across my chest?"

"When Ellen first found out she felt horrible for what she did to you," Nadia explained. "She was physically ill over the situation. She couldn't eat or sleep. She went to Ed's house to confront him. From what she told me later, it was lucky he had a fire extinguisher on hand or he'd be nothing more than a pile of ash. Her powers were so out of control, she said she almost burned his house down."

"What did he say? I'm sure Ed lied again," Willow muttered, trying to tamp down the anger coursing through her veins like battery acid.

"Not when it came to Daisy. He admitted everything, swore that they were in love. And that when her mother found out, she insisted her daughter go to the cops because she was technically still a minor," Nadia whispered.

By the time Nadia finished, Willow's chest was heaving. "Tell me what he said about me, Nadia. Did he finally come clean about the past?"

Nadia blinked and her eyes filled with tears. "He claimed that you'd been stalking him for months, and that you even threatened violence on

Ellen if he didn't leave her." After a few gasps, the room became eerily quiet again, each one of the women seemed to be hanging on Nadia's every word.

After Nadia wiped her eyes on her sleeve, she continued. "Ed said you were a bad seed, a troubled soul and that you'd only end up down a dark path that you'd never come back from. But no matter what he said, I didn't believe it then and I don't believe it now. I wish I'd spoken up on your behalf. Ellen knows she's wrong. That's why she's been purposely avoiding you."

"Thanks for telling me everything." Willow's throat constricted, Even after all these years, hearing Nadia reveal what she'd only suspected was like a dagger through the heart. The only one of the witches that knew the truth about Willow's past, and the real reasons she was here, was Ellen. It explained why she never spoke up on Willow's behalf. "This subject is a bitter pill for everyone involved. I suggest none of us bring it up after today."

Despite the burning sensation in the pit of her stomach, she needed to stay focused on her goal: stop a killer, avenge Maeve's death, and turn her life around. Then she'd finally prove Ed wrong.

"I was the only one who knew the truth until Agent Denopoulos confronted Ellen with the facts. I guess she figured it was time to come clean. I happened to be home the day Daisy's mom stopped by the coven. Ellen made me swear not to tell anyone. I guess she wanted to save face. It must be embarrassing to know the man you once shared a bed with was a total pedo. I mean, gross. I'm sorry, Willow," Nadia said, sounding sincere.

Willow let out a breath. "I'm glad Daisy had the guts to do what I never could. It sounds as if justice was finally served." She hoped the pain of those words didn't show on her face.

Nadia put her hand on top of Willow's. "That's not true. Daisy had someone who believed in her and fought for her. You didn't. I'm sorry, Willow. You were brave enough to get out of the situation. That counts for a lot."

Willow swallowed the lump in her throat, at a loss for words. She couldn't bring herself to look at Nadia. After several tense minutes, finally, she found the strength to respond. "My whole life was ruined because of this lie, but that's in the past. Let's focus on what I came here to do."

"None of us had any idea that your life was ruined, Willow," Saje whispered, touching her arm. "We just assumed you went to go live with your mother."

"We were all young, and foolish," added Nadia. "I'm sorry for everything."

After that, no one said a word. The truth hung in the room like stale air on a humid day. Willow simply nodded, wanting to crawl out of her skin. Once everyone finished their breakfast and loaded plates and mugs into the sink, she turned toward Nadia and Saje, needing to redirect the conversation. "What's your expert opinion on the spell?"

"I've done a little research," Nadia said, running her fingers across the page. "This spell was written by a witch by the name of Raven Degrassi. This town was named after her. From all accounts, she wrote this spell about a hundred and fifty years ago during a particularly violent witch hunt in Italy. There was a band of fae that raped and tortured members of Raven's family."

Nadia swallowed hard and continued. "Eventually, they burned them at the stake. Raven created this spell and a potion to destroy those who had hurt her loved ones. Her grimoire got passed down to other generations and it saved her remaining ancestors once they settled here in the States."

Intrigued, Willow nodded. "I've always known this town was rich in myth and lore, but I've never heard that particular tale. Do you think this potion will kill him?"

"I've been trying to figure out the ingredients, but it's pretty complex," added Saje. "I think with a few minor tweaks it could be powerful enough to destroy him. We don't have all of the ingredients she suggests here in Jersey, but there are things we could use as substitutes. I'd like you to take a look at Raven's spell and see if you recognize any of the words." She turned the book to face Willow.

"You, Gillian, and Maeve were the only witches who were taught in old Latin for the invocation of spells and enchantments." Nadia turned the page. "I asked Ellen, but she said you'd remember this kind of thing better than she would."

Saje leaned over Willow's shoulder. "I can't make out this word, 'animus'."

Willow glanced at the page. "It means soul."

"And what about this one, 'ex inferisnatas'?" asked Saje.

"It's not a direct translation, but it means being born out of the lower world."

"It's all starting to make sense." Nadia's eyes grew wide. "We have to banish his soul, not just his physical body, to the lower world."

"Great, it sounds like a piece of cake." Willow rolled her eyes, her excitement starting to fade.

"Why don't we take a break?" suggested Saje. "I have a few things to look up in the coven library and on my computer. I'll spread the word to meet back here, say in an hour, and let's see what we can come up with using our collective powers."

Willow nodded. "Sounds good."

Saje left the table, while Nadia remained and stared at the floor. Immediately, Willow picked up on her anxiety. "Look, Nadia, I think we've said all we need to. As far as I'm concerned, we've cleared the air as much as it's going to clear. We're working together on this one, right?"

"Yes, it's something else actually. I didn't want to mention it in front of everyone," Nadia muttered, refusing to look Willow in the eyes.

"Spit it out. What's this about anyway?"

"A conversation Agent Denopoulos was having with his boss and I'm afraid it involves you. You can link with me. Then you'll know I'm not lying. He said something about playing a role to get you to trust him."

Was Alex manipulating her this entire time to get her to cooperate? No way. She had to consider the source. Clearly this woman didn't care about her in the slightest. Guilt had driven her to tell the other women about Ed, not concern. If it had been anything more, she would have said something when she found out the truth. But then again, she had no way of getting ahold of her. Working for the Cabal had forced Willow to live on the down-low these past few years.

Still, she had to know for sure. She took Nadia's hands, allowing her to establish a link between them. Her skin tingled where they touched. The kitchen faded away. Nadia's memory played through Willow's mind like a bad B movie. There was no denying it. Hearing Alex betray her to Smith crushed Willow's heart. After she yanked her hands away from Nadia, the memory faded until she could see the kitchen once more.

She should've known. Willow could never trust men. Alex was no different. Why did she have to go and sleep with him? How could she have been so stupid?

Her stomach twisted with shame. She was still soaring on anger and adrenaline from their earlier conversation, but not enough to dull her pain. Alex's words started to sink in and became heavy like a sandbag to the chest. She attempted to inhale, gulping air into her lungs. But she couldn't get enough. Red pinpricks floated in her vision and all she could think about was getting the hell out of there as her eyes burned with big, fat tears.

CHAPTER 19

illow stood in the greenhouse, a mortar and pestle in one hand, and a photocopy of the vanquishing spell in the other. She placed the paper on the long butcher-block worktable, a splotch of candle wax and herbs smudged across the top. The only light came from the flicker of votives in the center of the table.

After meeting with Saje and Nadia, the three of them had spent the better part of the day, and most of the evening, poring over the spell. The list for the potion ingredients seemed endless. Now it was time to put their hard work to the test. The only catch was when said aloud, the incantation could be dangerous, deadly in fact.

If the vanquishing spell backfired it could destroy her soul as well if she didn't invoke it properly. A knot of tension settled in the pit of her stomach at what she was about to do. But at this point she was done waiting around for the killer to swoop in and take her. If he tried, at least this time she'd be ready. She wasn't going to ask the girls for any more of their help. How many more had to die before the fae was banished to the Underworld?

A streak of lightning drew her gaze to the floor-to-ceiling windows. A torrent of rain lashed at an inky black sky. Temporarily transfixed by the sight, she let out a long, deep breath and tried to chase the sensation of anxiety away.

Even with a handful of well-trained MBI agents guarding the coven, she didn't feel safe, not really. If the killer wanted to strike, she didn't think anyone could stop him. She thought about her *athame* strapped in her hip belt and tried to relax.

She reached for an old shawl off a hook on the wall and wrapped it around her shoulders to chase away the chill. Now she was caught in the throes of the storm. She had no choice but to make the best use of her time. Besides, she couldn't sleep anyway. Images of Alex swam behind her eyes. She needed to keep herself busy. It was the best way to keep her mind from focusing on her pain.

Alex felt nothing for her. Apparently, it was all an act, a ruse to keep her in check and under his controlling thumb. He'd never get past his distrust of witches. Why did she want to believe so badly that he would? Maybe her grief over Maeve had blinded her to the truth.

Her chest felt empty and cold. Refusing to indulge in self-pity any longer, she pulled the herbs from the shelves and got to work, grinding rosemary seeds, rue, and valerian root, along with a sprinkle of mugwort, into a fine dust.

When she was finished, she wiped her hands on her jeans and couldn't stop thinking she'd lost something precious. *Was it Alex? Or maybe it was hope.* She walked to the sink and filled a cauldron with water and set it on the stovetop.

Who was she kidding? She'd already fallen for him, hard. Fate, she always did have a sense of humor. Willow wanted a man who didn't want her back, not for more than a quick fling, anyway. She'd suspected as much from the very beginning. Then why did the truth have to hurt so badly? Maybe because of his disdain for everything she stood for.

The girl means nothing to me. I'm playing a role. Nothing has changed. Besides, you think I'd ever lie down with a witch? His words reverberated through her head and tied her stomach in knots.

She turned up the flame on the stove and tried to shake the fog from her brain. No, this was a good reality check. She couldn't afford to get lost in silly fantasies filled with hearts and flowers. Alex had almost made her forget the cruel reality of her past. She'd been abandoned, left to survive on the streets. And yet, somehow, she'd found a way to manage all on her own. She couldn't go soft now. She needed to keep her edge to defeat a killer. Maeve had to be avenged.

A loud mewling noise drew her attention to the fat black feline in the corner of the room. "Piewacket, is that really you?" She walked over, picked him up, and gave the cat a scratch behind the ears.

"Bless your little soul, you always could detect when I was sad." She nuzzled him close to her body as he meowed and licked her face. She gave the cat a kiss on the head before placing him back down on the floor. "You would never hurt a woman, would you, handsome?" Maybe she was destined to be an old cat lady herself. She pushed the depressing thought aside and decided to focus on her potion instead.

When she walked back to the butcher block, she poured all the freshly ground herbs into the cauldron of steaming water. She murmured a series of incantations and then waited for the water to boil before ladling the potion into a couple of glass bottles. She secured each one with a stopper.

With a sigh, she wiped the sweat from her brow and let the shawl slip from her shoulders. She was about to practice the spell before she cleaned up when a giant gust of wind and a hard lash of rain smacked against the greenhouse. The small structure shook on its hinges. The candles flickered and then blew out.

Piewacket mewled. "It's okay, Pie," she murmured into the pitch blackness. Hands shaking, she was about to flick her wrist to light the candle when a large hand closed over her mouth.

Instinctively, she elbowed her attacker in the ribs, which allowed her to break free from his hold. She heard a grunt as her fingers wrapped around the handle of her *athame*. She unsheathed the blade from her hip belt and pointed the tip at the broad shadow in front of her.

"Willow, what the hell are you doing? I'm sorry. I didn't mean to startle you. I was afraid you'd scream and wake up the whole damn house." Alex stood inches from the edge of her blade. His hulking shadow loomed over her in the darkness. From the rough edge to his voice, he wasn't happy about having a sword pointed at his throat.

"How did you find me out here?" she asked, her voice laced with anger.

"Your tracking device. Why are you out here all alone in the middle of the night? It's not safe." He flicked a light from his keychain and held it up, forcing her gaze to his gorgeous face. Even soaking wet and with his clothes plastered to his body, the man was sexy as sin and too dangerous for her peace of mind.

"I've been busy making a potion, one that should vanquish the killer for good." She purposely left out the part about how it might end up killing her as well. She didn't think he needed to hear that tidbit just yet. From now on, things between them could only be professional. Their interactions would be limited to the case, nothing more. She moved the tip of her blade from his throat to his chest. Why did she have an overwhelming urge to hurt him like he'd hurt her?

"Put the knife down, Willow." His eyes flashed in the dim light and she noticed his briefcase slung over his arm.

"I wonder," she said, pointing it directly at his heart. "If someone like you even has a heart. I'd venture a guess, if you do, it's probably as cold and hard as a block of ice."

His jaw clenched. "What's going on? What the hell are you talking about?"

"It doesn't matter. I'm here to do a job," she said, and sheathed her *athame* back in her belt. "There's no room for anything else. I had a little chat with Nadia. This is just a job, right? I mean nothing to you."

He didn't respond at first, instead he pulled a lighter from his pocket and lit the candles. "I don't know what she told you, but it was all taken out of context. I said some things I didn't mean." After he ran a hand through his wet hair, he shook his head, spraying her with rain drops. "I had no other choice. It was to protect you. You need to listen to me, Willow. I didn't want Smith to figure out the truth."

"Really? What's the truth? I'd love to hear it from your lips." She wished she could keep the bitterness out of her voice. She reached for a kitchen towel off the counter and tossed it at him.

He caught it and wiped his face, then laid it across the back of the sink. When he turned back to face her, his eyes flickered to hers. "I care about you. A lot."

Her pathetic heart sped up and began to pound. "Why should I believe you? You lied to me." She'd met enough liars to last a lifetime. She didn't need another one. "Why are you sneaking around here in the dead of night? What's going on?"

"I don't have time to explain." He let out a string of curses. "I'm afraid there's been another murder. The bastard killed another witch."

Her hands flew to her ears. "No, it can't be."

"I'm afraid so. I've been at the morgue all day." He placed his briefcase on one of the small tables. "I happened to be there going over the evidence records when the call came in. Smith had no choice but to let me stay and help. I know too much about this case to stand aside, and considering the circumstances, he agreed, at least in an unofficial capacity anyway."

"What happened?" she asked, sounding weary. Her anger drained away, a sense of horror taking over. Suddenly, whatever he'd said about her didn't matter at the moment.

"A farmer stumbled upon the decomposed body of a female in a shallow grave on his property less than twenty-four hours ago. It turns out she was a witch from a coven a few hours away. At first we didn't think it was the fae who killed her, because he broke his pattern of how he's been disposing of the bodies. But Tate confirmed she was killed with a three-inch-wide broadhead to the back of the neck from the bolt of a crossbow. Her disappearance was reported about two days ago. Listen to me, I need you to put aside everything you heard today and link with the trace evidence we recently found."

This was the first time Alex had used the term "link" to acknowledge her power. "Go on."

"There was a substance like grain and traces of hay under the nails of both Kimber and the latest vic. I suspect it's a farm, based on a combination of your visions and the evidence we've gathered so far. In one of his arrest records, the killer said hunting was his favorite hobby. It all fits, Willow. But you're the only one who can tell us where he's taking these women." Alex took a step closer and her heart hammered in her chest. "I need you." The deep timbre of his voice reverberated through every cell in her body.

She took a step away from him. "Let me see if I can pick up anything. I want to help."

"I'm sorry to make you do this. I wouldn't ask if I didn't think it could help us, but we're so close." Alex pulled a plastic container marked "trace evidence" from the inside of his briefcase. "I got a sample off his latest vic. Her name was Meadow Kruger."

"Meadow? She was here filling in at the circle for Gillian. She was just a kid." Her heart clenched.

"According to Tate, he must've killed her the night after he unsuccessfully tried to kidnap you and Gillian. She had marks on both of her wrists. It turns out they were rope burns."

"Dear Goddess, that's awful."

Alex slipped on a pair of gloves and opened the plastic container. He walked over to her and handed her a pair. She slipped them on and reached for the container. His fingers brushed hers, and heat shot up her arm. She ignored it and sank down in a slip-covered chair.

She squeezed her eyes shut as her fingers closed over the evidence. A combination of anticipation and nerves made her tremble. She tried to quiet her mind against the incessant pounding of her heart and the catch of her breath.

At first, all she could make out was a gray fuzziness like a spider web intricately woven over the images. All at once her breath left her body and she was there, breathing in the scents of hay and leather, mingled with a hint of manure.

The rough edges of the rope dug into her wrists and ankles. The pain was endless, hour after hour of burns scraped against her skin until it was raw and bloody. She turned toward the door and froze as it slowly creaked open. A flood of adrenaline rushed through her veins and made her lightheaded. This was it...he was coming to kill her this time. She sensed it with every breath left in her body.

Footsteps pounded on the floorboards, and a fresh wave of panic washed over her like a raging tidal wave. She used all her body weight to try to smash the chair backward onto the floor and roll away. But she was too late. He was there, directly behind her. She could smell his sweat and the hot tang of his breath on her neck. The stench of death clung to his clothing like a dirty veil.

"Now, Meadow, if you wanted me to set you free all you had to do was ask." He lifted her off the barn floor and set the chair upright. She recoiled as he bent down and kissed her on the neck.

He pulled out a knife and held the blade in front of her face. She sucked in a breath, preparing for the blow, but he cut the ropes at her ankles instead and then slashed the ones at her wrists.

She shook her head in disbelief. He was playing a game to trick her. She gulped for air. "W-why would you let me go?"

"Stop asking questions. You got your wish. Now you're free. Just be careful what you wish for," he said in a voice that made her blood run cold.

Heart pounding, she stood up and her legs wobbled beneath her. Shivering, she could barely feel her toes. She took a tentative step and pain shot up and down her legs. She tried to ignore the hot sting of pins and needles exploding in her feet.

"You're wasting time. Let's see how far you get." He stood back and surveyed her with a sneer.

She couldn't wait for her blood to start flowing again. She had no choice. She had to run. Once she brushed past the barn door to the outside, she sucked in shallow breaths. She couldn't remember the last time she had drawn in fresh air.

Trees and shrubs flew past her and became a blur. Her heart pounded painfully in her chest as she continued to run. Sobs escaped from her throat when she spotted a broken-down fence that led to a dirt road. If she could get past the edge then she could make it to the road. She stumbled and fell to the ground. Shaking from head to toe, she forced herself up.

Footsteps pounded through the dirt behind her, followed by the sound of creepy laughter that echoed through the trees. She kept going, running as far and as fast as she could. Overgrown patches of hay and grass grew up over the wooden slats of the fence. There were no animals or farm equipment anywhere in sight. Who would find her? She got to the edge of the gate when she heard a rush of wind. Too late.

He'd already released the bolt. She became vaguely aware of her body falling to the ground like a rock plummeting into the ocean.

Her bloodcurdling scream rang in her ears, followed by the clawing, gripping need to fight, to stay alive. Pain exploded over every inch of her body. Red-hot bursts of fire lashed across her skin. Flesh, muscle, and tendons ripped away from bone as blood rushed hot and heavy.

When she thought she'd die from the pain, his voice pounded in her ears and vibrated through her head. "I won't stop. I won't stop until you're all dead."

The bolt sank deeper into her flesh until numbness took over. A single tear slid from her eye as she drew her last breath, and then it was done.

Willow's eyes flew open. She blinked. Her entire body shook with aftershocks. "You're right." A sob escaped from her throat. "He's taking them to a farm, holding them prisoner inside a dilapidated barn. It was horrible. I witnessed the whole thing. He let Meadow go free and then hunted her like an animal before he killed her."

Breathing hard, she glanced over at Alex as he pounded the keyboard on his laptop and then turned the screen toward her. Maps flashed in front of her at lightning speed. "There are approximately four farms in a fifty-mile radius of here. Can you think of any detail, anything at all that would set this farm apart from the others?"

"I don't know," Willow said, shaking her head in frustration. "I saw a fence. It was rusted out and falling down, but there were letters on it, initials I think."

"I want you to think, Willow, what were the initials? Did you see them?"

She stood and began to pace. The images floated in and out of her brain like a movie on fast forward. "I'm not sure, but I think the same ones I saw on the belt buckle, SG. I still don't know what they mean or why I keep seeing them."

"I do." Alex continued to pound furiously on his keyboard and then rubbed his beard, as though lost deep in thought. "Take a look. Could this possibly be the place?" He turned the screen toward her again.

The image was grainy and dark. "I don't know," she said honestly. "It could be."

"Then it's worth a shot. You need to see this." He pressed a key and a moment later the name Stephen Griffiths flashed across the screen. "You pegged his initials from the start. I should've never doubted you."

She scanned over the personal history revealed in his file, mulling over every twisted detail. When she got to the part about his mother being a witch, her skin crawled. "He's a monster."

"I wish I didn't have to tell you at all, but you've earned the right to know." Alex pressed a warm hand on her arm. "There's something else. He was formerly employed by Saint Claire, but we still haven't figured out the connection, if there is one for that matter."

"What? Hold on. You think Saint Claire could be behind the murders? But why? I don't understand."

"I'm still trying to figure it out. You mentioned that the other witches were doing work for a local antique dealer. My friend Mulroney from the RHPD has been investigating the case. We compared notes and did some digging. We found out that it's a subsidiary of the Shadow Cabal."

She exhaled, trying to take in this new revelation. "This is like a never-ending nightmare. What can I do?"

"Nothing right now. I'll know more after I pay a visit to Stephen Griffiths." Alex turned off his computer, slid it inside the case and pulled out his keys. "I gotta go." Determination etched deep lines all over his handsome face.

"Hold on. Why aren't you calling Cayden or Brodie to go with you? Don't tell me you're planning to go to that house of horrors alone? Are you mad?"

"All of them are tied up right now. I'll text them on the way. There's no time to waste. I have to act now. There are three farms in the vicinity that fit your description. One is about twenty-five miles from where Meadow's body was found, and the other two are farther north."

"I'm going with you," she said, and grabbed her trench coat slung over the back of the chair. After she slipped it on, she swiped the potion bottles off the butcher block and tucked them in her pockets. "What are we waiting for?"

He shook his head. "Absolutely not. I can't take you on this one, Willow."

Could he really care? "What? You're not going alone. It's too dangerous."

"You're right. It's precisely the reason you're staying here." Alex took a step toward the worktable and braced his hands on either side of her, trapping her with his big, muscular body. The heat and concern in his eyes made her toes curl.

"I can protect myself, Alex. Besides, you can't go without backup." Her lips curved into a smile. "I'll just follow you anyway."

"Technically, I'm still off the case. I'm not supposed to be doing this. You're only making this harder for me." He glanced at her foot. "What about your ankle?"

"Good as new." She pulled out a small vial from her pocket and held it up. "I still have the healing potion Saje made for me in case it acts up."

"There's no arguing with you, is there?" He took a step back and pulled up his shirt. He had two enormous laser guns strapped in holsters to his hips. The man was packing serious heat. "This time, I won't hesitate. It won't be enough to kill him, but it'll knock him unconscious."

"That's where I come in. I douse him with the potion and chant the spell, which should send his ass straight to hell." Willow glanced out the window as they headed for the greenhouse door. The rain had finally stopped and yet the same icy sensation of dread was back, only tenfold. She shivered and lifted the collar up on her coat. "We better hurry. I have a feeling there's another storm coming."

CHAPTER 20

"We're here." Alex parked his truck at the end of a long gravel road that, according to his map, led to Stephen Griffith's property. He wasn't sure if this was the place or if there was any connection to Ven Pariah for that matter. But it was a solid lead, one that he planned to follow up on.

He killed the engine and stole a glance over at Willow. A sliver of moonlight silhouetted her profile and the slim column of her neck. "This farm's registered to a Samuel Griffiths."

"I'm getting a strong sense about this place," she mumbled and glanced out the window. "It's seriously giving me the creeps. Griffiths? You think it's his father?"

"It could be, or a relative he killed to take over their property. It wouldn't be the first time I've seen this kind of thing. I ran a search on my phone but there are too many Sam Griffiths to look through and I want to act fast."

Even in the dark, he could make out the tension in her features; her eyes were wide, her lips parted, and her hands were clenched at her sides. He'd been fighting the urge to pull her into his arms and kiss her senseless since the moment he saw her at the greenhouse. Every part of him wanted to reassure her of his feelings, but he couldn't, not yet anyway. There were other things at stake.

In a different time and place, he'd take her somewhere safe and make love to her until neither of them could think straight anymore, wipe all thoughts of death and crossbows from both their minds, but that would have to wait. The pulse hammered at her throat and her breath grew shallow, and he wondered if she sensed what he'd been thinking. "Are you ready to check it out?"

She'd been cold to him, the hurt raw and potent on her beautiful face. He wanted to tell her everything was going to be okay. But he wasn't sure he had it in him to say something that could be a lie, especially not to her.

"I'll follow your lead." Willow placed her hand on the door handle, and then stepped out into the darkness.

Alex slammed the door of the truck harder than he intended, hating the idea of putting her in danger once again. He flicked on his flashlight and glanced around at his surroundings. The fog was thick after the storm and it made visibility almost impossible. He inhaled and the scent of manure, hay, and wet grass instantly flared in his nostrils. *Let this be the place.*

Everywhere he looked, raindrops clung to the bare branches on the maple trees and heavy underbrush. He turned toward a small hill a few hundred yards away. "If this is indeed his lair then he'd be able to detect the truck from a higher vantage point. We have to cover it up." He started to reach for a few stray branches.

Willow touched his shoulder. "I can use a glamour." She whispered a spell and then flicked her wrist. Sure enough, his truck now resembled a giant boulder. He shook his head, his mind still trying to accept what he'd just witnessed. He didn't think he'd ever get used to magick. "What now?"

"Why don't we search for the barn you saw in your vision?"

They crossed through a muddy field, narrowly avoiding tree roots, low hanging branches, and giant rocks along the way. "Look there, up ahead." Willow pointed to a rise in the land and a chimney in the distance. Behind the structure, he could make out the faint outline of a small greenhouse.

When she turned back to face him, her eyes filled with fear. "Willow? What is it?"

"I'm picking up on a dark sensation and this weird scent. It's the same one that came over me that first day back at the coven. I wasn't sure what it meant."

"And now?"

"I think I've been picking up on Stephen Griffith's essence all along from my visions. What if he knew the girls? Everything's clicking into place. Alex, do you remember how Tate said the killer's shirt was made of hemp?"

"Yeah, but we were never able to trace it back to him. Why?"

"I'm starting to think Stephen Griffiths may be the guy who's been selling hemp seeds and herbs to the coven, which explains how he's had access to all of the women."

"Jesus Christ." Adrenaline coursed through his veins as he tucked his flashlight under his arm to pull out his cell. He pressed a button and Cayden answered on the first ring, sounding anxious. Alex relayed the details to him, and they talked for a few minutes before he ended the call. "What a clusterfuck. Cayden's on it. He's going to warn the other witches and assured me he'd keep the girls safe. Ellen hasn't been seen for a few hours, but that doesn't mean she's in danger necessarily." Alex shoved his phone back in his pocket.

Fear flashed in her eyes. "I hope you're right."

"Let's make sure this is the place before I call for backup. With the new murder, we're spread pretty thin." Not to mention, Smith would be pissed that he was even out here, especially if this led to a dead end.

She took another step and then stopped and held her sides as though in physical pain. "Willow? What's wrong? Are you okay?"

"Oh this is the place, all right," she said with a gasp. "I'm getting an energy vibration like a thunderbolt. I sense incredible fear and violence, especially in this area." When Willow tried to take another step something stuck to the bottom of her boot. "Ew, Alex, what is it?"

Alex touched a finger to the ground and sniffed. "It smells metallic, like blood. This must be where he killed them." Shaking his head, he pointed his flashlight at the ground and followed the bloody trail. He started to kneel to take some pictures and samples of the scene when the ground shifted beneath his feet. "Watch your step." He put his light down and placed his hands on the ground. Instantly they became wet. "There's something not right over here. The ground's still really soaked in this area. It feels as if it's going to give."

When he glanced up, her eyes filled with panic. "Alex, don't move."

Alex took a step back and the ground began to crumble beneath his feet. "Stay where you are." At the last minute, he wrapped his hands around the low-hanging branch of a tree and dangled in midair. Dirt, rocks and debris rushed toward him. It flew in his eyes and caught in his throat.

A surge of adrenaline coursed through his veins as he coughed and gagged. When he looked down, he came face to face with a twenty-foot-deep crevice. "It's a sinkhole." His hands were still wet from touching the ground and his fingers began to slip.

"I can't hold on." The next moment he fell headfirst into darkness. ***

Willow gaped open mouthed into the giant, yawning hole and continued to call out Alex's name, but he didn't answer. "Please let him be okay." She stood there, frozen to the spot, her heart thudding against her ribs, trying to figure out what to do. *What if he's dead?*

The thought was too painful to bear. When the wind kicked up and blew dirt in her mouth, it was like a mental slap. She had to call for help. No one knew they were here. She pulled out her cell, but the battery was dead. "Okay, think. Don't panic. A million spells flashed through her mind, but only one would work. She'd have to levitate him.

She unsheathed her *athame* and threw it on the ground. And just like when she was holding onto Gillian's ankles, she imagined she was weightless. After she chanted a quick spell, she floated as close to the crater as she could without falling in. "Hold on, Alex, I'm going to get you out of there."

Her hands shook as she pushed them together to form a ball of light. She pointed it into the hole and held her breath. Her heart squeezed when she spotted him in a crumpled heap at the bottom. Blood seeped from his head and covered his jacket. He didn't move, but he was still breathing. "I love you, dammit. I've never needed anything in my life, but I need you." Tears swam in her eyes.

She let the light float overhead while she closed her eyes and cleared her mind. Then she focused on controlling the wind. Cold air circled around her and flew in every direction. She concentrated on lifting and bending it with her will, and then chanted her spell.

"*Earth and air stir the breeze*
Let the elements carry you up through the trees.
This is my will, so mote it be."

Suddenly, the air moved at her command. With every gust and current, she became more aware of her ability to control the force and direction.

"Alex, I'm going to try to levitate you." Willow shouted over the gusts.

Even if he couldn't hear her, she had to at least try to reach him. She tuned into his energy while she kept the wind going. He was weak and fading in and out of consciousness.

"I've never moved anything as big as you. It's going to require a lot of concentration on both our parts. As hard as it might be, try to relax and imagine you're as light as a feather."

Sweat beaded on her forehead and her entire body swayed with the effort. For a moment, she thought she might pass out, but then his body slowly began to soar up through the air. "You're doing great. Keep coming."

The wind continued to blow all around them in a vortex. When Alex was about halfway out of the hole, he groaned and opened his eyes. "What the hell's going on?"

"Don't think. Try to focus on being light." She kept her hands lifted as he floated the rest of the way out. When he hovered a few feet above the ground, she shifted the airflow so it gently blew him over solid ground. He let out a huge sigh the minute his knees touched the grass. Before she could ask him where it hurt, he mumbled something about her vowing not to use magick on him and passed out cold.

CHAPTER 21

"We've got to get back to the truck, Alex." Willow dragged him by the collar through the fields and shrubs, hoping not to cause any further injuries, which was no easy task. She kept glancing over her shoulder to make sure Griffiths hadn't spotted them. It took all the last of her magick reserves to turn the boulder back into Alex's SUV.

She reached into his pocket for the key fob, clicked it, and opened the door. With the last of her strength, she pushed him into the seat, and then slammed the door. By the time she got into the driver's seat, Alex was grumbling under his breath. She sighed. That was a good sign. She glanced in the rearview mirror and a shadow moved through the trees.

Time to get the hell out of here. She started the engine and clicked a button on his dash. According to his GPS, they were several miles from the nearest hospital. She floored the gas, hoping she'd get there before she passed out.

After thirty minutes, she was exhausted, and could barely focus on the road from expending so much magick. Desperate for a place where they could rest far away from the farm, she spotted an empty hunting lodge on the side of the road. She exhaled with relief, and prayed it was empty.

Willow threw another log on the fire and rubbed her hands over the flames to chase away the chill. She glanced over her shoulder at Alex, who was sleeping soundly on the lodge's worn leather couch. A heavy wool blanket covered most of his body.

After she had gotten him into the house, she'd given him what was left of Saje's healing potion, still in her pocket from earlier.

She'd been forced to use the last of her magick on a spell to unlock the giant wooden doors and now could add breaking and entering to her list of misdemeanors.

Finally, Alex stirred. Color bloomed on his cheeks and lips. She turned back toward the fire and exhaled. It had been a close call. *Too close.*

"When was the last time you slept?" he croaked.

"Alex?" Willow turned and moved to the edge of the couch, then knelt beside him. "You're awake. How do you feel?"

"Groggy, as if I were run over by a semi-truck, and my throat feels like I swallowed a bag of marbles. But I'm alive, thanks to you." She handed him a bottle of water from the table and held it to his lips.

He took a long swig, and then glanced down at the bandages wrapped around his chest. He flinched when he touched his ribs. "What's with wrapping me up like a mummy?"

"I think you may have bruised a couple of ribs when you went flying into that damn hole." She'd removed what was left of his mud-stained jacket, shirt, and pants. Luckily, there was a hunting knife left behind. She used it to cut his old flannel into strips, since she'd accidently left her *athame* at the farm. She wrapped them around his ribs and tied the ends in a knot. "It's as though that maniac booby-trapped the place. Believe me, it could've been a lot worse."

Now in the light of day, she prayed Alex had been too out of it to hear her declaration of love. "Uh, about what happened, back at the farm, how much do you actually remember?"

Alex rubbed his forehead and kicked his legs out from under the blanket. "The nightmare's all starting to come back." He sat up and glanced around at the stuffed deer heads mounted on the wall and the antler chandelier. "Where are we?"

"It's an old hunting cabin. The place was empty. I figured we could squat here for the night." Willow had lit candles on the fireplace mantle, bathing the cavernous room in a soft, warm glow.

"From the looks of things, there hasn't been anyone here for a while, so there's not much food. I checked the cupboards. I found microwave popcorn if you're hungry, and I think I can rustle us up some tea."

He swallowed. His throat was still raw and tight. "I'd love something hot, but before you go, I'll need your phone. I'm guessing mine was smashed into a million pieces and still at the bottom of that damn pit. Someone needs to get over to the farm, ASAP."

"Uh, about the phone. I didn't have time to charge mine before we left. I'm sorry, Alex."

He frowned. "You're lucky I keep a backup in the glove box of the truck. Keeping yourself prepared at all times is the difference between life and death, Willow. You can't always use your hocus pocus to get out of every sticky situation." The moment he said the words he wished he could take them back. He sounded like an ass, but he never expected the whole op to turn into a total shitstorm.

"Hocus Pocus? Funny, you didn't think magick was a problem when it was saving your life."

"Willow," he muttered, running a hand though his unruly hair. "I didn't mean it like that. I'm grateful for everything you've done from the very beginning and especially for saving my life. I guess I'm not used to being on the receiving end of a rescue. It must be the cop in me."

"Is that what this is about?" She rolled her eyes. "Are you pissed a woman saved you or was it because that woman happened to be a witch?" She reached for her coat and walked over to the table to grab his keys. She muttered something along the lines of, "You're a chauvinistic, closed-minded dick." Then the door slammed shut behind her.

Willow sat on the edge of the hearth and squished her toes into the rug while Alex talked with Cayden and Smith in the other room. The pop and snap of the fire was somehow peaceful, and she finally started to relax.

The events over the last twenty-four hours burned away in the flames, slowly turning to ash. She picked up the blanket Alex had left behind and wrapped it around her shoulders.

"You look cozy."

She turned and found him standing behind her, holding two steaming mugs in his hands. "You need to stay off your feet and let the potion do its thing."

"Don't worry. I plan on it." His dark eyes smoldered and made a slow ache build between her thighs. Too bad she wasn't about to fall into his arms again, not this time.

"The team's headed out to the farm? Did you call the coven and warn them?" she asked, hoping all the women were safe.

"All taken care of. We still have agents guarding the house. I told them to put the place on lockdown. No one, and I do mean no one's allowed in or out."

She exhaled, trying to loosen the tight knot in the pit of her stomach. "What about Ellen?"

"No one's heard from her, but that doesn't necessarily mean she's in danger. You said she's never around much." His expression softened in the firelight, putting her at ease. "I'm sure she's fine."

Of course, he was probably right. Ellen was as tough as nails. What could happen to her? He crossed the room and placed her mug on a small table beside the fireplace. His hair was a mess, he needed a shave and still had remnants of cuts and scrapes on his face and chest, but he somehow managed to look mouthwatering. He sat down opposite her in an oversized chair and blew on his mug before taking a sip.

"What did you find out about Samuel Griffiths?" She picked up her tea and took a long, slow sip, savoring the sensation of warmth.

"Samuel Griffiths was the killer's paternal uncle." His face was half hidden in the shadows, but the tanned skin on his chest caught the glow of candlelight. Her pulse kicked up a notch every time she saw him without a shirt. Everything about the man was so primal, so male.

"He died about a year ago and left the farm to his only nephew." Alex lifted his arm to take a sip from his mug and winced in pain.

"And Griffiths took it over as a place to kill witches?" What a psycho. "We have to stop him, Alex. We can't just sit around here waiting for him to lash out again."

"I agree, but we need to be prepared first. We rest for a bit to get our strength back as you suggested, and then we head over there. I calculated Smith and Cayden are still a few hours away. Brodie's on the road. He was following up on a lead. He's going to meet us there. It should take us only about forty minutes from here. We have some time to regroup."

He let his gaze trail over her body and she crossed her arms in front of her chest defensively. After he put his mug down, he stood and ambled over to the fireplace. He took a seat next to her on the hearth, and his warm lips brushed her cheek. "Any ideas?" he asked in a husky voice and leaned closer. Too bad his charms wouldn't work on her, not now, not anymore.

"Whoa, not so fast, mister." She placed her hand on his chest to stop him. *Big mistake.* It was a solid wall of muscle. She suppressed a groan. "I'm still angry about the things Nadia overheard you say. If I hadn't brought it up first would you have come clean? I mean, do you even care that you hurt me?" She looked away, not used to leaving herself so open.

His finger lifted her chin. "After everything, I'm shocked you need to ask. Yes, I care. In fact, all I care about right now is keeping you safe, Willow, and making you mine." The lust in his eyes and the heat in his voice warmed her more than the fire, the tea, or even the thick wool blanket ever could.

Then again, he could be saying all this to make her feel better or to bury the stress and anguish of the last few hours in casual sex. He'd hurt her once. She didn't think her heart, or her ego, could take another blow. "Alex—"

Before she could protest, he pressed his lips to hers, his fingers delicately brushing her hair away from her face. At first the kiss was gentle and tentative. Then he sighed, and her body liquefied from the slow, torturous flicks of his tongue. She wanted to forget about the horrors she'd seen and get lost in the moment. But then what? No, she couldn't do this. Not again. She pulled away, breathing hard. "I can't."

His eyes were drowsy with lust. "I would never hurt you deliberately, Willow. I've told you I was trying to protect you."

"Protect me from what?"

"Smith caught on that there's something going on between us. He was ready to pull you from the case. I was afraid he'd send your file to the Council. I couldn't let that happen. I swear I didn't mean those things I said. What do I have to do to convince you?"

Her heart melted from his words. She couldn't bear the thought of him deliberately hurting her. When he reached out to caress her cheek, she sensed he was telling the truth. "I could think of a few things." A smile tugged at her lips.

"We have plenty of time to talk later." He pressed his thumb to her lips and rubbed it back and forth, stealing her breath. With a tug, he pulled the blanket away from her body, and his eyes latched onto her breasts. "Do you have any idea how much I want you? Forgive me."

"Alex." His name came out like a plea. He wrapped his hands in her hair and angled her head to the side to seal his lips over hers. Alex's kisses were like a drug, intoxicating and totally addictive. She was falling hard and fast, leaving herself vulnerable, again.

Alarm bells went off in her head. It took every ounce of willpower to pull away. "This was a bad idea. You say a few sweet words and think I'll fall into bed with you. I can't let you do the same thing to me, Alex. It hurt too much. No matter what we've been through together, the stakes are too high."

He trailed long fingers down her neck to her collarbone before he slowly unbuttoned her shirt and gently caressed her skin. "Let me make it up to you."

He brushed his knuckles over her breast, and she gasped, obliterating the last of her defenses. "You don't play fair."

"All I can think about right now is licking your breasts and sucking on your nipples. I want to dip my head between your thighs and make you come in my mouth. I want you to claw my back and moan my name when I'm buried deep inside you. I want you to put aside everything else and focus only on pleasure. Do you think you can do that?"

A whimper escaped from her lips. She was almost too aroused for words. More than anything, she wanted to forget all about death and pain. She wanted to pretend the nightmare she'd been living and breathing didn't exist. "How could I refuse?"

"Let me make love to you, Willow." She knew in her heart Alex was the only man who could give her the kind of pleasure she'd always craved. She didn't know what would happen tomorrow or the next day, or if either of them would be alive. One thing was clear: Alex was the only man who could fill the ache in her soul and make her forget. She wanted him too much to deny herself.

The last of her resistance shattered like broken glass. She pulled her shirt over her head and kicked off her boots, then peeled off her jeans. His pupils dilated with arousal as his gaze raked over her black lace bra.

His lips brushed hers in a sultry kiss. She swept her tongue into his mouth, aching for a deeper taste of him. The kiss went on and on, until they were both shaking and panting. Alex moved his lips down her neck, to her collarbone, and licked the top side of her breast.

He sucked her nipple through the lace of her bra and she arched up to meet him. "Your sexy lingerie turns me on. After you pulled your bra out of your suitcase the very first day back at the motel, I was never quite the same. I couldn't stop imagining you in all that black lace night after night. But the truth is all I could really think about was taking it off."

She unhooked the front clasp of her bra and threw it over her head. "Now you don't have to imagine anymore."

He growled. "Your breasts are beautiful."

She smiled, loving the quick race of her pulse and the flutter in her stomach. No one had ever made her feel like this. He dipped his head and teased her nipples with his tongue, starting with one then moving to the other.

An intense rush of heat swept over her, leaving her wet and achy between her legs. "Please, Alex. I need you." She was already so turned on, ready to implode at any minute.

He pressed his hard length against her wetness and Alex groaned low in his throat. "You have to be patient. First, I want these off." He hooked his fingers under the waistband of her panties. He pushed them down to her ankles, wincing as he bent. She kicked them aside and lay on the rug completely bare to him.

His eyes trailed over her body, making her feel like the most beautiful woman on Earth and he did exactly as promised. He massaged her legs, slowly kneading her flesh until she thought she'd go out of her mind. "I think you like teasing me."

"I like making you come." His words made her shiver. He hooked her legs over his shoulders and bent his head. He licked and sucked until she was moaning and squirming beneath him.

"Yes, right there." Alex continued his sensual assault, adding a finger until she thought she'd come apart from the pleasure of his lips alone. He rubbed his finger back and forth over her sensitive flesh until she was gripping the rug. "Alex, please. Ah, I'm going to come."

"That's it, baby. Give it to me." He gave her another long, slow lick and she flew over the edge. He lapped up the last of her orgasm until her entire body thrummed.

Breathing hard, she lifted up on her elbows to look at him. The way the pulse raced in his neck and the fearsome look in his eyes, made her want him inside her. He was the bravest man she'd ever known, and he was hers, at least for the moment anyway. "I want you, Alex."

"I'm yours." Her gaze trailed down to his strong, muscled thighs and the enormous bulge in his black boxers, and her heart stuttered. When he slid his underwear down and kicked them off, she gasped, taking in the sight of his naked body.

Goddess, he was too beautiful to bear, every woman's fantasy come to life. For as long as she lived, she didn't think she'd ever get tired of looking at him.

"Willow," he rasped and closed his eyes when she gripped his erection. She drew her hand up and down his length, and then bent to her knees.

"I thought I might return the favor." She smiled and took him into her mouth. He moaned low in his throat and the sexy sound made her slick with need. She sucked and licked, swirling her tongue over the base. He moaned her name and knotted his fingers in her hair. It was by far the hottest thing she'd ever witnessed.

"I need to be inside of you." He guided her over in front of the fire and laid her on the rug. The soft fur brushed against her skin and tickled her back. He hovered above her and she lifted her hips up in a silent plea. Her fingers tugged on his very fine ass as he moved to position himself against her opening.

Without warning, he grabbed her hips and pushed deep inside her to the root. She gasped at the sensation. Though he grimaced in pain, he pulled out and did it again. He rubbed his length against her sex, making every nerve ending zing to life. "Ah, baby, you're soaked, and that gets me so hard."

"I want to feel you, but you're hurt," she protested.

One arm around her, he shifted his position so she was on top.

She straddled him, careful not to make contact with his ribs. She slid down onto him, feeling as if she would break apart in a million, tiny pieces. "I love you deep inside me." She moved up and down, taking the lead. The intimacy of having him at this angle was unreal. She increased the pace. "Am I hurting you?"

He moaned and caressed her breasts. "Does it look as if I'm in pain? You feel so good, so right." His words were laced with passion and lust, but something else—something she didn't want to think too much about. No, she couldn't go there right now.

"You're going to make me come." She moved her hips, giving herself to him body and soul. Her fingers gripped his hair as he plunged in and out of her, turning her into a pile of mush. He kissed her in a rush. His hot tongue swept into her mouth as her orgasm crashed over her, swamping her with sensation.

"Oh God. Yes."

"I want you to be mine, Willow." The cords on his neck flexed in concentration as his head fell back in pure ecstasy.

"Yes, yours, baby. I'm yours." She wanted to satisfy her man in every way. The thought made a sob escape from her throat. After everything they'd been through, she loved that they were stronger together. *Mine.* All her fears about the future seem to melt away in the sheer ecstasy of the moment. Regaining control of her body, she moved up and down on Alex's length until she felt him burst over the edge as well. He let out a satisfied groan as he came apart.

Willow was spent. She collapsed beside him and sighed deep. How could she ever get over him—over this? He stayed buried in her, caressing her back and hips. There were a million words on the tip of her tongue, but they were swallowed to the back of her throat by a toe-curling kiss.

When she could feel her limbs again, she scooted off him while he stretched and reached for his phone off the hearth. He set his alarm, and then grabbed the blanket. After he threw it over them, he wrapped her in his arms like a treasure. "I need to sleep for a few minutes. I feel like I'm going to pass out again."

"Don't worry, I'll wake up." Willow would have to protect her heart and savor these few stolen moments of pleasure. She'd tuck them away in her memory to cherish forever, because once the killer got ahold of her the next time, she didn't think she'd be so lucky. She couldn't predict her own death, but she'd finally come to the realization any moment could be her last.

It was only a matter of time—she was the next witch to die.

CHAPTER 22

"*We're going to get you out of here, Ellen,*" *Alex whispered as he entered the dark, damp room where she was being held prisoner. She was bound and gagged, her eyes filled with fear. The sound of creepy laughter permeated the air and then the fae appeared, pointing his crossbow straight at Alex's head.*

"*I've waited a long time for this. Any last words, Alexandros Nicolas Denopolous, before you die?*"

Alex tried to draw his gun from the holster, but Griffiths was faster, releasing the bolt from his crossbow. The next moment, Alex lay in a pool of his own blood. His head lolled to the side of his body in an unnatural way, cut almost clean from his neck.

"No," Willow came awake with a shudder. Her entire body shook from head to toe. The vestiges of her dream still clung to her like a thousand clawing hands, making her question whether it had been a dream at all.

Could it be a vision of the future?

After all the stress she'd been through these last few weeks, maybe her mind was playing tricks on her—locked in a web of fear and perpetual violence. She shook her head hard to try to clear away the fog. And yet she could still picture the vivid color of the blood and sense the pain and fear pumping through Alex's veins as he drew in his last breath. If it had only been a dream, then why did the ache in her heart leave her reeling? She sensed deep down it was something more. The dream had been far too real.

Her last thought before she'd fallen asleep had been about her death; maybe she'd foretold Alex's instead. As much as she tried to ignore the signs, the ice cold dread in the pit of her stomach was palpable. She turned to find the man in question still sound asleep. His breaths were shallow and even. She sighed in relief. He looked peaceful...strong. It was hard to believe anything bad could happen to him. She shivered and realized the fire had burned out. Stiff, her entire body ached from expending so much magick in the last few days. She stood and stretched her sore muscles.

She spotted her bra and panties and was careful not to wake Alex as she slipped them on. With a quick glance over her shoulder, she picked up his phone and turned off the alarm. He might be mad as hell when he woke up, but at least she'd know he was safe.

She tiptoed toward the fireplace, threw a log in the grate and whispered an incantation for fire. Then with a flick of her wrist, it flamed to life. Alex's clothes were still spread out over the hearth, partially shredded and still caked with mud, but dry.

After she got dressed, she pushed her hands into her pockets and pulled out the vanquishing potion. She held up the tiny vial to the light. Miraculously, the glass was still intact. She shook the clear liquid, not a drop had seeped out. Maybe it wasn't a miracle at all. Maybe it was fate. Her mind drifted back to the images in her dream and she suddenly had a strong sense of *déjà vu*.

The more she thought about it, the more her dream seemed eerily familiar, like the time right before she had the vision about Kimber's death. Images swam in her head, and then everything became clear. Alex would risk his life to save Ellen and, in the end, he would die trying.

Dear Goddess, no—that meant Griffiths had her. As much as she disliked the woman, Willow couldn't stand the thought of Ellen being all alone and trapped in his clutches. They were both going to die. Willow sensed it deep down in her bones. But Alex was very much alive at the moment, which meant she could change the outcome of the future. Finally, she could end this ordeal once and for all. The solution sat in the palm of her hand.

This time she vowed not to let Griffiths hurt another innocent, especially not the man she loved. As much as she wished it wasn't true,

Willow's feelings were real. She couldn't change her past, but she could change the future.

Now was her chance to finally make things right. Despite the risk, she had to go after him. She pulled on her boots, grabbed Alex's keys and headed for the door. Her heart squeezed in her chest as she stole one last look at his sleeping form over her shoulder.

"*I love you*," she murmured. She'd already broken her vow to the Goddess to never use magick on him. She'd suffer the consequences to save his life. She whispered a sleeping spell to ensure that he wouldn't wake up and turned the knob on the door. Her throat choked with emotion and her eyes swam with tears, and she knew, deep down, she was saying goodbye.

Alex rubbed his eyes, still naked and tangled in the blanket on the floor. Sunlight spilled into the spacious room and a satisfied smile twisted at his lips. He couldn't remember the last time he'd slept so soundly.

A sense of contentment filled him in a way he'd never known before. He could almost still feel Willow's soft curves pressed against him and smell her perfume. He instantly grew hard. Memories of their lovemaking were still fresh in his mind. He loved the way her body molded to his when she was riding him.

If he could only wake up to her every morning, he'd be a happy man. The thought was equal parts scary and exciting, especially for a guy like him. Now he'd gone and fallen for a witch. But Willow was nothing like Velvet Laresh, he reminded himself, determined to leave the past where it belonged.

He reached out to her, but she was gone. "Willow." He called out her name again, but she didn't answer.

The room felt cold. His heart hammered in his chest and his gut told him something was wrong. He picked up his cell and let out a string of curses. The battery was dead. What time was it? The alarm had never gone off. He glanced over at where she'd left her clothes and boots, but they were gone. When did she leave? How had he not heard her?

How far could she get on foot? He rubbed the back of his head in bewilderment and glanced out the window as late morning sunlight peaked through the clouds. He guessed he'd been out cold for hours. *But how?* He'd never fall into such a deep sleep at such a critical time in an investigation. The answer hit him with the force of a sledgehammer.

Did she put a spell on me?

Anger sliced through his gut like the edge of a knife. His hands clenched into fists. He reached for his muddy jeans, pushed his legs into them and shoved on his boots. With a groan of frustration, he stood and walked around the room in search of his coat.

He didn't know what the hell Willow was up to. All he cared about was finding her. He walked to the couch and pulled on his coat sans his shirt. He picked up his gun off the end table and holstered it to his leg. He went to retrieve his keys and his heart rate spiked as reality struck.

She took my goddamn truck? She was going to put herself in danger yet again, and there wasn't a damn thing he could do to stop her.

CHAPTER 23

The moment Willow approached the property, every nerve ending in her body vibrated. She could sense the inherent evil within. As she pulled to the side of the road and got out of the truck, the energy all around her became dark and heavy like an invisible weight pressing down on her soul. She'd remember this place in her nightmares, the smell of the earth, and the way the trees parted in the distance. Gnarled branches twisted into foreboding shadows. Her skin burned, and her senses became overloaded.

Her heart pounded as her intuition tried to tell her body to run far away. But what choice did she have? Alex would die if she didn't do this—and probably Ellen too—and she couldn't live with that. She closed her eyes and tried to tune into Ellen's essence. She breathed in the air and sensed her presence. The bastard had gotten to her, which confirmed her dream had been real.

A million thoughts and emotions swirled through her head. Now it was her time to do something selfless for a change. This was her chance to finally right the wrongs of her past. Fate had brought her to this moment. And whatever happened from here on was on her terms; she'd stop this madman or die trying. Maeve would've done the same for her. Things had changed. Willow wasn't the same lost girl anymore. There was a certain sense of liberation in working for the good guys now. Pushing everything else out of her mind, she reached into her pocket, and her hand curled around the potion bottle. Willow swallowed the lump in her throat and hurried her steps. There was no time to waste—after all, she had a high priestess to save and a fae to kill.

The bottom of Alex's feet throbbed, and after walking for what seemed like hours, the soles of his boots were starting to come apart. His mouth was bone dry. And his ribs hurt like a mother. He didn't know how many miles he'd walked, but it wasn't enough. There was still no sign of the farm or of Willow, and as luck would have it, not a vehicle in sight.

What if I'm too late?

He was too lost in thought and too worried about Willow to see a van screech down the highway toward him at full speed. He jumped out of the way right before he became roadkill. The van spun its wheels and came to a screeching stop in front of him.

His hand flew up to shield his eyes from the glaring headlights. He wondered if he was hallucinating from lack of water and pure exhaustion when he caught a glimpse of a large blonde head with black horns behind the wheel. "Cayden?"

The door flew open and the demon jumped out. "Alex, where the hell have you been? This is seriously no time to go MIA on us, man."

"How did you find me?"

"The tracking devices. Smith and Brodie are headed to the farm and I came to find you." Cayden drew Willow's *athame* from behind his back and threw it to Alex, handle up. "I think this belongs to a friend of yours. What the hell are you waiting for? Let's go take the scumbag down."

Willow stopped to take a breath, a stitch burned in her side. Wheezing from running at full-speed through the grass, she slumped against a tree. The moment she made contact with the bark, she saw red. *Blood everywhere.* The tree held so much pain—and fear—a witness to all who'd been tortured and died here. She let go, forced air into her lungs, and continued forward.

The stench of death lingered in the air. She tasted it on her tongue and all the way to the back of her throat. When she crossed over an embankment, she spotted the greenhouse and a dilapidated barn in the distance. Despite the sunny day, the place looked as dark and desolate as it did in her vision.

Through the corner of her eye, she caught movement. She ducked under a tree branch, careful to keep out of sight as much as possible. Her heart pounded against her ribs. She told herself it was an animal and took a tentative step through a copse of trees. Now she could actually see the small barn to the left of the house clearly.

She blinked and images from her dream flooded her mind. She could still hear Ellen's scream ringing in her ears. She needed to get close enough to catch Griffiths off guard, get him away from Ellen, then throw the potion on him and chant the spell. And then he'd be obliterated for good, and she realized that was a big *if.*

"Here goes nothing," she murmured, got down onto her belly, and crawled to the barn. Rocks and sticks cut through her jeans and scraped against her skin. She bit down on her lip against the pain and kept going.

When she finally made it to the side of the barn, she got to her feet and ran inside. She spun around, but there was no sign of Ellen or the fae anywhere. "Ellen," she whispered, trying not to give herself away.

There was not a single window around the wooden walls. The place was dark and freezing cold. She pushed her hands together to form a ball of light and took a tentative step forward. She glanced at the rows of haystacks, hanging rakes, and farm equipment. Nothing looked out of the ordinary.

Every few seconds, she'd turn her head and glance over her shoulder, bracing herself against getting blindsided. Movement drew her attention to the back of the barn. Moving as silently as she could toward the source, she came to a filthy tarp hung like a door.

She pushed out a hand, trying to sense what was behind it, but all she picked up on was a sea of blackness. She took a step closer and the end of her ponytail tangled in the top of the tarp. She held her breath and stepped through it.

When she came out on the other side, she gasped and forced herself not to sink to her knees in shock. Blood splattered the barn walls like some kind of twisted mural. Row after row of crossbows and knives of varying lengths hung from hooks overhead, covered in dried blood. Splotches of blood even coated the dirt floor. She coughed and covered her mouth to keep from gagging. Pink Floyd's "Run Like Hell" played from speakers all around the room.

Willow wrapped her hand around a beam to get her bearings. The sensations of fear and death made her light-headed. Her senses tuned into the collective energy surrounding her and she trembled with physical pain. Shaking, she let go of the beam and took several long, deep breaths. The air was thick, heavy with the metallic smell of smoke along with a faint scent of blood and black magick.

Her gaze zeroed in on an altar set up on a cardboard box. She spotted a fabric poppet on top. It was wrapped with a lock of flaming red hair, which she instantly recognized as Ellen's. A single black candle burned beside it. Only the two together could bind a witch's powers completely.

Her hands began to shake. She took a step back and collided with the back of a table.

"Willow?"

She jumped and turned to find Ellen tied to a chair. Her head was slumped forward. Anger bubbled inside Willow's chest. She cursed, wishing she had her *athame* to cut her ropes. "We have to get you out of here."

"No," Ellen cried. "He'll kill us both. He used a piece of my hair and then gave me a potion that stripped my powers, and he'll do the same to you. Leave while you still can, before he gets back."

"Don't be ridiculous. I'm not leaving here without you," Willow whispered, trying to sound more convincing than she felt.

"You don't get it. You're no match for him." Ellen began to sob. Her usual bravado was gone, replaced with raw fear. "He's bat-shit crazy. Look what he did to the demon special agent." She tried to lift her head.

When Willow glanced up, she found Smith spread eagle, covered in blood and hanging from the rafters. "Dear Goddess." Her hand flew to her mouth. She sensed he was still alive, but barely. "Where's Brodie?" She rubbed her hands over her face to hide her expression of horror. When Ellen didn't respond, Willow chanted a series of healing spells for Smith, but her magick was still too depleted for it to do any good.

He was too high up to send her energy into his body. The only thing she could do right now was to try and save Ellen. "Listen to me. You have to be strong. You have to fight, and I will get us out of here." Willow whispered a spell to undo the knots, but they didn't budge. She dug her fingers into them and pulled. They seemed magickally enhanced somehow.

"We don't have much time."

"I need a knife or an object with a sharp point." Willow glanced around for anything to cut the ropes and climbed onto a chair. Her only hope was to use one of the crossbows.

Shock flashed in Ellen's eyes as Willow stepped down holding the weapon in her hands. "What are you doing?"

"Saving your ass." Willow bent and moved the tip of the broadhead back and forth against the ropes at Ellen's wrists, and then moved to the ones at her ankles.

"C'mon, hurry," Ellen pleaded, an edge of panic in her voice.

"Almost there." She'd cut the ties at one of Ellen's ankles and was onto the other one when a loud thud made Willow glance at the roof. Before she could finish cutting the last piece of rope, a dark shadow flew down, landed on the other side of the barn, and spread out its wings.

The fae smirked. "Well, well, it looks like we've got company."

CHAPTER 24

"Only cowards prey on innocent women. Does it make you feel more like a man?" Willow held the crossbow in front of her body like a shield, trying not to show fear. If she was getting out of this alive, she had to hold her own.

She got a good look at him, and it gave her chills. Long, dark hair hung past his collar. He was dressed in black from head to toe and reminded her of an avenging angel of death. Splatters of blood covered his shirt and pants.

"I'm afraid I have to correct you." Griffiths glanced from Ellen to her, letting his wings slowly retreat back into his body. "Ellen's far from innocent. In fact, she was a willing participant, a common whore. She's been flirting with me since my first visit to the coven. She was the one who came onto me," he said, pointing in Ellen's direction.

"She made it clear from the start she'd come back to my place and screw me. It's amazing the degrading lengths some women will go to for a handsome face and a muscular body. All you have to do is ask a woman a few questions about herself and then tell her she's hot and *voila.*"

"Well you'd know all about whores wouldn't you? Wasn't your mother a whore, Stephen? Stephen Griffiths, right? Didn't she bring her johns to your home? Is that why you're such a twisted bastard?" A stab of anxiety pricked her chest.

"Shut your mouth, witch." Pink Floyd's "Run Like Hell" continued to play softly in the background, over and over again on a continuous loop. Next to her, Willow could hear Ellen's heaving breaths and quiet sobs. No matter what bad blood lay between them, she didn't deserve this.

Now, after everything, Willow wasn't sure if Ellen had managed to get the rest of the ropes off. Then again, what help would she be if she did? Willow stole a glance over at the high priestess and her heart sank. Her powers were bound, and she looked weak and dehydrated, probably in a state of shock. She turned back to face him again and gulped at the look of pure evil blazing in his eyes. "Did Saint Claire hire you to kill the witches?" The question was why, but she would work up to that. She had to, because if he had hired him, even Griffith's death wouldn't mean the coven was safe.

He smiled and it made her gut twist with revulsion. "When he figured out Maeve Donovan was blabbing her mouth to your boyfriend, he hired me to get rid of her. Funny," he said with a bitter laugh. "It turned out pretty well when I absorbed her powers after I killed her. After that, one witch just wasn't enough."

A surge of rage shot though her veins. "You bastard!" Willow's fingers were white-knuckled around the handle of the crossbow. "You'll pay for her death." She pulled on the trigger and waited for the bolt to release, but nothing happened. *Oh shit.*

"I'm counting on it," he said with a sneer. "My crossbow's magickally enhanced to work only on my command."

She dropped the offending weapon and lifted her hands in front of her body. "What's the reason for killing the others," she said though clenched teeth.

"I've been keeping an eye on the coven for months," he muttered in a gruff voice and walked to the altar. He lifted his shirt and pointed to his belt buckle, edging closer. "I was able to use this as a shield to keep the cops and the MBI off the radar. Well, until you came along, and now I'm afraid I have to get rid of you too."

"You'll never get the chance. Other agents will be swarming the place any minute." Her eyes darted toward the barn door, but there was still no sign of anyone.

"I'm afraid not soon enough. I got some of your hairs off the tarp. I put tape on it for this very reason." When he picked up one of the poppets and wrapped her hair around it, her breaths became shallow. The bastard was going to try and bind her powers.

"I witnessed firsthand how the witches were able to use their magick to locate jewelry and artwork." He lit a black candle, sending plumes of smoke around the room. "I reported back to Saint Claire and he thought that kind of export business could be lucrative for his own distribution channels." The cloying stench of death began to close in and Willow got the distinct impression that time was running out.

Alex had mentioned something about checking out crates in Port Jersey. Could they be filled with drugs? "Is that how Saint Claire's been distributing smack under the radar and getting it past the authorities? He was stashing drugs in the antiques?"

"Imagine my surprise when the cops started showing up at the coven." He paused before meeting her eyes. "I had no choice but to kill anyone involved to keep them quiet. I was paid handsomely. Bodies keep showing up and the police still haven't managed to catch me. What a joke."

Her stomach twisted with anger. "Then this was all about money?"

He vehemently shook his head. "It was never about the money. I had a witch for a mother." His voice caught with emotion. "She was everything to me. My father didn't approve of her vocation and slit her throat right in front of me to punish her. I watched her blood run all over the floor." He stared off into space, wrapped up in the disturbing memory. "I tried to save her, but she died in my arms. She had to pay for her sins just like the rest of you."

"No one here has done anything to you. You're murdering innocents for something your father did. But it'll never bring your mother back." What was the point of trying to reason with him? Ellen was right. He was bat-shit crazy. But Willow had to distract him so she could get close enough to throw the potion on him. She inched closer. "It's time to get over your hatred and let us go."

"Save the dime store analysis. I've been going to shrinks my whole life." When he twisted the poppet in his hands, her heart began to pound. "They only want to medicate me and put me behind bars."

"It's where you belong. You have to stop hurting women." *I need to get closer.*

"I regret that I'll have to hurt you, Willow. A witch like you is a rare find. You possess beauty, matched by physical strength, and a strong will.

I've been fantasizing about breaking that will from the first moment I saw you at the club." His creepy smile made her gut twist with revulsion. "It's the only reason I didn't kill you."

"Sorry to ruin your plans, but you won't get the chance, because I plan on destroying you, obliterating your soul, in fact." Her voice belied the fact that her knees were wobbling together.

"Do you now?" His eyes gleamed with a maniacal curiosity as he circled her like fresh prey. "I'm fascinated." He tilted his head to the side. "I bet you'd be a real whore in bed, too. Maybe I should ask Agent Denopoulous. I'm surprised he's not here at this very minute busting down the door trying to rescue his beloved."

"Go to hell."

"I could tell by the pathetic look in his eyes that night outside the club. He wouldn't shoot me because he was afraid he'd hit you. I promise to make him suffer. There's something you should know about me. I never go back on my word. Isn't that right, Ellen? Didn't I promise to make you scream?"

"You tricked me." Ellen lifted her head and began to sob even louder.

"Stop talking to her and don't you dare say anything about Alex. He's brave and kind, as opposed to someone like you, who's evil through and through." Willow needed to get close enough to throw the potion on him. If he was quick and managed to invoke a spell to bind her powers, then she and Ellen were doomed.

"Ah, did I strike a nerve? Is Agent Denopoulous your Achilles' heel? How interesting. I could have fun with this. Imagine when he finds you dead with your flesh missing? I can't wait to see the look on his face." His boots made crunching noises on the barn floor, reminding her of his proximity.

Not close enough, not yet.

"At least I have people who care about me." And for the first time since she'd come back to Raven's Hollow, she realized she did. "Who do you have to keep you warm at night? One of these?" She pointed to the crossbow on the floor.

C'mon Ellen, I need you. I have the vanquishing potion. She whispered to her telepathically, hoping and praying she was tuned into her.

"Your sentiments are moving," he growled. "Not."

She'd never come across a creature whose eyes were so cold and menacing, two black, soulless pits. She swallowed hard and pushed the troubling thought to the back of her mind. "You can't function in society and you could probably never get a girl without using black magick or violence on her. I used to despise you, but now I only pity you."

By the flare of his nostrils and the look of pure rage burning in his eyes, her plan seemed to be working. He took a step toward her. "Enough talk. First, I'm going to kill Ellen while you watch. Then you can witness what will happen to you when I consume her body and absorb her powers. I can't wait to do the same to you. I'm willing to bet you taste delicious."

Willow's whole body trembled. She shoved her hand in her pocket to wrap her fingers around the potion vial. She kept it curled in her fist and retained a fighting stance. "You think I'm going to give in without a fight? My fists will do fine."

He arched his brows. "You have balls."

Chest heaving, she took a step toward him. This was her last chance. It was do or die. "Are you going to engage me or do you only 'get off' shooting women in the back when they aren't looking?"

"You want me to fight you?" He laughed, a low, menacing sound that made her stomach churn. "It would be like using a cannon to kill a fly. But then again, I've never been one to turn down a lady, especially a pretty one," he muttered.

Before Willow knew what was happening, he was on her, shoving her to the barn floor. His strength took her by surprise and for a moment, she panicked.

In one quick move, he pulled both her hands above her head and started to rip off her jeans. "I didn't plan on screwing you first, but I need to teach you a lesson."

"Get off me." She tried to kick him, but his body crushed tightly against hers, and she couldn't move. Frustrated, she screamed in his ear at the top of her lungs and his eyes flashed with rage.

"I don't need a crossbow to kill you. I can do it with my bare hands." He let go of hers and covered her mouth and nose.

She gasped and tried to breathe, but he cut off all her airflow. Her mind reeled. This was it! She was going to die!

Suddenly, he let go of her and his eyes bulged from their sockets. Ellen appeared behind him holding a piece of rope around his neck. She pulled, hard. The fae's weight lifted off her slightly. His arms flailed over his head in an attempt to claw at Ellen's face.

"Do it now!" Ellen screamed.

Willow crawled out from under him and scooted backward. She uncorked the potion and threw it in his face. Realization flared in his eyes as she chanted the spell.

"A fae born from evil your end is near
For taking lives and inciting fear
I ask for help from the winds that blow
To banish you to the world below
On this plane you can no longer dwell
Death takes your soul with this spell
This is my will so mote it be."

Ellen chanted the words with her the second round through. On the third chant, he screamed in agony. His body pulsed and turned bright orange. The stench of burning hair, flesh, and bone filled the air. Fire overtook him from the inside out as his body slowly turned to ash, leaving a pile on the barn floor.

A gust of wind circled around his ashes. Moments later, a group of small creatures in black cloaks appeared. When they dropped their hoods, Willow resisted the urge to scream. Red eyes peeked out from their twisted, skeletal faces. The ashes flew around and dissolved into their collective bodies. Without uttering a word, they sank into the floor in a haze of smoke, back to the Underworld.

Shaking from head to toe, Willow cried and laughed at the same time. "Finally, we did it." She looked up at Ellen, who was pale and trembling, still holding the rope she used to strangle the fae in her hands. "It's okay. He's dead. He's really gone."

"He's dead?" Ellen blinked as if she'd been in a daze, then dropped the rope and began to cry hysterically. She came over and hugged Willow. They held on to each other before both of them slumped down on the barn floor.

"Dear Goddess, Smith, I almost forgot about him." Willow got to her feet. "We have to get him down."

"We can take it from here." A deep male voice echoed from the other side of the barn. Willow turned to find Cayden and Alex running toward them with Gillian, Delilah, Nadia, Arabella, Belinda and Saje clamoring not far behind.

When Cayden spotted Smith, his ice-blue eyes flared to red. He made a hissing noise and his face shifted, resembling that of a monster all gnarled up with red skin and bulging muscles. His teeth lengthened into fangs, his features transformed, changing into his full-on demonic rage face. Alex ran over, and together, they stacked bales of hay to use as a makeshift ladder. Cayden climbed up with incredible stealth and speed and cut Smith's ropes with a knife. Once he was free, Cayden flung Smith over his shoulder, careful not to hook him with a horn. He climbed down and laid the commander on a bed of hay.

Slowly, Cayden's face and demeanor reverted back to normal. "He's still breathing, but he needs medical attention."

"We got it covered," Nadia chimed in as she made her way over to Smith.

Cayden held a hand out. "Wait just a minute." He looked to Alex. "Can we trust them?"

Alex nodded at him, but his gaze went to Willow as he answered. "Absolutely." He kneeled next to Smith, using a towel to stop the bleeding.

Cayden dropped his arm and let Nadia approach Smith. She sat next to him and began chanting a healing spell. Saje appeared next to her and moved her hands up and down Smith's battered body to add her power to mend his wounds. When his skin began to knit itself back together, she poured a potion into his mouth.

After a moment, he coughed and started to come to. "What the hell's going on? What are you feeding me?"

Nadie lifted his wrist and checked his pulse "He's going to be fine."

Everyone let out a collective breath.

Saje turned to face Willow. "After Alex called Agent Teague, we did a divination spell and tracked Ellen here. Somehow, you managed to stop the evil that fell upon us and in essence, changed the future. You used your powers for good, Willow, and by doing so, altered your karma. May all good come to you times three. Blessed be."

As Alex tried to make his way over to her, a group of uniformed cops, including his friend Mulroney, filed into the room. Together, they began the task of taking pictures and collecting evidence. "If you hadn't told me how to make the potion and if Nadia hadn't helped me write the spell, I could've never vanquished him. Now he's toast."

"It's about time." Saje smiled and went back to treating Smith, who was sitting up and mumbling orders. He was already starting to look agitated. Willow sighed with relief and figured it was a good sign.

The music continued to play through the speakers, forcing her hands over her ears. "Will someone please cut the twisted jam," Willow shouted, having had her fill of Pink Floyd's "Run Like Hell" to last a lifetime.

When the music stopped, Willow turned toward the rustle of footsteps behind her as a new team of agents rushed in, along with more men in blue from the RHPD. The women went over to Ellen next, sent her a healing spell, and then fed her a potion for the remainder of her wounds.

Willow's eyes locked with Alex's from across the room. "I'm okay," she mouthed with a smile.

His hot gaze trailed over her, as though looking for signs that she was telling the truth. A swirl of emotions swam in his eyes, fear, anger, need, and maybe even love. "We need to talk," he mouthed back and started to make his way toward her in the crowd.

Before he could fight his way through, Ellen came rushing toward her and grabbed her by the shoulders and squeezed. Tears streamed down her face. "We'd probably all be dead if it wasn't for you, brave girl. I'm sorry for everything, but especially for being a foolish, prideful witch and holding the past against you for so many years. I always suspected Ed was a louse, but I didn't want to believe it."

Speechless, emotion clogged Willow's throat. Gillian must've overheard their conversation because she glanced from Willow to Ellen and back again with a guilty expression on her face.

Gillian walked over and embraced Willow in a bone-crushing hug, then released her. "Thank you again for saving my life and now Ellen's. I can probably never repay you for what you did, but here's a start. I heard what Saje said about karma and it's high time I corrected mine once and for all. I have to take some responsibility for Ellen kicking you out." She glanced at the floor. "I spread a lot of nasty gossip about you and Ed, without hearing your side of the story. I turned against you. My dad left my mom for a much younger woman, and I let that whole situation influence my behavior and my judgement toward you. I was wrong. And now I finally understand what it's like to be accused of something you didn't do." After she finished, her face turned red with shame.

Willow's heart thudded against her ribs upon hearing Gillian's apology after all these years. "My life tuned into a shit show after you spread those rumors. I don't know what to say."

"How about you forgive me?" A sad smile spread across Gillian's pretty face.

"After everything? I don't know." Willow could've sworn the room fell silent. All eyes seemed to focus on her. She could forgive, but she'd never forget. Then again, after everything maybe it was high time to put the past behind her and start fresh. "I have to move forward. I'm starting a new chapter from today on. According to Saje, I've changed my karma. I think Maeve would've wanted me to make peace with you."

"There will always be a place for you at the coven, Willow," Ellen chimed in. "Having you back at the coven has made me realize how much I've missed you," she said, wiping the tears from her eyes with the back of her hand.

"We all did," Gillian said, sounding sincere.

The next moment the tall, striking vampire friend of Alex's, Detective Mulroney, cut through the crowd. His pale blue eyes locked onto Gillian's, and Willow saw wariness and heat. Gillian turned as though she could sense him behind her and froze. "Hmm, I'm sensing that he has something to do with whatever you were wrongly accused of," Willow whispered, curious to get the real scoop on that one.

Before Gillian could respond, Alex walked over and placed a warm hand at the small of Willow's back. "If you'll excuse us, ladies." He then glanced at the vampire, who was standing a few feet behind him. "Give me a minute, Garrett."

Garrett nodded and walked back in the other direction.

"Let's finish this conversation later. I'm sure you two have things to discuss, and so do we," Ellen said, leading Gillian away by the arm.

"Are you really okay?" Alex kept his hand on her back and led her to a corner under a hayloft. He stopped and turned to face her, taking in the cuts and scrapes and dried blood on her hands.

"Nothing one of Saje's potions can't fix." Willow let out a deep breath and felt light and almost giddy, as if an enormous weight had been lifted. She started to wrap her arms around his neck, but Alex pulled away and flashed a stern, accusatory glare. "What is it? I thought you'd be happy. The killer's dead and can never hurt anyone else again."

"Of course I am, but he could've killed you. It's sheer luck that he didn't." His eyes flared with anger.

"I'd like to think there was some skill involved." She smiled and crossed her arms over her chest.

"Why did you take off? Have you always bucked authority? You deliberately disobeyed orders. You stole my frigging truck for God's sake, although it shouldn't surprise me."

"Whoa, what the hell is that supposed to mean? I had a vision. I saw Griffiths kill you, Alex, I had to stop him and took matters into my own hands."

"By breaking every rule and code of conduct in the process? He could've killed both of you." He let out a ragged breath and she sensed his pain.

"What is it? Alex?"

"We found Brodie in a cottage attached to the property. He's dead. The bastard got him in the back of the head."

Her gut twisted with grief. Shaking, Willow touched Alex's arm and he flinched away from her. "Oh, Alex, I'm sorry. I had no idea."

"If I hadn't been under a sleeping spell I could've been here." He ran a hand through his unruly mop of dark hair. "Maybe he'd still be alive."

"You don't know that," she said, shaking her head. "This was his time, Alex."

"Don't give me your philosophical witchy crap," he snapped. "You completely undermined my authority."

"Is that what this is about? Usurping your authority? I guess nothing has changed between us?" she asked in utter disbelief.

"Did you or did you not put me under a spell and use magick on me?"

Tears pricked at her eyes. She bit down on her lip to keep them from flowing freely. "Yes, but it was for your own good."

"I'll be the one to decide what's for my own good." The hard rasp of his voice made her stomach churn.

"I feel horrible about Brodie. I never meant for something like this to happen. I was trying to protect you. I killed that maniac, and you're here with me alive and well and so is Ellen."

"Yes, and I'm grateful. The entire agency will be indebted to you for your services."

Why did he sound so cold and detached, so clinical? "Alex?"

"You know how I feel about witchcraft and magick." He took a step closer until they were nose to nose and for one crazy moment she thought he might kiss her.

"What Velvet Laresh did to you and your partner will always come between us, won't it?"

There was an unbearable silence that hung in the air. Alex's stance was hard, rigid. Her joy deflated faster than a kite caught in a windstorm. "I think you've just given me my answer."

"We still have to take down Saint Claire. We'll need to get more information about his various organizations from you. I filled Cayden in on the way over. I want to act fast before word gets out about Griffiths' death. We'll be questioning you in the morning, then you'll be free to go. Your record will be erased clean."

He'd never get over the fact that she was a witch. She lifted her chin in defiance as though every word wasn't like a sword through her heart. "I guess there's nothing left to say." She took a step back, needing to get as far away from him as possible. "We were thrown together due to extenuating circumstances. This case is almost over and so are we."

He nodded. "It's probably for the best. You and I are from different worlds. It was crazy for me to think this could ever work." People were starting to stare at them. "I can't talk about this anymore. I better go. I need to wrap up and I've got a week's worth of paperwork to fill out."

His gaze swept over every inch of her as though committing her image to memory. He turned and walked toward the cluster of agents gathered in the center of the barn and didn't bother to look back. She stood there, staring at his back, her heart shattering into a million pieces.

Delilah walked over and put her arm around her shoulders. "Willow? Is everything okay? What can I do?"

Willow waited until Alex was out of sight, and then let the tears fall. Now she understood the consequences for breaking a vow to the Goddess. She gave her the chance to save Alex's life, but in the end, Willow would lose him in the bargain. She didn't think she'd ever be okay again. She squeezed her eyes shut against the pain. "Get me out of here."

CHAPTER 25

"Where's everyone?" Alex turned toward Cayden and took a seat across from him at the kitchen table. "I've never seen the coven this empty." He reached for an apple from the basket and took a bite.

Even in the middle of the night, there was typically a flutter of activity and a throng of witches milling around. Alex stole a glance over his shoulder, hoping Willow would miraculously appear in the kitchen in need of a midnight snack.

After he sighed with disappointment, he turned back to face Cayden again. It was probably for the best. He needed to keep his distance from her anyway. "No one around here ever seems to sleep."

"Apparently, they all went to a Wiccan celebration," Cayden muttered, his eyes glued to his computer screen.

The grandfather clock in the hallway chimed, reminding him of the late hour.

"Then I guess we have the whole place to ourselves." Alex planned to grab a quick bite and call it a night. Now that Ven Pariah was dead, his services here at the coven were no longer required, although the case was still officially open until Tristan Saint Claire's reign of terror ended and he was behind bars.

Cayden glanced up and frowned. "I keep looking at the door, expecting Brodie to walk through it."

"Yeah, but he's never going to again, is he?" His anger surged. "If Willow hadn't put me under a damn spell and stolen my truck, I could've been there sooner. I could've saved him." Alex got to his feet and pitched his apple into the trash.

"You need to stop blaming Willow and stop blaming yourself. I read your report," Cayden said, pointing at his screen. "She thought she was protecting you and a member of this coven. She did the job you and Smith hired her to do."

"What about Brodie? Who was protecting him? I just got back from Brooklyn. I broke the news to his family and dropped off his stuff. It was awful," Alex said, remembering the horrorstruck look in his mother's eyes. "How the hell are you supposed to tell a mother her only son is dead, murdered by a madman? He was twenty-nine years old. He had his whole life ahead of him. Brodie's dad died a few years ago. Needless to say, she didn't take the news well. This whole thing is like history repeating itself in this really awful way."

"I'm sorry if this dredged up the whole ordeal with your old partner." Cayden's gaze narrowed. "You should've let me go."

"When Pete was killed, I had to tell his wife. He left behind a three-year-old little girl." His gut twisted at the memory.

"Man, you never know when it's your time. I'm going to try to make a stop in Brooklyn and pay my respects to Brodie's family when this case is wrapped." Cayden glanced back to his computer and began to pound on his keyboard.

"His mom wants to make the funeral next week. I'm helping her with the arrangements." Alex ran a hand over his beard and exhaled.

"We can go together. Look, I know this must be hard for you, but look at what can happen in the blink of an eye. I'm not trying to get in the middle of you and Willow, but I know you. If you don't make things right with her, you'll always regret it."

Alex's jaw clenched. "Stay out of this, Cayden."

"Hell, I admit her methods are unorthodox, but at the end of the day, she got the job done. Who's to say any of us could've done anything differently? Granted, she started out pretty shady, but you have to look at all the good she's managed to do in a short span of time. She saved three lives, including yours, which has to count for something. Demons believe in a form of karma similar to witches. Did you ever think in the grand scheme of things, maybe it was Brodie's time? You would've ended up going after Willow and then you'd be the one dead, bro, not him. Besides, who knows what he'll accomplish in his next life."

"Not you too?" Alex scowled, walked back to the table, and sat down, his grief now replaced with annoyance. "Do you actually believe in all that woo-woo crap?"

"And what if I do? Sometimes you've got to believe in things that are bigger than yourself. Let go of the past. It has no place in your present and if you're not careful, it'll shape your future." Cayden shut his computer and stood up from the table. "I just finished my last report. I'm done here."

"Thank you, Deepak Chopra." A part of him knew Cayden was right. Alex wanted to blame someone for Brodie's death. Willow was the obvious choice. But as far as he was concerned, it didn't change a thing.

"I'd love nothing more than to sit here and trade insults with you, but I'm too damn tired." Cayden chuckled. "I'm heading out. Are you coming? I can fill you in on the details of the op on Saint Claire's headquarters." It had been three long, grueling days since they'd been to that farm and yet it had felt like months. Being away from Willow didn't help.

"Nah, it's too late, I figured I'd crash here for the night. I'll clear out the rest of my stuff in the morning. Tell me the plan before you go." After tonight, Alex didn't know when he'd see Willow again. His stomach knotted at the thought. Even if they couldn't continue what they'd started, it still didn't make things any easier. He missed talking to her, laughing with her, and making love to her. He just missed Willow, period.

"You sure that's the only reason?"

Not that he'd ever admit it to Cayden, but he wished he'd said and done things differently. Well, he guessed hindsight was twenty-twenty at this point. He'd purposely avoided running into her at every turn, and fortunately for him, Cayden had agreed to get the scoop on her inside knowledge of Saint Claire's various organizations.

Alex smirked. "Of course I'm sure."

Willow had even agreed to go to the port with Garett and had managed the unthinkable—confirmed that drugs were indeed hidden in a shit-ton of crates inside the cargo hold.

Cayden knitted his brows together. "If you say so. Are you ready for tomorrow? Is everything in place?"

"I went undercover to the gallery as a janitor and planted video surveillance throughout the building."

"It'll come in handy when we pay them a visit." Cayden pulled out his phone. "I downloaded this schematic a couple of hours ago. Check it out. Saint Claire's minions convene in a warehouse that's owned and operated by Prestige Art Gallery. It's a subsidiary of the Shadow Cabal."

"Damn, he's an ingenious bastard. Where do these boxes actually go?" Alex picked up a water bottle on the counter and twisted off the cap.

"Our IT guys broke through his firewall and accessed his hard drive. According to his logs, these boxes go to galleries and museums all over the country. You name it and he's got a foothold somewhere," Cayden said and shoved his phone in his pocket.

Willow had been telling the truth from the start. She never knew about the drugs. "It's no wonder he's managed to expand his operation in a short span of time. He's been dealing to the people with money and means, not only the junkies strung out on the corner," Alex said, shaking his head in disgust. "I never imagined that he was the monster behind the murders all along."

"He has too much at stake to let anyone get in his way." Cayden zipped his jacket and picked up his duffle bag off the floor. "We've got a hell of a lot of ground to cover, but all the details are in place."

"What makes you think this op will go down smoothly?" Alex glanced at his watch and exhaled. It was less than twenty-fours away. Would they be ready in time?

"The RHPD has reported the case to the FBI. We're working together on this baby. We'll have undercover agents from both agencies spread out, combing all the galleries, art museums, and ports from here to Brooklyn in the next twenty-four hours. Trust me, they'll be arresting people first and asking questions later. We convene at Saint Claire's headquarters at nine o'clock sharp."

"I hope you're right," Alex grumbled. "I have a bad feeling about this."

"We've been working toward this for months. His operation is about to go up in flames and all because of Willow." Cayden smiled. "She really came through for us on this one."

"I don't want to talk about her, okay?" Alex took a sip from his water and slammed the bottle down harder than he intended.

"Here's an idea, why don't you stop sulking and go apologize."

"I don't need someone with your track record with women giving me advice," Alex snapped. "Besides, I've told you already, there's nothing going on between us anymore. Now it's all about the case."

"If you say so, but it's your loss." Cayden shrugged. "She's funny, smart, resourceful, and smoking-hot. Too bad you had to go acting like a stubborn fuckwad and screw things up. Then again, you've opened the door for me," he said, puffing out his enormous chest.

Alex was across the table faster than Cayden could blink. He shoved his partner's six-and-a-half foot frame into the wall. "I don't care if you are a demon. So help me God, if you go near her, I'll rip those horns off your damn head and turn them into earrings. Do I make myself clear? And who the hell are you calling a fuckwad?"

"Jealous much?" Cayden burst into laughter. "It's easy to press your buttons where she's concerned. That was a test, my friend, and you failed miserably."

Footsteps sounded behind them. "I didn't think anyone else was here. I heard shouting. Is everything okay?"

Alex turned to see Willow standing in the doorway. A slice of moonlight streamed in through the Palladian window, silhouetting her face and accentuating the glossy strands of her red hair. He quickly stepped in front of Cayden to block his view of her.

His eyes roamed over her body and his mouth went dry. She wore a short, black lacy nightgown with a robe that barely closed over her breasts. "Fine. I hope we didn't wake you."

"No. I couldn't sleep." Clearly, she wasn't expecting to see anyone at this time of the night from the way she fumbled with the tie at her waist. But it was too late. He'd already seen the outline of her breasts, even caught a glimpse of her pink nipples pushing through the lace panel of her nightgown. The front of his jeans grew painfully tight.

She was so beautiful, standing there with sleep still in her eyes and moonlight licking her skin. Her lips parted, and Alex had a sudden urge to taste. He wanted to sweep her into his arms and kiss her ripe mouth, pull down her nightgown and fondle her breasts. Alex blinked, trying to rein in his libido and hide his shock at seeing her in the flesh after three long days.

Why did it feel more like three years? And why does my chest suddenly feel tight?

Cayden cleared his throat and Alex realized he'd been staring... fantasizing. "I was just leaving." His partner walked out the kitchen door and Alex swore he could still hear him laughing.

Willow froze as she gazed up at Alex's gorgeous face. When the shock wore off, her whole body started to shake. She pressed her hand against the wall to steady herself. Never in a million years did she expect to find him standing in the kitchen in the middle of the night. She hadn't seen him in days. "I assumed you moved out. What are you still doing here?" she asked, trying to sound casual.

"I'm picking up the rest of my stuff, grabbing a quick bite, and then heading out at the crack of dawn, if that's okay with you," he said in a snarky voice.

"Sure. It's a free country." Willow crossed into the kitchen and opened the fridge. Her heart pounded as she pulled out a water bottle. She twisted off the cap and took a swig. She wiped her mouth with the back of her hand and tried to act casual.

"This doesn't have to be weird. We're both adults. I think we can handle being in the same room together, don't you?" he said with an edge to his voice.

"I agree." *Nope, not weird at all.* She glanced over at him, expecting his eyes to be cold and angry. Instead they were hot and confused as they trailed over her body.

She squared her shoulders, trying not to show how badly she was hurting inside. He didn't need to know that she hadn't eaten or slept in days or that she'd been crying nonstop. In the blink of an eye, he'd crushed her heart to smithereens. She refused to give him any more power than he already had over her. "I'll be quick and get out of your way."

"Take your time. I'm in no rush."

Goddess, she wasn't ready to face him, not yet. She hadn't worked up the courage or practiced what she'd say if she did. And to make matters worse, she couldn't be any more vulnerable, standing there in her current state of undress, barefoot and half naked, with her face scrubbed free of makeup.

All of her usual armor was gone. But running from the room didn't seem appropriate. She walked to the island, a safe distance away, and her stomach growled loudly. She glanced around for anything to munch on and caught him gazing at her out of the corner of her eye. "What?"

"You should eat something," he mumbled and motioned to the fridge. "How come you're not at the ritual?"

"I was too tired. I thought it might be a good time to catch up on some sleep. As it turns out, killing a fae and obliterating his soul can knock the stuffing out of a girl," she said with a smile and ducked into the butler's pantry to catch her breath. She leaned up against the door and placed a hand over her pounding heart.

She swallowed hard and picked up a bag of pretzels. When she calmed her nerves, she made her way back to the island. She reached for a bowl from an overhead cabinet and sat down on a barstool. She dumped half the bag in it, took a handful and pushed the rest to the center of the island in offering. It felt strange to sit here with him and act as if they'd meant nothing to each other.

"Are you okay?" Alex folded his arms across his chest, drawing her gaze to broad shoulders and sculpted biceps. Somehow the room seemed smaller.

"I'm managing. How about you?"

"I'd say about the same?" He pulled out a carton of milk from the fridge and a container of leftovers. He set them on the counter and then reached for a glass from the cabinet. "I haven't had a lot of downtime." Anger rolled off him in waves. "I've been pretty busy trying to wrap up the loose ends on the murders, help plan a funeral for one of my closest friends, not to mention bust up a drug ring run by a criminal mastermind."

"This can't be easy for you." She'd never seen him this tense and angry. It killed her to stay rooted to the spot. Despite how badly he'd hurt her, she wanted to go to him and make everything okay. "Alex, I'm truly sorry about Brodie. Is there anything I can do or say right now to make it better? Maybe lighten the mood?"

"I don't feel like laughing or making jokes right now." He leaned against the counter and frowned. "Not when one of our own is dead."

"Alex? You're still blaming me for Brodie's death?" Before he could respond, she stood up from the island and closed the distance between them. "Well, guess what? It wasn't my fault. I didn't kill Brodie. A maniac by the name of Stephen Griffiths did. Stop blaming me for his death, and it's time to stop blaming yourself too."

His eyes flashed fire at her. "So I've been told. Excuse me. I think I lost my appetite." He brushed past her, and she stopped him by grabbing his arm.

"Sometimes bad things happen to innocents, good people who don't deserve to die. And those who are left behind, they're the ones who suffer the most. We're filled with rage and betrayal. We want to blame someone to take away the pain, but trust me, it won't do any good and it won't bring him back. No good comes from living in the past. We can't change it. In fact, your hostility will only besmirch Brodie's memory and all the good he accomplished in his life. All that negative energy's toxic and flows out into the universe. It's like black sludge on the soul." She let go of his arm and exhaled, bracing for his backlash.

A swirl of emotions clouded his eyes. "Enough with the lecture, okay? What if I could've saved him? You took that chance away from me, and away from him."

"Listen to me, Alex. I only did it to protect you, not to hurt Brodie. Would it have been better if it had been you who died? I would've never let that happen," she whispered, pouring all the pain, all the hurt of the last few days, and the love she felt for him into her words.

"He didn't deserve to die." Alex shook his head and his eyes softened.

"None of this makes any sense. Brodie knew the risks involved when he set foot on that farm. He died protecting the innocent. He was a great agent and a great man, er, demon." She rubbed his back, gliding her fingers across his worn tee shirt.

She felt the anger dissipating from his body. Confusion and grief started to take over. She sent peaceful energy to him, hoping it would help. It wasn't using magick on him, exactly.

"Yeah, he was brave as hell and I never heard him complain or say a bad word about anyone. Everyone loved the guy. He'll be missed by a lot of people. I guess I've been blaming myself for a lot of things for a long time. I never realized the extent of it until now."

"Epiphanies can be a real kick in the ass. I've had a few of them myself recently."

They stared at each other for several minutes, neither one saying a word. Willow was the first one to break the awkward silence. "What are you really doing here in the middle of the night?"

His eyes locked on her mouth. It was as though all the oxygen had been sucked out of the room. "I told you already. I came to get the rest of my stuff." His voice came out hoarse.

"I see." Then he didn't come back to see her or say goodbye. After tomorrow, she wondered if she'd ever see him again. Her chest ached thinking about it.

"Are you still hungry?" he asked in his deep, sultry voice, the one he used when he was doing wicked things to her with his tongue.

She pushed her thighs together, trying to deny the effect he had on her body. She'd finally accepted the fact that they couldn't be together. Surely, he was talking about food, not sex.

"Starving. All I ended up eating today was a bag of chips and a stale Hershey bar I dug out of the bottom of my purse. The food here is awful."

"I've never seen anyone so tiny eat so much junk." He chuckled and walked back to the fridge. The sound of his laughter healed a piece of her soul. After he opened the door and peered inside, he turned back to face her once more. "There's eggs and cheese left from the other day." He pulled them out, along with mushrooms and peppers. Then set everything on the counter. "How about I make us some omelets?"

She refused to get her hopes up. It was a meal between two people trying to make their way back to friendship, nothing more. "Sounds good. What can I do to help?" She walked over to the counter to stand beside him.

"I hear you're good with a knife." He smiled and pushed over the mushrooms and peppers. "You can chop."

"Glad to see you can still make a joke." After she pulled out a cutting board and a knife from the butcher block, she sliced into a pepper.

"Yeah, me too. How's Ellen holding up after the whole ordeal? You two finally make peace?" He pulled a bowl from the kitchen drawer.

"It was a long time coming. I still don't think it has all hit her yet, the murders, her kidnap." Willow sighed, still not able to believe it was all real. "She's been keeping pretty busy, which is probably a good thing. There's been quite a flurry of commotion around the house. The press got wind of what happened and a reporter by the name of Summer Styler stopped by here this morning."

"Hold on, wasn't she the same woman who was at the scene when Kimber's body was found?" He poured oil into the pan and spread it around.

"Yeah, and I think she may have gotten me on camera while she was here." She frowned. "The last thing I need right now is to have my face plastered across the evening news. It'll lead Saint Claire right to me."

Concern flickered in his eyes. "He's got other things on his plate right now. I doubt he's tuning into the news."

"I'm probably being paranoid. I mean, what are the chances?" Willow resumed chopping the remainder of the vegetables and tried to push away the knot in the pit of her stomach.

They worked in silence for several minutes, standing shoulder to shoulder. She started to relax from the sizzle of oil in the pan and the steady pounding of the blade hitting the wood. When she finished chopping, she put the knife down and watched Alex crack eggs into a bowl and beat them with a whisk. "I'm impressed. You look as if you know what you're doing."

"I've always been good with my hands," he said with a wink.

Don't I know it! Her face flamed. She could think of a million ways he could pleasure her with those big, strong hands of his. She wanted him so much her body ached with physical pain. Standing this close to him certainly didn't help matters. It only made her want him more.

He grinned. "Get your mind out of the gutter. I was referring to working in construction before I became a cop." He reached over, deliberately brushing up against her as he scraped the vegetables off the cutting board and into the pan. His clean, musky scent made her head spin.

To an outsider, they probably looked content, two lovers about to enjoy a meal together after a healthy bout of sex. But right now nothing could be further from the truth. "Did the map of Saint Claire's operations help? What were you able to find out?"

"Yes. Thank you. But I'm afraid that information's classified." Alex scooped the omelets out of the pan with a spatula and set them on plates. "The good news is you're officially a civilian again. You're free."

"I've waited a long time to hear those words." Why did she think there'd be more satisfaction in them when she did? Instead they left a hollow feeling in the pit of her stomach. "Until Saint Claire's dead I'll never be free. What's going down? Don't you think I have a right to know? I've gotten you this far." She pulled out silverware from one of the kitchen drawers and placed it on the counter, along with a couple of napkins. They both took seats at the island.

"The less you know at this point, the better. It's for your safety." He stabbed his fork into a piece of omelet and took a bite.

She wanted to argue, but from the determination in his voice and the set of his jaw, she sensed she wouldn't get anywhere with him if she did. She took a bite of her omelet instead. She closed her eyes, savoring the taste. "You've been holding out on me. This is delicious. You never told me you could cook."

Their gazes locked and held. "There are a lot of things I've neglected to tell you."

A part of her wanted to press further and yet another part of her decided to leave well enough alone. "Do you think Saint Claire will come after me? What aren't you telling me, Alex?"

"I've assigned an agent to safeguard you for the next forty-eight hours until he's either dead or behind bars." Alex reached out to caress her cheek. "Don't worry, you're safe. I'd never let him hurt you." His words were possessive, and primal. "Can we change the subject?" he asked and dropped his hand.

"What would you like to talk about?"

"How about your plans? What will you do after the case is wrapped up? Are you planning to go back to Salem?"

She could've sworn she heard his sharp intake of breath waiting for her reply. Sitting here alone with him, cooking and sharing a meal was a huge mistake. It made things feel too intimate and only reinforced how much she missed him—how much she loved him.

"There's nothing for me here. I've told you, I'm a gypsy. I don't stay in one place for long." She got up from the barstool and placed her dish in the sink. "I'm not sure how many jobs there are in Salem for an unemployed witch who used to work for a big-time criminal. I've saved a little money. I should be okay until I find something."

"I wiped your record clean, as promised." He stood and placed his plate next to hers, then bracketed his hands on either side of her, trapping her with his massive body. "This is your chance to start over. Why not find a job here in Raven's Hollow and put down roots? You don't have to leave if you don't want to."

"You make it all sound simple."

"Hey, it is simple." He ran his thumb over her bottom lip and her pulse quickened. "I've missed you."

"Alex?" She pressed a hand against the solid wall of his chest and tried to break away from him, but he kept her there by pressing his hips into hers. He groaned at the contact. His eyes swept over her and made her shiver.

"Do you have any idea how beautiful you look right now?" His erection pressed against her thigh and her hips jerked in response. She cursed her traitorous body.

"What do you want me to say? You're giving me all these mixed signals and it's confusing as hell. We broke up, remember?" She couldn't keep the hurt out of her voice.

He cupped her face in both his hands. "Willow, I love you."

Shock rippled through her, setting every nerve ending into overdrive. "Whoa, what did you say?"

Passion and love burned in his eyes. "You heard me. I'm in love with you and have been from the start. I didn't plan on it and tried like hell to keep this from happening. But I can't fight it anymore. What I feel for you is all consuming. My love for you, hell, it burns inside of me. The thought of Griffiths, or anyone, hurting you or touching a hair on your head sent me into a tailspin. I said things I didn't mean out of anger and fear for your well-being. I'm sorry. You're mine, Willow, mine to protect, mine to love. Can you ever forgive me?"

Tears clogged her throat and spilled down her cheeks. He brushed them away with his thumbs. No man had ever declared his love in such a romantic, sincere way. She wanted to believe him with all her heart, but she couldn't risk him breaking hers again. She was so confused it made her head spin. She didn't know what to believe anymore. "What am I supposed to say, Alex?"

"Don't say anything." He dipped his head and caught her lips in a long, slow kiss. His mouth was warm and soft. The taste of him made tears prick her eyes. Being with him like this was a balm on her soul. As much as she didn't want to get her hopes up, she needed him like she needed air.

She moaned when his tongue darted into her mouth, stealing her breath and her ability to form a coherent thought.

There was nothing gentle about his kiss; it was raw and hungry, like a man who'd been lost in the desert and was in desperate need of water. She thought her knees might buckle from the taste and feel of his mouth. She slid her arms around his neck and hung on for dear life.

He broke the kiss and whispered, "You're mine." He slid the straps of her nightgown down. By the time his mouth found hers again, she was breathing hard and digging her fingers into his back, urging him on. He trailed kisses along her neck and nipped at her shoulder

"Do you have any idea how badly you hurt me, Alex?" she murmured, knotting her fingers in his hair.

"I never meant to. I want to make it up to you. Let me." He pushed the silk down further so her breasts were exposed to the cold air. Her nipples tightened. He groaned and bent his head and licked her breast and sucked on her nipple.

An intense rush of heat swept over her and pooled at her thighs. "I need you," he murmured, lifting his head to look into her eyes. "Tell me you feel the same way." Before she could respond, he began to suck and tease her other nipple. All she could do was whimper.

"Oh you're going to pay, big time." She ached for him, lost in the wild scent of his cologne. She pulled him up by the collar of his tee shirt and pushed it over his head. She ran her hands over his broad chest and shoulders, loving the silky texture of his skin.

Her hand skated lower and unzipped his jeans, then pushed his boxers down. He kicked off his shoes and stepped out of his pants, pushing them off to the side. She stared at his rock-hard length and licked her lips.

He was beautiful down there, wide and thick with silken skin, and a smattering of dark hair. How could she ever live without this, without him? "I guess you did miss me. Let's see how much. I'm going to drive you out of your mind as payback."

"Willow." She got to her knees and licked him. He hissed out a breath and shoved his fingers in her hair. Her mouth closed over his straining cock while she stroked her hand back and forth. His taste and his scent were the most erotic things in the world.

His head fell back with a groan. Watching him made her sex throb. "I'm going to take you hard." He lifted her off the floor and sealed his hot mouth over hers again in a kiss that stole her breath. "I need inside you, now." He angled his hips against hers.

She responded by nipping at his ear. "Yes, yes. I can't wait any longer." She wanted him inside her.

He lifted her up and she wrapped her legs around his waist. He stumbled through the kitchen to the nearest door. He pushed it open and fumbled with the light on the wall and she realized they were in the butler's pantry.

"We would've never made it upstairs." She kissed him again and a hot rush of desire coursed through her veins. He shut the door and pressed her up against it. His fingers sailed up her thighs, caressing, exploring. "Alex."

By the time he slid her panties down, she was drenched and shaking. He pressed a finger inside her and she shuddered against the impulse to buck her hips. Every nerve ending zinged to life.

He curled a finger inside of her. She moaned into his neck as he explored her folds. He continued to rub back and forth, increasing the pressure. Tension coiled in her belly "Yes! Please, don't stop."

She was ready to beg if she had to. She threw her head back as a rainbow of light filled her vision as she broke apart. She rode out the waves of pleasure, bucking her hips and whispering incoherent words. When she finally caught her breath, she wrapped her hand around the width of his erection and stroked. "Now it's your turn.

He groaned. "I would love to savor this moment and take it slow, but I don't think it's happening."

She pushed her hips forward and found the slick head of his erection. She nipped at his lower lip. "Slow can be extremely overrated." She couldn't wait to have him inside her.

"Good, then we agree on something for a change." He nipped and kissed the shell of her ear and slid into her. His kisses trailed down her neck as he pushed deeper, stealing her breath. He continued to push to the root, thrusting in and out of her. "I know you love me too, even if you can't say it out loud. I can see it in your eyes when you look at me." The truth in his words made tears burn her eyes.

She was skittering on dangerous territory with him, but at the moment she didn't care. Maybe this was just some unfinished business between them, a good, healthy bout of hot, sweaty sex before they went their separate ways. But could she ever walk away with her heart intact? *Maybe I'm kidding myself.* She clawed at his back, not able to get enough.

"I love you. I'll always love you, Willow. Look at me."

And when she did, she could see the love reflected in his eyes. His words were her undoing. She was about to break apart again when he increased his pace, making her lose her mind. He forced her gaze to his by lifting her chin, deepening their connection and searing her heart. She became lost somewhere between pleasure and pain.

"Alex." He reached down and slid his thumb over her bud until her body began to convulse with pleasure. "I'm so close."

"Come for me, Willow. I want to feel you."

She cried out when his hips bucked. She was shattering from the inside out. He pumped harder and then they flew over the edge together. His face was buried in her neck, fingers tangled in her hair. Her body became boneless in his arms.

He pressed his forehead to hers while he was still inside her. "I didn't mean to take you like a rutting animal. I couldn't help myself."

Still panting, she smiled up at him. "You don't see me complaining." It was true. She couldn't complain. Alex's lovemaking took her to new heights sexually, emotionally, and she feared, if she let herself, she could easily become addicted to the man. But she'd learned her lesson the hard way.

As far as she was concerned, his declaration of love didn't change a thing, because she knew from experience, sometimes love wasn't enough. As much as she wished it weren't so, she feared their relationship was doomed.

CHAPTER 26

"*W*here are we going?" Willow asked Delilah as they walked along Washington Street in the downtown section of Hoboken. Businesspeople hurried past, carrying steaming cups, as well as moms wheeling toddlers in fancy strollers. Exhaust fumes mingled with the scent of freshly brewed coffee. Sirens blared, horns honked, and the hiss of trains rushed past.

"You'll see soon enough. It's a surprise." Delilah smiled and shoved her hands in the pockets of her black, wool trench coat. She waved at a few people Willow didn't recognize as they made their way down the busy street.

Nick, a sexy demon whom Alex had assigned to trail her every move, followed at a safe distance behind them. She turned and waved, but he pretended not to notice and maintained his stony expression. "I'm not much for surprises. Seeing Nick standing at the foot of my bed this morning is about all I can take for one day. Somehow I managed to convince him to wait downstairs while I showered and changed."

Delilah laughed. "This one you're going to like. Promise."

"I'm holding you to it for getting me up this early." Willow stifled a yawn. To say she'd gotten zero sleep the night before was an understatement. After almost spontaneously combusting in the butler's pantry, she took Alex back to her room. They ended up making love until dawn, not able to get enough of each other. She flushed at the memory. For the moment, all seemed right in the world for a change.

Her phone beeped. She pulled it out and glanced at the screen. It was a text from Alex. *Stay far away from Saint Claire's headquarters and don't go out alone. xoxo. Alex*

How could she? Not with an overzealous demon practically glued to her side. Her heart lurched in her chest. What danger was Alex getting himself into this time? Willow shoved her phone back in her jacket pocket.

"What's the deal with the demon?" Delilah asked, angling her head in Nick's direction. "I mean, don't get me wrong, it's not every day a gorgeous male tags along on my errands, but the killer's dead. Why do we need MBI protection? Are you still in danger?"

For as long as Tristan Saint Claire lived and breathed, she'd be looking over her shoulder. But she didn't need to worry Delilah with all the sordid details. She'd been through enough over the last few weeks. Death took its toll on everyone, even the strong ones. "Pay no attention to him." Willow waved a hand in the air. "It's Alex being overprotective. Something big is going down on a case I've been assisting him with and it's at a boiling point. I think he's being overly cautious."

Concern flashed in Delilah's eyes. "I hope you're right."

A part of Willow felt like a fool, walking around with a personal bodyguard, but Alex didn't give her much of a choice in the matter. All morning long she'd heard a buzzing in her head and couldn't shake the feeling that someone other than Nick was following her every move. She linked her arm in Delilah's to assuage her fears. "We've got a seven-foot-tall demon trained to kill looking out for us. What could go wrong?"

"Why does it sound like you're tempting fate?" Delilah asked, her brow furrowed in concern.

"Nonsense. I can't remember the last time I had a day out. I need this. We both do." Besides, it would be a damn shame to let such a crisp, sunny day go to waste. Maybe after everything, she was imagining things.

In any case, she refused to let it ruin her morning. Willow glanced up and down the streets at the colorful canopies and the twinkle lights displayed in the store windows. "I almost forgot how quaint the downtown can be." In all the years she'd come back here to meet Maeve, it had always been at some out-of-the-way greasy pit, or a sleazy bar.

With every café and shop they passed, she got an instant rush of nostalgia, pulling her back in time to life before she worked for the Cabal—before she lost a part of her soul, her innocence. *Can I really ever move forward, or am I kidding myself?*

"It doesn't take a psychic to see you're distracted." Delilah stopped in front of an empty store with a "For Rent" sign in the window. She placed a gloved hand on Willow's shoulder. "We can bag this for now and grab coffee and talk if you'd like."

"I'll admit, I have a lot on my mind right now, but I refuse to let it interfere with our outing, or your surprise. Let's grab the coffee later." Willow forced a smile. Last night she'd promised Alex she'd stay out of his way. She couldn't go back on her word now. Besides, she was no longer working for the MBI. She wondered where it left things between them. Even after his admission of love, she still wasn't sure what it meant, or if they had a future together.

If she were a realist, she'd forget about him and pretend they'd never met, chalk it up to the best sex of her life and move on. Too bad her heart wouldn't let her. "What's the deal with this place?" She glanced at the sign.

"It's my future." Delilah pulled out a key and turned the lock. "I stopped by the realtor's. She couldn't meet me this morning, but she said I could have a look at the place."

"Whoa, then I can't wait to see what's inside." Willow followed Delilah into the enormous empty space. She coughed as she glanced around at the dust motes and thick cobwebs hanging from the ceiling. She heard a tap on the glass and bodyguard Nick appeared at the window.

"What do you think? Granted, this place is in serious need of bleach and some elbow grease, but can you see the potential? Picture a cabinet over there filled with crystals." Delilah pointed to the far corner of the room. "And one next to it filled with wands and scrying bowls, maybe Tarot cards. I'd like to stock fresh herbs for potions and make my own candles for spell casting. I thought I might even carry some of my special soaps and lotions."

"You want to turn this into a magick shop?"

"Exactly" Willow couldn't miss the excitement in her voice. "You said this was something you've always dreamed of doing. This has been my dream for as long as I can remember too."

"Wow, I'm impressed. You've got it all figured out. This is exactly what the downtown needs. What brought this all on?"

"I've spent the last couple of years living at the coven under Ellen's tutelage. Now I feel as if I've learned enough to go out on my own." Delilah leaned against the counter, took off her gloves, and unraveled her scarf. "I want my own place."

"I'm happy for you, Delilah. This is great. Everyone deserves to follow their dreams." Why did Willow suddenly feel so lost and confused about her own future? She was a psychic who didn't have the first clue where her life was headed. She'd laugh at the irony if the situation wasn't so ridiculous.

"You're right. Everyone does deserve to follow her dreams. But I don't plan on doing this alone. I'm thinking more along the lines of a group effort. I'm going to ask all the girls in the coven. I figure we could pool our money and share in the responsibilities and the profits. Everyone has something to contribute." She motioned around the store. "What do you think? I got the feeling you might want to stick around. The store could sure use a great psychic."

"Hold on, are you asking me to go into business with you?" Willow walked up and stood beside her, shaking her head in disbelief. "You can't be serious? There are things you don't know about me, about my past."

"Look, Willow, we don't know each other that well, and I get that you've faced hard times, but you're a good person. I sensed it right away. I'm not asking for a resume. I've seen what you can do. I'm offering you a chance to be your own boss. What do you say?"

Her heart leaped. After everything she'd been through, Willow never imagined going in on a legitimate business or being her own boss. Deep down, she wanted to stay in Raven's Hollow, start fresh, and explore this thing between her and Alex. Even if she got hurt, he was worth the effort. "I have no experience running a business, and there's something I need to put out on the table. You say you don't care about my past, but you might feel differently after you find out what I've done—what I was."

"Whatever you did can't be changed. I'm a Wiccan at heart. It's not up to me to judge. Besides, think of how many lives you saved. In my humble opinion, your good deeds more than make up for any past sins." Delilah reached out and squeezed her shoulder. "Do you need time to think it through?"

Before Willow could respond, loud voices made them both turn toward the door. Nick was yelling at two hulking figures with red eyes and short black horns. Her heart sank when she noticed two intertwined circle tattoos emblazoned across their beefy arms. It was Saint Claire's symbol. *He sent his flunkies. How did they find me?* Crap, the newscast.

Her eyes locked with the larger of the two demons. He flashed a set of razor sharp teeth at her, and then pounded his fist on the glass. Her gaze darted to Nick. His enormous body was poised to fight, but the other two overpowered him, thrusting kicks and fists into his head and chest. "We need to get out of here."

Delilah screamed. "What's going on? Who the hell are those goons? Why are they beating up Nick?"

"I'm not sure," Willow lied, taking a step back and grabbing Delilah by the arm. "Is there a back entrance to this place?" She tried to keep the panic out of her voice and failed.

"I don't know." Delilah started to shake.

"Go find one. Now." Willow sent her a mild shock of energy.

Delilah disappeared toward the back of the store while Willow figured out a plan of escape. She reached for her *athame,* but it was gone, left back at the coven. Damn. She frantically glanced around the empty room in search of a weapon, but only found a couple of small rocks and a broken piece of stone. She picked them up off the floor and stuffed the pieces in her coat pocket. Willow glanced over at Nick and covered her mouth with her hands.

Blood dripped from the side of his face and nose. The poor guy was getting his ass kicked. She wished she could help him, but she had to protect Delilah. When one of the demons turned toward her, Nick used it to his advantage, thrusting his knee into his crotch. The demon grunted and dropped to his knees writhing in pain. The other demon roared and tackled Nick, sending him careening through the plate glass window.

Willow ducked behind the counter. She covered her face with her hands as shards of glass flew through the air.

"C'mon, this way." Delilah helped her off the floor. Willow didn't look back but could hear thunderous footsteps pound behind them.

Together, they ran to the back of the store and up a spiral staircase. Her boot caught on one of the steps and Willow stumbled, coming face to face with a massive head and razor-sharp horns. The demon growled and grabbed her by the hair. She reached into her pocket and jabbed the broken piece of stone into his eye. He roared and let go of her.

"Hurry!" Delilah yelled from the top of the stairs.

"Where the hell are we going?" Willow climbed up and followed her through another door, this one led to the outside. A burst of icy cold air hit her in the face and blew her hair in every direction. Goddess, they were on the roof. *I hate heights.* Panic gripped her like an iron fist. She swayed and couldn't seem to catch her breath or get her bearings.

"Willow, we have to climb down." Delilah pointed to a ladder.

When Willow glanced over the side of the building, all the air left her lungs. Black spots swirled in front of her eyes. "N-no, I can't. It's too high."

"Yes, you can. It's our only way out. We can cut through a back alley and hide. I called Ellen. She's on her way with the cavalry." Delilah ran to the side of the building and climbed down to the first rung of the ladder. "Let's go."

Willow had barely registered her voice. Adrenaline was flooding her body and she couldn't move. It wasn't until she heard footsteps thunder up the stairs that she snapped out of her fog. She flicked her wrist and the door slammed shut. She flicked it again and the lock clicked into place.

Fists pounded on the door. Power rippled through the air like a bolt of lightning. Already she sensed the demons breaking through her spell. Her magick wouldn't hold long. She channeled all the energy in her mind and body on keeping the door shut. She began to shake. "You have to go without me. Please, save yourself. It's me they're after."

"Don't look down and you'll be fine. Trust me." Fear choked Delilah's voice.

The door began to squeak on its hinges and Willow held on. Despite the chilly day, sweat dripped from her forehead and seeped through her heavy wool coat. *Can't hold on much longer.* "You need to go."

Tears streamed down Delilah's cheeks. "They'll kill you."

"I...can...handle...myself," she choked. "But I can't do that and protect you. Go find Ellen and the other girls. I'm begging you."

Finally, Delilah nodded and climbed down the ladder. Willow continued to hold the door shut, using all her energy reserves, focusing the last dregs of her magick until Delilah was safely on the street and running far away from the building.

Her body collapsed onto the concrete as the door burst open. Footsteps pounded across the rooftop with so much force, Willow swore the two demons left indentations in the concrete. A giant hand wrapped around her throat and lifted her off the ground. She gasped for air and kicked out with her leg, aiming for the groin.

"That's going to cost you," muttered the demon closest to her. Blood dripped from the corner of his eye where she'd jabbed him with the rock. "Payback will be swift and deadly, but like a pink frosted cupcake compared to what Tristan Saint Claire has planned for you. Time to pay a visit to your old boss."

CHAPTER 27

"*I*'m parked in the rear of the gallery. We're clear on this end," Alex whispered into his microphone. He was crouched inside the cab of the delivery truck, his eyes trained on the loading dock of the Prestige Art Gallery. Clad in a faded brown uniform, he pulled down the bill of his cap to cover his face and adjusted his earpiece.

He was waiting to get the go-ahead from Cayden to go in the back of the gallery. His partner was positioned inside, undercover as a customer. Antsy as hell, he tapped his foot in agitation. "What's happening in there?"

"My tie's friggin' strangling me and these shoes are two sizes too small," Cayden muttered. "There's a mortal security guard packing heat parked at the front. He's giving me dirty looks. Oh, and the curator is a hot female who keeps crinkling her nose at me as if she smells something rotten under her designer heels. But other than that, it's a helluva good time. We should've switched places on this one. You would've been more convincing at this sort of thing."

"You need to distract them while I sneak in the back." His plan was to drop off a stack of empty boxes, then pick up the ones delivered from Saint Claire's warehouse that contained the drugs and get out of there fast. It was dangerous as hell, not to mention a long shot, but the best they had to go on right now.

"The curator's on the phone, but I can feel her eyes on me. I'm doing my best to fawn all over ugly splotches of paint splattered across a canvas with a price tag of fifteen big ones. I think we're in the wrong business."

Instinctively, his hand shot to his broken ribs where a stab of pain still lingered every time he expelled a breath. "Yeah, we're not in it for the money. It's all about the glory," Alex said, not able to keep the sarcasm from his voice. "Make sure she doesn't go in the back. Let's get this over with." All they needed to do was confiscate the drugs inside the shipping boxes and then they'd convene at the warehouse and make their arrests.

Anxiety twisted in his gut when he glanced at his watch. At this precise moment, at least a dozen or so other agents were doing the same thing—spread out to Saint Claire's various drug-smuggling operations—ready to take him down.

If all went as planned, his ring would come to a screeching halt. Alex's only sense of comfort in all this was assigning Nick to protect Willow. The demon had a good track record with the agency. He'd keep her out of harm's way.

There was a crash, followed by a lady's scream and lots of shouting. Alex pulled his earpiece away from his ear and winced. He waited a beat and pushed the plastic piece back in. "What the hell did you do? Cayden?"

"Shit, I accidently knocked down this hideous sculpture of a dude with a huge penis and a bird's face off one of the pedestals. Now the ice queen's motioning toward the security guard and they're both headed this way. You're clear for now. Go. You better be fast. I can only pull this off for so long. They're looking at me like I should be in a straitjacket."

"Smooth. Smith's going to have a shit fit." Alex slung his duffle bag over his shoulder and popped the trunk. He pulled out the dolly, loaded it with the empty boxes, and wheeled it up the ramp onto the loading dock. "Okay, I'm moving as we speak."

"My horns are blocking the guard's view of the security feed."

"Don't move until I tell you I'm clear." Alex glanced over his shoulder to make sure there was no one around and placed a sticky note over the camera. He pulled a magnetic strip with an electronic sensor from his bag. He pasted the strip over the alarm system and held his breath. Thousands of numbers blinked on the panel before the device beeped several times.

The back door slid open with a hiss, allowing him to step inside the gallery. He took a quick sweep of the cluttered stockroom and headed for the corner closest to the door. He unloaded the empty boxes and stacked them against the wall. "I'm in."

"She's making me pay. I handed over my credit card and it got declined, only two left in my wallet. We've got a short window before one of them calls the cops, and then we'll be in the middle of a shit storm. Hurry up. I moved away from the counter, and I'm pretending to admire another hideous painting."

"You think this is easy? I'm looking for his logo. Two intertwined circles, right? What the hell does it mean anyway?"

"The symbol's Demonish. It means power wields power," Cayden whispered back. "Check on the side or the bottom of the boxes."

Stacks and stacks of different sized cartons filled the small space. Alex kicked a box to the side in frustration. He recalled seeing the symbol in Saint Claire's file, but never thought to ask about the significance. "How poetic."

"Last one was declined. How we doing back there? The security dude's yelling into his walkie-talkie. I think I've overstayed my welcome."

"You have to distract them a bit longer. Keep acting crazy. How hard can it be?" Alex pushed another stack of boxes to the side and cursed. "Still no luck."

Cayden groaned. "Time to execute Plan B."

"Now might be a good time to fill me in on Plan B." There were rustling noises, followed by a pop and lots of commotion.

"Liquid ketamine. Don't worry. The stuff doesn't work on demons. But it's super potent on humans. The good news is those two will be out cold for a while."

His heart began to pound. "And the bad news?"

"The stuff spreads fast. Let's hope you get out before it does. I'm meeting you in the back. I have a feeling we're about to have company."

"It spreads? How long?"

"My guess, three minutes, give or take. Tick tock."

"Nothing like a little pressure on the job to get the blood pumping," Alex muttered, hoping like hell he didn't pass out before he found the right ones. His hands began to shake as he lifted another box and threw it against the wall.

Finally, he dug through three larger ones and found the logo stamped into the shipping labels. "Got them. Meet me in the truck." He loaded them onto his dolly, slipped out the back door and removed the strip from the panel. After he pulled off the sticky note from the camera, he glanced over his shoulder to make sure he was clear before heading down the ramp.

He stopped halfway down, pulled a razor blade from his back pocket and knelt next to the boxes. He cut the packing tape in one quick swipe. Underneath the handfuls of bubble wrap and layers of tissue paper, there was nothing but a fancy oil painting. "Could Saint Claire be hiding the drugs inside the art? Cayden, are you there?"

When he didn't respond, Alex cut open the back of the frame and found what looked like at least a kilo of heroin in a plastic bag taped to the back of the canvas. Willow was spot on. He ripped open the bag, dipped his pinky in, and put the white stuff to his lips. He cursed then spit on the ground. *Paydirt.*

"Going somewhere?"

Alex looked up. Three guys in navy-blue street cleaning uniforms blocked his path, standing at the end of the ramp. Alex stared open-mouthed at the Glock now pointed at his face, an FBI standard issue. "Hmm, Saint Claire even has the government on his payroll?" He got to his feet and stepped in front of the dolly. He lifted his arms in surrender. "Easy, boys. I'm not here to get in a pissing match. We all have our jobs to do. Surely, we can work this out." Even if he stalled until Cayden showed up, they were still out numbered. "Besides, three against one?"

The biggest of the three walked toward him and tried to look over Alex's shoulder at the boxes. "Step aside, and I'm warning you, do it slowly. I wouldn't want to blow a hole in the side of your body. The blood might get all over the sidewalk and then we'll be in the middle of a messy investigation."

The encroaching piece of shit kept his Glock pointed at Alex's face, which gave him zero chance to pull his gun from his ankle strap. "Let's talk about this. We have agents planted at every one of Saint Claire's drug smuggling sites." Alex inwardly cursed and did what he was told. "It's only a matter of time before it all comes crashing down. Hey, it's still not too late to switch back to the good guys and help the rest of us take him down."

"Working for the good guys is overrated and the pay sucks," the big guy said with a scowl. He patted Alex down and grabbed his laser gun out of his holster. "What other goodies do you have on you?"

Where the hell was Cayden? If he didn't get here soon Alex was going to lose whatever evidence they had collected. A buzzing noise came through his earpiece and made him hiss out a breath. Before he could stop him, the bastard pulled off Alex's cap and ripped the earpiece from his ear. "I don't think you'll need this." Now he was truly screwed.

A loud boom made them both turn toward the end of the loading dock. Smoke and ashes flew everywhere. The stench of burned flesh lingered in the air. When the haze cleared, the other two agents who'd been standing at the bottom of the ramp were gone, turned into a pile of dust, only their navy-blue uniforms remained.

"Sorry I'm late to the party." Cayden stood at the end of the dock, his M15 laser focused on the chest of the guy still holding a gun to Alex's head.

But before Cayden could get out a shot, Alex screamed, "Hold your fire." Alex held up his hands as if he were surrendering, then turned and punched the guy as hard as he could, landing a jab straight to the jaw. His body crumbled to the ground like a dead weight.

Alex bent to pick up his Glock and put it in his waistband. He retrieved his laser gun and his earpiece. "Don't think you'll need these," he said, mimicking the man's earlier words and sarcasm. "I hope it was worth it, you sonofabitch."

His gaze moved to Cayden who was jogging up the ramp. "Nice of you to show up. What the hell took you so long?" He took in his partner's ripped clothes and the blood streaking his face and chest. "What happened to you?"

"I got here as soon as I could. I got jumped by two of Saint Claire's humans the second I came out of the gallery. But I don't think we'll be hearing from them again." He shoved his laser back in his coat.

"Are you nuts? You didn't need to totally obliterate them, or those poor bastards. They could've talked." Alex angled his head toward the two piles of ash left on the loading dock. "Smith's going to castrate you. Do you have any idea the red tape he'll be facing? There aren't even bodies for an autopsy. Those two were FBI."

"It was unavoidable. I'll put a call into dispatch from the van. The FBI can send someone to clean up its own mess. We have to go. Now."

"Did I miss something? I lost communication for a sec." Alex ran a hand through his hair, taking in the macabre scene.

"It's bad and keeps getting worse I'm afraid. We've lost five of our own and have two agents down. Saint Claire was onto us all along. Our guys walked into a deathtrap." Cayden huffed out a breath and refused to look him in the eye.

"What aren't you're telling me?"

"One of the agents who went down was Nick. He's still alive, but he's critical. He has a broken nose, broken ribs and a fractured skull. He's lost a lot of blood thanks to Saint Claire's demons. They've got Willow. Shit, I'm sorry, Alex."

He sucked in a breath and gripped the handle of the dolly until his knuckles turned white. His mind blurred. *Willow?* "How the hell could this happen?" He gaped at Cayden in bewilderment. "Do we have any idea where they've taken her?"

Cayden shook his head, his expression bleak. "I know how much you want to go after her, Alex, but you can't. Smith ordered us to load up the boxes and confiscate the contents of Saint Claire's private plane. It's in a hangar of the Raven's Hollow airport and about to take off for South America. We don't know if he's actually on it or he's got his top scumbag in charge at the helm, but either way, we believe a good portion of the smack in those shipping boxes is in the cargo hold. If we don't stop him, he'll get away for good and his drug business will continue to expand."

"What about Smith? Why can't he meet you there?"

"Smith's on his way to Saint Claire's estate to see if he's cleaning out his safe, so he can nail him. We're down agents. I need you on this."

His gut twisted. If he didn't go with Cayden, he'd let Saint Claire walk away scot-free. The most heinous of all murdering drug lords would start his cartel up in another town. How many more would die or become addicted to drugs because of him? Gus was one of the lucky ones, but there were plenty of others who weren't so lucky. And without substantial evidence, it would be impossible to convict him in any court—mage, human, or otherwise.

His heart sank. But if Alex didn't go after Willow, she was as good as dead. "I can't. I have to save Willow."

"Listen to me, there's a helipad about a mile away." Cayden pointed toward a row of buildings in the distance. "Smith sent a chopper to pick us up. We go bust Saint Claire, then we go find your woman."

Alex glanced at the boxes. "This would be enough to send him to jail for a long time. It may not be the major bust we were hoping for, but it's something. I can't risk her life. I have to go after Willow."

"You love her, don't you? I can see it in your eyes."

"I do. I can't lose her, not now. C'mon, I'll drop you at the helipad." His heart began to pound as he wheeled the dolly down the ramp. "I've got to figure out a way to find her. Even if I have to go to every one of the businesses on the map Willow drew for us. I still have a copy in the truck."

"What about the tracking device you put on Willow? Did you ever remove it?" Cayden asked, opening the back door and loading the boxes in the back of the van.

"I never had a chance." Hope bloomed in his chest. Alex pulled out his cell and pressed a button. Sure enough, a black ping showed Willow was at the warehouse. He sighed with relief and shut the hatch. "I've got to go save my woman."

Alex jumped into the driver seat, slammed the door, and floored the gas. He'd never been a religious man, but he figured this was as good a time as any to offer a silent prayer to let her be safe. He said one to the Goddess, just for good measure. And he vowed that if she came out of this okay he would never judge magick or witches again.

Hang on, Willow. I'm coming for you.

CHAPTER 28

*W*illow cracked her eye open, and pain exploded on the side of her head and along her jaw. When she tried to glance at her surroundings, all she could make out were shadows that seemed to creep up the dusky walls.

Shivering, she couldn't stop her teeth from gnashing. She managed to glance down at herself. Her clothes were tattered and hanging from her body in shreds. With great effort, she lifted her head and gazed around the cavernous room.

The only sound came from the steady drip of water hitting a concrete floor. The damp stench of mildew flared in her nose and her throat.

Her entire body ached as if she'd been run over by a bulldozer at full speed. She tried to stretch out her limbs but realized as fear knotted in her stomach that she was suspended from the ceiling.

Her hands were bound behind her back with chains. She focused her energy and used what little strength she had left to break free of their hold, but the chains didn't budge. *Lead.* No wonder she felt so weak and confused. What little magick she had left from fighting off Saint Claire's minions had been completely drained.

Now her mind was fuzzy and she couldn't remember a thing after she'd been snatched from the roof of that building. She tried to think of a spell to break free, but nothing came to her. Letters and words circled around in her head like alphabet soup.

"Let me out of here," she screamed at the top of her lungs until she was hoarse and thoroughly pissed.

"There's no air and no one cares." The words whispered through the room like a verse from a creepy nursery rhyme. Shadows seeped out of the walls and circled around her. Three sylphs appeared, choking the breath from her lungs. Their ghoulish bodies zoomed across the room in a flurry of gray mist.

A door creaked open and then closed. The clatter of footsteps thumped across the concrete floor. "Well, look who we have here." A tall, broad shadow walked over and stood in front of her. His bald head and short red horns cut through the darkness like a floodlight. Tristan Saint Claire snapped his fingers and the sylphs dissipated and floated away into the walls.

Coughing, she gasped for air. She took slow, steady breaths until her chest finally stopped heaving. Angry tears stung the back of her eyes and clogged in her throat. She spat next to his feet, barely missing his suede Bruno Magli loafers. "Now you've got me here. What the hell do you want?"

"Willow McCray." He snapped his fingers again and a ball of light appeared in the palm of his hand and floated to the ceiling, illuminating the dank room. She glanced around and realized they were in the basement of his warehouse. At least he hadn't taken her far. Maybe Alex would still be able to find her before it was too late. While she could handle herself in most situations, working with Alex had made her realize it was okay to lean on someone you cared about. It wasn't a show of weakness, but a sign of strength.

"I would say it's great to see you again, but I'm afraid you're on my shit list at the moment." He rubbed his hand over a cut on her knee and she winced in pain. "I'm not fond of beating up on a skirt. Even I have a code, but my guys said you tried to claw out their eyes and kick them in the 'nads. What do you expect? You've been a bad girl, Willow. I'm afraid it has come to this." He shook his horned head, looking disappointed. "You worked for me for a long time. You were like the daughter I never had."

A bitter laugh bubbled up from her throat. "You sent out a hit on me and had your thugs smack me around. You murdered my best friend and two other innocents. If that's how you treat your loved ones, I'd hate to see how you treat your enemies."

His brows rose, causing an eleven to form between his horns. "Ah, you always could cut through the bullshit and get straight to the point. I didn't want those witches talking to the cops. They would've ruined everything, and I couldn't let that happen," he said shaking his bald head. "I hear you've been doing a lot of talking to the MBI, even working for them as a psychic. You've switched sides? I doubt it'll last long. A pretty leopard like you doesn't change her very tainted spots. What are they offering you for giving away all my secrets?"

"What if I told you they weren't offering me a thing? Maybe I did this on my own to see you rot behind bars."

His smile didn't reach his eyes. "I should kill you right now for your insolence." A vein pulsed in his forehead. "Now you've caused a hell a lot of trouble for me." He began to pace back and forth and pulled out his phone. The fabric of his fine silk suit made a whispering sound as he passed.

"You're too late. The evil empire you've worked so hard to create is being dismantled as we speak. Even if you kill me, it won't stop what has already been put into motion."

His lip curled into a sneer. "The only reason you're not in a trash bag floating along the Hudson is because you're worth more to me alive than dead. I can bargain for your life. You're like a dirty penny that keeps showing up. Let's see how much you're worth."

Before she could tell him to shove it, the door above them burst open and heavy footsteps pounded down the staircase. One by one, FBI agents, along with men and women from the RHPD, descended on the scene, carrying high-powered rifles and shields.

Saint Claire snapped his fingers and the sylphs floated out of the walls toward them. Shouts and screams reverberated through the room. His security detail, the thugs who had manhandled her, rushed down as well. In a matter of minutes, the room erupted in chaos.

She blinked back tears when she saw Alex descending the stairs and running toward her. He called out her name, but she was too weak to answer. When Saint Claire turned to watch the fight break out, Willow used the distraction in her favor. *I'm not going down without a fight.*

Before the sylphs could get to Alex, she lashed out with her feet, hitting

Saint Claire in the back of the knees. He stumbled forward and she kicked again, hitting him in the back of his skull. He groaned and fell face first onto the concrete floor. She heard a crack and figured she must've broken his nose. He let out a sting of curses, and when he lifted his head and turned, his face was covered in blood. "You little witch. I'm afraid you're more of a liability than a bargaining chip. Goodbye, Willow." The demon snapped his fingers, and an energy ball made of blue light zoomed through the air and smacked her in the chest.

"No!" Pain exploded through every cell in her body. She screamed in agony and started to convulse.

When her eyes started to close, death's shadow appeared holding a bouquet of black roses and wearing a crown of thorns. She tried to scream, but a suffocating darkness closed in like a noose around her throat. Numbness took hold of her body and then one last breath slipped from her lips. It was too late. Willow couldn't fight *him* any longer.

When Alex's gaze locked on Willow's limp form dangling from the ceiling like an animal at a slaughterhouse, his gut twisted with fear. Demon special agents rushed in behind him, along with several FBI. Across the room, the men in blue were getting the life choked out of them by a mysterious gray mist floating through the air. He couldn't help them, not now. He had to go to her, he had to save her.

He bent his head and tried to fight through the commotion. He spotted Saint Claire on his knees across the room. Before he could reach for his gun, the demon threw a ball of blue fire in his direction. Alex ducked just before it hit him in the face.

The next moment a blast shook the building and forced Alex to cover his ears. He looked over at Saint Claire, spread out, in a crumbled heap. He breathed a sigh of relief, but it was short- lived. He needed to get to Willow. He shouted her name, making his way toward her.

"I thought you might need backup. It turns out I was right." Alex turned to see Smith standing behind him with a smoking M15 in his grip.

"Smith? What are you doing here? I thought you were at Saint Claire's place?"

"I didn't mean to kill him. I planned on bringing him in for questioning, but the blast forced his energy ball right back at him. We confiscated what we needed. I let the FBI handle the rest. I rushed over here." Smith holstered his gun and turned in Willow's direction. "Let's get her down."

Together, they ran to Willow and Smith used his brute strength to remove the chains from her wrists. Alex was filled with a crushing pain as he pulled her down and held her in his arms. Her body was limp and lifeless, ice cold. Her pulse was nonexistent and she wasn't breathing.

He kissed her temple and cradled her in his arms. "Come back to me. I love you. I can't lose you." How could she die on him now? He hugged her to his chest. "Willow, wake up." He brought his nose to her hair to inhale her scent. "Someone call an ambulance." The moment he said the words, his brain clicked into action.

After he laid her flat, he pressed his hands on her chest about to apply CPR when Smith kneeled beside him and shook his horned head. "I'm afraid that won't revive her. Nothing can reverse the damage of a fire ball or bring back the dead, except, maybe a powerful spell." Smith angled his head toward the stairs, which was now clear. "Go. You don't have much time."

There was only one place Alex could take her where someone might be able to bring her back. Without a moment to spare, he lifted her and ran toward the door.

"I'll take things from here," Smith called out. "Get her healed."

There had to be a way to save her.

By the time Alex got to the coven, Willow's lips had turned blue. He barreled through the front doors, headed to the kitchen and laid her down on one of the butcher-block surfaces. He'd placed a call to Ellen from the car so the witches would be ready when they got there.

Ellen glanced down at Willow's limp, lifeless form, and tears slid down her cheeks. "I'm so sorry, Alex. I fear even magick can't bring her back."

"No, you have to try." He was ready to beg if he had to. He'd do anything to save her. He'd been hoping and praying that the witches could bring her back.

"Even I don't have that kind of power," Ellen said in a choked voice.

Willow's skin was pure ashen now. Saje and Nadia rushed into the kitchen holding a variety of potion bottles. "Whatever the demon did to her we can't seem to undo," Nadia whispered beside him and touched his shoulder.

Tristan Saint Claire's drug ring had been successfully dismantled. According to the alert on his phone, all of his dirty operations had screeched to a crashing halt. His thugs were either dead or behind bars. The one thing he'd been working toward for months, and years. All of it meant nothing without Willow. "Please, can you keep trying? I'm begging you."

The women nodded and attempted to get a potion into her mouth with a dropper. He'd scorned magick for the better part of his adult life, and now he was asking Ellen and the other witches to do the unthinkable, resurrect the dead.

Arabella, Delilah, and Gillian walked in and gathered around Willow. They bent their heads in sorrow. "You can't reanimate a body," Arabella whispered. When she glanced up, her face was pale with grief.

He only wished it had been him and not Willow who'd been in that basement. If only he could go back in time and save her. "My sole purpose during this bust was to keep her out of the way and now she's gone."

Gillian came over to his side and squeezed his hand. "Hold on, Alex. There might be a way to bring Willow back. Granted, it's unorthodox as hell, but it might actually work. You have the power to save her, but you'll need to give Willow something precious."

His heart leaped. "Whatever it is, I agree. I'll do anything."

"Willow saved my life and now it's my turn to save hers. This spell requires an ancient form of magick. There's only one way to bring her back." Gillian looked up at him and tilted her head to the side. "You have to agree to give Willow a piece of your soul."

With a wave of her hands, Ellen lit seven white candles along with long sticks of incense and formed a circle around Willow's lifeless form. All of the witches clasped hands and motioned for Alex to go to the center. He let out a long, deep breath and closed his eyes.

The witches began to chant from an ancient text about life and bringing the spirit back into the body. At first, nothing happened, except the brush of air on the back of his neck. He said a silent prayer to the powers that be and begged for forgiveness. He asked for Willow to be spared.

"Please come back to me, to this life," he whispered.

"Alex, you need to talk to her." Gillian glanced up at him and smiled. "Magick takes on many forms. It's not only spells and charms, but it's also love and light, hope and beauty. Let all the love you feel for her carry the spell. Try to focus your mind and your intentions."

He hadn't changed out of his delivery uniform and still had the stench of Saint Claire's greasy warehouse on him. The scent competed with the fresh flowers and the fragrant hint of citrus and jasmine. He pushed the thought from his mind and focused on her instead.

"I love you, Willow. I've never loved anyone like I love you." His voice choked with emotion. Alex cleared his throat. "Before you came into my life, I was filled with bitterness. My heart was cold and empty, and then I met you and I've changed forever for the better. Somehow you managed to open me up and made me see how wonderful life could be. I don't want to lose you. I can't." The candles flickered and the wind kicked up.

"Keep it up, Alex." Gillian whispered. "There's powerful magick in your heart." He went to her side, reached for her hand and squeezed.

Alex fought the grief twisting his heart. All around him the women continued to chant the spell over and over again. The room vibrated with power. His body began to shake, and it felt as if an invisible thread were being pulled from his chest. White spots flickered in front of his eyes and swirled around the room. He wondered if the specks were pieces of his soul floating into Willow's body. He got the sensation that it was splitting in two. As scary and strange as it felt, he hoped that was what was happening, because it meant she would live.

"Did you see that?" Arabella asked. "I thought I saw Willow's chest rise. The spell must be working. Don't stop chanting."

Their voices grew to a fevered pitch. Wind swooped into the room, circled around and made their hair blow in every direction. Already he could feel the magick pulse against his skin, and to his shock, it wasn't at all unpleasant. "Willow?"

Color flooded her cheeks. Willow coughed and slowly opened her eyes. She glanced around and started to sit up. "Where am I?" She blinked like she was waking up from a dream. "What's going on?" The women let out a collective gasp, cheered, cried, and high fived all around.

"How do you feel?" Alex asked with a huge grin. He moved his hand behind her back to support her. "Don't try to move."

"Strange. I had the weirdest dream. I was floating between this world and suspended in the afterlife." Willow winced in pain as she tried to sit up more.

"Shh, take it easy, baby." He pressed his arm under her neck and eased her back down.

"A part of me doesn't think it was a dream at all," she murmured and rubbed her chest.

"You're here with me, alive." Alex bent down to kiss her cheeks, her temples, and her lips, tears clogging his throat.

"Did I die?"

"I'll tell you all about it, but not right now. I'm taking you home with me and never letting you go. I thought I lost you." Alex buried his face in her neck, inhaling her scent, feeling his heart beat again.

"I'm not going anywhere. I love you, Alex, with all my heart and soul."

EPILOGUE

SIX MONTHS LATER

The grand opening of Bell, Book, and Candle was a raucous celebration of magick, friendship, and tremendous hard work. All the girls had worked their butts off to make this come together in a short period of time.

"Business is definitely booming," Willow murmured, and pulled a box filled with different colored taper candles onto one of the glass cases. She glanced around the store and smiled. People milled in and out and circled onto the sidewalk. The place was exactly as Delilah had envisioned it to be, with a few added twists. Now there was a room in the back for Tarot card readings, astrological charts, and even séances.

Willow spent the majority of her time working at the front of the store and loved helping young witches pick the right tools to perfect their craft. She'd started to build a decent-sized clientele that came in for spell-work and private readings.

Her gaze locked with Delilah's from across the room. She was floating around the shop, shaking hands and helping customers. She was a natural in this type of setting. The combination of her patience and kindness drew witches into the store in droves.

Over the past couple of months, they'd gotten extremely close and talked on the phone almost every day. Now she considered Delilah one of her closest friends, confidante, and now she could add business partner to the list.

The door swished open and Alex, Smith, and Cayden made their way through the crowd. Alex walked over and kissed her cheek. "How's it going, babe?"

"Great. Everything's going as planned, even better than expected. We've sold out of the majority of our stock. The potions and soaps are flying off the shelves."

"I'm glad to hear all your dreams are coming true." Even after all these months his smile still made her heart pound.

"Oh, I could think of a few things to add to the list," she said in a breathy voice.

He leaned over the counter and whispered close to her ear. "You just wait. I have a surprise for you."

Since the night she'd technically died, she'd moved into Alex's spacious two-bedroom condo on the other side of town. From that point on, they'd spent every waking moment together. Each night when they got home from work, and as Alex's schedule allowed, they'd spend hours talking, laughing, cooking together, and making love.

Each day when Willow woke up and snuggled in his arms, she thought life couldn't get any better. There were still times when she waited for the other shoe to drop, but thanks to all the amazing things happening in her life, those times were few and far between.

Finally, she began to accept that there could be good in her world. She figured it was the least she could do after Alex had accepted and even welcomed magick into his.

Ellen passed in front of them holding a basket of crystals. She tripped over something on the floor and the basket started to fly out of her hands, but Smith caught it midair. She turned and kissed the demon on the cheek. Smith smiled and they walked to the corner of the store, deep in conversation.

"Hold on, did you just see what I did? Could those two...? Nah." Alex shook his head.

Willow shrugged. "Hey, you never know. Everyone deserves a shot at love. Besides, she'll be good for him. She'll loosen him up a bit."

"Yeah, let's hope he can handle her," Alex said with a laugh.

The day's festivities weren't over yet. After Willow and Alex left the store, they headed to Hope House. The two had started the organization as a safe house for runaways and teens hooked on drugs.

Both had worked tirelessly on the project's inception and had come together to put all the finishing touches on the place. After making several requests to a few local businesses for donations, and organizing fundraisers, they were able to rent a space downtown.

The hot, sunny July day was perfect for digging around in the garden. Willow kneeled on the ground and was now covered in dirt. The sun beat down on her face and made her smile.

Over the last several weeks, she'd planted three trees in honor of Maeve, Kimber, and Meadow. She was pulling out the weeds from the soil when Alex walked over to her and knelt on the ground next to her. He was holding something behind his back.

"Hey handsome."

"Hey, yourself." Alex brushed his lips to hers and she sighed, never getting enough of his sultry kisses.

"Almost ready to get out of here?"

"You have to check this out." Willow pointed to the three mounds of dirt. "I've finally taken your advice and decided to put down roots." The first sign of green was sprouting up from the dirt. "What do you have there?

"Your surprise."

"What kind of surprise?" After she brushed her hands on her jeans, she peeked over his shoulder. "Don't keep me in suspense."

He pulled a small crate from behind his back. A soft mewling emanated from inside of it. "Well, you did say you've always wanted a kitten."

"What? Are you kidding me?" Willow opened the top and pulled out a small, jet black ball of fur. "Oh, Alex." Tears stung her eyes. "He's perfect. Thank you."

"What will you name him?" Alex scratched him behind the ears.

"How about Brodie?

A wide grin spread across his face. "Good choice. I got him a special collar. What do you think?"

When Willow held him up, something gleamed brightly in the sunlight. Her heart stuttered when she realized it was a diamond ring. "Alex?"

"Allow me." He unfastened the diamond from Brodie's collar and slipped the ring on her finger. Tears slid down her cheeks as she looked at the ring up close for the first time. It was an antique platinum setting, a round diamond with small rubies set into the band. "It's beautiful."

"This belonged to my paternal grandmother. My grandfather gave it to her right before they came to this country. I figure it was good luck since they were married for fifty-two years. Will you marry me, Willow, and make me the happiest man on Earth?"

"Yes, yes." She wrapped her arms around his neck and kissed him deeply. She lifted her hand up to admire the ring, still not able to believe how beautiful and happy her life had turned out, and it kept getting better by the minute. More tears streamed down her cheeks. "I love you so much."

"I love you, too. Forever. Let's go home. I want to show you how much and celebrate our engagement, naked," he whispered and kissed her ring finger.

They had a lifetime to celebrate and love each other, but that didn't mean she didn't plan on getting started right away. "What are we waiting for?"

***

Thank you for reading! Did you enjoy? Please add your review because nothing helps an author more and encourages readers to take a chance on a book than a review.

And don't miss the book 2 of the *Raven Hollow Coven* series, MIDNIGHT TEMPTATION, available now. Turn the page for a sneak peek!

Also be sure to sign up for the City Owl Press newsletter to receive notice of all book releases!

SNEAK PEEK OF MIDNIGHT TEMPTATION

It only made sense that certain protocols needed to be followed when attending a supernatural speed dating event: like how long you could check someone out for it to be considered socially acceptable. Three seconds, maybe four—tops.

When Gillian Howe tried to imagine sounding clever to a complete stranger in the span of five minutes, her stomach twisted into knots. Of course, there was the drink rule to consider. How many should you consume? One probably wasn't enough to take the edge off. Two might loosen you up enough to keep from getting tongue-tied during the stretches of awkward silences. By the time you got to three and were well on your way to getting sloppy drunk, it wouldn't matter anyway.

Fortunately, she didn't have to worry too much about it or go through the paces of said mini-dates. But that didn't mean she couldn't do her part from the sidelines.

Tonight, her job was to match each of Hoboken's fourteen supernatural and human singles brave enough to attend this event with a card from her tarot deck. And for those lucky enough to find a match, they were eligible for a full couple's reading.

Her breath caught as she glanced around the W's hotel lobby, struck by the cool, modern décor. One wall was comprised entirely of glass and the other of sleek wood paneling. Enormous rectangular fixtures shimmering with black and silver lights hung like floating sentries from the ceiling. Black leather chairs and cushioned benches with red pillows were artfully displayed on top of a black marble floor.

The room started to fill up with human and demon males dressed in fine cut suits. The only trouble with the latter, hot as they were, most demons had egos even bigger than their hulking physiques.

The ladies looked chic decked out in little black dresses, while some wore glittery tops with leather pants and uber-high heels. One by one, they made their way over to the bar, and like the rest of the living room, it was blinged out in silver and black. Sinatra crooned from overhead speakers, setting the perfect mood for the evening.

Instinctively, Gillian tugged at the hem of her short, black, lace dress, starting to feel a little self-conscious. She'd gotten a steal on it even by H&M's standards. The deep V in the front was currently being held together by a safety pin and a prayer, but it was all she could afford at the moment.

"What constitutes as clever first date conversation anyway?"

Gillian recognized the soft, feminine voice. She turned toward her business partner and best friend Saje. They ran a small magick shop with a group of other witches from their coven.

She took a seat next to her on a red baguette. The familiar aroma of Saje's perfume filled the air. Even that didn't relax Gillian.

With damp hands and her heart racing, Gillian placed several tarot decks on one of the small lacquered tables and began to shuffle the cards. Magick, pure and bright pulsed beneath her fingertips. Gillian looked up. "I think I'm the wrong person to ask, but I'm guessing, 'do I have spinach in my teeth' is probably a major no-no."

Saje chuckled, easing some of Gillian's tension away. Different colored strands of beads adorned Saje's neck. She wore a flowy print dress that complimented her petite frame, and high wedges on her feet. Her outfit screamed Boho-chic, and perfect for cohosting a speed dating event. She opened a small cooler and unloaded a cocktail shaker and mason jars filled with pink colored liquid. A mischievous gleam flashed in her eyes.

"Trust me, anyone who drinks some of my special brew will be inclined to follow their deepest desires, and see hearts and flowers in their eyes, not spinach."

"I always wondered where the old adage "love is blind" comes from. Now I know." Gillian cut the decks and began arranging her cards face down in a diamond pattern.

"Don't let your cousin Brooke hear you say that. I'm sure it would be considered sacrilege in some dating ritual handbook." Saje shot her an evil grin as she pulled a hair tie from her wrist and swept her long, dark hair up in a messy bun.

"Funny, I didn't know there was one." But if anyone had a copy it would be Brooke. Speed dating for charity was her baby. Coined matchmaker to the millennial crowd, Brooke believed everyone deserved love, and that one perfect person was out there once the stars aligned and timing collided with physical attraction in some cosmic way. Gillian, on the other hand, wasn't so sure.

"Brooke's the eternal optimist in the family. She got the gene I never inherited," Gillian said with a smirk. "Seriously though, what have you brewed up for us tonight, nothing too potent I hope?"

"It's a special blend of lavender, crushed rose petals, grapefruit juice, and a pinch of vodka." Saje gave her a reassuring smile. "Trust me, there's nothing to worry about. I used a spell for general romantic feelings to blossom for those who are already into each other. This will just give them a gentle push so they can see through the clouds of their self-doubt. Think of it as a way to make their potential match's clear. As long as we're on the subject of love, have you ever considered…"

Gillian shook her head, amused. "Hey, I thought Brooke was the official matchmaker for the night. Besides, I want tonight to be all about the charity." Now that everyone in their friend group seemed to be pairing up, her love life continued to be a hot topic amongst her coven mates. They'd been planning this night for months, selling tickets, and posting the event on their websites, and social media. The purpose was to raise funds for Gillian's charity, Hope Club, along with their corporate sponsor, Kurt Lawrence of The Lawrence Cancer Support Network. The cause was near and dear to Gillian's heart. Gillian knew what it was like to watch a loved one get sick and feel helpless. At least now she could do something proactive. Besides, this event would be great promo for their magick shop, not to mention fodder for her weekly podcast, Eat, Tarot, Love.

After Gillian lit seven votive candles for luck, she spread some business cards and pens with the charity logos on the table. She glanced at her watch and then at Saje. "We'd better finish setting up, this party's about to go full gear any minute now. Let me help you."

When she bent down to pull out a funnel from Saje's bag, her heel slipped off her foot.

"I love the outfit, especially the shoes." Saje pointed to Gillian's feet. "Although, they do seem a tad big."

"Sorry, I should've asked first, but they matched the dress." Gillian adjusted the strap on her borrowed stiletto. Saje was the only one in their coven whose feet were bigger than hers. That's what you did when you lived with a house full of women, you shared everything, nothing was off-limits, and closets were no exception.

Saje tilted her head to the side. "Are you okay? I'm picking up on some major stress vibes from you."

The question made Gillian's skin flush with a mist of nervous perspiration. The trouble with having a psychic for a best friend was you couldn't keep anything to yourself. "Sorry. I guess I'm a little off my game tonight."

This was the first time they'd done something like this and Gillian was still uneasy about the whole thing. In fact, she'd stayed up half the night tossing and turning, not able to pinpoint exactly what was off. Now she felt like a total zombie. She'd used half a tube of concealer to cover the matching luggage under her eyes.

But that wasn't the only thing keeping her awake. She couldn't shake the sense of emptiness and longing, twisting inside her. Pushing her uneasiness to the back of her mind, she refused to venture into a dark place tonight.

"This is supposed to be fun, remember?" Saje unscrewed the tops of the mason jars, and together, they went to work filling wine glasses with her potion.

"You're right of course. At the risk of sounding like a walking contradiction, does anyone fall in love the old-fashioned way these days?" This said by a woman who had zero prospects of her own.

"What about Willow? She fell in love the old fashion way." Saje pointed out. Their mutual friend and former coven mate was about to tie the knot to her gorgeous, special agent boyfriend.

Alex proposed to Willow a few months back. Now their engagement party was just a week away and Gillian still didn't have a date. But Willow wasn't the only one who'd been brought to her knees by the L word. Saje had fallen ass over elbow in love with one of Alex's coworkers.

Gillian wasn't sure what was flowing through the water of Raven's Hollow these days. But it seemed like all of her friends were pairing off and blissfully happy. The click-clack of heels made her glance over her shoulder, catching the eye of the event hostess for the evening. "Almost ready to go?"

"I just need a minute." Brooke walked up to their table looking like the picture of class in a red sheath dress and matching Louboutin's. Her wavy blonde hair was pulled up in an elegant chignon. With her fresh face, blue eyes, and fair skin, Brooke was Gillian's polar opposite. Gillian had been told she was exotic looking, which took some time to grow into, especially as a teenager. But now, as an adult, she'd learned to embrace her olive skin, dark eyes and wavy, brown hair, grateful she'd inherited something from her mom.

Her cousin set down her tote bag, then reached inside to pull out score sheets and name tags. "Since you two are speed dating virgins, I want to give you a quick run-through of what to expect," Brooke said with a bemused expression on her face. "Once the guests have arrived and the format is explained to them, each person will get a tarot card and a sample love potion—at which point they can embark on their dates."

Even if Gillian wasn't thrilled about the choice of tonight's venue, she still planned to benefit from the publicity this event would bring in for the shop and her charity. Having a corporate sponsor would be a huge boon on both fronts.

As much as she loved working at the shop, she needed to branch out on her own. She'd become too dependent on her friends. It was time to spread her wings and fly. Her ultimate goal was to combine her communications background with her gift for the tarot and launch a weekly radio show, which was slowly turning into an all-out obsession. She loved helping people realize their potential in love, career, and relationships through her readings. And radio was a great medium to reach a large audience. Hopefully, tonight would help her take a step in that direction.

"Crap, I forgot the decorations," Brooke shouted, pulling Gillian out of her fog.

"I've got them right here." Saje set the plastic bag on the table. The sound of voices drifted over from the bar. People lined up and made their way toward the tables. Everyone looked excited, some a little terrified, not that Gillian could blame them.

"Let me get those for you. Why don't you greet the guests," Gillian whispered to Brooke. With one hand full of streamers, Gillian reached inside the bag for the scissors and tape. After she climbed on top of a chair, she twisted the ends and taped them around a wooden pillar.

Suddenly, all the hairs on the back of her neck stood on end. Her whole body tensed. The chatter and music became muffled. Her eyes flickered across the lobby in search of who, or what had caught her attention.

Then she saw *him*.

Six-feet-three inches of tall, dark, and brooding stood at the front desk. Detective Garrett Mulroney? What the hell was he doing here? Seeing him again after all these months sent a jolt of shock rippling through her.

His gaze locked with hers, and for a moment she forgot to breathe. They both stood there staring at each other. It was as though he could see beneath her armor, the kind she wore under the little black dress.

The word handsome didn't even begin to describe him. Mythological titans like Adonis and Poseidon came to mind, males so stunning, they couldn't possibly be real. But then she thought of other words too, like arrogant, brash...controlling, she could go on.

Mulroney crossed the lobby with a confidant gait, his long legs eating up the distance between them in a few easy strides. Her heart hammered in her chest with every step.

Every female head turned to catch a glimpse of the vampire. The closer he got, the more her body became hyperaware of his presence. He kept his thick head of dark hair short on the sides and longer in the front. The cut showed off the angles and hard lines of his face. Sexy stubble darkened a square jaw, and he looked every bit as dangerous as she remembered. Long, and lean, Gillian could make out the ripple of sinewy muscle beneath the jacket of his grey suit. In the past, she'd always been attracted to the artistic types. So, there was no good reason why she was drawn to this rough-hewn alpha.

But Goddess help her, he was magnificent.

Laughter drifted out from the bar and that's when she realized she was still standing on a chair, gawking at him like some lovesick schoolgirl. She went to step down and her foot slipped out from one of her strappy sandals. Before she could fall sideways onto the marble, two strong arms wrapped around her waist, and caught her in midair.

When she looked up and into Mulroney's ice-blue eyes, her heart gave a little flutter. Apparently, the legends about vampires having preternatural speed and strength were real. But then as his gaze filled with a kind of raw, primal desire, she had no doubt the steamy ones about them possessing a certain sexual allure also rang true.

"You're lucky you didn't break your neck," Mulroney whispered close to her ear and set her on her feet. "What are you doing here tonight, Miss Howe?" The deep rumble of his voice did funny things to her insides.

"I could ask you the same question." Gillian grabbed the scissors and scotch tape off the table, then shoved them in her black, beaded bag. "If you must know, I'm working," Gillian snapped. Ever since the prickly detective had been assigned to investigate the robbery of one of her clients, a local antique dealer, their paths had collided on more than one occasion.

Mulroney's eyes did a slow sweep of her from the tips of her three-inch heels to the top of her head. Goosebumps instantly spread across her flesh. Gillian wanted to squirm from the flagrant perusal, but remained still, refusing to give him the satisfaction. Why would she? After all, he had tried to ruin her life. "Interesting work attire," he murmured.

Her hands clenched at her sides, fighting the urge to tug on her dress again. "I'm sure you didn't walk over here to comment on my choice of clothing. To what do I owe the unexpected *pleasure*?" she asked with a healthy dose of sarcasm.

"Trust me, this wasn't planned," he said in a gruff voice, refusing to look her in the eye.

Gillian couldn't help remembering the day he and his partner had showed up at the coven. Peppering her with questions and unwarranted accusations, they'd invaded her safe space, conjuring that too familiar lash of shame, reminding her of the days when the neighbors used to call the cops to keep her parents from an all-out war.

He kept his hands stuffed in his pockets, his stance casual, but he wasn't fooling anyone. There was no mistaking the predatory way he kept checking out the people strolling by like only a cop would. She followed his gaze as it took in every detail, restless with intensity, before finally landing on their banner. "Is this a private fundraiser?"

She nodded, not in the mood to elaborate. "Are you here in an official capacity? What's the matter, no real criminals on the streets tonight?" Or maybe this was personal and he was meeting someone. He'd worked with Alex on several cases, and according to Willow, he was a confirmed bachelor, not that she had inquired or anything.

"A quick word, please, Miss Howe. We need to talk." The object of her unhealthy obsession ignored her questions and reached for her elbow, pulling her off to the side. His touch seared through the thin material of her dress, leaving a hot flush along her skin. At five-foot-seven, she wasn't exactly short, but even in her heels, he towered over her.

"Hold on. I'm kind of busy right now. What's this about?" Gillian demanded, catching a whiff of his masculine scent, a blend of sandalwood, and clean laundry. She fought the urge to sigh and glared at him instead.

"You shouldn't be here." Mulroney glanced over at the couple's tables scattered with rose petals, floating candles, bowls of heart-shaped chocolates, and the Lawrence Charity placards. He turned back to face her and scowled. "I want you to leave. Now."

"Excuse me?" His words knocked Gillian off-center and before she could process them, an attractive female vampire with dark hair pulled in a tight ponytail walked up to Mulroney and placed a hand on his arm.

"It's time. We need to go." A surge of irrational jealousy coursed through Gillian's veins like battery acid.

For a split second he hesitated, his gaze still fixed on Gillian, and she sensed some kind of inner battle raging inside him. Then he gave her a curt nod and walked away. Her heart sank.

Brooke approached and crossed her arms over her chest. "What was that all about?"

Not sure what to make of their twisted interaction, or of Mulroney's ominous words for that matter, Gillian sucked in a quivering breath, and let it out. "No idea."

Don't stop now. Keep reading with your copy of MIDNIGHT TEMPTATION available now.

And sign up for Shari Nichol's newsletter to get all the news, giveaways, excerpts, and more!

Don't miss more of *Ravens Hollow Coven* series
with book two, MIDNIGHT TEMPTATION, available now, and find
more from Shari Nichols at sharinicholsauthor.com

When tarot card reader Gillian Howe hosts a supernatural speed dating
event, she's hopeful to discover her chance at love.

Making the perfect match is her passion. Too bad she can't find one for
herself.

A chance encounter with a wealthy vampire soon finds her plunged into a
secret society of trancing, blood bonds, and human escort rings. She'll need
help to survive, but the vampire detective is the last person she
wants...even if he is scorching hot.

Garrett Mulroney has dealt with his share of the supernatural. His sire
tried to force him into a life of debauchery, but he chose to uphold
the law.

The fact that the one woman he can't seem to get out of his lust-filled
dreams is at the center of his investigation doesn't bode well. It's a good
thing she hates his guts, because it helps douse his growing desire for her
and focus on the case. But when Gillian's cousin is kidnapped into the Du
Sang Brotherhood, she becomes the prime witness.

Now they're forced to put their differences aside and go undercover by
pretending to be a couple. The more time they spend together, the more
Garrett wants her in his life—and in his bed.

Will they be able to develop the love and trust needed to take down the
Brotherhood or become its next victim?

Please sign up for the City Owl Press newsletter for chances to win special subscriber-only contests and giveaways as well as receiving information on upcoming releases and special excerpts.

All reviews are **welcome** and **appreciated**. Please consider leaving one on your favorite social media and book buying sites.

For books in the world of romance and speculative fiction that embody Innovation, Creativity, and Affordability, check out City Owl Press at www.cityowlpress.com.

ACKNOWLEDGMENTS

I would like to thank my editor, Heather McCorkle for giving me this opportunity, and breathing new life into these characters. I'm so grateful. To my critique partners, Mary Kate Schweiger and Stacey Wilke, I could've never finished this book without all the red pen and endless feedback. Thank you! I would like to offer a special thank you to Nancy, for always reminding me what friendship means.

ABOUT THE AUTHOR

Shari Nichols grew up in a small town in Connecticut where haunted houses, ghosts and Ouija boards were common place, spurring her fascination with all things paranormal. Ever since she read her first Barbara Cartland novel, her life-long dream has been to write sexy, romantic stories. When she's not writing, she's reading, going to the gym, or hanging out with family and friends.

She lives in New Jersey with her husband, two children, and her golden retriever. Shari's a member of Romance Writers of America, New Jersey Romance Writers, Liberty States Fiction Writers and Fantasy, Futuristic, and Paranormal Romance Writers. Sign up for her newsletter here.

Awards: Golden Leaf Finalist, NJ Author Best Book Finalist, The Beverley Award, HOLT Medallion Finalist, Literary Titan Silver Medal Winner.

sharinicholsauthor.com

facebook.com/sharinicholsauthor
twitter.com/Shari_Nich
instagram.com/shari_nichols

ABOUT THE PUBLISHER

City Owl Press is a cutting edge indie publishing company, bringing the world of romance and speculative fiction to discerning readers.

Escape Your World. Get Lost in Ours!

www.cityowlpress.com

facebook.com/YourCityOwlPress

twitter.com/cityowlpress

instagram.com/cityowlbooks

pinterest.com/cityowlpress

www.ingramcontent.com/pod-product-compliance
Lightning Source LLC
Chambersburg PA
CBHW031207020726
47499CB00002B/517